Mr. Darcy's Rival

D1715655

by

KARA LOUISE

ISBN: 978-1512053531

Cover Images: Dreamstime.com
Cover Design by Kara Louise

Published by Heartworks Publication
Printed in the United States of America

Library of Congress Cataloging-in-Publication Data

Kara Louise
Mr. Darcy's Rival

A Note to my Readers ~

I have several people I wish to thank who were a great help in
getting this book written and into your hands.
First and foremost, I am indebted to Jane Austen
for her original work and wonderful characters.
Thanks also to Mary Anne Hinz, Gayle Mills, and Sienna North
for their comments and edits,
and to all those who have a special place in their hearts
for Jane Austen's characters and stories to continue.

I hope you enjoy *Mr. Darcy's Rival.*

Dedication ~

This book is dedicated to my granddaughter, Aisley,
who hopefully will come to love Jane Austen's novels
as much as her grandmother does!

Chapter 1

Elizabeth sat quietly in the carriage across from Sir William Lucas; his youngest daughter, Maria, sat beside her. The tall, robust gentleman chatted incessantly about the good match his eldest daughter, Charlotte, had made to Mr. Collins, and it took every ounce of willpower Elizabeth possessed to display a charming smile and not refute his nonsense. She was grateful she had brought along a book and could, at least, pretend she was captivated by the novel. In truth, his ramblings, coupled with the carriage jarring over ruts in the road, made it difficult for her to attend to the words. She hoped they would soon arrive at Hunsford parsonage, the home of Mr. and Mrs. Collins.

Sir William's lofty praises about his daughter's marriage held no weight to Elizabeth's opinions and sentiments regarding the match. She considered Mr. Collins a foolish man and believed her friend had acted out of desperation for her unmarried state rather than from sound judgement, and surely not from love. Charlotte had reassured her, however, that she had acted in a completely reasonable manner in accepting the clergyman's offer of marriage just days after Elizabeth had refused his offer for *her* hand.

Elizabeth hoped she could enjoy Charlotte's company without too much interruption from her husband. She was curious as to how her friend was faring. She gave a slight shudder as she contemplated how her own mother had insisted she marry Mr. Collins when he had made her the offer. Fortunately, Elizabeth's father had countered her mother's mandate, and her refusal was permitted, nay, even greatly encouraged, by him.

Elizabeth would be a full month here, and despite looking forward to spending time with her friend, the mere presence of Mr. Collins would afford her little pleasure. She wondered whether she would soon be counting the days before she returned home. A heaviness weighed down upon her; she deeply felt the loss of

Charlotte as her closest friend. Marrying Mr. Collins had not only moved her fifty miles away, but Charlotte was now subject to the whims of one of the most ridiculous men Elizabeth had ever met.

Marrying solely to be married and settled well was not something Elizabeth desired. She wondered if she would ever meet an honourable man who would love her and whom she would love in return with all her heart.

Her thoughts turned to her sweet Jane, and how she and Charles Bingley had formed an attachment last autumn. Yet he had left their neighbourhood without so much as taking his leave. She was now in London, hoping to see him and determine what had happened to so radically change his opinion of her.

Elizabeth's brows narrowed. She could not think of any reasonable explanation as to why he would leave in such a hurried fashion with no further communication. She began to wonder if there was a decent gentleman anywhere in all of England. Even Mr. Bingley's friend, Mr. Darcy, despite being rich and handsome, had proven to be arrogant, uncivil, and ill-mannered, provoking her highest disapproval and censure.

Sir William pointed out the window. "Ah, here we are. Is it not a most charming home? Hunsford certainly suits our Charlotte."

"It is lovely," Elizabeth replied with little enthusiasm.

"It looks smaller than I thought it would be," Maria said, leaning across Elizabeth's lap to peer out.

"It will suit them for now. They shall not have to live here forever, you know."

Elizabeth felt her insides tighten as she fisted her hands. He may not have meant it, but it certainly sounded as though Sir William was referring to Mr. Collins's fortunate situation as the heir presumptive to Longbourn, her family home, which would become his upon the death of her father. It was something she tried not to think about, but that was difficult, as her mother never ceased mentioning it.

As the carriage pulled up to the front of the parsonage and came to a halt, Mr. and Mrs. Collins rushed out to greet their guests. Seeing Charlotte again brought a smile to Elizabeth's face, even though her friend was on the arm of Mr. Collins.

After the threesome stepped down from the carriage, Elizabeth held back, allowing Charlotte to hug her father and sister. Once Charlotte had greeted them properly, she took the few steps to Elizabeth and reached out for her hands.

"Welcome to Hunsford, Elizabeth."

"Good day, my dear friend! How are you?" Elizabeth asked.

"I am doing well, and everything is perfect as I now have family and my best friend here." She squeezed Elizabeth's hands and then slipped one arm through hers, guiding her towards Mr. Collins, who gave a slight bow.

"Cousin Elizabeth, it is good to see you. I am certain you will find Charlotte has found her life here to be one of great contentment and delight."

Elizabeth felt Charlotte's arm tighten about hers. "I am sure she has," she replied politely.

"Let us all go inside, shall we?" Mr. Collins said to his guests. "I know you are eager to see our humble abode!"

There was a quick tour of the small, but cosy, home. In each room they viewed, Mr. Collins praised Lady Catherine, who apparently had done much to improve it. Afterwards, Elizabeth, Charlotte, and Maria took tea in the sitting room while Sir William and Mr. Collins toured the gardens. Elizabeth thought the home was well laid out, as there were several rooms Charlotte could use if she wished to avoid her husband's company.

"How was the journey?" Charlotte asked. "Did you find it to be long and arduous?"

"Not at all," Elizabeth replied. "Time passes quickly when you anticipate arriving at your destination."

Charlotte laughed. "I sometimes find it passes more slowly when you are looking forward to it, and passes all too quickly when you are dreading your arrival."

Elizabeth smiled, wondering if Charlotte had dreaded coming to her new home after she and Mr. Collins were married.

"It would have been much more pleasant if our carriage had ridden more smoothly!" Maria exclaimed.

Charlotte patted her sister's arm. "There are so many more ruts in the road since the recent rains. I think even the finest carriage would have difficulty offering its occupants a smooth ride."

"I thought we would never arrive, and Father talked

continually," Maria complained. "Lizzy had a book to read, but I had no choice but to sit there and listen to him."

"You could have read a book, as well," Charlotte said. "Certainly one of your gothic novels would have sufficed."

Maria stood up and made her way across the room. "It still would have been a long journey." She drew close to the window, looking to the right and left. After a few moments she went to the next window, which looked out in a different direction. "Charlotte, there is someone out there talking with Father and Mr. Collins." She turned around. "Do you know who it is?"

Charlotte set her teacup down and rose to her feet. "It could be Lady Catherine de Bourgh."

"No, it cannot be her. It is a gentleman! And from here, he looks to be quite handsome!" Maria pressed her face closer to the window. "He is medium height, quite slender, a little shorter than Father, and has light brown hair."

Elizabeth raised a brow and looked at her friend. "Charlotte, you did not inform me about any handsome men in the immediate area. What secrets are you keeping from me?"

Charlotte moved across the room to join her sister. "It sounds like Lady Catherine's nephew, Matthew Rickland."

Elizabeth looked at her, a question on her face. "Then is he Mr. Darcy's cousin?"

Charlotte shook her head. "No, he is Sir Lewis de Bourgh's sister's son."

Elizabeth followed Charlotte to the window and looked out. "You are correct, Maria. He does appear handsome from here, but perhaps Charlotte will tell us he grows less so the closer he gets."

"On the contrary. If you promise not to tell my husband, I believe you will see he improves in appearance as he draws near." Charlotte let out a long sigh. "And he is a most proper gentleman, with open and amiable manners."

"Well, this is splendid, indeed!" Elizabeth said. "Has he been here long?"

"A few days." Charlotte slowly turned to Elizabeth with a sly smile. "I understand he plans to stay a full month, just as you are."

"Does he indeed?" Elizabeth widened her eyes with a smile, which quickly disappeared in feigned disappointment. "Perhaps he is here for purposes other than to be admired by three young ladies, but rather by one particular lady."

"Lizzy, whatever do you mean?"

"He may be here to secure Lady Catherine's daughter's hand in marriage. Perhaps he heard she has been promised to her other cousin, Mr. Darcy, and he has come to convince her otherwise."

"I truly do not believe that is the case."

Elizabeth winked at Maria. "Are you certain he did not come to duel with Mr. Darcy over their cousin?"

"Lizzy, be serious. He has not come to secure Miss de Bourgh's hand in marriage. I doubt even Mr. Darcy intends to do so."

"Do you, now?"

Charlotte bit her lip. "It pains me to speak so, but she hardly ever talks, choosing to spend her time doing her studies or some such thing in a journal she carries with her everywhere. I doubt she would meet Mr. Darcy's rigorous expectations."

"Could anyone?" Elizabeth laughed.

"That I cannot answer, but I am quite certain you will enjoy Mr. Rickland's company."

"I certainly hope so," Elizabeth said with a quick smile

Charlotte smiled. "Lady Catherine must have discovered our guests had arrived and sent him over to extend a welcome."

Elizabeth clasped her hands. "How kind of her!"

Charlotte chuckled. "Not so much kindness, but curiosity." She gave Elizabeth a pointed look. "I would not be surprised if he has come with an invitation to Rosings. Lady Catherine has been most curious about the woman who brazenly turned down her clergyman's offer of marriage."

Elizabeth let out a groan. "Oh, Charlotte! Do you suppose she will whip me with forty lashes?"

The front door opened, and the women heard the men approaching as their voices and footsteps grew louder.

Charlotte took her friend's hand and patted it. "No, Lizzy. Lady Catherine enjoys giving verbal lashings, instead." She turned to the door. "Mr. Collins, I see we have another guest!"

"My dear Charlotte, Lady Catherine has condescended to have her nephew pay us a call!" He clasped his hands together and rocked back and forth on his heels. "Is this not splendid?"

Matthew Rickland stepped in alongside the two men. He had a pleasing countenance, a ready smile, and his overall appearance added greatly to his favour.

"Yes, Lady Catherine is very kind. Welcome, Mr. Rickland. May I introduce my good friend, Miss Elizabeth Bennet, and my sister, Miss Maria Lucas?"

Mr. Rickland nodded his head and gave a slight bow to both ladies. Elizabeth felt a slight flutter when his strikingly blue eyes met hers. His eyes were deep set and seemed to dance as he spoke.

"Miss Bennet, Miss Lucas, it is my pleasure. I hope you had a pleasant journey."

"We did, thank you," Elizabeth said.

"We were about to have some refreshment, Mr. Rickland. Would you care to join us?" Charlotte asked.

"I have no pressing engagements. I would be delighted."

Charlotte directed everyone to the drawing room, while she stayed back to give some instructions to her maid. Mr. Rickland took a seat next to Elizabeth.

She leaned forward, clasping her hands. "Mr. Rickland, I am eager to meet your aunt. I have heard from my friend and her husband how attentive she is to their comfort."

Mr. Rickland took in a deep breath and let it out with a soft chuckle. "Oh, yes, she is attentive to nearly everyone… and their *comfort*." He smiled and directed his glance towards Mr. and Mrs. Collins. "I hope Mrs. Collins is not offended by my aunt's…" He fisted his hand and brought it up to his lips, clearing his throat. "…*excessive* attention."

Elizabeth smiled and was interrupted from responding as Charlotte walked over and sat down to join them.

"Mrs. Collins," Mr. Rickland began, "my visit this afternoon is not merely to pay a call, but to extend an invitation from my aunt to you and your guests to dine with us tomorrow. We would be delighted if you would join us."

Mr. Collins, who was standing at his wife's side, gasped at the news, and a broad smile matched his wide eyes. He briefly bowed his head as he said, "We are extremely obliged to you and Lady Catherine for such an honour."

Mr. Rickland told them when they would be expected.

Elizabeth watched his face reflect amusement as Mr. Collins answered with endless prattle, extolling Lady Catherine's goodness to his humble family.

When Mr. Collins finally seemed content that Lady Catherine's nephew was assured of his gratitude, he ceased. His silence also coincided with the arrival of the refreshments.

As they enjoyed the food and drink, their conversation covered a variety of subjects. Mr. Rickland informed them he had come to Rosings to discuss his estate with Lady Catherine's steward. Elizabeth found Mr. Rickland to be intelligent but not boastful, humorous but not ridiculous, and amiable and polite. In many ways he was quite the opposite of Lady Catherine's *other* nephew.

As Charlotte and Elizabeth were conversing with Mr. Collins and Sir William, Mr. Rickland turned to Maria, who was sitting quietly across from them. "Tell me, Miss Lucas, have you ever been to Kent prior to this visit?"

Maria blushed and shook her head. Elizabeth, who would much rather have been conversing with him than Mr. Collins, turned and watched in admiration as Mr. Rickland engaged the young girl in conversation. Maria's natural shyness prevented her from giving more than two-word answers, but Mr. Rickland persevered.

As the two conversed, Elizabeth appreciated him for being patient with Maria and asking questions she could readily answer without fear of saying something wrong.

She was lost in her thoughts when she realized Mr. Rickland had turned back to her, waiting for a response.

"And what is your opinion, Miss Bennet?"

Elizabeth felt a warmth flood her cheeks as she realized she had no idea of what they were now speaking. Or perhaps the blush was due to his smile, which she noticed was slightly crooked, but seemed to touch every feature in his face.

"Pray forgive me, Mr. Rickland, but I was not following your conversation. What opinion did you wish to hear? I warn you, I have opinions enough for everyone in this room, and I am always willing to voice them!"

"I would be delighted to hear them all, but for now, we were discussing whether a natural landscaping is preferable to an artificially manicured setting." He leaned in towards her. "Miss

Lucas does not seem to have an inclination either way. Do you have a preference?"

"I do have a strong opinion on the subject," Elizabeth said with a smile. "I am more inclined to prefer a natural landscape. I have seen many a bush that looks nothing like its intended form because someone got carried away with pruning shears!"

Maria's eyes widened, and she covered her open mouth with her hand, shaking her head as she did.

Mr. Rickland lowered his head. "Then I fear you will not approve of my aunt's meticulous and precise gardening practices. I was telling Miss Lucas that Lady Catherine insists everything be pruned and clipped to her exact specifications. She thinks there is no finer garden than hers and does not take criticism lightly." A smile betrayed his caution.

"I shall pay her the highest compliment for her garden, then, and you two shall be the only ones who know I am not speaking the truth."

"Your secret is safe with me!" Mr. Rickland stood up and gave a quick bow to the two young ladies. "If you will excuse me, I fear I must return to Rosings. My aunt will send out the militia to look for me if I am not there to do her bidding when she has need of it." He gave Charlotte a short bow. "Thank you for the tea and cake. I look forward to seeing all of you tomorrow."

"We look forward to it, as well," Charlotte said.

Mr. Collins took a step towards their guest. "Please convey to Lady Catherine how deeply humbled and honoured we are at her condescension. We cannot thank her enough for the invitation."

Mr. Collins gave a deep bow, and Elizabeth did not miss the slight smirk on Mr. Rickland's face.

"I shall."

He stepped out the door, with Mr. Collins and Sir William following close on his heels. Elizabeth let out a long sigh. "Oh, Charlotte, Mr. Rickland is such a pleasant young man. I think I shall greatly enjoy my stay here!"

Chapter 2

Elizabeth awoke early the next morning as the light began to filter through the sheer window coverings in her room. She sat up and stretched, a wide smile forming on her face. She felt a rather surprising anticipation of the day's events. How odd that she was actually looking forward to dining at Rosings with the inimitable Lady Catherine de Bourgh. But it was not her cousin's patroness she looked forward to seeing.

She smiled and bit her lip as she pondered being in company with Mr. Rickland again. She readily admitted to herself that she enjoyed his conversation yesterday and hoped there would be more opportunities to get to know him better.

She swung her feet over the side of the bed and walked to the window, peering out. The sun was coming up over the distant rise, and the few clouds hanging in the sky were edged in reds and oranges.

Her eyes scanned out over the small garden, a large grove and park beyond it, and in the other direction, some woods in the distance. She had not yet seen Rosings, but had conjured up an image of a cold, dreary structure, with an exterior that was rigid and harsh. *Much like Mr. Darcy*, she thought. And Mr. Rickland's description of the gardens being overly manicured would certainly fit in well with the image she had drawn in her mind. She nodded as she thought of Mr. Darcy being manicured into the strict mould of a wealthy man of the upper class, who had little tolerance for those beneath him.

She bit her lips as she considered her acquaintance with Mr. Rickland may have softened the harsh image of Rosings in her mind… *just a little*. She looked forward to seeing him again later. This day could not pass quickly enough.

~~*

Despite finding her thoughts straying frequently to Mr. Rickland, Elizabeth enjoyed her time with Charlotte and Maria. Mr. Collins spent the morning and a portion of the afternoon at church getting ready for Sunday and also with some parishioners he needed to visit. Elizabeth deemed it fortunate that he did not feel the necessity to entertain his guests. She had already had enough of his hospitality.

Sir William kept to himself, reading in the small Hunsford library or walking about in the garden. Elizabeth determined he likely did the same when he was home at Lucas Lodge.

Elizabeth and Charlotte found it necessary to reassure Maria several times before leaving for Rosings that the behaviour she normally exhibited was all Lady Catherine required and she ought not to fret about it. The poor girl had worried herself into quite a state.

"If you are uncertain whether or not to say something," offered Charlotte, "then remain silent. I find that is best."

Elizabeth chuckled to herself, as she doubted Maria would be able to formulate a single thought in Lady Catherine's presence, let alone articulate any words.

Later that day, as she was getting ready for her first visit to Rosings, Elizabeth sat at the dressing table brushing her hair as she pondered Mr. Rickland. What did she think of him and what did he think of her? He had certainly been polite and amiable. His personality was engaging and his manners were impeccable. She truly enjoyed his company.

She gave her head a slight toss and crossed her arms in front of her. She determined she would simply enjoy Mr. Rickland's company for however long it lasted.

Elizabeth chose one of her finer dresses to wear for their first visit. Mr. Collins had assured his guests earlier in the day that they were not to be uneasy about their clothing, as Lady Catherine and her daughter would understand they would not have the elegance of dress equal to the inhabitants of Rosings Park. Laughing at the thought of Lady Catherine comparing fabrics and lace over dinner, Elizabeth put a final pin in her hair to keep it up. She moistened her fingers and ran them across her eyebrows to shape them, and then joined the others downstairs.

As they walked to Rosings, Mr. Collins chattered incessantly, but Elizabeth did not hear one word. When they crossed the lane and the great manor came into view, Elizabeth stifled a gasp at the gardens surrounding it, and her lips curled in a smile. Precisely pruned bushes and trees stood like uniformed sentinels at attention, guarding the home against those unworthy of Lady Catherine's condescension. They were certainly as Mr. Rickland described, even more so. Elizabeth raised a brow as she thought of Mr. Darcy standing stiffly at a window or mantel. Perhaps he too, in a like manner, was guarding himself against the degradation of a society he deemed beneath him.

They moved along the stone and gravel path to the large front door while Mr. Collins gave an animated account of the grandeur of the windows in the front of the house, the fine stone sculptures originally brought from Italy, the many chimneys, and of course, the meticulously manicured gardens. What Elizabeth noticed, however, was a turret at the far west end, with windows at the top looking out in every direction. She smiled as she thought of peering out from the lofty vantage point.

Before he knocked, Mr. Collins looked at Elizabeth and Maria with a slight grimace. "Lady Catherine is one of the finest ladies you will likely ever meet. I know you are not accustomed to being in the company of someone in such an elevated position, and I beg you to be on your utmost best behaviour." His admonition did nothing to diminish Maria's fears. In fact, it appeared he was completely unaware of them. He gave a quick bow, nodded his head, and then turned to knock.

Elizabeth's jaw tightened, and she forced herself to think of how she would behave in Mr. Rickland's presence so as not to be tempted to do exactly the opposite of what Mr. Collins asked.

The large door creaked open, and a tall, elderly butler greeted them. He slowly ushered them into a grand, marbled entrance hall. Sir William and Maria seemed as awestruck as Elizabeth was. She had never seen anything like it; however, she would not wish it for herself. It was far too pretentious and extravagant. Mr. Collins seemed pleased by everyone's silent admiration.

They were about to walk down the hall when Mr. Rickland

appeared. He briskly approached them with outstretched arms. "Greetings and welcome to Rosings! If you will follow me, my aunt is expecting you." He nodded to the butler, turned, and led the way down through an ante-chamber and into a spacious room.

Elizabeth felt a hand wrap tightly about her arm, and she looked back to see Maria's pale face. She patted the young girl's hand. "You shall perform well enough, Maria. Do not fear what you may, in truth, have no reason to dread."

"Oh, but I know she is going to find fault with me!" Maria said in a hushed voice.

Elizabeth gave her an encouraging smile. "Maria, if she finds any fault with you, imagine what she shall think of me! But fear not, if she even attempts to reprimand you for anything, I shall stand up for you!"

Maria took in a deep breath. "Oh, Elizabeth, pray do not say such things! I know that would make it so much worse!"

As they came to the door, Elizabeth felt Maria pause. She gave the girl a smile and an encouraging pull. "Just smile sweetly at her. No one can find fault with a smile," Elizabeth said with only a small doubt as to whether it was true for Lady Catherine.

They entered a large drawing room with wide windows. Dark, heavy draperies were opened enough to allow in only a small ray of sunlight. Lady Catherine sat majestically in a large chair, her arms resting in her lap. She tilted her head as the party approached and bade them enter with a slight wave of the closed fan she held in her hand. Narrowed eyes followed them as they walked in.

"I assume these are your guests, Mr. Collins."

Mr. Collins gave a deep bow. "Yes, your ladyship. Mrs. Collins shall make the introductions, if you please."

Charlotte stepped forward and curtseyed. "May I present to you my father, Sir William Lucas; my sister, Miss Maria Lucas; and my friend from Longbourn, Miss Elizabeth Bennet?"

She then turned to her guests. "This is our esteemed patroness, Lady Catherine de Bourgh; her daughter, Miss Anne de Bourgh; and Mrs. Jenkinson, Miss de Bourgh's companion."

Elizabeth and Maria curtseyed, and Sir William gave a low bow. Elizabeth looked at Miss de Bourgh and could not reconcile this young woman, who was destined to marry Mr. Darcy, as one he would deem suitable. She had connections and a fortune, certainly, but she could not imagine he would align himself with someone as pale and sickly as this young woman. A small coverlet was over her lap, and despite looking up at the guests, she offered only the barest smile and little acknowledgement.

Elizabeth deemed her to be *much* like Mr. Darcy, however, in the manner of her greeting.

Elizabeth noticed her holding a small book in her lap, which she surmised to be a journal of some sort. She wondered if it contained lessons assigned by Mrs. Jenkinson. Elizabeth smiled. Perhaps they were lessons on how to be a mistress of a great estate – like Pemberley!

Maria seemed unable to say anything, but Elizabeth and Sir William expressed their pleasure in making the acquaintance.

Lady Catherine tilted her head, narrowed her eyes, and looked pointedly at Elizabeth, as if she was about to say something. Instead, she extended her hands towards a sofa and some chairs. "You may be seated."

"We are all honoured to have been invited to dine with you," Mr. Collins said with another bow, this time a quick, short one, before taking a seat himself.

There was at first simple and civil conversation. It was apparent Lady Catherine enjoyed speaking in a most authoritative tone, even when it was about something as mundane as the weather. Elizabeth could readily imagine her arguing with storm clouds that dared rain on a day she did not deem suitable.

Once the safe subjects – the weather, the roads, and everyone's good health and comfort – had been discussed, Mr. Collins invited his party to the window to admire the view of the gardens. Lady Catherine remained seated, but seemed to wait expectantly for the compliments.

As Elizabeth gazed out, she felt someone come up behind her and knew immediately that it was Mr. Rickland.

"Is this not the most splendid garden you have ever seen?" Mr. Collins asked with a wide sweep of his hand. He looked directly at Elizabeth. "I think you will agree, my dear cousin, that such splendour is rarely seen."

Mr. Rickland walked around her and leaned casually against the wall. "Yes, Miss Bennet," he said with a mischievous glint in his eye and a hint of a smile. "I would enjoy hearing your opinion of it."

"Indeed it is… unlike anything I have ever seen." She turned to Lady Catherine. "I can certainly understand the pride you have in this garden. You must be most attentive to its care."

"I am," Lady Catherine said with a deep and slow nod of her head. "But it is still too early in the season to fully appreciate its beauty. If you see it in the summer, I am certain you would find it even more beautiful."

"It is my loss, as I shall be gone by then," she replied.

"You handled that splendidly, Miss Bennet," whispered Mr. Rickland, as they returned to their seats.

This time Elizabeth looked at him and met his smile with one of her own. She glanced at Miss de Bourgh, who had been watching them. The young lady then opened her book and began writing in it, seemingly not interested at all in the conversation that flowed about the room.

After a bit more casual conversation, they were led into the dining room. Elizabeth was pleased Mr. Rickland was seated across from her. Mr. Collins proudly took his place at Lady Catherine's side.

Much of the conversation around the table consisted of praise for each excellent course served, although Sir William and Mr. Collins seemed to care more for eating than speaking. Charlotte seemed inclined to attend to Lady Catherine, making an occasional attempt to bring Maria into the conversation, while Miss de Bourgh said little.

Elizabeth was grateful for Mr. Rickland's conversation. She enjoyed the rapport between them and the attentiveness he showed her.

He knew the exact time to look up at her and lift a single brow when he knew she would be stifling a giggle as she delicately wiped the corners of her mouth with her napkin. It usually occurred when Sir William echoed the praises that Mr. Collins regularly bestowed upon Lady Catherine, for he said little else.

At length, Elizabeth's curiosity for Miss de Bourgh prompted her to address her. "Miss de Bourgh, I noticed you were doing a great deal of writing earlier. Is there anything in particular you write about?"

Anne slowly turned and studied Elizabeth for a moment. She spoke softly and tentatively. "No, nothing in particular. I merely like to record my observations."

Elizabeth smiled, believing she was not particularly shy, simply not inclined to verbosity. She had an intelligent, discerning look in her eyes. Elizabeth assumed that was the end of their conversation, but a moment later, Anne continued.

"While some may have the talent to draw or paint a scene in a sitting room or parlour, I prefer instead to describe it in words."

Elizabeth looked at her in amazement, attempting to avoid displaying the surprise she felt. This young lady, who rarely spoke, instead favoured the written word. "Would there be an opportunity for me to read anything you have written? I would dearly love to see how you described us." Elizabeth smiled. "I assume you were sketching our characters in the drawing room."

Anne suddenly blushed. "Oh, dear, I fear I could not... no."

Elizabeth gave her an understanding nod. She thought back to the attempts she had made at drawing a picture and felt very much the same – she would not wish for anyone to see it.

Mr. Rickland prevented any further discussion, as he leaned forward. "Tell me, Miss Bennet," he glanced at his aunt and then looked back. "Do you play a musical instrument?"

Elizabeth smiled and tilted her head. "I do play the pianoforte, but my ability is nothing about which I can boast."

"You must decide, then, whether to admit it to my aunt, for she shall most certainly request you to perform a piece after dinner."

Elizabeth nodded graciously. "I thank you for the warning, but if she wishes it, I believe I can muster up the courage." She leaned forward. "As long as you can all muster the courage to listen!"

Mr. Rickland smiled with satisfaction. "Splendid! I look forward to hearing you play."

Elizabeth brought a napkin up to her mouth and furtively spoke to Anne. "Unfortunately, I may be forced to expose my poor talent before everyone."

Anne responded with a smile. "It is never easy to place oneself in a position where one's talents are judged. I trust you shall perform admirably."

"I appreciate your confidence, bearing in mind you have never heard me play!" Elizabeth said with a laugh.

Anne's eyes turned to Elizabeth's hands. "You have nice long fingers, Miss Bennet. You can easily reach the keys." Anne lifted up her hands and gave them a turn, looking at the front and back. "My short fingers, unfortunately, were never suited to playing well. No matter how hard I tried..." Her voice trailed off.

Elizabeth smiled, but not before noticing a look of regret that passed across Anne's face as her gaze turned briefly to her mother.

As the ladies returned to the parlour, Lady Catherine did indeed ask Elizabeth if she played, and she answered that she did a little. Mr. Rickland knew his aunt well.

"You may select a single piece to play when the men return. The music is next to the instrument. After you have performed, we shall set up the card-tables."

As Elizabeth looked through the ample selection of music, she listened to Lady Catherine advise Charlotte on the management of her domestic concerns. She was even more convinced if it were her receiving these admonitions, she would not have been able to hold her tongue and politely acquiesce as Charlotte did.

She found a piece of music she knew fairly well and placed it on the piano before returning to the other ladies.

Lady Catherine then began an interrogation of Elizabeth, asking about her family, sisters, and education. Upon discovering she and her four sisters had not had a governess, Lady Catherine exclaimed with forceful astonishment that she had never heard anything so absurd. Elizabeth was grateful the men returned, bringing an end to the conversation.

Mr. Rickland immediately looked from his aunt to Elizabeth. She surmised he must have seen her frustrated countenance, for he pressed his lips together and raised a brow in her direction. He then smiled and said, "Miss Bennet, I understand you play the pianoforte. Would you do us the honour of performing?"

Lady Catherine waved her fan through the air. "Yes, she has already selected a song."

As Elizabeth stood up and walked to the pianoforte, Mr. Rickland followed her. "May I assist by turning the pages?"

Elizabeth sat down at the instrument and straightened the music. She looked up at Mr. Rickland and smiled. "Thank you."

Elizabeth played the piece well enough to receive a modest applause at the conclusion. As the servants came in and set up the tables for cards, Lady Catherine felt it incumbent on her to continue questioning Elizabeth.

"Miss Bennet, I understand Longbourn is entailed to Mr. Collins. While it is favourable for him, I certainly do not see the occasion to entail estates from the female line. Rosings is not so. Was your father not able sire any sons?"

Elizabeth let out a surprised laugh. "He had no sons, Ma'am, only five daughters, and you cannot expect me to know whether he was able to or not. I assume only the Good Lord would have such information."

Lady Catherine narrowed her brows and shook her head. "I find it highly imprudent to have five daughters when the home is entailed to the male line."

Elizabeth opened her mouth to protest, but said nothing when she glanced at Mr. Collins and saw his face was white with what she could only imagine to be dread as to how she might answer. A look at Mr. Rickland's face, however, betrayed his displeasure in his aunt's comments.

"Yes, highly imprudent. I cannot imagine what he was thinking," she finally said with a feigned look of regret.

Mr. Rickland began to cough, but Elizabeth was quite certain it was only done to conceal a laugh.

After more discussion about her sisters and whether or not they were all out, Lady Catherine concluded by declaring Elizabeth gave her opinion decidedly for so young a person.

Elizabeth was grateful for the diversion of cards, where most conversation was then restricted to each party of four and dealt mainly with the game. She was thankful she was not placed at Lady Catherine's table, but disappointed she was not at the same table as Mr. Rickland. She was greatly enjoying his company.

She could, however, observe him when she looked up at her partner and was fairly certain on more than one occasion, he was also looking at her. At least she hoped so.

Chapter 3

The next morning after getting dressed, Elizabeth went downstairs and was greeted by pleasant aromas coming from the kitchen. Charlotte was already there and asked Elizabeth to join her in the drawing room for some time alone before the whole household was up.

"What did you think of Lady Catherine?" Charlotte asked her.

Elizabeth pressed her lips together and raised her brows. After a moment, she said, "She is much as I expected her." She laughed and shook her head. "Maybe even more so."

They then spoke about Miss de Bourgh and conjectured about her writing, what Mr. Darcy must think of being promised in marriage to her, and her illness, as she had coughed quite a bit the previous evening.

Mr. Rickland was discussed a great deal, and both expressed delight in his company and that he afforded them great pleasure.

It was well after ten o'clock before Elizabeth finally stepped outdoors. She was determined to explore the park and grove instead of going in the direction of the woods. She decided not to venture there until she was more familiar with the area. She ought not to get lost on only her third day here.

As she walked towards the shelter of a hedgerow, she chided herself for not being able to stop the thoughts of Mr. Rickland that engulfed her. The night before, she had been grateful for his reassuring presence in the austere company of his aunt, and then later, it was all she could do to keep her attention on the game of casino her table played. On more than one occasion she had looked up to see him gazing at her, often with a smile on his face. Since he was at the table with Mr. Collins, she had surmised it was because of some bit of foolishness her cousin might be saying, but she could not help but hope it was because of her.

As she contemplated Charlotte's situation being married to Mr.

Collins, she wondered whether or not her friend was truly content. She did not seem particularly unhappy, and yet there was certainly something amiss. In her conversations with Charlotte about her life now, her dear friend spoke little of her husband, but when she did, there was neither praise nor criticism. She also spoke of him with little emotion. Elizabeth was certain if she were married to someone she loved and respected, he would be a large part of her ardent narrative.

Elizabeth ran her fingers across an overgrown bush, pulling some leaves off as she did. She sighed as she contemplated whether she would want a home with so great a number of rooms she would be able to hide from her husband when she did not wish to see him. She hoped that would not be necessary. She would like to think a small, four-room house would be sufficient if she and her husband shared a deep and abiding love for one another.

Elizabeth came upon a rise that looked down on Hunsford parsonage and the stark and stately Rosings. She leaned against a tree, enjoying the view. In addition to the two homes, she could see the steeple of the church, and then beyond was a cluster of small homes in the nearby village. Looking across in the opposite direction, she could see a wide expanse of dense woods.

It was quite serene up here, and she was eager to further survey her new surroundings, but knew she ought to be returning. As she set off to return to the parsonage, she heard a familiar voice call her name. Turning, she saw Mr. Rickland.

"Miss Bennet! I thought that was you."

"It is, indeed. I wished to do a little exploring. Do you also enjoy a morning stroll?"

"As long as it is not too early." He breathed in deeply. "We could not ask for finer weather, especially in the spring. We are quite fortunate in that we missed a good deal of the seasonal rains a few weeks back. When I arrived, my aunt did nothing but complain about not being able to go out due to all the mud!"

"I have been known to walk with nary a concern for either the rain or mud," Elizabeth announced.

"Indeed?" He fingered his chin and arched his brows. "Are you telling me the delightful young lady with whom I visited in the drawing room of the parsonage and at Rosings yesterday is not as refined as I was led to believe?"

"I suppose," said Elizabeth with a smile, "that would depend on one's definition of refined."

"Granted. May I ask what your definition is?"

Elizabeth shook her head. "No, you must first tell me your definition, sir."

"Hmm, well, I would say a refined woman knows the right words to speak in any situation; she is gracious and poised, intelligent, and most importantly, makes a gentleman feel he is the only one she has eyes for when they are dancing."

"Oh, dear, by that definition I fear I fail miserably," Elizabeth laughed. "I must confess I often *speak my mind most decidedly*. As for dancing, I have danced no less than two dances in the past six months where I am certain I did not evoke that response." She crossed her arms emphatically in front of her. "Not only that, it is the last thing I would have *wanted* those two gentlemen to feel about me as we danced."

"Unfortunate for them," he said. "But I am not quite finished with my definition."

"I am not certain I can bear to hear anymore."

"I would also add that a refined woman has a sense of humour, enjoys taking walks – even in the rain and mud – and is *not* afraid to express her many opinions."

Elizabeth clasped her hands behind her and looked down. She knew the smile on her face echoed the joy she experienced in Mr. Rickland's presence. She lifted her eyes, meeting his.

Mr. Rickland extended his arm for her to take as they began walking. "I hope you were not terribly offended by all my aunt said to you yesterday."

"Oh, not at all."

"She has a… well, how shall I say this… she certainly feels it is incumbent upon her to scrutinize each guest and make her opinions known when she believes they can benefit from her excellent advice."

"I see," laughed Elizabeth. She brought a finger up to her lip, tapping it. "She is correct, however. I do express my opinions too decidedly. There are times when I simply cannot keep from saying what is on my mind in spite of my best efforts."

He lifted a single brow and nodded. "Yes, but I would venture to say you do not pry into others' affairs and offer unsolicited advice." He stopped and looked down as the heel of his boot scraped across the dirt. "While it may appear she takes delight in finding fault in others, I believe she thinks she is improving the person by mentioning it."

"Perhaps." Elizabeth let go of his arm and swung her arms out. "It is a beautiful day!"

Mr. Rickland leaned against a nearby tree trunk. "Changing the subject?" He chuckled.

"A more pleasant, safer subject, I think."

"Indeed, but first I must relay some regrettable news. At least it is regrettable to me."

"What is it?"

"I have some business in town and will be away for several days, possibly a full week. I know my aunt likely will invite you for tea again before I return, and therefore, I must apologize in advance for anything she may say."

Elizabeth shook her head with a laugh. "As I informed you earlier, you have no need to apologize to me for your aunt."

Mr. Rickland regarded Elizabeth with his deep-set blue eyes. "This may be hard to believe, but I think my aunt enjoys your company. I know she enjoys the conversation. You add a bit of..." He paused and looked at her, pinching his brows in concentration.

"Startling frankness?" Elizabeth suggested.

"Not at all. I would call it a lively intelligence."

"You are too gracious. I doubt that is what she would call it."

"Well, as you said, it is a beautiful day. May I escort you back? I should like to take my leave of everyone before departing." He offered Elizabeth his arm again, and the two walked the short distance back to the parsonage.

~~*

Once Mr. Rickland had departed for London, Elizabeth felt his absence greatly. His intelligent and lively conversation had provided them with much diversion. Charlotte expressed her hope he would return directly, and even Maria spoke of feeling the loss of him.

They were invited for tea at Rosings a few days later, on the day before Sir William was to return to Hertfordshire. As Lady Catherine again pried into Charlotte's handling of her household and sought to learn more about Elizabeth's family, she remembered Mr. Rickland's apologies, which gave her the ability to respond more graciously than she felt.

She was delighted to have the opportunity after the tea had been served, to sit next to Anne in a corner of the room by themselves. Mrs. Jenkinson worked on an intricate piece of stitchery nearby.

"Miss de Bourgh, have you done much writing today?"

The young lady shook her head. "No. As much as I try, I have had little inspiration of late."

"What do you find that inspires you?" Elizabeth asked softly.

A sly smile appeared on Anne's face, and she looked around as if to make sure no one could hear her. "Observing interesting characters and conversation, coupled with an interesting story."

Elizabeth let out a deep sigh. "I fear we must be quite boring."

Anne shook her head, and a slight blush touched her cheeks. "Not so much. Perhaps I shall have a bit of inspiration three days from now."

Elizabeth laughed. "Now you have me intrigued!"

Three Days Later

Colonel Richard Fitzwilliam reclined comfortably in the carriage, his legs stretched out at an angle as far as he could without tangling with his cousin's feet. His head had fallen back, and he made loud gurgling noises as he breathed in and out.

Fitzwilliam Darcy was annoyed. The drive to Rosings had taken longer than expected because the roads were in such disrepair. Even if he had wished to sleep, it would have been impossible due to his cousin's incessant snoring.

But probably more than that, he was not looking forward to this visit. For four years, he and his cousin had made the trip to

Rosings every Easter, but he found it to be more and more disconcerting with each passing year. Most likely it was because Lady Catherine was declaring more adamantly that he must marry Anne; a wish his aunt – and unfortunately his mother – had hoped for from the time he and his cousin were infants. And he was feeling more and more disinclined to do their bidding.

As he stared out the window at the small village that signalled they were about an hour away from Rosings, he blew out a puff of air. He wished he had settled this ridiculous notion his aunt had about joining their two estates through marriage years ago. Whether or not his mother would yet have wished it were she still alive, he would never know, but he could not marry Anne. He had never reconciled this frail, quiet, young lady to the woman he had always envisioned as Mistress of Pemberley. It was not that he disliked Anne; when they were younger, they had gotten along quite well. She was sweet and kind. He did not care for her in the way he wanted to care for the woman he married. He wished to love his wife, much as he had come to love…

He shuddered and shook his head. He could not allow such thoughts. They only tormented him. Despite making every attempt to put Miss Elizabeth Bennet out of his mind these past few months, he still could not imagine anyone else as the woman he would love and marry.

He took in a deep breath and let it out in a soft moan.

"There you go again. Darcy, I have never heard you sigh so much in your life!"

"I thought you were asleep. And it was not a sigh." Darcy had not mentioned one word about Elizabeth to his cousin and did not wish to speak of her now. "I was merely hoping to waken you. Your snoring is appalling!"

Fitzwilliam chuckled. "So I have been told, but I have yet to hear it myself."

"Trust me, you do snore."

Fitzwilliam shrugged his shoulders lightly and glanced out the window. "We shall be there shortly."

"Yes."

"Is your heart beating thunderously in anticipation of seeing your promised one again after so long a time?" Fitzwilliam asked with a teasing glance.

Darcy flashed him a threatening look. "The last thing I need is for you to join forces with our aunt in this absurd notion."

"But you must remember your mother wished a marriage between you and Anne, as well. You would not want to disappoint her, would you?"

Darcy's face darkened. "If my mother did indeed wish it, it was because she did not know how... how unsuitable our cousin would be as Mistress." Darcy shook his head. "I need you to be an ally for *me*, not my aunt."

"Then you must make an attempt to set things straight with her," Colonel Fitzwilliam grumbled. "How can I be an ally when you do nothing?"

"I intend to make it clear to her whilst we are here that I will *not* be marrying Anne."

Fitzwilliam crossed his arms in front of him and huffed. "As you declare you will do every year."

"This time I mean to do it. My patience is wearing thin. With her *and* with you!"

The colonel stretched out his arms and legs, emitting a loud groan. "You had best get it done so Anne can get over her broken heart and set her sights on someone else."

"I doubt it will break her heart."

"Has she ever told you she does *not* want to marry you?"

"She would never defy her mother, but I can assure you she has never expressed any partiality towards me, in either words or in expression."

"Perhaps she writes down all her feelings of love in her journals as she cannot bring herself to say them aloud."

Darcy shook his head. "If that were even near to the truth, it would still not make her suitable to me. I have seen nothing that indicates to me she has anything close to love or affection for me."

"I beg to differ. I believe I saw something when she was... about sixteen years old."

"That was a long time ago. We have a mutual respect for each other, but certainly not love." Darcy clenched his jaw. This was not altogether true, as it was last year he attempted to discuss it with Anne, but she stopped him before he could even utter the words. He hoped she was not longing for him to declare himself to her.

Fitzwilliam leaned forward. "Love is important to you, is it not?"

"What do you mean?"

"If I recollect, this was the issue with the friend you were telling me about. You discouraged him from declaring his love to a young lady because you felt she did not exhibit much affection towards him."

"Yes, but there was more to it than that."

"Ah, yes. Her family was unsuitable." Fitzwilliam clicked his tongue. "And you felt it incumbent upon yourself to advise him of this. Was he so besotted with her he was not able to judge for himself?"

"He merely needed a little prod in the right direction through some wise counsel from those whom he looks up to and who could view the situation more objectively."

'If you ask me," the colonel began, "I do not have much respect for this friend of yours if he can be swayed so readily. Remind me never to confide in you when I find myself captivated by a young lady."

"You, I believe, already know the type of woman you can and cannot marry. Bingley's family has new money, and he has not yet fully realized the danger in which he might find himself when a pretty young woman sets her eyes on his fortune." Darcy cleared his throat and wrung his hands together. "Or a young lady's mother seeks him out for that reason."

"You are too persuasive for your own good, Darcy." The colonel leaned forward and clasped his hands. "But I now know why you are not yet married. It is either because you are waiting for the right time to ask for Anne's hand or you dissuade yourself out of every eligible woman who comes your way! I am certain you talked yourself out of Miss Grace Strathern, but I cannot conceive of what argument you used."

"Miss Strathern?"

Fitzwilliam tilted his head towards his cousin, giving him a pointed look. "I recently heard some rumours circulating about you and Miss Strathern, while you were in London these past few months. She would certainly qualify as a suitable Mistress of Pemberley."

Darcy stiffened and turned his head away from his cousin and towards the window. "It is true she is tolerable…" Darcy paused and tightened his jaw as he recollected referring to Elizabeth the same way. "I did visit her family on two occasions, and our paths crossed several other times while I was in London. But…" his voice trailed off.

"But what? I am most curious what faults you find with her."

Darcy shook his head. "She may be most suitable in connections and breeding, but there were things about her…" Darcy knew he would never be able to put into words how he felt. It was mainly due to the comparisons he now made to Elizabeth.

"Heavens, Darcy! She is beautiful, gracious, and would step easily into the role of Mistress of Pemberley. What could you possibly not like about her? She is perfectly agreeable."

Darcy turned back towards Fitzwilliam. "She is *too* agreeable."

"How can a woman be too agreeable?"

"She agrees with everything I say. I feel as though I do not truly know who she is, what her true opinions are. She either has no opinions or seeks to please me by wholly agreeing with mine." Darcy paused and took in a deep breath. "She was not able to engage my affections."

"Ha!" Fitzwilliam laughed. "Engage your affections! This is preposterous! If Miss Strathern cannot engage your affections, I am at a loss to know who can."

Darcy was silent. He knew it was useless to discuss this further.

Colonel Fitzwilliam looked out the window. "We are passing the parsonage; we shall be at Rosings soon." He began gathering up his belongings.

Darcy glanced out the window as well, wondering if his cousin knew how close to the truth he was when he accused him of talking himself out of an affection. But it was not just Miss Strathern. As he had persuaded Bingley against Miss Jane Bennet, he had been persuading himself against her sister, as well. He let out a huff.

"There you go again!"

"No," Darcy laughed, trying to shrug it off. "You said we were passing the parsonage. I was merely thinking of our aunt's new clergyman, Mr. Collins. I actually met him in Hertfordshire last autumn. He was visiting his family; he even attended the Netherfield Ball Bingley and his sister hosted." Darcy shook his head. "Odd character. I cannot wait for you to meet him!"

"Truly? I look forward to it."

As the two cousins were looking out, they saw a gentleman walking towards Hunsford.

"Is that him, there?" asked the colonel.

Darcy narrowed his eyes. "No, that man is too thin. I cannot... wait, is that not Rickland? Did you know he was going to be visiting Aunt Catherine over Easter?"

Fitzwilliam leaned towards the window to get a better look as they passed. "You may be correct. I had not heard he was going to be here, but then we are not always apprised of every detail when we come."

"It has been several years since I have seen the man. At least he will provide us with a little more diversion than what we are accustomed to here."

"I certainly hope so." Fitzwilliam clapped his hands. "Perhaps our stay will prove to be more interesting than usual."

Chapter 4

Elizabeth waited with fanciful expectation and fervent hopes that Mr. Rickland would pay a call at the parsonage now that he had returned from London. She chided herself for such thoughts and feelings for a gentleman she barely knew. It was so unlike her, but she wholly enjoyed his company, and he added a great deal of liveliness to her stay here.

Mr. Collins had informed the ladies the previous evening the esteemed gentleman had returned to Rosings and would certainly wait on them today. Elizabeth decided to wear her pale blue morning dress. While it was not one of her finer gowns, she felt it complimented her skin and hair colour, and brought out the blue in her eyes. She tossed her head slightly as she looked in the mirror. She wondered whether Mr. Rickland would even notice. She hoped so.

A few hours later, when Mr. Rickland was announced, Elizabeth felt her heart begin to race. He walked into the sitting room with confident steps, greeting first Charlotte, and then Elizabeth and Maria.

"Welcome back, Mr. Rickland," Charlotte said. "Please come in and join us. I regret my husband is visiting some of the parishioners." She stole a sly glance at Elizabeth. "I hope you will find us a suitable substitute and be inclined to stay and visit."

Rickland smiled and nodded. "What gentleman would not enjoy being in the company of three charming ladies?"

"How was your time in London?" Elizabeth asked.

"I actually was surprised to find myself thinking how much I would prefer to be here! Normally I look for any excuse to be away from this place." He put up his hand. "Please do not mistake my intent. I truly care for my aunt, but my previous visits have not been as... delightful... as this one has been." He gave Elizabeth a pointed look.

Elizabeth shook her head. "Pray take care, Mr. Rickland, I do not think Miss Lucas has ever heard such blatant flirting in all her life."

He leaned towards the young girl. "You will find men say the most ridiculous things when in the presence of a pretty lady. And when there are three, he cannot be held accountable."

Maria blushed, as everyone expected. She opened her mouth as if to speak, but apparently changed her mind and closed it again directly.

"Would you care for something to eat or drink?" Charlotte directed Mr. Rickland's gaze towards an apple nut cake. "I must say it is quite delicious."

Mr. Rickland put up a hand. "I must decline. On my way here I saw a carriage pass into Rosings Park bearing Lady Catherine's other two nephews. I must return to greet them. I only came to inform you of my return."

Elizabeth felt her heart pound, as much for Mr. Rickland's kindness as out of fear it was Mr. Darcy who had just arrived.

"Lady Catherine's nephews?" Elizabeth asked.

Mr. Rickland turned to her. "Her brother's son, Colonel Fitzwilliam, and her sister's son, Mr. Darcy."

The three ladies looked at each other and then back at Mr. Rickland. "We are acquainted with Mr. Darcy," Charlotte said in answer to his questioning look. "He came to Hertfordshire with his friend who leased a house in our neighbourhood."

"Did he?" he asked. "Were you much in his company?" He directed his question to Elizabeth.

"Occasionally." Elizabeth would like to have added, *"Much to my dismay."*

"Indeed, it is a small world," he said. "The two men normally stay here several weeks, and if they are anything like me, they will look for something to occupy their time away from Rosings."

Mr. Rickland stood up and gave a short bow. "Thank you, ladies, for the company. I hope to see you again soon." He gave a wave of his hand. "There is no need to get up. I shall see myself to the door."

As soon as he stepped out of the room, the ladies looked again at each other. "Mr. Darcy!" Charlotte said. "This should prove interesting."

Elizabeth let out a mocking laugh. "I highly doubt he will set foot in here, Charlotte. You know how much he despises me. I imagine we shall never see him."

"I am certain he does not despise you, Elizabeth."

"If he did not despise me, he certainly took great delight in looking upon me only to find fault." She pounded her clasped hands onto her lap and let out a sigh. "And I have so been enjoying Mr. Rickland's charming company."

A wide smile appeared on Charlotte's face. "I am glad to hear it, Lizzy. He is such a nice looking gentleman and so amiable. I was hoping you did."

"He is far more agreeable than his cousin – or whatever Mr. Darcy is to him." She turned to Charlotte and gave her head a few sharp nods. "I can guarantee if Mr. Darcy deigns to pay us a call, he shall stand at that window, looking out on the garden, glancing over only to look down on us."

"I never found him as impossible as you did, Lizzy."

Elizabeth laughed. "That is because he did not mortify you by claiming you were merely tolerable and not handsome enough to tempt him to dance."

Charlotte shook her head. "That was ill-mannered of him, especially with you standing close enough to overhear, but at length, he must have come to change his opinion of you. He did ask you to dance, remember?"

Elizabeth narrowed her eyes at her friend. "How could I forget? It was the worst dance of my whole life." She let out an exasperated huff as she considered her dance with Mr. Collins was worse, but she would not confess that to Charlotte.

"Is he a poor dancer?" Maria asked.

"On the contrary, he is an excellent dancer." Elizabeth took in a deep breath and massaged her forehead with her fingers. "He has the most infuriating talent of knowing exactly what to say to raise my ire." Looking back at Charlotte, she said, "I hope we will not have to see him often while he is here."

As Elizabeth pondered Mr. Darcy's arrival, she suddenly realized it was three days ago Anne mentioned she might have more inspiration for writing at that time. She slowly shook her head. She knew little about what moved one to be motivated in their writing, but felt fairly certain the arrival of one's true love would likely provide plenty of inspiration for the young lady.

~~*

Colonel Fitzwilliam and Mr. Darcy stepped into their aunt's house, waiting for the expected effusive greeting. Darcy could almost count the seconds it would take for her to let out a jubilant cry and come rushing towards them after they were announced.

"Now!" Colonel Fitzwilliam said, a moment before her cry was heard.

"You are good, Cousin. I was two seconds behind."

The two men greeted their aunt when she stepped out of the sitting room. Her arms were stretched out to them, and she took one hand of each nephew, squeezing them tightly within her long, bony fingers. Her hands shook slightly, but she had a firm grip. "It is good to see you, both. I despaired you would never arrive! Come, let us go to the drawing room! Anne has been eagerly waiting to see you." Her wrinkled face revealed a smile, but Darcy took it as more conspiratorial than friendly.

They followed her back to the sitting room where Anne sat with Mrs. Jenkinson. When she looked up and saw them enter, she slowly closed the journal in which she had been writing. A faint smile appeared. Colonel Fitzwilliam approached her first and took her hand. "It is good to see you, Anne." He leaned over to kiss it.

He stepped away to allow Darcy to greet her. Darcy took her small hand and cradled it in his. "It is good to see you, Anne. I hope you are well." He did not kiss it, but squeezed her hand before he released it.

"Sit down and tell us how you have been! Poor Anne will likely tire soon." Lady Catherine looked at Darcy apologetically. "Your visit is all she has talked about for some time. She always looks forward to seeing you."

Darcy did not know if his aunt was speaking with more hope than truth, but he did not miss his cousin's smirk. He attempted to smile at his aunt. "If she needs to go to her room to rest, we will understand."

"Come in and sit down. Richard, you must be weary after being so long overseas. Did your regiment see much action?"

"We did, Aunt."

She waved her hand through the air. "I do not wish to hear about it."

Fitzwilliam smiled. "No need to worry. Even if you did wish to hear, I would refuse to tell you about it!"

As the two men sat down, Colonel Fitzwilliam said to his aunt, "We thought we saw someone crossing the lane from Rosings to Hunsford. Was that Matthew Rickland?"

Lady Catherine nodded. "Indeed it was! I am delighted he was able to visit while you are here. He came over a week ago, but returned last evening from a short trip to London. He will be pleased to know you have arrived."

"Yes, I am!" Rickland stepped into the room. "Tell me, how long it has been?"

Colonel Fitzwilliam and Darcy stood to greet him.

"It has been at least four years," Darcy replied. "I saw you in London the year after my good father died."

"That is right," Rickland said. "I fear I knew not what to say to you. I knew you were still grieving, and I felt completely inadequate."

"Then we are even," Darcy replied. "I knew not how to be good company around people who were not as gravely affected by his death as I was. I wrongly assumed everyone ought to feel the same depth of grief I felt." Darcy gave a head a slight shake. "And shortly after, you lost your father."

"Indeed, I did."

Darcy smiled. "Hopefully this visit will be a much improved one for all of us."

"I am certain it shall!" Rickland replied.

"We saw you walking to the parsonage," the colonel said. "You did not stay long."

"No, I noticed your carriage pass, so I kept my visit short." Rickland suddenly turned to Darcy. "It appears you are known at Hunsford."

"Yes, I met Mr. Collins in Hertfordshire."

"But it was Mrs. Collins who informed me of her acquaintance with you."

"Mrs. Collins? He was not married when I last saw him." Darcy looked confused. "Did he marry someone from Hertfordshire?" Darcy's insides tightened as a fleeting thought presented itself that it might have been Elizabeth.

"Yes, yes he did."

Darcy drew in a breath, holding it until Rickland told him the name of the lady he had married.

"Her name is Charlotte. Charlotte Lucas, before she married him."

"Charlotte Lucas?" Darcy released his held breath, feeling greatly relieved. He shook his head, however, at the news. "I have to admit I am rather surprised."

"Her sister and friend are visiting and also claimed an acquaintance with you."

Darcy's heart leapt. He was not certain whether he wanted it to be Elizabeth… or not.

"Her friend is Miss Elizabeth Bennet." Rickland raised his brow. "A pleasant young lady. Are you acquainted with her?"

Darcy did not trust himself to speak. He nodded an affirmative as his jaw was so tightly clamped he could not have opened his mouth had he wished to. He quickly turned away and heard not another word Rickland said. His mouth was suddenly dry, and his mind whirled with thoughts. He had tried so hard to put her out of his heart and mind, and now on a visit to his aunt – something he did each year – he discovers she is just next door!

"I am quite surprised she chose to come, after what she did to poor Mr. Collins!" Lady Catherine said in an angry tone.

The men all turned their heads, looking at her questioningly.

"What could she have done to Mr. Collins?" Rickland asked. "They seem perfectly amiable when I have seen them."

"I am certain it is only due to her friendship with his wife, but I find the whole circumstance imprudent on her part." Lady Catherine clucked her tongue twice to the cadence of her tapping fan on the arm of the chair. "She gave no thought to the welfare of her family."

Darcy was curious. He normally did not appreciate the gossip his aunt relayed to them, but usually it was about people he did not know… or care about. This time it was different.

Darcy's aunt directed her gaze and words at him. "Surely you were aware of what happened as it occurred in Hertfordshire. I am certain you must. Mr. Collins informed me of your presence there. Miss Bennet's parents were understandably angry, and he was convinced the whole of the neighbourhood talked about it."

Darcy wondered how much of his aunt's words were her own conjecture or whether Mr. Collins had elaborated in some way. He tried to think of what may have taken place to cause such an uproar, but he could not recollect anything. Finally he said, "I know not of what you are speaking. I am not aware of anything untoward that occurred."

Rickland and Colonel Fitzwilliam looked from Darcy to their aunt and back, hoping to discover what had taken place.

Lady Catherine looked surprised at her nephew's apparent ignorance. She pounded her fan into her hand. "Miss Bennet refused his offer. You know her home is entailed to Mr. Collins as there are no sons, and accepting his proposal of marriage would have been the wise thing for her to do, keeping Longbourn in the family."

Darcy dropped his jaw, and his eyes widened in disbelief. "Mr. Collins asked for *her* hand in marriage?"

"He most certainly did. I cannot imagine what she was thinking to have done such a thing," Lady Catherine huffed. "Her parents ought to have insisted upon it."

"I am completely surprised," Rickland said, a sly smile forming. "I had no idea."

Darcy narrowed his eyes, trying to comprehend all this. "And then… how is it he married her friend, Miss Lucas?" He shook his head. "How did that come about?"

Lady Catherine's face clouded over, and she pinched her brows in displeasure. "He certainly could not remain at Longbourn after being so humiliated, so Mrs. Collins, then Miss Lucas, invited him to her home, where she extended to him the respect he was not shown by Miss Bennet."

Darcy could not attend to the conversation that followed. His mind whirled with thoughts of Elizabeth being across the lane, as well as her refusing an offer of marriage from Mr. Collins.

After failing in several attempts to rid his mind of these thoughts and pay attention, Darcy stood. "If you will excuse me, Aunt, I would like to freshen up." He gave a short bow, turned slightly to Anne and nodded his head.

As he walked out, Colonel Fitzwilliam echoed Darcy's words and joined him. They walked up the wide staircase and soon Rickland was at their side, as well.

"Are you gentlemen willing to visit Hunsford? This news makes me respect Miss Bennet so much more!" Rickland let out a soft chuckle. "When I said I was surprised, I had not a hint Mr. Collins had first asked for her hand. What I did not say was having met Mr. Collins, I was *not* surprised she refused his offer." He laughed again. "But I am certainly glad she did!"

"Now you two have me intrigued as to the kind of character this Collins is. And I am even more intrigued by this young lady, as well. What say you, Darcy? Shall we visit?"

Darcy knew he could not sequester himself from Elizabeth the whole time he was here. He might as well get their first encounter over with. "Yes. Pray allow me some time. Shall we meet in half an hour?"

"A half an hour it is, then!" With that, Rickland walked back down the stairs, and the two men continued to their rooms.

Darcy walked numbly into his chamber, where his valet was putting away his clothes.

"Give me a moment to myself, Jenkins. I shall call for you shortly."

"Yes, sir."

When Jenkins left, Darcy braced his arms on the back of a chair. He wondered when Collins had asked for Elizabeth's hand. He shook his head. He had not heard anything about it, and as Bingley had almost always been with her sister, he knew if it had happened while they were there, he would have known.

It must have been after they had departed Netherfield for London. Collins was likely acquainted with the fact everyone anticipated an engagement between Bingley and Jane Bennet. Elizabeth would have been his next choice – although not his wisest.

Darcy collapsed into the chair. He knew Elizabeth well enough to realise she never would have been happy with Mr. Collins. For her to refuse him as she did, however, took away a source of security for her family. He narrowed his eyes and winced. It was especially so, now the much anticipated – and hoped for – engagement between Bingley and her sister had not occurred.

"I have not seen her in almost five months. How is it I seem to be no closer to forgetting her than when I departed Netherfield? Obviously, Fitzwilliam was in error. I was *not* persuasive enough towards myself," he muttered softly.

He closed his eyes and leaned his head back. He had done everything in his power these past five months to try to forget her and believed he had succeeded. Until about twenty minutes ago. The rush of all those feelings he thought he had quelled forcefully assaulted him.

He cradled his jaw with his hand, wondering whether these feelings were merely the surprise of hearing she was here. He shook his head, and his fist came down hard against the arm of the chair.

"She is completely unsuitable for me!" He let out a huff. "It cannot be that difficult to conquer these feelings I have for her!"

Darcy stood up, tightening his jaw and fists. "I shall treat her with complete indifference and free myself from the hold she has over me once and for all!"

He fortified himself with a deep breath. "The sooner I get this first visit over with, the better off I shall be!" He went to the door and called for his valet.

Chapter 5

At Hunsford parsonage the three ladies spoke of nothing but their increased opportunity for entertainment with the two additional men arriving at Rosings. Elizabeth, while not convinced Mr. Darcy would add a *delightful* diversion, owned he might provide an *amusing* one. She looked forward to watching him interact with Miss de Bourgh. Would his cousin devote more time to writing, being inspired by his presence, or would she listen intently to his every word?

She was also curious about his cousin, Colonel Fitzwilliam. Would he be as proud and haughty as Mr. Darcy, or would he be as kind and polite as Mr. Rickland?

The ladies did not have long to wait. They were quite surprised when Mr. Collins rushed in – completely spent of breath – to inform them the three illustrious gentlemen were even now on their way, having entered the lane from Rosings.

He rushed over to straighten a picture on the wall. "Hurry and tidy things. We must offer them refreshment! Call the maid!"

"There is no need to panic," Mrs. Collins strongly advised with a directed look at her husband. "Everything is in good order, and we have tea and cake to offer them."

"Good!" He patted his heart in either fatigue or reassurance, yet he seemed agitated still. He walked to the window and looked out.

Mrs. Collins leaned over to Elizabeth, shaking her head. "I try to keep something on hand at all times in case we have guests or for those times Mr. Collins is called upon to pay a visit. I like to send something along."

Elizabeth smiled at her friend. She had pursed her lips to conceal her smile as she watched Mr. Collins fret about the three gentlemen on their way. It had certainly surprised him they were coming to call so soon after their arrival, but in truth, it surprised Elizabeth even more.

She tilted her head as she looked at Charlotte. "I wonder if Mr. Rickland suggested they visit. I cannot imagine Mr. Darcy coming here on his own accord so soon after arriving at Rosings. The two gentlemen could barely have had time to sufficiently greet their aunt! Could Mr. Collins be mistaken?"

The sound of the door-bell proved Mr. Collins was not in error. They all stood and waited for the gentlemen to be shown into the drawing room. Mr. Rickland stepped in first, followed by Mr. Darcy and then his cousin. The three men stood abreast of each other, and introductions were made.

Elizabeth could not help but notice the genial smiles on the faces of Mr. Rickland and Colonel Fitzwilliam, while Mr. Darcy's expression was sombre and seemed to reflect a wish that he were anywhere but here. He glanced at her when she was introduced to Colonel Fitzwilliam, but then quickly turned his eyes to Charlotte and complimented her home.

Charlotte invited them to sit and asked the maid to bring in the refreshments.

Elizabeth watched the men and thought to herself she was going to enjoy comparing their differences. Mr. Rickland was obviously the most comfortable and sat leaning slightly forward with his arms resting on his legs, his hands clasped lightly. His engaging smile and the twinkle in his eyes suggested a familiarity and pleasure in his surroundings. And as had been the rule, he was most inclined to enter into conversation with the residents of the parsonage.

In the middle sat Mr. Darcy, upright and stiff, and not at all inclined to smile. Elizabeth caught his eyes fixed upon her when she occasionally glanced at him, but he seemed distracted. He did not seem engaged by any of the conversation. His hands rested upon his legs, his fingers tapping lightly; likely a habit he exhibited when ill at ease. He remained, for the most part, silent.

On his other side sat Colonel Fitzwilliam, an odd mixture of the other two. He sat as upright as his cousin, but it was likely due more to his military training. He entered into conversation directly, and Elizabeth noticed a smile appeared readily and frequently. While he would not be described as particularly handsome, he had a rugged friendliness and gentlemanly politeness that was quite attractive.

They spoke of the pleasant weather, the upcoming Easter holiday, and a musical soiree the Collinses and their guests had been invited to attend the Saturday following Easter. Elizabeth smiled as she began to consider the men seated on either side of Mr. Darcy. In her mind's eye, they served as bookends, propping him up. The thought of them being quite stylish bookends, with the unfortunate task of holding up a large, dull book, brought a smile to her lips.

The only person in the room who was more silent than Mr. Darcy was Maria, who seemed as much in awe of these gentlemen as she was of Lady Catherine.

When the subject turned to London, Elizabeth decided she would inquire if Mr. Darcy had seen her sister, Jane.

He turned to her, and his brows pinched together. "No," he answered in a somewhat disconcerted manner. "I have… not been so fortunate as to see her."

He seemed unwilling to speak further on the subject; he almost appeared discomfited, as if the question disturbed him. She wondered how much he knew about what had prompted Mr. Bingley to leave Netherfield so abruptly and not return. She was almost certain he was completely aware of the motives behind his friend's actions.

"Are you much in town, Miss Bennet?" Colonel Fitzwilliam asked as he leaned forward, an affable smile lighting his face.

"Not as much as I would like. My aunt and uncle reside there, so I do have the opportunity on occasion." She tilted her head and smiled. "I enjoy the bustle of the people on the streets and all the fine shops, of course, but there is nothing that gives me greater pleasure than attending the theatre or a concert."

"There is nothing finer," Colonel Fitzwilliam said. "It is what I miss most when I am away."

Elizabeth pressed her lips together and then added, "I am always delighted to return home to the country, however."

Mr. Rickland took the opportunity to tell the ladies Colonel Fitzwilliam had just returned from having fought the French.

"Oh!" Charlotte said, delicately covering her mouth with her hand. "Were you on the battlefield? I hope you were spared from witnessing or experiencing anything too terrible."

Colonel Fitzwilliam smiled. "I appreciate your concern, Mrs. Collins. But I make it a practice not to speak to ladies of my war experiences. I hope you do not mind my not answering your question, for I do not wish for any speculation one way or another."

"That is considerate of you, Colonel Fitzwilliam," Charlotte replied with an appreciative nod.

Elizabeth enjoyed the addition of Colonel Fitzwilliam. He had a demeanour that was much more appealing and engaging than his cousin. He and Mr. Rickland, sitting comfortably on either side of Mr. Darcy, seemed to accentuate the latter's stiff and aloof manner.

"Do the three of you make a regular habit of visiting your aunt together?" Elizabeth asked, wondering if they often saw each other. She looked at each, but then turned back to Mr. Darcy, wondering if he might chance a response.

"Darcy and I have visited our aunt at Easter together for the past several years," the colonel replied. "We were pleasantly surprised to see Rickland was here."

"It has been at least four years since we have been in each other's company," Rickland added. He turned to Darcy. "I am actually surprised we do not encounter each other more often when we are in town."

"I am not surprised. It is quite large," Darcy said.

"True," Rickland said. "And if I recollect correctly, you prefer the quiet and solitude of Pemberley over the excitement and busyness of London society."

"No, not entirely." Darcy replied tersely. "I enjoy London and all it has to offer, but then I am always pleased to return home to the country." He cast a quick glance at Elizabeth, with something that almost resembled a smile.

Conversation slowed as everyone enjoyed the tea and cakes. Elizabeth caught Mr. Darcy's eyes on her on several occasions, and she was convinced he was still finding fault with her, although… There was a difference in his looks, but she could not quite determine what it was. She inwardly smiled. Perhaps his aunt had already expressed her displeasure with the outspoken friend of

Mrs. Collins's.

But in her defence, she could readily proclaim she and Mr. Darcy's intended had enjoyed some good conversation, and she felt honoured Miss de Bourgh considered her a friend. Oh, she could not wait to see how the two behaved around each other.

~~*

As the men walked back to Rosings, Rickland and Fitzwilliam spoke with great admiration of the pleasant company at the parsonage. But Darcy's mind and heart were so full, he could not attend to their words.

It was useless. He had made a futile attempt at reining in his feelings for Elizabeth, but as soon as he had seen her, he was lost in her warm smile, exuberant laugh, and her fine eyes. She had looked stunning in the blue dress she was wearing, and the attractiveness of her every feature seemed heightened. He felt as though he were trying to swim against a strong current as he fought the rush of those strong feelings. He was making no progress; in fact, he was sinking into the depths of admiration for her!

He nearly took in a deep breath, but checked himself, knowing his cousin would almost certainly comment on it. He forced himself to breathe evenly as he thought about seeing Elizabeth for the first time again after so many months. Could his heart beat any more forcefully or every rational thought disappear so quickly? She was standing in front of him, and all the resolve to expunge her from his heart and mind had vanished.

He absently kicked at a rock in the path as he recollected his father's grief at the death of his mother. They had loved each other deeply, and his father's despondency had frightened him. He had become – for a short while – someone Darcy did not even recognize.

When he was still quite young, he had determined he would marry a woman suitable to be his wife and Mistress of Pemberley, perhaps even Anne. He would allow others to marry for love, but not him. He had actually found it preferable, as the suitable women he met hardly made any lasting impression on his heart.

They were either too shy or too scheming, too coy or too cunning, or too avaricious with nary a thought of being generous to others. That was until he met Elizabeth Bennet!

This woman, whom he deemed only tolerable the first time he saw her, whose family members occasionally exhibited the most inappropriate behaviour, and who lived in a country manor entailed away to a cousin, unwittingly and quite surprisingly had become embedded within the very fibres of his heart. From the moment he had declared she was not handsome enough to tempt him, he had not been able to dismiss her from his thoughts.

"Darcy, are you not paying attention?" Colonel Fitzwilliam gave his cousin a nudge.

"I am sorry. Pray, forgive me. What were you saying?"

Rickland stepped in front of Darcy and stopped. "We were talking about Miss Elizabeth Bennet. What is your opinion of her?"

Darcy searched his mind for something to say that would not sound contrived. "She seems a pleasant young lady."

"I heartily concur," Rickland said, "but that is an odd thing to say about someone with whom you are already acquainted."

"Well, yes, I... I am, although it is not a particularly close acquaintance. But everything I saw of her indicated she was a... pleasant young lady." He realized he was fisting his hands so tightly his fingers hurt.

"I think I am going to enjoy our visit this year. It will add so much to our days when we can pay a call on the whole party at the parsonage and when they are invited to Rosings," Colonel Fitzwilliam said with a smile.

"And Miss Bennet, in particular!" declared Rickland. "The few times Aunt has invited Mr. and Mrs. Collins and their guests to Rosings to dine or for tea, it has been a most enjoyable time. Miss Bennet is not at all intimidated by our aunt, and actually enjoys a lively debate with her." Rickland laughed. "It has been most amusing."

Darcy suddenly found himself jealous of the time Rickland had been here with Elizabeth. Did she challenge his opinions like she had his own? Had she raised that single brow and lifted her lips in a smile directed at Rickland as she had to him? Did she wish to sketch Rickland's character as she had attempted to sketch his?

Darcy frowned. That reminded him of his last evening with her before he left Hertfordshire. They had ended their dance at the Netherfield Ball, and it had not gone well. He felt his jaw tighten and wondered again what Wickham had said to cause her to be so angry with him. He could only imagine, and as the men started to walk again, he speculated about what lies Wickham could have told her.

He looked down at the ground as he walked, shaking his head, wondering… wondering.

"I would like that," Darcy heard Colonel Fitzwilliam say. "Splendid idea! What do you think, Darcy?"

Darcy closed his eyes trying to recall what Rickland had said. The last thing he remembered him saying was that he was amused by how Elizabeth had not been intimidated by their aunt. After that, he had become lost in his thoughts about her. He could not allow them to know he was not paying attention, again.

"I would… like that, as well." Darcy hoped he was admitting to something he truly would enjoy.

"Good!" Rickland clapped his hands together. "You are the one to discuss it with our aunt! She will do almost anything you ask her to do."

Darcy grimaced. *Of what is he speaking?*

"I doubt I have such powers of persuasion," he replied cautiously. "Rickland, you have been here longer and are better acquainted with her mood at the moment."

Colonel Fitzwilliam stopped and grabbed Darcy's shoulder. "But Darcy, you only need to tell Aunt Catherine you think this will be beneficial for Anne. Think how enjoyable a musical soiree would be. I would wager our cousin would truly enjoy going."

Darcy's eyes widened. *How did they go from talking about Elizabeth to talking about attending the musical soiree?*

"It will be a small, informal gathering, and I hope there will be some dancing." Mr. Rickland had a wide smile on his face. With a slow nod he added, "I am certain an invitation has come to Rosings. If someone in the neighbourhood is hosting any entertainment, they know they had best extend an invitation to Her Ladyship."

Darcy's thoughts turned again to Elizabeth as he considered having another dance with her, hopefully an improvement on their last one. But he did not like the idea of encouraging his aunt to accept the invitation for her daughter's sake. "You know Anne is barely allowed to step outside, and heaven forbid that she go out in the evening. I admit I like the idea, but I strongly doubt our aunt will agree."

"No worry, Darcy. We shall all encourage Aunt Catherine in the matter. She only needs to hear you wish to attend," Fitzwilliam said. He added with a chuckle, "Perhaps we can ensure there are a few other eligible gentlemen to whom Anne can be introduced. This might be exactly what you both need to get out from under Aunt Catherine's expectations for your marriage."

Rickland laughed a little too enthusiastically for Darcy's peace of mind. "I would have thought in the four years since we have seen each other, the issue of your betrothal would have been resolved… one way or the other!"

Rickland slapped his hand on Colonel Fitzwilliam's shoulder. "Do you know, Colonel, whether your esteemed cousin is still contemplating going through with this arranged marriage to Anne, or is he merely waiting for the right lady to come along before he decides?"

The colonel chuckled. "We were talking about that on our way here." He leaned over as if to whisper to Rickland. "Apparently he is even immune to the beautiful Miss Grace Strathern."

"You are aware I can hear you, Fitzwilliam!" Darcy's voice was edged in frustration.

"Miss Strathern?" Rickland's face reflected great astonishment at such a thing. "Darcy, she is all that is beautiful. Perfection itself!" He shook his head. "Please do not tell me she has welcomed your attentions but you are disinclined to welcome hers!"

Darcy clenched his jaw. Neither of these men would understand. "This is something I am in no mood to discuss."

"As you wish," Rickland said, turning to walk on. "But please, do speak to our aunt about the soiree, Darcy. It shall be a fine thing to add to our visit."

"Are you planning to stay long?" Colonel Fitzwilliam asked.

Rickland shrugged his shoulders. "I have no pressing engagements. As long as the two of you are here, I think I might as well stay." He turned to look at Darcy. "How shall it be, Darcy? Will you inquire of our aunt about the soiree?"

Darcy could not help but consider with pleasure the notion of having another dance with Elizabeth. At the mere thought of it, his heart pounded. He wondered silently, however, how his resolve had disappeared so quickly. He had hoped his heart would be safe from her. He had been in her presence no longer than half an hour, and he was as captivated and drawn to her as he had been in Hertfordshire.

"I suppose there is no harm in trying," Darcy said, as calmly as he could manage.

Chapter 6

The next morning Darcy awoke after a restless night; thoughts of Elizabeth kept him from sleep. He summoned his valet, and as he waited for Jenkins to select his clothes, he peered out the window, looking towards Hunsford. He drew in a deep breath and leaned lightly against the frame. Despite not sleeping well, he felt a sense of joyful expectation. He shook his head at that, but it was exactly how he felt. All because of Miss Elizabeth Bennet.

He thought back to the previous evening. When he and the other two gentlemen had joined their aunt and cousin in the drawing room, it was all he could do to concentrate on the conversation. Elizabeth was foremost on his mind, and he was not able to think of anything else. Fortunately he had a book with him and kept his eyes on the page. He hoped no one noticed he was not turning the pages as often as he normally did.

Retiring early so he could clear his mind in the solitary quiet of his chambers was of no benefit. The feelings that arose with every thought of Elizabeth forbade any rational argument against her. It was also to no avail when he finally blew out the candle and closed his eyes for the night. If awake, she was in his every thought; when he slept, she invaded his dreams.

As he looked out the window, he saw movement on the lane, drawing his attention. His heart began to pound as he pondered whether it might be Elizabeth. He knew from the time she spent at Netherfield with her ailing sister she enjoyed walking in the early hours of the day. If he set out to meet her, it would give him a greatly desired opportunity to spend some time alone with her, as he recollected Rickland was not an early riser. A scowl darkened his face as he considered while he initially had welcomed Rickland's presence here, now he wished Rickland gone.

When the men had gathered in the study after dining, Rickland would have no other topic of conversation than Elizabeth. He did not mind Fitzwilliam's praise of her, but with Rickland, it was another matter. The man had been a little too enthusiastic about her presence here and how delightful she was.

Darcy unwittingly let out an audible growl.

"Pardon me, sir?" his valet asked.

Darcy quickly turned, chiding himself for letting his thoughts become so forceful. "Oh, nothing, Jenkins."

Once dressed, he hurried down the winding staircase and walked to the front door, ignoring the tantalizing aroma of food being prepared in the kitchen. He stepped out and glanced up at the gathering clouds, hoping they would not bring rain. More than that, however, he hoped the rains would not come before he came upon Elizabeth.

Before setting off, he stepped back in and grabbed an umbrella, in case they found themselves in a downpour. He smiled at the thought.

His pace increased as he drew closer to the lane. He looked around, hoping to see her lovely figure, wondering which direction she might have taken. A movement to his left caught his eye, and his breath caught when he saw her strolling towards the small meadow leading out to the woods. He began walking in her direction, enjoying the few moments of being able to watch her without her knowing his eyes were upon her.

She stopped and picked a few wildflowers, bringing them up to her nose. This allowed him to draw nearer. She seemed unsure which way to walk next and glanced about her. It was then she looked his way.

She turned her head, as if she was about to continue on, but then paused. He took the opportunity to walk determinedly up to her and stopped several steps short of her.

"Good morning, Miss Bennet."

Elizabeth nodded her head. "Mr. Darcy."

"I see you are taking advantage of the weather before the rain sets in."

"Will it rain, do you think?" she asked, with a tilt of her head.

"I can almost guarantee it. I can feel it and practically smell it."

Elizabeth chuckled. "Truly? I see you are well prepared." She glanced at his umbrella.

He lifted it up and then poked it into the ground, much like a walking stick. "It does serve a twofold purpose." He nodded his head in the direction Elizabeth had been going. "Shall we walk?"

Elizabeth lifted her eyes and seemed to extend to him a rather hesitant, but oh so pleasant, smile. She gave her head a slight shake. "Pray, I would not wish to disturb you if you were in search of a solitary walk this morning."

"You would by no means disturb me," he said, admiring the curls bouncing around her face as she spoke. "I do not necessarily walk alone because I wish to. My cousin is not much of a walker, although he takes a yearly stroll about the park before we leave, and Mr. Rickland is not an early riser." He stole a glance at Elizabeth to see if she had any reaction to this.

"Not many people are. In my family only my father and I enjoy the early morning."

"The others do not know what they are missing," he said softly. "The sunrises at Pemberley are incomparable." He glanced down at her. "Perhaps I favour the sunrise because it is visible from the home. As the sun sets on the other side of the ridge behind Pemberley, it cannot be readily seen unless you climb to its top."

"Is it an easy climb?" Elizabeth asked.

"I believe it would be easy enough for you. It is neither too high, nor too steep."

A look of confusion passed across Elizabeth's face, and Darcy suddenly wondered if he had spoken too presumptuously. He had so often imagined her walking the grounds of Pemberley that he wished for her to appreciate them even though she had never seen them.

They walked quietly for several minutes, Darcy savouring her presence at his side. He was grateful for the easy silence between them.

At length, Elizabeth stopped. "If you do not mind, Mr. Darcy, I must turn back. You may continue on if you wish."

"No, I ought to return, as well. My aunt serves the breakfast meal at precisely nine o'clock."

They turned, and after more silence, Elizabeth finally said, "I have not had many opportunities to walk since coming here, but this has become my favourite destination. I love walking through the meadow to the woods and out to the plateau."

"You have good taste, Miss Bennet, especially now the wildflowers have begun to bloom."

Elizabeth nodded. "Yes, perhaps that is the reason I am partial to it."

"Only take care in the woods. My cousin and I got lost in them once, despite having come here for years."

"Thank you, sir. I shall heed your warning."

A few raindrops began to fall, and Darcy quickly opened the umbrella, holding it over their heads. "You see, Miss Bennet? The rains have come." He extended his arm for her to take.

"Indeed you were correct," Elizabeth said with a sigh of resignation, slipping her hand around his arm.

They continued to walk in silence to the lane that separated the Hunsford Parsonage and Rosings. The rain began to pound against the umbrella, and the wind picked up, forcing Darcy to hold the umbrella tightly to keep it from blowing away.

"It appears to be quite a storm." Mr. Darcy smiled. "I shall see you to the door so you do not get unduly wet."

They reached the house, and Elizabeth hurried up the steps. "Thank you, Mr. Darcy. I appreciate the use of your umbrella."

Darcy nodded. "It has been my pleasure."

She dipped a polite curtsey, and Darcy watched her walk into the small house. His heart had pounded the duration of the walk, and it was not due to exercise. He was pleased and felt confident she had confided to him this was her favourite walk so he would seek her out again. And he most definitely would. Their walks in the morning would belong to the two of them alone.

~~*

There was an abundant, steady rain for three full days. It rained so significantly it looked to be a solid sheet of water cascading off the roof of the parsonage. The wind whipped the trees and howled like wolves. At times it felt as though the rain would come through the slate tiles of the roof or the wind would blow down the door. There was no choice but to stay indoors and visit with those in residence at the parsonage. Unfortunately, that meant there were no visits with the gentlemen from Rosings.

Finally, on the third day, the clouds scattered and the sun shined brightly. How vivid was the difference, Elizabeth thought, as she gazed out the window in her room. The haze of grey overspreading the landscape had given way to a bright blue sky, brilliant sunlight, and green leaves and grass revelling in the recent moisture and warmth. She rested her arms on the sill of the window as she took in the pleasant sight. She looked towards Rosings and wondered whether the men would venture across the lane, which she presumed would be quite muddy. One thing was certain – Hunsford had been excessively dull without them.

At the sound of voices, Elizabeth went downstairs. She found Charlotte in her sitting room and heard Mr. Collins practicing his sermon in his library.

Charlotte noticed Elizabeth glance in the direction of his booming voice. "He does not wish to go to the church yet because of the mud, so he is practicing here. He does not do that often."

"If we listen in, can we stay home from church on Sunday?"

"Elizabeth, it is Easter." Charlotte gave her friend a reproachful look.

"Yes, I was only teasing. I am sure it will be a lovely service."

"My favourite service of the year. Even more than Christmas Eve," Charlotte said. "There is something about the thought of forgiveness and how it makes things right – between men and also between men and the good Lord."

A fleeting thought of Mr. Darcy came to Elizabeth's mind, of how she had held on to his insult from their first meeting, feeling resentment towards him that followed her everywhere. She was able to smile, however, as she realized she actually could be amicable towards him – especially when in Mr. Rickland's presence.

"Is Maria awake yet?"

Charlotte shook her head. "I believe she would sleep all day if she was allowed to." She clucked her tongue. "If she has not shown herself in half an hour, I will send the maid to waken her."

At that moment Mr. Collins came out of his study. "I am going to Rosings, my dear Charlotte. Lady Catherine wishes to see the notes for my sermon and offer her excellent advice." He looked at

Elizabeth. "I am fortunate to have a patroness who is excessively attentive to the sermons I preach to the parishioners. She demands only the best, and I try to oblige her." He emphasized this with several wags of his finger. "I shall return later."

"Take care of the mud, dear," Charlotte advised him as he walked out the door.

As Elizabeth watched him leave, she wondered whether there was any area of their life in which Lady Catherine did not give her opinion. A smile came to Elizabeth's face as she thought of possibly one, hoping her advice did not touch on the subject of the marriage bed, although she was quite certain she had advised them of the wisdom of promptly producing an heir.

The two ladies enjoyed an hour's intimate tête-à-tête, and finally Maria joined them. They talked of the change in weather and conjectured whether or not the rain might return. Elizabeth mused when the men – particularly Mr. Rickland – might return to pay them a call.

She furrowed her brows as she reprimanded herself for thinking so much about him. He may, after all, not have any interest in her other than enjoying her company. He may even have an arranged marriage to some young lady, perhaps a cousin, as Mr. Darcy had. She knew that as an heir to a small manor, he might wish to marry a lady of means to secure his wealth. She had no wealth to offer a man, and yet she had never felt the need to marry a man with a large fortune. She would only hope for a nice, modest home and enough money for the basic necessities – and a little pin money for herself.

Her thoughts were interrupted by the return of Mr. Collins. "Ladies! Ladies! The gentlemen will be here shortly. They claim to have some delightful news! I am all anticipation!"

Elizabeth glanced down and smiled at his bare feet.

"They are coming this way in all the mud?" Charlotte asked.

"Indeed, it is shockingly muddy. I took my shoes off directly, and I must now repair to my room for a clean pair before they arrive." Mr. Collins clasped his hands together in a dramatic gesture. "Her ladyship has certainly seen fit to display to our guests such condescension." He quickly stepped out of the room.

Charlotte turned to Elizabeth with a lift in her brows. "They are walking across the lane in all that mud to pay us a call? I am surprised, although I have my suspicions why."

Elizabeth laughed softly. "I am certain the men have been confined indoors far too long."

"Whatever you believe the reason to be, I am delighted you and my sister have been afforded a most enjoyable time." She turned to Maria. "Are you enjoying your visit?"

Maria nodded enthusiastically. "I am, but I wish I knew what to say around them!"

Charlotte laughed. "One day you shall, Maria." She looked at Elizabeth. "And you?"

"I confess my time here has been quite enjoyable, Charlotte," Elizabeth said. "You know me well enough to realise the men have added greatly to my pleasure, but it is enough that I have been with you, my dear friend." Elizabeth reached over and took Charlotte's hand, squeezing it.

"And I am certain there is one gentleman whose company you particularly enjoy." Charlotte smiled at Elizabeth and placed her other hand on top of hers. "Take care, Lizzy, not to lose your heart to the wrong man."

Elizabeth tilted her head at her friend and was about to ask what she meant when Mr. Collins returned.

"I saw the men arrive. I shall go see to them."

It was quite some time before the group entered the drawing room, and everyone seemed pleased with this overdue reunion. Elizabeth noticed even Mr. Darcy wore a smile.

Mr. Collins displayed an expression of sheer satisfaction, as if it was due to him they were being shown such consideration.

The three men came and stood before the ladies and bowed, and the ladies curtseyed in return. They all sat down, and Mr. Collins seemed the most eager to hear what the men had come to say. If anyone needed to learn patience, it was him. But they did not have to wait long.

"The last time we were here… it seems ages ago," Mr. Rickland began with a laugh. "We talked a little about the musical soiree the Saturday after Easter. We spoke with our aunt and discovered she also received an invitation. While she does not often attend these events, she has agreed we all should go." He raised his brows and looked directly at Elizabeth. "We hope you are all planning to attend, as well."

"Indeed, we are," Mr. Collins answered with a deep nod of his head.

"Yes," added Charlotte. "We are looking forward to it."

"Shall there be a variety of music, do you think?" Elizabeth asked.

"Knowing the hosts, our aunt believes there will likely be some instrumental pieces as well as soloists."

"Shall there be dancing?" Maria asked, but immediately lowering her head as a blush covered her cheeks.

"I certainly hope so," Rickland exclaimed. "Possibly only a few sets, but we shall dance all the same." He looked at Elizabeth with eagerness on his face.

"But shall Mr. Darcy dance?" Elizabeth turned to him with a raised brow. "Has your opinion of dancing changed since the evening at Lucas Lodge?"

"And what is my cousin's opinion of dancing?" The colonel chuckled as he looked from Darcy back to Elizabeth. "I would dearly like to know. Our paths rarely cross in a ballroom. At least, recently they have not."

"If I recollect correctly, when we first met, I observed him dance no more than four dances when ladies had to sit out because gentlemen were scarce. And those dances were with the two ladies in his own party."

"Scandalous!" exclaimed Fitzwilliam. "And how do you account for this, Cousin?"

"I had only arrived and had not at that time the honour of knowing any lady in the assembly beyond my party."

Elizabeth shook her head and turned her gaze to Mr. Rickland. "And no one can be introduced at a ball?" She smiled and added, "Perhaps that is a new rule of good society that has begun in London but has not yet made it to the country."

Mr. Rickland returned her smile. "If it is, I have not heard of it. What is the purpose of a ball if not to make new acquaintances?"

Mr. Darcy tightened his jaw. "While it may be the object of some to make new acquaintances, I fear I am ill-qualified to recommend myself to strangers."

Elizabeth waved her hand through the air. "Well, I shall not dispute your opinion of yourself, but I also recollect you saying to Sir William Lucas you disliked the amusement of dancing in general."

Darcy's brows narrowed as if he was contemplating what to say. Elizabeth felt she had probably teased him enough, but for some reason she enjoyed watching him struggle through his discomfiture.

"If you recollect, Miss Bennet, I was more than willing to dance with you at Lucas Lodge, but you are the one who refused."

Elizabeth chuckled. "Yes, I confess I did."

Darcy leaned in a little. "And then you refused to dance a reel with me at Netherfield. It was not until the Netherfield Ball that you finally consented to be my partner."

"Goodness, Darcy!" Mr. Rickland exclaimed. "I thought you said you were only slightly acquainted with Miss Bennet."

Elizabeth looked at Mr. Darcy, feeling a great deal of confusion and, for reasons she could not determine, slightly hurt. She guessed by his flushed face and downcast eyes that he was rather embarrassed. Elizabeth licked her lips and sat upright. "I am certain Mr. Darcy has many close acquaintances, and while we were in each other's company in Hertfordshire for a little over two months, to him that would qualify me as merely a slight acquaintance."

"Miss Bennet, I hope you will allow me to make up for my cousin's poor manners. Please say you will dance with me at the soiree." Colonel Fitzwilliam looked at her with pleading, but apologetic, eyes.

"Thank you. I would be happy to." She smiled as she answered him.

"And I hope you shall agree to dance one with me," Mr. Rickland quickly offered. "I have looked forward to a dance with you since we began talking about it. Promise me you will!"

"I should enjoy it, Mr. Rickland."

It was quiet for a moment, and Elizabeth felt all the awkwardness Mr. Darcy must feel. She hoped he would not give in to the silent expectation of also asking her to dance.

"Miss Bennet," he said softly, "I would ask you allow *me* to make up for my own poor behaviour in Hertfordshire. Please say you will dance one with me, as well."

Elizabeth looked up at him. If Mr. Rickland had displayed a pleading look, Mr. Darcy's was tortured. It would have been so much easier for both of them if he had not asked her.

"Certainly, Mr. Darcy," she replied with all the civility she could muster.

The rest of the visit passed uneventfully, but still pleasantly. The men also asked Charlotte and Maria to dance with them, and then they talked of the recent rains and their hope nothing would interfere with their plans to attend the soiree in a little over a week.

Chapter 7

Elizabeth sat in the drawing room with Charlotte and Maria. They each quietly worked on stitchery. There had been no invitations to Rosings or visits from the gentlemen for the past three days. It was not because of rains, for the skies were blue and the air was warming with the promise of spring. No, it was due to a shooting party the men had been invited to on a neighbouring manor.

She shook her head as she pondered how unfortunate it had been, however, when she had taken her morning walks each of those mornings, she had encountered Mr. Darcy. As she worked her needle in and out of the fabric, she pondered how it could be that their paths continually crossed. She could not understand how Mr. Darcy had not taken her meaning when she told him the woods had become her favourite place to walk.

She had certainly sensed his discomfiture at having to walk with her that first morning. His silence was exceedingly loud and crystal clear, and she was more than willing to grant him the silence he most certainly seemed to prefer.

She could not believe he still chose to walk out into the woods, knowing full well their paths might cross. Elizabeth had to surmise that since the woods were so extensive, he believed he would have little chance of encountering her. She determined he must have been as exasperated as she was.

But despite having to suffer his presence at her side, she had enjoyed the walk. The woods were deep with a variety of trees, some tall and some short, and the newly budding leaves seemed to enjoy waving about in the breeze. The birds had added their voices, as if looking forward to each new spring day.

Elizabeth mused that the world about her was more vocal than the man beside her. She let out a soft huff.

"Is everything all right, Lizzy?" Charlotte asked.

Elizabeth looked up. "Yes. I ... I merely pulled the thread too

60

quickly through the fabric, and it knotted." She looked down and pretended to work on untying a knot and then continued stitching.

She tried to set her mind back to her needlework, but her thoughts kept returning to their walks. She found it odd she actually found him interesting when he conversed. She occasionally was able to get him to enter into a lively discussion about two particular subjects. He seemed to enjoy talking about books he had read and Pemberley. He had intrigued her when he spoke about his country home. It was apparent he was quite proud of it and loved it, but she could only attribute his motive for such elaborate narratives was that he wished to boast to her about it. She let out a soft chuckle, however, as she considered by his description of it, she would likely find it quite lovely.

Later that day, the ladies all commented on how impatient they were for the men to return. Elizabeth chided this unknown neighbour for planning a hunt while she was visiting, thereby removing a major source of enjoyment from the ladies at the parsonage. They all laughed as Charlotte accused her of sounding much like Lady Catherine.

Elizabeth took to heart at least she would see Mr. Rickland on Easter Sunday, and she looked forward to attending the musical soiree with the gentlemen.

Mr. Rickland, Mr. Darcy, and Colonel Fitzwilliam finally paid them a visit the day before Easter.

They had a lively discussion of the shooting party and how each had enjoyed their share of success and failure each day. They were not able to stay long at the parsonage, as it began to rain. They took their leave, bidding the ladies farewell and assuring them they looked forward to seeing them at church the next day.

Easter Sunday dawned with nary a cloud in the sky. It had only rained sporadically the day before, so the roads and paths were not exceptionally muddy.

Elizabeth paid more than her usual attention to the sermon this particular morning, being aware Lady Catherine had some say in its preparation. She attempted to determine which parts might have been from her cousin and which parts from his patroness. There was a commendable balance between exhorting the parishioners to give, visit the poor and sickly, and encouraging them to be honest and upright, while trusting the good Lord for the wisdom and strength to do those things.

After the service, Lady Catherine and her daughter stood alongside Mr. and Mrs. Collins and greeted the congregation as they stepped out of the church, while the three gentlemen stood aside with Elizabeth and Maria.

"I am rather surprised." Rickland leaned in towards Elizabeth, but spoke so the three others could hear. "Mr. Collins delivered quite an exceptional Easter sermon."

Elizabeth nodded in agreement. "I was thinking the same thing, myself! I believe he put a lot of thought into it."

"Quite so!" declared the colonel. "And it was short enough to get us dismissed a few minutes early!"

"I believe we have your aunt to thank for at least some of it," Elizabeth said. "Apparently Mr. Collins has Lady Catherine give him her appraisal and offer suggestions to improve his sermon once he has written it."

"I had no idea!" Mr. Rickland said. "But I would wager she does not offer suggestions, but directives."

Elizabeth tilted her head and laughed. "But is it her design to make the sermons longer or shorter, I wonder?"

"Ha!" Colonel Fitzwilliam turned to Darcy. "I would love to know!"

"I would hope," Mr. Darcy said solemnly, "she is more concerned with the content of the sermon than the length of it." He turned to his cousin. "And you ought to be paying heed to the sermon instead of the hands on your pocket watch."

Elizabeth watched Colonel Fitzwilliam's brows lower for a brief moment. When a gentleman stepped up to Mr. Darcy and addressed him, drawing his attention away, Colonel Fitzwilliam chuckled. "So you see, Miss Bennet, while my cousin and I are very close, in many ways we are quite different."

"I have noticed," she said with a laugh. "You seem always to be on the lookout for a diversion, while he seems always to be on the lookout for something to disparage."

Mr. Rickland was quick to add, "He has always been that way, has he not?" He shook his head. "He seems to have an absolute notion of what is right and wrong, allowing for little disagreement."

Elizabeth stole a glance at the object of their discussion as he spoke with the gentleman who had approached him. The gentleman was doing most of the talking. Mr. Darcy merely nodded his head every now and again and did not seem to be at all engaged in what the man was saying.

She smiled as she thought of his initial conversation with Mr. Collins at the Netherfield Ball. She had been so mortified to see her cousin approach him without any formal introduction, and despite having a close connection with his aunt, she was well aware Mr. Darcy did not appreciate this breach in etiquette. Yes, he certainly had a strong sense of what was proper in polite society and would tolerate nothing less.

After a few moments of silence, Colonel Fitzwilliam added, "But I suppose he has every right to expect it of others if he abides by the rules himself. And he does. I have yet to see him behave inappropriately in the company of others."

Elizabeth had to bite her lip to keep from mentioning all the times she had witnessed his rude behaviour in Hertfordshire.

When the gentleman to whom he was talking walked away, Darcy returned to the group.

"Who was that?" his cousin asked.

"Mr. Adamson, who is hosting the soiree this Saturday. He wanted to inform me he and his wife would be delighted to introduce their daughter to me. You remember her – the one who sang a solo at church on Easter Sunday three years ago at the sweet, tender age of sixteen."

"I fear I do not recall her."

"No need to worry about that. Neither do I."

Colonel Fitzwilliam crossed his arms in front of him. "Heavens! Lady Catherine will not be pleased to know a local gentleman is seeking to introduce you to a daughter who is of marrying age!" He let out a bellowing laugh. "No, she shall not be pleased at all!"

Darcy frowned at this, and Elizabeth wondered if the remark was said to remind Mr. Darcy his intended was Lady Catherine's own daughter.

The great woman then called to her nephews. The church had emptied, and everyone else had dispersed. Mr. Darcy and Mr.

Rickland said their goodbyes and stepped away. Colonel Fitzwilliam leaned over to Elizabeth and whispered, "You notice how that gentleman called for Darcy alone? This happens all the time to him. But to me, never."

"And do you not mind?" Elizabeth asked.

"Mind? I am elated. I have no interest in trying to fend off all the marriage-minded mothers and fathers who wish to introduce me to their lovely daughters!"

Elizabeth smiled as Colonel Fitzwilliam walked away. The three men were each so different from one another. She could not help but wonder if the same thing happened often to Mr. Rickland, despite not having the fortune Mr. Darcy had. She finally concluded if someone had to choose between the two men, Mr. Darcy's fortune might be the deciding factor to someone interested in wealth alone, but Mr. Rickland had the advantage in open and easy manners.

She shook her head slowly as she walked over to Charlotte and her husband. *Mr. Darcy likely has women vying for his affections wherever he goes,* she thought to herself. "Worry not, sir," she whispered. "You have nothing to fear from me in that quarter. A gentleman's fortune is not as important to me as his character and integrity."

~~*

As the carriage returned to Rosings, Darcy felt a great deal of discomfiture. He had been disappointed when Mr. Adamson approached him to talk, drawing him away from enjoying Elizabeth's presence. He was also irritated at the man for making known his wish of introducing him to his daughter.

He had practically been holding his breath when Fitzwilliam mentioned their aunt's displeasure in his being introduced to a young lady of marriageable age. The last thing he wanted was for him to mention his aunt's expectation for him to marry his cousin Anne. He could endure his cousin's teasing when it was between the two of them, but he found it difficult to laugh about it when in the company of others, particularly Miss Elizabeth Bennet.

He stared out the window as the others chatted amongst themselves. Only he and Anne were silent. He turned to look across the carriage at his cousin and saw her looking at him with more perception than he had ever noticed before. He felt as though she knew everything about him, and he quickly turned away.

A sick feeling swelled inside as he considered what he had never wanted to believe. Perhaps Anne did truly care for him – love him, even – and was still anticipating him to ask for her hand. But he did not return those feelings. He told Fitzwilliam he was going to settle the whole misapprehension on this visit, and yet he had not broached the subject. With the feelings he had for Elizabeth, and having a relentlessly building desire to ask for her hand, he could not allow Anne or his aunt to continue to hope for a marriage between them.

His eyes shot wide open. Ask for Elizabeth's hand! Had it come to this? His heart began to pound as he considered this monumental step. Although he looked out the window, he wondered whether Anne's eyes were upon him, aware of his every thought. He made every effort to take slow, even breaths as he considered what this would mean.

He forced himself to think sensibly on this matter. He had certainly imagined her walking by his side on the grounds at Pemberley. During those months after they departed Netherfield, she had invaded his thoughts when he least expected it. He had to continually remind himself how unsuitable she was for him. But then, just as strongly, he would argue how suitable she would be stepping into the role of Mistress of Pemberley – but more importantly, as his wife. Her unsuitability had more to do with the expectations of others. To him, she was everything suitable!

He had made a futile attempt with Miss Strathern. He had known this young lady for several years. She was beautiful, had good connections, gracious manners, and would be most suitable as Mistress of Pemberley. But would she be everything he wished for in a wife?

No, she would not, he thought adamantly to himself. *She would satisfy others' expectations, but not mine!*

He gave his head a quick shake and briefly closed his eyes. As he began to blow out a puff of air, he stopped.

He turned his head slowly back towards the others to see Anne was still watching him. He met her gaze and noticed her slight smile. He swallowed hard, wondering if the smile was meant for him. A surge of guilt flooded him, as he suddenly realized how thoughtless he had been all these years avoiding the conversation that would be difficult, but was most needed.

His eyes turned to Rickland, who seemed to have a rather permanent smile etched on his face. He quickly turned back to the window, feeling a sudden flame of jealousy burn inside.

Rickland. The man certainly knew how to engage everyone in conversation. He was much like Bingley in that he could talk to anyone about anything. But was he singling Elizabeth out with the intention of securing her affections?

Darcy shifted in his seat, and his brows pinched together. He suspected Elizabeth enjoyed the man's company, but was she losing her heart to him? Was Rickland merely being sociable, or was his heart as captivated by her as his own was? He began tapping his fingers against his leg, but upon noticing it, clasped his hands tightly together.

He had the advantage of making her acquaintance first, although Rickland had the advantage of having recently spent a good amount of time with her before he and Fitzwilliam had arrived. Dare he think he had the advantage of wealth and connections over Rickland? He absently shook his head. Elizabeth would think nothing of those things, although he believed she would appreciate them once she had them.

His musings were interrupted by his aunt. "I have invited Mr. and Mrs. Collins and their guests to join us this afternoon." She brushed her daughter's sleeve with her gloved hand, as if she were wiping off some dirt. "Everyone else I invited had other plans. Such a disappointment. The rains this week certainly curtailed all visits. I am so grateful to you, my nephews, for if it were not for your presence here, I would have been most seriously displeased with nothing to occupy my time."

Darcy readily noticed Rickland's smile broaden as their aunt relayed this information.

"Will they be dining with us?" Rickland asked.

Lady Catherine waved a hand through the air. "No, no. They already had plans for their Easter meal. They shall partake of tea and a light dessert with us later today."

"Splendid!" Rickland exclaimed. "These persistent rains and the shooting party have kept us from their most delightful company far too long!"

Darcy silently agreed, while at the same time believing Rickland was displaying a little too much enthusiasm.

His eyes turned to Anne, who continued to watch him, and he quickly looked away.

~~*

That afternoon, the Hunsford party arrived none too soon for the gentlemen's satisfaction. Darcy had grown increasingly impatient for their arrival, which Fitzwilliam readily noticed. The tapping of his fingers or foot received a look from his cousin, and at one point, a nudge. He finally repaired to his chambers to await the party.

He returned to the parlour before their expected arrival. He had come to learn Mr. Collins was prompt, which pleased his aunt considerably. The bell announced their arrival at exactly the hour. Darcy took a deep breath, tugged at his coat, and straightened his neckcloth as he rose with the other gentlemen. He could think of nothing he wished to do more than spend time in Elizabeth's company and he hoped she was as eager to spend time with him, as well.

As the party walked into the parlour, Darcy fixed his eyes on Elizabeth. Each time he saw her, he was more convinced of her suitability. He thought her more beautiful than ever. How could he have considered her only tolerable the first time he saw her? He could barely breathe as he considered she was the handsomest woman of his acquaintance. He could not prevent the smile that began in his heart and turned his lips upward.

Rickland stepped forward and cheerfully greeted the party. Darcy found himself just as quickly gritting his teeth as Elizabeth bestowed upon him one of her ready smiles. His cousin followed, coming up alongside of Rickland and making a short bow to the ladies.

"We have all been anxiously awaiting your arrival," he said.

Then leaning close to the ladies he added, "This ragtag group of gentlemen is always in great need of the refined and most pleasant company of lovely ladies."

Darcy stepped forward with a formal bow. "Ladies, welcome." While he addressed all three ladies, his eyes stayed on Elizabeth.

"Come in!" Lady Catherine's voice echoed throughout the large chamber, and she motioned the same with her fan.

Mr. and Mrs. Collins entered first, taking the seats next to Lady Catherine, which put Charlotte next to Mr. Rickland. Maria sat on the other side of him, which left either a chair next to Mr. Darcy or one next to Miss de Bourgh. Elizabeth decided she would sit next to Anne and see if she could engage her in conversation.

Polite conversations amongst the different parties began, which allowed Elizabeth the opportunity to speak with Miss de Bourgh.

"Will we see you at the musical soiree this Saturday?" Elizabeth asked.

The young lady looked at her with wide eyes and a ready smile.

She nodded slowly. "I hope to be able to attend for a little while, at least."

Elizabeth smiled. "I look forward to seeing you there. Do you enjoy music?"

Again she nodded. "I do, but I neither play nor sing."

Elizabeth smiled sweetly. "But you have talent in other areas."

Anne's brows pinched together. "In other areas?"

Elizabeth pursed her lips together. "I am quite certain you excel in writing. You spend a great amount of time at it."

Anne's smile showed a hint of resignation. "It is something I enjoy. I cannot speak of my proficiency at it."

Elizabeth leaned in towards her. "I would truly enjoy seeing how you describe something with your words. Your secret would remain safe with me."

Anne's eyes widened. "Oh, I could not."

Elizabeth shook her head. "I promise not to laugh."

Anne looked about her, as if to see whether anyone was listening. Once assured no one was paying attention, she whispered softly, "Miss Bennet, no one knows. No one can know I write... stories."

"Truly?"

A blush painted Anne's pale cheeks, and she nodded. "But I beg you not to say anything to anyone. My mother does not know, and she would be upset if she were to find out. Only Mrs. Jenkinson is aware I write, and she encouraged me because she feels I have a gift. She sent my stories off to her... off to a publisher in London, and two of them have been published."

Elizabeth had never seen the young lady so animated, and she could hardly credit what she had been told. She looked up and saw Mr. Darcy's eyes upon them, his brow narrowed. Perhaps he was concerned she was poisoning his intended's mind with tales of living in a simple country neighbourhood.

She leaned in to Miss de Bourgh. "What type of stories do you write? Are they children's stories?"

Anne shook her head, her blush growing deeper. "No, I write love stories. But they are not published under my name. I could never..."

Elizabeth reached over and took her hand. "I have never met an author!" she said in a hushed whisper. "I am delighted with your accomplishment! Would you tell me under what name your books are published? I would love to read one, and I promise not to give away your secret."

Anne's brows knit together. "I do not know if I should..."

"Of what are you speaking?" Lady Catherine's voice boomed from the other side of Elizabeth as her fan slapped down into her palm.

Elizabeth turned. She did not know whether she was addressing Anne or herself. After a moment of silence, Elizabeth decided to answer. "We were speaking about the musical soiree and how much Miss de Bourgh enjoys music."

Lady Catherine narrowed her eyes. "But unfortunately she does not play an instrument. She enjoys listening. You will play for us, Miss Bennet? I should like to hear you play again. You may play two songs for us."

Elizabeth nodded. "I shall be happy to." She gave a friendly nod to Anne, who returned it with a smile. *Well, I am not certain I would wish Mr. Darcy on her,* she thought, *but she may turn out to be the perfect wife for him, after all. He will enjoy many a silent evening in her company whilst she writes. Oh, it shall be a happy union, indeed!*

Elizabeth walked over to the pianoforte and began looking through the selection of music. Mr. Rickland was soon by her side, assisting her in her choice. Colonel Fitzwilliam then came and stood on her other side.

"Since I am to play two pieces," Elizabeth said, "you each may pick one. But I do reserve the right of refusing your selection if I deem it too difficult."

Elizabeth suddenly felt someone come and stand behind her. She knew from the scowl on Mr. Rickland's face it was Mr. Darcy.

She turned her head slightly towards him, noticing his arms folded across his chest. "Did you come all this way to select a piece of music for me to play, Mr. Darcy? I fear your aunt has allowed me but two pieces, and I have already asked Mr. Rickland and Colonel Fitzwilliam to select them." She sent him a remorseful look.

"I trust whatever pieces of music they select, you will perform quite well, Miss Bennet."

Elizabeth turned to Colonel Fitzwilliam with a smile. "Mr. Darcy would have you believe I am more proficient at playing than I truly am and can play anything handed to me."

"As I can attest, she plays splendidly. Here is a favourite of mine," Mr. Rickland announced, handing her Pleyel's *Sonatina in D Major*.

"And may we hear you play this?" Colonel Fitzwilliam held out to her Haydn's *Sonata in G Major*.

"I doubt I shall be able to do either of these songs justice," Elizabeth said. "But perhaps I can manage if I play them a little slower than written." She moved to the pianoforte and sat down, flanked on either side by the two men. Darcy stood on the other side of the piano, looking across at her. She looked up at him. "Please do not flinch in any way when you hear my errors. I know there shall be some. Fortunately," she said, looking to her left and then her right, "I will see neither of the two men at my side when they grimace or shudder."

"I shall do no such thing!" Rickland exclaimed. "I will enjoy each note!"

"As will I, Miss Bennet," Mr. Darcy assured her softly.

Elizabeth took in a deep breath and began. She played the first two pages rather slowly, but she soon felt confident in her fingering and sped it up a little. She made several minor errors, but no one seemed to notice, even Lady Catherine.

When the last note of the final song sounded, she was rewarded with a soft applause and words of praise from the men.

Everyone was then treated with a delectable assortment of desserts to choose from and enjoy.

After they had finished, Lady Catherine casually looked towards the window. "It is nearing dusk. Mr. Collins, you ought to get everyone home before dark."

Mr. Collins shot up out of his chair and clasped his hands. "Yes! Yes! Come, we shall not keep you any longer." With a bow and a generous thank you to his hosts, he then gestured for his party to stand, and he began walking out of the room.

As Elizabeth walked past Anne, she whispered, "I greatly enjoyed talking with you, Miss de Bourgh."

Anne smiled and reached out her hand. Elizabeth took it and realized a piece of paper had been pressed into it. She looked down at Anne with a question on her lips, but Anne shook her head.

Elizabeth nodded knowingly. Anne did not want her to look at it in front of everyone, so she slipped it into her pocket.

Later, after they returned to Hunsford and Elizabeth finally was in the solitude of her room, she pulled out the slip of paper. On it was written a name, *N. D. Berg.*

Chapter 8

The next morning, Elizabeth was disappointed she could not venture out due to a light shower and hoped it would soon pass. Perhaps if she waited and set out later, she might encounter Mr. Rickland instead of Mr. Darcy. She picked up the book she had been reading last night and opened it to the page where, instead of her bookmark, Anne's secret note held her place.

Elizabeth looked down at the small piece of paper and smiled. Oh, she had knowledge of a most astonishing and private piece of information. She wondered what Mr. Darcy would think if he knew his intended bride was a writer. Especially a writer of love stories. She determined as soon as she returned home, she would do all she could to secure one of *N. D. Berg's* novels.

She went downstairs and joined Charlotte in the parlour, where they enjoyed tea and conversation.

The rain was brief, but it was not until after ten o'clock that it stopped. Mr. Collins left for the church, and Elizabeth noticed the sun shine finally filtering through the window.

"Charlotte, I think I shall take a short walk. I believe the rain clouds have moved on, and I so long for a stroll."

"I would join you, Elizabeth, but I fear it is too muddy for my taste. Mr. Collins would not be happy if he discovered I was out walking in the mud. Maria, of course, will have none of it."

"I shall be quite all right. I think I will take a book with me and find a nice secluded place to read."

As she left the parsonage and entered the lane, she saw two gentlemen setting out in the direction of the park. She reasoned it was probably Mr. Darcy and Colonel Fitzwilliam, but as she studied them, she realized she was only partially correct. It was indeed, Colonel Fitzwilliam, but the gentleman accompanying him was not Mr. Darcy, but Mr. Rickland. She hurried in their direction.

The two men stopped and faced each other, speaking quite animatedly. At length, Colonel Fitzwilliam looked over, noticing Elizabeth drawing near.

"Miss Bennet!" he exclaimed. "This is a pleasant surprise."

"I thank you. I am delighted the rain has stopped."

"It has cleared up nicely," Fitzwilliam added. "In what direction were you planning to go?"

"I thought I would stroll about the park."

"One of my favourite destinations," Fitzwilliam said cheerfully. "I always take a walk about the park on my last day here, but Rickland asked me to join him this morning."

"You have brought a book with you. What are you reading?" Mr. Rickland asked.

"It is *The Old Manor House* by Charlotte Turner Smith."

Mr. Rickland laughed. "Ahh, so are you enjoying it? I cannot say I have read any novels written by a woman."

Elizabeth tilted her head. "Do you think they ought not to write? If they have the talent and the opportunity..."

"I do not see the harm for a lady to write," began Colonel Fitzwilliam, "when she has no other source of income, but I am not of the opinion a lady of consequence ought to write. I believe I would draw the line there."

"But by not allowing women to write, might you not be depriving the world of a wonderful story?" Elizabeth tilted her head at him with a smile.

Colonel Fitzwilliam shook his head. "No, it is not for a fine lady to do. I would never be able to read a novel written by a lady."

"That is unfortunate. I am enjoying *The Old Manor House* every bit as much as I have enjoyed anything written by a man."

"I believe if a woman has the talent," Rickland offered, "she ought to have the same opportunity as a man to get a book published."

Elizabeth nodded and said, "Thank you."

"But..." Rickland began as he put up his hand. "I must maintain most men would not read it."

Colonel Fitzwilliam maintained his assertion a fine lady ought not to write, while Elizabeth held fast to her opinions.

"You all appear to be engaged in an enthusiastic discussion!" Mr. Darcy suddenly appeared, coming towards them.

Elizabeth gave her head a slight shake as she considered, once again, she must encounter him. She looked at him with a single raised brow. "Perhaps you have come to settle our disagreement. Amongst the three of us, we cannot agree."

"I would be happy to express my opinion, but I cannot guarantee you will all be of one accord once you hear it. What is the nature of this disagreement?"

"We were discussing whether a lady ought to be allowed to write without its being considered improper." Elizabeth was most interested in his opinion and held out the book for him to see the title and author.

"Hmm," he murmured. "I can guess what your different opinions are. I know Charlotte Turner Smith was raised in a wealthy home, but after she married, her husband squandered their money. They were unable to pay their debts leading to their incarceration in Fleet Prison. She began writing to help support her family of a dozen children, I believe."

Elizabeth folded her arms in front of her. "And do you believe she had the right to do that?"

In her case, yes. But I do not believe it should be an occupation of a lady of the higher circles."

Elizabeth let out a huff as Colonel Fitzwilliam laughed. "So the two of us agree. Sorry, Miss Bennet, but there are some ladies who simply should not write."

Elizabeth pursed her lips, wondering what Mr. Darcy would think of his cousin – his intended – authoring books.

"I shall not be dissuaded from my opinion. I believe a lady, whoever she may be, if she has the talent, should be able to do whatever she wishes. Men should not be the only ones who can do as they please."

"I fully agree!" Mr. Rickland said.

Elizabeth smiled at him and then directed her eyes to Mr. Darcy. "Why should a woman only be able to pen stories if she needs the money? What if she had a fortune, had everything she could wish for, but only this gave her any true enjoyment?"

Mr. Darcy studied her for a moment and then said, "I see no

harm in a lady writing, but publishing it would be another matter. Let her write her stories for the enjoyment of herself, her family, and friends."

Elizabeth wished to argue her point more fully but felt it was something he and Miss de Bourgh would have to work through once they were married. She felt a bit sorry for Anne, wondering how Mr. Darcy's views would affect her secret love for writing. She diplomatically concluded with, "We shall have to agree we all have our own opinion on the matter."

"I think that is best," agreed Colonel Fitzwilliam. "I concede there shall always be extenuating circumstances, so we must not make broad judgments without knowing all the facts."

"Thank you, Colonel," Elizabeth said, nodding her head.

He then turned to Darcy. "You are walking later than usual this morning."

Darcy nodded. "I had intended to set out as soon as the rain let up, but Mr. Lowell asked to speak with me."

Rickland turned quickly to him. "What would our aunt's steward want to talk about with you?"

Darcy shook his head. "He has a habit of soliciting my opinions when I visit and keeping me abreast of the concerns of the estate."

Elizabeth noticed Mr. Darcy fix his eyes on Mr. Rickland, who blew out a puff of air and suddenly turned to address her.

"I am so looking forward to Saturday's musical soiree, Miss Bennet. It shall likely be a most enjoyable evening."

Everyone was of the same mind. Both Mr. Rickland and Colonel Fitzwilliam chatted happily with her about it while Mr. Darcy said little.

Elizabeth joined the men as they walked back towards Rosings and Hunsford. She would not complain that her walk this morning would be much shorter than she was used to, for having the cheerfulness of Mr. Rickland and the polite attention of Colonel Fitzwilliam made up for the solemn silence of Mr. Darcy.

She could not help but wonder, however, if Lady Catherine's steward was required to keep Mr. Darcy informed about the estate since he was to marry Anne. And was Mr. Rickland jealous Mr. Darcy was being consulted and not himself? There had certainly been something in his manner that seemed to indicate he was not wholly pleased.

~~*

The gentlemen came to Hunsford for short visits the following two mornings. Lady Catherine had previous engagements, so there were no invitations to Rosings.

Later, after their visit on the second day, Mr. Rickland returned to the parsonage alone. This was a pleasant surprise to Elizabeth. It had been a while since she had been able to enjoy his company without the other two gentlemen.

"Good afternoon, Mr. Rickland," Charlotte said as she invited him in. "You have none of your companions with you?"

"I truly cannot say where they are. I suppose they might be out and about together. My aunt and her daughter had an appointment somewhere, and I found myself quite alone. There is nothing I would rather have done than come here. I hope you do not mind a second visit."

"Of course not," Charlotte replied.

They talked of the pleasant weather and how beautiful spring was with all the flowers blooming.

"Yes," Elizabeth said. "I was outside admiring the flowers in the garden. Some of them smell so lovely. This is my favourite time of the year."

"I believe you are right, Miss Bennet," Mr. Rickland concurred with a smile. He looked down at the book in her hand. "Have you finished your book yet?"

"I have not. My friend keeps me busy enough that I find little time to read."

Charlotte looked at Mr. Rickland. "I must confess we do talk a great deal. I fear we are both taking advantage of our time together before she returns home. Our parting will come far too soon."

They continued to talk for a considerable time of home and family, and at length Elizabeth asked, "Mr. Rickland, I am most curious about the turret on the west end of Rosings. Do you know what is up there?"

Mr. Rickland jumped to his feet. "I do! Would you ladies like to go see it? The prospect from that height cannot be surpassed, and not only that, there is a telescope in it allowing you to see for miles in all directions."

"I should like that very much!" Elizabeth said, clasping her hands together. "Charlotte, Maria, would you like to join us?"

Charlotte shook her head. "I will decline, but I am certain Maria would enjoy it." She turned to her sister. "The two of you can go, and I will wait here for you."

As the three walked across the lane to Rosings, Mr. Rickland told them more about the turret. "Lady Catherine does not allow anyone to mention the turret, as that is where her husband died."

Maria's eyes widened, and she came to a halt. "Really? He died up in the turret? Do they know what happened to him?" Her face paled as she was likely imagining all the horrors that may have transpired to bring about his death. Elizabeth knew her to be fond of Gothic novels.

Mr. Rickland gave a quick wink to Elizabeth. "Now that you mention it, his death was odd. No one missed him for three days, and when he was found, he had been stabbed several times and he had written three initials with his own blood before he died." He shook his head slowly and let out a moan. "Dreadful affair."

Maria began to shake. "I think I shall return to the parsonage. I do not want to go up anymore." She turned to leave, but stopped and looked back. "Whose initials did he write?"

Mr. Rickland and Elizabeth began to laugh. "I was teasing, Miss Lucas. He did die there, but strictly from natural causes. The turret is perfectly harmless!"

"No terror shall befall us, Maria," Elizabeth assured her.

"I shall protect you both!" Mr. Rickland said gallantly, striking a pose as if he wielded a sword. "But to own the truth, my aunt insists no one is to mention the turret in her or her daughter's presence, nor does she want anyone to access it, but sometimes we sneak up anyway."

Once they were at Rosings, they had to walk to the west end of the manor and take the stairs to the third floor. Rickland led them to a spiral staircase.

"Oh, my!" Elizabeth said. "I have never seen anything like this!" She began to take the stairs quickly, eager to reach the turret. As she began climbing, she heard Maria begin to express her doubts again.

"It looks ominous up there," Maria said. "I read a book once where a castle had a spiral staircase." She shuddered. "Frightful things happened to those who took those steps to the top."

Elizabeth halted with the intention of encouraging her, but then continued her climb when she heard Mr. Rickland's gentle voice soothe the young girl. "I promise you, no harm will befall you. It is light and bright and quite cheery once you enter the turret."

Elizabeth reached the top of the stairs and took the few steps to the door, which was slightly ajar. She gave it a gentle push and walked in. The sight of the surrounding windows looking out in every direction delighted her. Unfortunately, she was looking to the right as she turned to walk to the left.

She suddenly hurled forward, having tripped on an immovable object. Before she could even turn her head to see what had caused her to stumble, arms went about her, preventing her fall. She inexplicably found herself on Mr. Darcy's lap.

Their eyes met and locked. Elizabeth's mouth opened wide in surprise, while Mr. Darcy seemed to lean slightly towards her.

He stared silently at her for a moment, appearing somewhat dazed, still holding her tight.

Elizabeth gasped at the sight before her. Mr. Darcy was reclining in a chair, quite informally attired. He wore only a shirt and breeches. The sleeves of his shirt were unbuttoned and rolled up, and his legs were stretched out before him. It was his feet over which she had tripped.

It appeared he had fallen asleep reading, as Elizabeth also found herself sitting on a book.

When Mr. Darcy did not immediately let go, Elizabeth said firmly, "I believe, Mr. Darcy, you may release me now. I should be steady on my feet... as long as yours are out of the way."

He shook his head and removed his arms from about her, but not before Mr. Rickland and Maria stepped in. The young lady gasped, and a blush tinged her cheeks.

"Darcy! Unhand Miss Bennet immediately!" Rickland demanded.

Elizabeth quickly stood up and stepped away. "I tripped..."

"And I caught her," Darcy added. He stood up and looked

down at himself, suddenly remembering how he was dressed. "Pray forgive my attire. I did not expect anyone to join me here."

"So it seems." Mr. Rickland frowned, and his brows pinched together. "Well, Darcy, it appears this is the second time being up in the turret has contributed to your behaving rather shamefully."

Darcy clenched his jaw. "It would have been more shameful had I not caught her. What would you have had me do, leave her to fall?"

"I am quite all right," Elizabeth said. "Mr. Darcy acted in all prudence and was most proper." She paused and then lifted a single brow and smiled. "As to this other offense, he alone must defend himself, for I know not what it was, but I fear," she said with a soft chuckle, glancing down at his attire, "we cannot extend any mercy towards him for his clothing." She turned to Mr. Rickland. "And what *was* that first offense he committed?"

Mr. Rickland leaned against the wall and crossed his arms in front of him. "I understand he and his two cousins came up here without permission when they were younger, greatly upsetting my uncle." He glared at Darcy, and in an accusing voice, asked, "And were you found holding Anne in your lap that day?"

Darcy's jaw tensed. "Anne and I were no more than eight, and Fitzwilliam was ten. We were playing war, and came up here to shoot at our enemies."

"And using our uncle's brand new telescope, if I recollect."

Elizabeth let out a soft laugh. "Were there many enemies, Mr. Darcy? Did you save Rosings from marauding enemy troops?"

Darcy pinched his lips together. "I like to think we did. At that age, it was fun, but I confess, I should have known better."

"So Mr. Darcy has exonerated himself in two of the three offenses." Elizabeth gave a toss of her head. "I suppose he can also be forgiven for dressing so informally as he did not anticipate encountering anyone."

"That is true, and I appreciate your clemency. My aunt will not step foot in the turret because it is where our uncle died. They found him in the chair. At first they thought him asleep, he looked so peaceful."

"In that chair?" Maria gasped and took a step back.

"Actually, no," Darcy said. We thought it best to get rid of that chair, and I bought a new one. But she will still not come up here and forbids Anne to. If we do not come up here, no one will." He looked at Rickland. "I assume they are from home."

Rickland nodded. "They are."

"That is a shame. The view from up here is beautiful." Elizabeth pointed to the telescope. "May I look through it?"

Darcy extended his arm, and Elizabeth walked over to it. She leaned down and looked through the eyepiece. "Oh!" she said suddenly. "It is aimed directly at the parsonage garden!" She began to laugh. "I can see Mr. Collins meticulously picking weeds!" She pulled back and eyed Mr. Darcy. "Can it be you were spying on him to discover his secrets to gardening?"

Darcy's mouth twitched, and he gave his head a quick shake.

"I hope you do not suspect him of being an enemy." She looked back through the telescope and swivelled it around.

"May I see?" Maria asked.

Elizabeth stepped away, allowing her to look through it. She then turned back to Mr. Darcy with a taunting look. "I certainly hope you do not consider *me* an enemy, as I was out in the garden earlier, as well!"

Mr. Darcy's posture stiffened. "I certainly do not."

Elizabeth could readily see his discomfiture at being teased and turned back to look out towards the park. "If I had a turret, I would likely stay up in it all day!" She laughed. "Of course I would require a telescope." She gave her head a quick shake. "And a good book."

"An excellent prospect would be beneficial, as well," Mr. Rickland added. He then turned to Darcy, and Elizabeth noticed an accusatory tone in his voice, despite speaking again to her. "I think perhaps *you* should find other things to look at than a parsonage *garden*."

Chapter 9

That evening Darcy sat in the drawing room with a book in his hands. He could not concentrate on a single word as he thought again and again about his encounter with Elizabeth in the turret.

He had fallen asleep while reading after looking through the telescope. When Elizabeth had stumbled over his outstretched legs, he awakened, reacting instantly. After seeing it was her, it took him a moment to realize he was awake, as she often invaded his dreams. His eyes widened as he considered how close he had come to leaning over and kissing her. Fortunately, he did not; however, he may have held her a moment longer than what would be deemed proper.

She had been gracious in explaining to Rickland how she had stumbled and he had caught her. It was unfortunate she had fallen into his lap but only because Rickland had then walked in. As far as he was concerned, he greatly enjoyed briefly holding her in his arms. They remained up in the turret for nearly an hour, and she seemed to take delight in scrutinizing the prospect from every angle.

He forced himself to turn the page of his book. It would not do to have his cousin notice he was not devouring the book, as he normally did.

Despite being so different from the type of woman others expected him to marry – and even the type of woman *he* expected to marry – he could not put Miss Elizabeth Bennet out of his thoughts.

Since he had come to Kent, each encounter had revealed more and more about her he found engaging. She had such lively intelligence, a quick sense of humour, and then there were her very fine eyes. She took delight in such simple things. He could readily see how the other two men admired her. He was certain Fitzwilliam would heartily approve a marriage between himself and

Elizabeth.

He thought of Rickland and grumbled. Ever since returning from their walk yesterday, the man's attitude towards him had altered. He either avoided him, ignored him, or when he could do neither, he was blatantly uncivil to him.

It was worse after the incident in the turret. Rickland had not directly accused him of anything, but Darcy knew he had been angry when it was discovered the telescope was pointed directly at the parsonage. He wished to defend his actions, but he could not. It was true he merely happened to see Elizabeth walking outside the parsonage in the garden. He watched her lean over to smell the flowers. As he had watched her, he could readily imagine her walking through the flower garden at Pemberley, and he chose not to look away.

She had had such a lovely look upon her face. She was alone and appeared most content. He would like to believe it was due to him. Were her affections as engaged with him as his were with her? The joy he saw written in her face and in the liveliness of her movements was certainly how she made him feel. He had never felt so much joy in the presence of a woman. Only Georgiana came close.

Darcy lifted his eyes and looked at Rickland. He wondered, for the first time, if the man had more than a passing interest in Elizabeth. Could he be a rival for her affections? He shook his head. He had readily seen from the beginning Rickland enjoyed Elizabeth's company, but he attributed it to her lively and engaging manners. He surmised Rickland would not have any real interest in a woman unless she had a great fortune. He bit his lip and furrowed his brow as he contemplated this.

"Is the book that bad?" Colonel Fitzwilliam suddenly asked. "Or are you just in a foul mood this evening?"

"No, I am not in a foul mood. I am rather..." He clenched his jaw. "My mind is engaged in a dilemma of sorts."

He could not prevent his gaze from going over to Rickland, who was seated next to Lady Catherine, listening inattentively to her most recent complaints. Out of the corner of his eye he noticed Anne looking at him. When he looked her way, she met his gaze for a moment before looking back down to begin writing again.

"A dilemma, eh?" The colonel asked, apparently curious for more information.

Darcy shook his head. "Nothing of great import." He looked back at his book and abruptly turned the page, despite not having read it. He gripped the book tightly as he considered his last statement. On the contrary, it *was* of great import, if he were to make an offer of marriage to Miss Elizabeth Bennet.

~~*

The following morning Elizabeth came downstairs and was surprised to see Charlotte was already up. She sat to talk with her before setting out on a walk.

"Good morning, Lizzy," Charlotte said. "I must tell you how much Maria enjoyed going up into the turret yesterday with you and Mr. Rickland. She talked about it all evening after you went to your room."

"It is a lovely view from up there, but poor Maria was a little worried, after hearing that is where Sir Lewis died."

"She reads too many Gothic novels, I believe."

"She must have a vivid imagination. There was nothing frightening about it at all!" Elizabeth laughed.

"She told me Mr. Darcy was up there."

"Yes, he was," Elizabeth said with a laugh. "I imagine she told you about my unexpected encounter with him?"

Charlotte nodded and took a sip of her tea. "She did." She set the teacup back into its saucer and folded her hands in her lap. "Lizzy, has either Mr. Rickland or Mr. Darcy made any profession of admiration for you?"

Elizabeth's eyes opened wide, and her jaw dropped. "Heavens, Charlotte. What would have given you the idea that either would?"

Charlotte leaned forward. "I cannot help but notice certain looks between you and them and between the two of them."

Elizabeth laughed. "Now I think *your* imagination is too vivid! Perhaps *you* are reading too many novels that are filled with romance!" She shook her head. "I have certainly been enjoying Mr. Rickland's company, and I believe he is enjoying mine, but there is nothing more to it. As for Mr. Darcy, I cannot conceive of him having any real affection for me. He is merely being polite, which does seem quite unusual for him, having seen how he behaved in Hertfordshire." She stood up to leave. "Now erase those silly notions from your head, dear friend!"

Charlotte smiled. "You know I do not read romantic stories, Lizzy, for you know I am not romantic. I am merely making an observation."

"And you are perfectly entitled to your opinions in your observations, but I highly doubt any of these men, including Colonel Fitzwilliam, have any particular fondness for me." She turned to walk out the door.

As she stepped out, she heard Charlotte say, "Do not be so certain, Lizzy."

Elizabeth hurried down the lane, grateful no one was in sight. She hoped this morning she could escape Mr. Darcy's company. She had to laugh at the memory of the incident in the turret the day before. She knew he had been embarrassed at being found in such a casual state of attire, but he seemed to quickly forget he was without coat and vest. There was something else, however, in being caught with her in his lap. She chuckled. He was likely mortified, although he hid that most admirably.

She thought about Charlotte's words regarding the two gentlemen and shook her head. "Certainly not!" she said softly, taking in a deep breath and delighting in the fresh morning air. She turned towards the woods when she heard her name called.

"Miss Bennet!"

Elizabeth stopped and closed her eyes, before turning to see Mr. Darcy walking towards her. His long legs quickly brought him to her side.

She forced a smile and shook her head. A soft sigh escaped as she considered she could not succeed in taking a single walk without encountering him.

When he reached her, she tilted her head and said in the most civil manner she could muster, "Good morning, Mr. Darcy."

"Do you have a preference for your walk this morning?"

Elizabeth let out a chuckle. Of course she did. *Alone!*

"I am setting out to the woods this morning. There is so much to explore there, and I think I prefer it above all else here."

"Then to the woods it is."

Elizabeth found it difficult this morning to make idle conversation, as Charlotte's words remained with her. He, however, did not remain silent for long.

"I believe, Miss Bennet, you would enjoy the woods at Pemberley," he said. "My father had a portion thinned out to help their growth, but his secondary purpose was to put in some winding paths along a stream that runs through. He had several bridges built across the water to allow one to get from one side to the other at different locations."

Elizabeth turned her head away from Mr. Darcy so he would not see the surprise on her face as he again began speaking to her about Pemberley. "I am certain it is quite lovely, Mr. Darcy."

Darcy nodded with a smile. "Both my parents enjoyed walking and would bring me along with them when I was younger. They would point things out along the way, teaching me the names of flowers and birds. It was a special time for me to be with them instead of my nanny or governess. I think that is why I enjoy walking so much. I hope someday to instil that love in my children." He looked down at her and smiled, drawing in a deep breath and letting it out slowly.

Elizabeth wondered whether his children would also learn to look down on those who were not their equal. She knew better than to speak it aloud.

Instead, she said, "Merely trying to engender a particular interest in your children does not always guarantee success. My poor father tried to pass along the love of reading to each of his five daughters. Obviously, he was not successful with all."

"But he was successful with you."

Elizabeth nodded in agreement, but shuddered at his soft, mellow voice. "He was."

"I think you would find the library at Pemberley much to your liking. While I cannot take credit for the vast collection of books within it, I am rather proud of it."

She glanced up at him. He was looking down at her with a warm smile. She let out a soft, nervous laugh, and then, with a teasing smile of her own, she challenged him with a single raised brow. "But does the library at Pemberley have any books written by a woman?"

"I do not doubt it has, although I cannot say for certain."

Elizabeth was actually surprised he conceded this. "Perhaps you have read some unknowingly."

"Why do you say that?"

Elizabeth shook her head and looked straight ahead. "Because perhaps it is so looked down upon, a lady might use a man's name in getting her work published."

"Would a lady actually go to such lengths?"

Elizabeth laughed. "Oh, yes. If she is determined enough, she might hide this accomplishment from her whole family and have it published under a completely different name."

Darcy stopped and stared down at her. "You would not, I think, have done such a thing."

With a shake of her head she said, "Oh, no! I would most definitely tell my family and publish it using my *real* name."

She gave him one of her endearing smiles, turned, and walked on.

"Yes, I imagine you would," Darcy said softly.

In a few strides, Darcy caught up to her, and they continued on in silence. Their walk took them to an area dense with trees. The wind, sounding like a song, stirred up the newly leafing trees, while last year's fallen leaves and twigs crunched underfoot.

Elizabeth suddenly stopped.

"Is something wrong, Miss Bennet?"

She put her finger to her lips. "Shh," she said. "Listen. It sounds like an orchestra is playing. So many different instruments, and it is as if they have completely surrounded us."

Elizabeth tilted her head back and forth and hummed, as if to sing along.

"An orchestra playing? Miss Bennet, would you care to dance?"

Elizabeth froze. She was not certain she understood him correctly. "Pardon me?"

"Dance... to the music of the singing birds and the wind through the trees..."

Elizabeth laughed nervously. "Oh, Mr. Darcy, you are full of surprises. But I fear you shall have to wait until the soiree for our dance." She began to walk on, still laughing. "Dancing in the woods, indeed!"

While her words were teasing, she suddenly felt confused. She wished Charlotte had not spoken of her suspicions, for now she was weighing everything Mr. Darcy said and did by them. She needed to put such a ludicrous thought – that Mr. Darcy might be singling her out – from her mind!

~~*

The next morning dawned clear, the sun brightly declaring its arrival as it rose on the horizon. As the light streamed into his room, Darcy rolled away from the window to give his eyes time to adjust to the brightness.

He kept his eyes closed, for it was easier to imagine Elizabeth's face behind his eyelids. He had thought of nothing but her the day before. He could not get enough of her teasing smile and laugh, twinkling eyes, and single raised brow.

He could readily forgive his aunt for keeping them occupied yesterday, thus preventing any visits with those at the parsonage, due to his walk with Elizabeth earlier that morning. He actually preferred that to sharing her with Rickland and Fitzwilliam.

He rolled back over towards the window and opened his eyes. He slept with the curtains open so he would waken with the sun, and he wondered whether Elizabeth did, as well. There were so many things about her that were so similar to him. And so many that were pleasingly different. Not a day passed that he did not find something more to love in her.

He swung his legs out from under the coverlet and sat up, stretching out his arms. His morning walk with Elizabeth – alone – was the only thing he found himself looking forward to.

As his valet prepared his clothing for the day, Darcy stared out the window, and he could think of nothing but Elizabeth. When he was away from her, his heart and his life seemed hopelessly empty. What would happen when he and his cousin returned to London? When would he see her again?

He took in a deep breath and brought a fisted hand up to his chin. He tapped it a few times as he thought of the musical soiree in two days. He looked forward to dancing with Elizabeth, but more than that…

Darcy's eyes widened. *Of course!*

He turned quickly away as he pondered the feasibility of his idea. Yes! It would take care of several things. Asking for Elizabeth's hand before the soiree would solve a number of issues splendidly!

First of all, their engagement could be announced at the soiree. That would settle once and for all his aunt's mistaken assumption that he was going to marry her daughter! And it would take care of Mr. Adamson's groundless hope that introducing him to his daughter might lead to an engagement. Finally, it would ensure his being able to see Elizabeth again after they both departed Kent. He could even stop and talk to her father before she returned to Longbourn.

Darcy heard loud footsteps outside the door and wondered whether his cousin was already up. The servants normally walked much more quietly. He hoped he could sneak out without being stopped by him, so he decided to wait a few minutes to make sure. He knew if it was his cousin, he would go straight to the dining room for some strong coffee.

It was a fine morning, and although he was getting a late start, he hoped he would encounter Elizabeth, if not in the woods, then returning from them. The moment had finally arrived. He had revelled in Elizabeth's close presence, her smile and laugh, her scent, and her sparkling eyes long enough. This morning he would ask for her hand and would soon have the woman his heart yearned for as his wife!

Once his valet stepped out, and before leaving his chambers, Darcy stepped in front of the mirror and tugged his coat. Taking in a deep breath, he ran his fingers around the collar, attempting to loosen the sudden constriction of his neckcloth. His mouth was dry, and his heart pounded thunderously within his chest.

Darcy hurried downstairs, and his long strides brought him to the front door and down the front steps. He was grateful he did not see his cousin, and stopped and breathed in deeply. He had never felt so alive. And joyful. It had been a long time since he had truly felt happy! He could almost laugh, but at the moment he was too nervous!

He pinched his brows as he realized he had not even considered what he would say to Elizabeth when he asked for her hand. He could not take the time now to prepare the words. His heart was so full; they would come when he needed them.

Once he reached the lane, he slowed down, for he knew now she could not return without seeing him. He would follow the path from there to the woods.

As he approached the woods, he continually looked about him in case she had walked elsewhere. He narrowed his eyes and turned in every direction, hoping to see her step out from behind one of the many trees or bushes.

He stopped, taking off his hat, and ran his fingers through his hair, practically digging them into his scalp. He looked about him again and finally saw some movement in the grove. Ah! There she was!

When he came upon her, she had taken a seat upon a fallen log. She held what looked to be a letter in her hand and was reading it intently. He knew she would not notice him unless she glanced up.

As he drew closer to her, he was unexpectedly assaulted by a sudden sense of duty, and even more surprising, the nervousness he felt earlier had not left him. He shook his head to dislodge these tormentors from their attack. His determination fought against his fears, and his heart waged war against his duty. He knew Elizabeth was the woman he wanted as his wife. He had known from practically their first encounter in Hertfordshire. She challenged him, intellectually and surprisingly, in countering his opinions. He enjoyed the thought-provoking conversations he had with her, and she did not oblige him by agreeing with everything he said.

He fisted his hand several times, straightened his shoulders, and suddenly wondered how to get her attention without startling her. He stopped a few steps away from her. He could almost reach out and touch her. As he contemplated how much he desired to do so, she let out a long sigh and slowly lifted her head.

Darcy had no time to think about how he would make his presence known. "Miss Bennet, I... good morning!"

She turned her head towards the sound of his voice; her eyes were wide in surprise. "Mr. Darcy, I did not see you."

"Pray forgive me. I did not mean to startle you." He watched as she quickly folded the letter and slipped it into the pocket of her dress. "I did not mean to interrupt you, either."

"There is no need to apologize. You neither startled nor interrupted me." She turned her eyes down to her hands, which she folded in her lap. "I am only reading again a letter from Jane I received earlier."

Darcy came around and stood in front of her. Now that he faced her, he could not bring a single thought to his mind. How could his heart feel so full and his mind be so void? He took in a deep breath to calm himself.

"Miss Bennet, I hope you do not mind. Do you have a moment? There is something of great import about which I should like to speak with you."

Chapter 10

"You wish to speak with me?" Elizabeth seemed somewhat unsettled, which did nothing to calm his nerves. He had hoped for a reassuring smile.

Darcy looked down, giving his head a shake. When he looked up and into Elizabeth's sparkling eyes, he began, "In vain have I struggled. It will not do. My...

"Darcy! Miss Bennet!"

Darcy spun his head around to find Fitzwilliam and Rickland walking briskly towards them.

"Good morning!" A beaming smile lit Elizabeth's face. "I see we are all of the same mind to take a stroll this morning."

Rickland hurried to her side and sat down next to her. "It is a beautiful morning! And after such rains as we have had, one must not take for granted the next day will be as fine."

Darcy felt his head begin to spin as he fought anger and frustration at both Rickland and his cousin. He looked at Fitzwilliam. "You are not normally a walker, and yet I encounter you twice in almost as many days?" His question sounded more accusatory than he would have liked.

"Rickland wished to speak with me," replied Colonel Fitzwilliam softly so only Darcy could hear. "We keep being interrupted, so we set out again this morning."

Darcy listened but his mind was elsewhere. What was he to do now? He glanced at Elizabeth and wondered if she felt the same vexation as he did at the interruption. Did she suspect he was about to offer for her hand? Was she hoping he would?

Colonel Fitzwilliam turned and brought a foot up to the log and leaned down, resting his arms on his bent leg. "Miss Bennet, I must say this visit to our aunt's has certainly been made more enjoyable by your company and that of your friend and her sister."

"I thank you, Colonel. I can honestly say all of you have made my visit here more enjoyable than I could have imagined." She glanced up at the men with a gracious smile.

"If I could but convince my cousin to delay our departure next week, you know I would. But you see, Miss Bennet, I am at his beck and call."

"I see," she said, with a forlorn look. "We shall have to somehow endure without you." Elizabeth turned to Darcy. "Your cousin cannot convince you to delay your departure?"

"Unfortunately, I cannot, as much as I would like to." He gave her a quick, knowing smile. "I would remain if I could."

"He is correct, Miss Bennet," Colonel Fitzwilliam added. "It is because of me we are required to leave. He ensures my prompt and timely return to London."

"He takes prodigious care of you," Elizabeth said. "A valuable cousin, indeed."

"Oh, but he is good towards all who know him. Whether relation or friend, he looks out for their best interest. Why, he even took great delight in telling me how late last autumn he separated a young man from an attachment to a young lady whose family was very much…"

"Fitzwilliam!" Darcy's heart began to pound. He could not believe what his cousin was saying. "That is enough!"

"He is also modest!" laughed the colonel. "You had every reason to congratulate yourself as you said her family was unsuitable for this young man."

Darcy watched in horror as Elizabeth's face paled and her eyes widened in comprehension. She knew exactly to whom his cousin referred. Anger darkened the eyes she flashed at him.

He shook his head, as if trying to deny it, although he could not. He needed to explain it to her, but he could not formulate any coherent thought that would explain his actions in a way Elizabeth would understand.

Before he could reply, Elizabeth unleashed her wrath upon him.

"And what right do you have, Mr. Darcy, in making a decision like this for your *friend*?"

Darcy opened his mouth, but no words came out.

Rickland narrowed his eyes at Darcy. "It is surprising to me, as

92

well, Darcy. Why would you interfere in such a manner?"

"Now give my cousin credit. He did not believe the young lady returned this gentleman's affections."

"And is he an accurate judge of affections?" Elizabeth asked in a mocking tone. "Can he see into the heart of a lady?"

Darcy's mouth was dry, but he knew he must defend his actions. "I observed no outward display of affection on her part."

Elizabeth looked directly at him. "And is it up to you to rightly determine her degree of affection? To decide for your friend whether or not her family is suitable? Could your friend not make that decision himself?"

"Miss Bennet, I..."

Elizabeth put up a hand to stop him. "I shall never fully understand you, Mr. Darcy; nor do I care to. One thing I do know – your interference is inexcusable. You may believe because of your wealth and connections you have a right to subject those you deem beneath you to bend to your control. But we no longer live in the Dark Ages, and whatever your motive was in separating them, your reasoning behind it was faulty."

Darcy met Elizabeth's dark, stormy eyes. He had seen her flash those eyes at him before, but now he could readily see how much angrier she was than he had ever known her to be.

Before he could make any justification, she lowered her eyes and said softly, "I feel a headache coming on." She turned to Mr. Rickland. "Would you please escort me back to the parsonage?"

"Certainly." Rickland stood up and took her hand, bringing her to her feet. "Please excuse us." He shot Darcy a look of disgust, and the two walked away.

Darcy could barely begin to comprehend what had just occurred. His cousin looked at him with a questioning glance. "What was that all about? I knew Miss Bennet disliked you, but her reaction was more severe than I ever would have expected."

Darcy jerked his head around in disbelief. "What do you mean you knew she disliked me?"

Fitzwilliam blew out a puff of air. "It has been apparent from the moment I first made her acquaintance that she barely tolerates your company. Darcy, you cannot tell me you were not aware of her opinion of you." He paused and looked in the direction the couple walked. "But this was certainly not what I expected. I thought she would laugh at it, as she has laughed at other things you have done."

Darcy felt as if the ground beneath him was about to give away. His head swam with what his cousin had now revealed to Elizabeth and this unforeseen intelligence he imparted to him. He shook his head as he tried to make sense of it all. How could he have not seen what others had readily seen? How could he have believed Elizabeth returned his regard when, in truth, she loathed him? She had laughed at him! He wondered what had truly been her opinion of him and what must she think of him now!

Darcy did not trust himself to speak. His feelings waged war within. He felt anger at his cousin for mentioning something he had not expected him to share with anyone else, grief for allowing himself to love a woman who did not return that love, frustration with himself for being so blind, and jealousy at Rickland for being the one Elizabeth wished to have comfort her.

"Darcy? Would you care to please explain?"

Darcy turned to his cousin, who had been silently waiting for an answer. He knew not how to disguise the anguish that was likely written on his face.

"It was her sister. Her eldest sister, Jane, was the young lady from whom I separated Bingley."

Colonel Fitzwilliam's jaw dropped. "Heavens, Darcy! No wonder she was angry! I had no idea. Pray, forgive me."

Darcy waved a hand through the air. "You had no way of knowing." He peered at his cousin through lowered brows.

Fitzwilliam watched him for a moment as if pondering something. Finally, he said, "Darcy, before Rickland and I came upon you and Miss Bennet, he asked me something I initially thought odd."

"What was that?"

"He asked whether you had feelings of affection towards Miss Bennet."

Darcy took a deep breath, afraid to even look at his cousin. "And... and what did you tell him?"

"I laughed. I told him there is something between the two of you, but it is certainly *not* affection."

Darcy turned away from his cousin, rubbing his jaw. He scuffed the ground with the heel of his boot.

"Darcy, am I correct in that assumption, or did I misspeak in that matter, as well?"

Darcy closed his eyes, and when he opened them, he saw his cousin had stepped around and now stood in front of him. He pinched the bridge of his nose, looking at the ground as he did, and nodded his head.

"Lord, Darcy. I had no idea!"

"I am grateful for that. I would not have wished you to divulge the matters pertaining to my heart to Rickland."

"If you had told me, both of your feelings for Miss Elizabeth Bennet and the lady involved in your... your..."

"Go ahead and say it, Fitzwilliam. My interference."

Fitzwilliam tossed his head. "If you had told me it was her sister, I would not have made such a blunder."

"There is a lot I should have done differently. And the blunder, as you call it, can for the most part be attributed to me."

"Do you want to start at the beginning?"

"I would rather not."

"Darcy, I cannot imagine what you could have done to earn a lady's contempt. In particular, Miss Elizabeth Bennet's!"

When Darcy did not answer, Fitzwilliam continued. "I can certainly understand she is angered now, but what offenses could you have committed before this? Especially if you harboured feelings of affection for her."

Darcy began walking. "I am in no mood to discuss this."

"You are angry with me, and I take full responsibility for my share in this. But please help me understand!"

Darcy stopped abruptly and turned to look at his cousin. "The less you know, the better. I do not want you talking to Rickland about my feelings for Miss Bennet. He is under the misapprehension I do not have any feelings of affection for her, and I would prefer we leave it that way." He fisted his hands and let out a long sigh.

"Ahh. Those sighs emanating from you; I now know why."

Darcy chose to ignore his cousin's remark. "Did Rickland indicate *he* likes Miss Bennet?"

"She is very likeable. We *all* like her, Darcy. Rickland, me, and even our aunt, believe it or not. But I doubt you are referring to *that* kind of liking." He shook his head. "He did not give me any indication his feelings for her are strong in that way. He is much like me in that he has to consider marriage to a lady with at least a moderate fortune."

"I would not wish for Miss Bennet to be misled and hurt by him. Why would he ask to speak with you about my interest in her if *he* were not interested?"

"I believed he was merely curious." The colonel shook his head. "Perhaps I was wrong *there*, as well."

Darcy was silent for a moment and then said, "I should like to leave on the morrow. I can make an excuse to our aunt, but I cannot remain here."

Fitzwilliam rubbed his chin. "As much as I hate to leave the pleasant company we have enjoyed here, I would have to agree." He folded his arms across his chest. "But I am still interested in hearing how this all came about."

Darcy let out an exasperated huff. "We shall have a long carriage ride on the morrow. One day removed might make me more inclined to discuss this with you." He began to walk away, and then stopped. "But I would not count on it."

~~*

Elizabeth had politely taken Rickland's proffered arm as they walked away. She was grateful for it as she felt she needed his strength to keep from crumbling to the ground in distress. It was all she could do to speak calmly and rationally.

She briefly told Mr. Rickland about her sister and Mr. Bingley. All along she had placed the blame on Caroline Bingley for her brother's sudden departure and change of heart, believing her to be responsible for keeping him from returning to Netherfield. Hearing it was due in large part to Mr. Darcy had been a shocking revelation.

She had actually found Mr. Darcy to be a bit more tolerable here than when she had seen him in Hertfordshire. He seemed more relaxed and less inclined to distance himself from and look down upon those he deemed beneath him. But this new information about him was beyond her ability to forgive.

Mr. Rickland was all politeness as he walked in silence with her. Elizabeth was certain he must have felt the heaviness of her heart as well as the heavier weight upon his arm. He placed his other hand over hers.

After a few moments, he said, "There are times when I do not understand Lady Catherine's other nephew, and I can be grateful I do not have to call him a true cousin. What he did was inexcusable, and I can offer no justification for his behaviour, only regret it caused you and your sister a great deal of hurt."

"Thank you, Mr. Rickland. You certainly owe me no apologies for what he has done."

He patted her hand gently. "While I wholly enjoy Colonel Fitzwilliam's company, Darcy can sometimes wield his wealth and connections with nary a thought for others."

Elizabeth silently nodded. After a few moments she said, "He barely acknowledged those in our neighbourhood. While Mr. Bingley was friendly, gracious, and accommodating, Mr. Darcy usually stood off by himself, refusing to speak to anyone."

"He seems... I may be wrong, but he seems to enjoy your company."

She let out a dubious laugh. "I doubt he does. Perhaps he only wishes to appear agreeable in the presence of his aunt and cousin. For you heard what Colonel Fitzwilliam said. Mr. Darcy thinks my family unsuitable. He must consider me unsuitable, as well."

"That was wrong of him."

Elizabeth sighed. "My family may have its share of oddities, but no more than any other family. And it was not as if Mr. Bingley had never met my family. He seemed perfectly at ease with them."

"Darcy likely has strict criteria by which he judges others." Rickland let out a chuckle. "I would not be surprised if he has a list and checks each person he meets against it. If they do not meet all of his standards, he deems them unsuitable."

Elizabeth attempted to laugh. "We did have a conversation one evening about his idea of an accomplished woman. The list of requirements was quite extensive."

"Were he to meet every eligible woman in all of England, I

believe he still would not find a woman suitable for him."

Elizabeth sighed. "And he has every right to have a certain expectation for himself, but I do not agree with his thinking that he has a right to inflict his standard on others."

"You have spoken my thoughts exactly!" Rickland stopped and looked at her. His eyes narrowed as he said, "Perhaps it is due to the expectations in his family of his marrying Anne. He is forced to find fault with every other lady." He jutted his jaw. "Oh, perhaps you were not aware of this."

Elizabeth laughed. "Oh, indeed I was, and the more I come to know Miss de Bourgh, the more I am convinced he will have many surprises once they marry."

Rickland smiled, and they continued on. When they reached the parsonage, Mr. Rickland asked if he could see her in.

"No, thank you. I should like some time alone."

He took her hand and squeezed it. "I certainly understand. Let me know if there is anything else I can do."

Elizabeth smiled and walked to the door. She went straight to her room, grateful she did not encounter Charlotte, Maria, or Mr. Collins. She sat on her bed, and her tears began to fall.

She reached into her pocket and pulled out the letter from Jane that had arrived before she left on her walk. She wiped away the tears filling her eyes so she could read her sister's words.

Our dear aunt has been so gracious to me and allowed me the time alone I have needed to try to understand why Mr. Bingley did not come to see me after I visited his sister. I know time will heal my grieving heart, but right now I wonder how that healing will ever happen and how long it will take.

Elizabeth shook her head as she readily sensed the despair in Jane's letter. Her anger at Mr. Darcy deepened as she considered her sister's broken heart.

"Oh, my dearest Jane, it grieves me you are suffering so severely all because of Mr. Darcy's inexcusable actions! I so wish there was something I could do!"

Chapter 11

There was little conversation between Darcy and his cousin while they made their way back to Rosings. As they walked up the steps to the front door, Darcy tugged on his cousin's arm.

"I shall be in my room for the remainder of the day. Please make my apologies to our aunt, but I cannot bear anyone's company for a while. I shall come down when we dine."

"She will not be pleased. When are you going to inform her we are leaving in the morning?"

Darcy tensed his jaw and gave his head a quick shake. "I shall tell her this evening *after* we have dined."

They entered the house, and Darcy turned abruptly in the direction of the stairs, leaving Fitzwilliam to bear Lady Catherine's wrath and make excuses for his cousin's absence.

Upon entering his chambers, Darcy encountered his valet, who was hanging up some recently washed and pressed garments. "Do you have need of anything, sir?"

"No, no, Jenkins. I would prefer some time alone. I am not well. You are dismissed for the remainder of the day."

"I am sorry to hear you are unwell. Is there anything I can get for your comfort?"

Darcy shook his head. "Not now. But there has been a change of plans. The colonel and I are departing in the morning. You may pack my bags when I have gone down to dine."

His valet nodded his head and accepted the news without question. "Yes, sir. I shall be in my quarters packing my things if you change your mind and have need of anything."

Darcy thanked him, and Jenkins left. Darcy was grateful he did not have to inform his valet – or anyone for that matter – he was suffering from a shattered heart and a complete assault on who he thought he was and what he thought he knew.

Darcy collapsed into a chair, leaned his head back, and closed his eyes. His fingers tapped nervously on the arm of the chair as he felt all the disillusionment of the past hour battering him.

It seemed an impossible effort even to breathe, as he felt such a heaviness encompass him. His feelings for Elizabeth, which had only increased while in her presence here, were in turmoil. He loved her. Deeply. He thought it odd his intense affection and regard for her were as strong as they had ever been, despite discovering she had despised him all along. And how much more she must loathe him *now*! He had been so wrong about her returning his affections! He closed his eyes as he considered how poor a judge he was of a woman's partiality for a man.

He pounded his chin with his closed fist. Apparently he had also been wrong about Jane Bennet's affections for Bingley.

He took in a deep breath and held it as he contemplated he had nearly asked for Elizabeth's hand in marriage. He had been confident she would accept him. He had suffered no doubt whatsoever! He could only thank the good Lord he had been prevented from doing so and making a complete fool of himself.

He would have done anything for Elizabeth. He had wished to cherish her and walk with her through the woods at Pemberley and dance with her at balls. He had envisioned her by his side with friends at parties and the theatre, as well as alone with him in the Pemberley library or drawing room… or sharing his bed. His mouth went dry, and he closed his eyes. Would he be able to put her out of his thoughts, mind, and especially, his heart?

~~*

Darcy finally came out of his chambers in time to join the family for the evening meal. If it had been at all possible, he would have departed immediately, but he could not. It was bad enough he was going to have to inform his aunt he and his cousin were leaving on the morrow, a full week early. She would not be happy.

When he walked into the parlour, where everyone was waiting for the meal to be served, he greeted them with a quick bow. He readily noticed Fitzwilliam's questioning scrutiny and Rickland's accusatory gaze. His aunt tapped her folded fan into her palm, a sure indication she was not pleased.

"You have been absent all day. Fitzwilliam claims you are unwell."

Darcy looked down. He hated to lie, but after a moment he reminded himself he was, in all truth, unwell. "That is correct, Aunt Catherine. Indeed, I am not well." He glanced over at Rickland, who looked down, giving a slight shake of his head.

"All you need is a good meal. Eat hearty, and you shall feel better directly."

Dinner was quieter than usual. Anne said nothing, merely glancing up at her cousins occasionally. The three gentlemen said little, which allowed Lady Catherine to fill the silence, savouring the uninterrupted opportunity to air her opinions and grievances. Darcy had little appetite and even less desire for company. It was all he could do to remain seated and civil throughout the meal.

Later, when they gathered again in the parlour, Darcy stood and approached his aunt. He gave his cousin a pointed glance, silently beseeching him for his support, if required.

"Dear Aunt, I fear I have some bad news. Something has arisen requiring Fitzwilliam and me to leave Rosings in the morning."

"Tomorrow?" Lady Catherine propped both hands on the arms of the chair and leaned forward. "You cannot be serious!"

"I am indeed serious, and I am truly sorry if this causes you grief. But it cannot be helped."

"What reason can there possibly be?" Lady Catherine asked; her lowered brows and creased forehead revealed her indignation. "This is not to be borne! You will stay until a week from Saturday as you had planned, and I will hear no more of it!"

"I am sorry, Aunt, but we will leave on the morrow."

Lady Catherine took in a few deep breaths. She leaned back in her chair and pointed her fan at him. "This is merely some whim of yours, and I am not used to submitting to any person's whims. You will remain here, and we shall speak no more of it."

Darcy shook his head. "I fear I cannot."

Lady Catherine narrowed her eyes at her nephew, as if trying to determine the real reason behind the sudden departure whilst attempting to prepare her next argument. Finally, she shook her head. "You cannot miss the soiree. Anne has been looking forward to a dance with you. You cannot disappoint her."

Darcy looked over at Anne, who was sitting quietly across the room writing feverishly in her journal. He thought of his earlier intention that he would be engaged to Elizabeth by now, and this whole misunderstanding of their being intended for each other would be at an end.

"Anne, pray forgive me. Perhaps some other time."

Anne looked up at Darcy and smiled weakly. "I understand." She then looked back down and began writing again. He did not think she looked particularly grief stricken over it.

"You have seriously displeased me." Lady Catherine turned to Fitzwilliam. "And what have you to say on this matter? Have you tried to talk any sense into your cousin? Certainly *you* understand what is owed me by my nephews."

"Oh, we do, Aunt, but we must leave on the morrow."

She turned to Rickland. "*You* are not leaving, are you?"

Rickland smiled, glancing only briefly at Darcy. "Oh, no. I intend to stay as long as I can. I am truly enjoying myself here."

"And well you should!"

Darcy looked from Rickland back to his aunt. "If you will excuse me, as I said earlier, I am unwell and shall be in my chambers for the remainder of the night. I do not wish to be disturbed." He looked at Fitzwilliam. "I shall see you in the morning. I hope to depart no later than nine o'clock."

"Wait!" Lady Catherine exclaimed, her face red and her hands shaking in anger. "I will not..."

Darcy gave a quick bow and stepped out of the parlour, hurrying to his room. He would leave it to his cousin to smooth things over with their aunt.

When he entered his room, his valet was there.

"I have finished packing, sir. Is there anything I can do for you? Are you going back down this evening?"

"No, I shall be in my chambers the remainder of the evening and wish to be left alone."

"Yes, sir." Jenkins stepped to the door. "I will await your call."

"Thank you."

Darcy sat down and dropped his head into his hands. He raked his fingers through his hair as he tried to comprehend how wrong he had been. Not about loving Elizabeth. He still felt she was the one woman he would always love and cherish. He had erred only in believing she returned his affections.

He lifted his head and leaned back. Looking at the desk in front of him, he saw some sheets of stationery and a quill and bottle of ink. He reached for the quill and twirled it between his fingers.

He thought of penning a letter to Elizabeth, explaining his actions and asking for her forgiveness. But no, he could not present her with a letter. It would be improper, and she would likely throw it away before reading it. Yet he was accustomed to writing letters, especially to Georgiana, and in them expressing those feelings he could not always convey in spoken words. But what he truly wished to say in a letter to Elizabeth, he could never deliver into her hands.

He leaned forward and slowly opened the bottle of ink. Nodding his head, he thought, *But there is no harm in writing a letter for my own peace of mind. Miss Elizabeth Bennet need never see it.*

He sat up straight in the chair and dipped the quill into the ink. He brought it down on the fine piece of linen stationery.

Miss Elizabeth Bennet,

Be not alarmed, madam, thinking I shall attempt to place this letter in your hands. Doing so would benefit neither of us and would put your reputation at risk. I am not penning these words for your eyes to see, but to salve my own feelings and expectations, which earlier today suffered quite a shock.

The sentiments which you expressed regarding my actions and my character were by no means without provocation. You accused me of an offense of which, on the surface, I own I am guilty. That I separated my friend Bingley from your sister is true. I admit to being quite proud of my success. But I must give an account of my reasons – and this is why you shall not see this letter – because there is one particular reason which was not mentioned in our argument today. It gave greater impetus to my actions than did the other two.

One reason I separated Mr. Bingley from your sister is because I noticed no partiality on her part. I did not perceive her heart was touched as deeply as his. I readily noticed Bingley greatly preferred your elder sister to any other woman in the county. But it was at the Netherfield Ball I was made acquainted, by Sir Williams Lucas's information, that Bingley's attentions to your sister had given rise to a general expectation of marriage. I had seen my friend in love many times before, but upon watching him thereafter, I came to the conclusion his partiality was beyond anything I had ever witnessed in him. Unfortunately, I witnessed only open, cheerful, and friendly looks and manners on the part of your sister, no returned partiality at all.

You informed me, rather emphatically, that my reasoning for separating them was faulty. As you know your sister better than I do, I assume you believe her to have loved him. If this is indeed the case, I admit I was wrong. I apologize for my error.

The other reason expressed was the unsuitability of your family. I do not wish to pain you, but there were on more than one occasion displays of total want of propriety by your mother, your three younger sisters, and occasionally even by your father. I would console you, however, with praise for you and your elder sister; neither of you are included in this censure. You both behaved honourably and sensibly.

My third reason for separating the couple is the principal reason I can never present this letter to you. It is likely the strongest of the reasons, but one which cannot be made known to you: I had come to ardently admire and love you. I had not set out to fall in love with you when I first met you, but the more I found myself in your presence, the stronger those feelings became. It was when you expressed your doubt as to my only knowing six accomplished women that I found myself utterly captivated. Your liveliness and wit – even at my expense – brought a refreshing joy to my life.

The days you spent at Netherfield nursing your sister were tortuous for me. I wished so much to publicly declare the depth of my feelings, but I was torn by a sense of honour and duty to my family because you were not of the sphere in which I should marry.

Of all these things I ask your forgiveness, except for coming to love you.

I do not regret loving you, for you made me feel alive again after so many years of loneliness. You filled me with a joy beyond my comprehension merely by being in your presence. As the day of the Netherfield Ball drew closer, the sole direction of my thoughts was to ask you to dance. Unfortunately, I came away from that dance with innumerable emotions, none of which were what I had hoped and expected to feel.

When we departed Netherfield, I was intent on removing myself from your presence even more than I was on separating my friend from your sister. I grew up with a sense of duty that is likely much stronger than anything Bingley would ever need to feel. But I knew if he and your sister married, I would be frequently thrown into your company. I realized (however right or wrong) I ought not to entertain thoughts of marriage to a lovely lady from Hertfordshire with little fortune and no connections.

What I did not expect, however, was encountering you five months later here in Kent. When I walked into the parsonage that first day and saw you, I realized my feelings for you had not waned, but were as strong ever. You wore a light blue dress that caused the blue in your eyes to sparkle and your skin to glow. I realized there was no hope for me to conquer those feelings I had tried to erase. I was a man lost in the depths of love.

With each encounter my feelings grew stronger. I longed each day to see your smile and enjoy your lively, intelligent wit. Every morning I looked for you as I walked, hoping to have you by my side. I could never confess to you that on more than one occasion I wished to pull you close to me into a warm embrace and lean down to kiss your inviting lips.

I wanted nothing more than to share with you my hopes and dreams, which included having you walk by my side at Pemberley. I decided I cared nothing for family duty, and it became my main object to ask for your hand. That is what I was about to do when we were interrupted by Rickland and Fitzwilliam in the grove.

Apparently I have been blind – or perhaps naïve – as to what your true feelings for me were. It was only later, when I was alone with my cousin, that he helped me comprehend your opinion of me. Even before you came to hear of my part in separating Bingley and your sister, you had an intense dislike of me. I had been blinded by my fervent love for you and believed what I wanted to believe rather than what was in truth before my very eyes.

I imagine your opinion of me was somehow influenced or perhaps strengthened by Wickham poisoning your mind with accusations against me. I know not what he said, but he is a man who cannot be trusted. I can only testify, along with Colonel Fitzwilliam, that he nearly ruined a member of our family and has squandered fully the monies provided to him would have enabled him to make something of his life. But I will not take the time here to dwell on his faults. I will only say I hope he does not further impose himself on you and deceive you with more of his lies.

There is one more thing I would wish to warn you about. But no, if I were to say anything about Mr. Rickland, I would be committing again that same act of interference which before you felt was so wrong of me.

I feel like a fool. Not for having loved you, but for not realizing you despised me all this time. I am ashamed of those actions you found to be so abhorrent; I only wish I could make things right. You were — nay, you are — the one woman to whom I felt I could give my whole heart and soul — for all eternity.

Writing this has eased a small portion of the pain in my heart.

May God bless you in all you endeavour to do.
Fitzwilliam Darcy

Darcy looked down at the letter. He knew it would be a long time before all the pain ceased. No matter where he went or what he did, a vivid memory of Elizabeth would be there taunting and accusing him.

His fingers tapped the table, and he looked at the coals burning in the hearth. He would burn this letter and hope the flames would sear the wounds that now tortured him. He folded it up, looking one last time at her name at the top. *Miss Elizabeth Bennet.*

He stood up slowly, holding the fine sheets of folded linen stationery in his hand. For a moment he wished he did not have to burn them. He wished Elizabeth could read this and know how he truly felt. Would that make any difference at all?

He shook his head. No. Her opinion of him was decided. She had finished sketching his character. And it was not pretty.

As he began to walk towards the fireplace, there was a knock at the door. Darcy looked at the door and then down at the letter. Instead of tossing it into the fireplace, he stuffed it, along with the other sheets of blank stationary, into his satchel.

"Darcy! It is Fitzwilliam. May I come in?"

"A moment, please!" Darcy quickly closed the satchel, walked to the door, and opened it.

Chapter 12

Colonel Fitzwilliam stomped into the room. "You are in my debt, Cousin. You owe me a lifetime of favours for all I have done for you."

"What?" Darcy asked, afraid to hear his cousin's reply.

"Not what! Who! Our aunt!"

"Is she still angry?"

"Of course, she is angry. I was, however, able to convince her Georgiana requested our immediate return. I *confided* this to her when Rickland was out of the room, telling her it was a highly sensitive matter, and we needed to be there for her."

"Did she not ask what the matter was?"

Colonel Fitzwilliam shook his head. "Rickland came back into the room, and I left soon after. You," Fitzwilliam jabbed Darcy in the chest with his finger, "can conjure up something more to tell her on the morrow when she inquires. Which I am certain she shall."

"I shall tell her it is none of her business," Darcy replied.

Fitzwilliam rolled his eyes. "She is of the opinion *everything* is her business, if you have not quite comprehended that in your eight and twenty years."

Darcy drew in a breath. "I thank you, Fitzwilliam. For remaining a faithful friend when I act like a fool and for being a faithful cousin in dealing with Aunt Catherine when I deserted you."

Fitzwilliam smiled smugly. "As I said, you owe me!" He sat down and looked about the room. "Now pull out some glasses and that brandy you have hidden somewhere in here. I need something to take the edge off my nerves!"

~~*

Darcy awoke the next morning with a terrible headache. His valet came in to make the final preparations for their departure and was surprised to find him still in bed. He worked quietly about the room as Darcy began to stir and slurred a greeting.

"Good morning, sir. I have your clothes set out for the day. I hope you approve. Shall I draw you a bath?"

Darcy slowly lifted his head and let it fall back down onto the pillow. "Yes, but give me a few minutes."

Jenkins nodded and stepped out of the room.

Darcy rubbed his forehead, giving his head a shake. He remembered drinking with his cousin, but little else. He and Fitzwilliam had imbibed a bit more brandy than they normally did, and his mind was vacant, his recollection of the evening a blur. There was something teasing his memory, but it was just out of reach.

It was… Darcy bolted upright in his bed, and then as his head began to throb, he placed both open palms around the back of his head, fearing it might fall off. He closed his eyes as the room began to spin. The memory of yesterday, Elizabeth's accusations, and his discovery of her contempt, assaulted him forcefully.

He attempted to recall his conversation with Fitzwilliam as they sat together drinking last night and wondered how much he had told him.

He knew his cousin had, by means of the brandy, set out to loosen his tongue about all that had happened concerning Elizabeth. It was certainly much easier talking to him about his faults with an incoherent mind and a slightly deadened sense of anguish.

He shook his head. It mattered not. They would be back in London later today, and she would be out of his life. That thought did little to alleviate his pain. In fact, it made it worse.

He slowly pulled himself out of bed, taking care lest he stumble or aggravate the throbbing in his head. He walked to the window and could not help but immediately glance towards the parsonage. He swallowed, although his mouth was uncomfortably dry.

He looked in the other direction and noticed the trees swaying in a strong wind. The sky was clear except for a line of clouds on the horizon. They were in the eastern sky, the opposite direction they would be traveling, so it should not impede them.

He closed his eyes to fend off a wave of grief as he thought about Elizabeth; a pain as deep as if he had lost a close family member to death. But behind his closed eyes, Elizabeth's face and fine eyes appeared as real as if she were right in front of him. As her eyes turned dark and accusatory, he quickly opened his own. He shook his head, hoping and praying time and distance would erase those vivid images and ease his pain.

~~*

When Darcy was dressed, he reluctantly walked downstairs to face his aunt. He knew she likely would still be furious about their early departure, but no set down or threats would change his mind. He was departing today!

He came into the dining room to find his aunt alone. He was rather surprised – and greatly relieved – she did not assault him with her determination they remain, but instead asked him if he felt she could be of use to his sister. Darcy looked at her not quite understanding what she meant, but then remembered his cousin had fabricated a story about Georgiana needing their assistance.

"No, I…" Darcy took in a deep breath, searching for the right words. "If we find ourselves in need of your good counsel, Aunt, we shall notify you immediately."

A satisfied smile spread across her face. "I knew you would. Just let me know. I shall be more than happy to come at once and offer whatever advice I can provide."

"Yes, I am quite certain you would." Darcy sat down and was served a cup of coffee. "Where are Fitzwilliam and Rickland?"

"Fitzwilliam wanted to take his leave of Mr. and Mrs. Collins and their guests. Rickland accompanied him." She lifted her napkin and dabbed her mouth. "He claimed you were still unwell and thought it best you not join him. He was going to express your apologies for not coming yourself."

"That is good of him," Darcy said, greatly appreciating how Fitzwilliam thought of everything. He visited with his aunt for only a few more minutes, eating a biscuit and some fruit, and then returned to his room to await his cousin's return.

When Fitzwilliam came to Darcy's chambers, he inquired after him, giving him a knowing look, as if he already knew the answer. Darcy mumbled that he felt well enough, but was certain his cousin doubted it. After the amount of drink Darcy had imbibed the previous night, the colonel would know he would not be himself for some time.

"Did Rickland remain at Hunsford?" Darcy asked, hoping to sound uninterested.

Fitzwilliam took in a deep breath. "Yes." He walked over and grasped his cousin's shoulder. "It will be better once we leave."

Darcy nodded but doubted the truth of that.

As they prepared to set out, Darcy gathered those belongings he wanted with him in the carriage. He brought his great coat in case they encountered rain, his satchel so he could tend to some work, and some books to read. He truly did not feel like reading but knew that might be the one thing that would rid his thoughts of Elizabeth. He knew not what he might be in the mood to read, so he had looked through the small bookshelf in his chambers. He picked out a history book and a biography of poets and their poetry. He hoped one of the books would engage him.

The two men paid their respects to Lady Catherine and Anne. Fortunately, Mr. Rickland had not yet returned from Hunsford so Darcy did not have to face him. But regrettably, that meant he was spending more time with Elizabeth. Darcy's jaw tightened at the mere thought of it.

They stepped outside to see the two Pemberley carriages waiting, ready to transport them. They would travel in the larger, more luxurious one, while the luggage, his valet, and two other menservants would ride in the other.

A maid from the kitchen brought out a basket filled with a variety of food to eat on the way. She was walking towards the carriage and had stepped up alongside Darcy and Fitzwilliam when a strong gust of wind caused her to turn her face against it, and she stumbled, crashing into Darcy.

He dropped his coat, satchel, and books as he reached out his arms to straighten her and the basket. When he was satisfied she was balanced, he looked down and let out a frustrated huff. The flap on his satchel had not been securely shut, and papers from inside were flying everywhere. The wind picked some up, carrying them hither and thither. He quickly picked up his satchel and asked Fitzwilliam if he would be so kind as to gather his coat and the books and put them into the carriage while he scrambled to retrieve the papers.

Jenkins, who had brought down the final valise, handed it off to a coachman and helped. Darcy looked at the wad of papers in his hand as his valet handed him what he had picked up.

"Thank you, Jenkins. I think this is all. I see no more." He walked over to Fitzwilliam, who was also looking around.

"Do you have everything, Cousin?" Fitzwilliam asked. "I believe I saw some papers fly off in that direction under the carriage."

Darcy stooped down to look. "No, I see nothing. I believe I have recovered everything."

As they walked the short distance to the carriage, Darcy grasped his cousin's arm. "Thank you for everything, Fitzwilliam. You certainly made a persuasive argument to our aunt in favour of us taking our leave this morning."

Fitzwilliam nodded his head. "You can thank her devotion to Georgiana and her concern for her well-being."

As they were about to get into the carriage, they noticed a rider approach the house. A young man hopped off the horse and walked up to the door.

Darcy paused. "I wonder if it might be a post from Georgiana. I have been expecting something from her." He looked back towards the house.

"Perhaps you had best go see, for if it is from Georgiana and left in Aunt Catherine's hands, she is likely to open it and discover nothing is amiss with her."

Darcy nodded and hurried to the door. He passed the post rider who was returning to his horse and stepped in, placing his satchel on a small table inside the door. He was a few steps behind the butler, who was carrying the missive on a salver to the parlour.

"A letter for you, Lady Catherine."

Darcy stopped in the doorway, stepping to the side of the butler. His aunt looked up. "Did you forget something, Nephew?"

"No, I saw the post rider and wondered if it might be more

news from Georgiana."

"It is not."

"I thought it may have been another letter from her." Darcy narrowed his brows. "If a missive comes later today from her, would you please send it on immediately to me at Suncrest House?" He hoped in this way, if Georgiana had written, his aunt would not be inclined to open the missive and read it. But if she did, at least he would be gone.

"I shall. I do hope she will able to join you the next time you visit."

"We shall see." He gave a bow to his aunt.

He walked back outside and climbed into his carriage, tapping on the front. "On our way!" He looked across at his cousin. "No snoring, please. I need some rest. My head is throbbing, and I hope to get some sleep so I can get some work done later."

"You left some work unfinished back there," Fitzwilliam said, pointing behind him to Rosings.

Darcy scowled at him.

Fitzwilliam lifted his hands and asked, "What was that look for?" He shook his head and turned to the window. "Things remain exactly as they did before we arrived despite your avowal you would end this whole misunderstanding between our aunt, Anne, and yourself."

"Unforeseen circumstances arose."

Colonel Fitzwilliam leaned back and stretched out his legs. "They most certainly did." Closing his eyes, he said, "Would you be so kind as to awaken me when we arrive?"

~~*

Elizabeth welcomed the visit Colonel Fitzwilliam had paid that morning along with Mr. Rickland. She was grateful Mr. Darcy had not accompanied them so she did not have to feign civility towards him. She had not mentioned anything to Charlotte about what had occurred the previous day; she was certain the two gentlemen would be polite enough not to bring it up.

Mr. Rickland decided to remain at Hunsford with the ladies when Colonel Fitzwilliam returned to Rosings. They had an enjoyable visit, much like before Mr. Darcy and his cousin had arrived. He remained for another hour and then excused himself, claiming his aunt would likely be in need of him. Elizabeth believed he remained long enough to be certain Mr. Darcy had already departed before he returned.

After enjoying some tea and biscuits, Elizabeth found herself in need of a stroll. She had not been able to walk earlier due to the men's visit, and it was a lovely, warm day; the only thing she might have to complain about was the wind.

"I shall return shortly, Charlotte. I hope to be back within the hour."

"I wish you would not walk about on your own, but I know you have done it for as long as I can remember. Be careful and keep an eye on the horizon. I believe a storm is heading our way!"

"I shall take care," she said with a laugh.

Elizabeth stepped out and breathed in deeply. She looked about her and knew at once she would not walk the park. Not after the events that had taken place there yesterday. No, she was in the mood for her favourite walk. She would set out for the woods and explore a little more. At least she knew Mr. Darcy was no longer here to intrude upon her.

She walked along the lane separating Rosings and Hunsford and peered through the shrubbery to see all was quiet. She smiled and shook her head at the manicured shrubs standing guard, bringing to mind thoughts of the rigid Mr. Darcy. She surmised he and Colonel Fitzwilliam were now gone.

A gust of wind ruffled the leaves around her, and she looked down to see a small swirl of leaves and dirt spinning up and then just as quickly collapsing to the ground. She smiled and picked up a leaf, bringing it up to her face so it tickled her nose. As she dropped it, the breeze picked it up, and she watched it twist and turn as it floated softly down into the base of a bush. She lowered her brows as she noticed a folded piece of paper tucked nearby.

She walked over and leaned down, picking up a fine piece of stationery. She turned it over in her hands, noticed writing on it, and began to unfold it. Her eyes widened, and she gasped as she saw at the top, written in fine penmanship, was her name, *Miss Elizabeth Bennet.*

"What...?"

Her heart began to pound as she slowly opened it to find a letter written on both sides of the fine linen. She quickly turned it over and read the signature at the bottom. She came to a halt as she saw the name – *Fitzwilliam Darcy*!

Elizabeth looked about her, fearing someone might have seen her pick it up. She could not imagine why he would have written her a letter or why it was blowing around out here! Her heart pounded as she began to read his words. She slowly brought her hand up and placed her fingers over her mouth. Her eyes widened as she realized he never intended for her to read the missive.

Miss Elizabeth Bennet,

Be not alarmed, madam, thinking I shall attempt to place this letter in your hands. I am not putting down these words for your eyes to see, but to salve my own feelings and expectations, which yesterday suffered quite a shock.

Elizabeth began to walk quickly towards the woods. She grasped the letter with both hands as they had begun to shake. She pondered whether or not to read it; she knew it would be wrong for her to read the words he had not intended her to see. She should not be reading a letter from him even if he *had* intended her to read it and had placed it in her hands! She knew he was likely angry with her for her accusations the day before, but her own curiosity for answers would not allow her *not* to read it!

Chapter 13

Darcy abruptly opened his eyes, giving his head a shake and trying to determine what had wakened him. He knew he had been exhausted, but was actually surprised how quickly sleep had overtaken him. Earlier, when Fitzwilliam had closed his eyes, Darcy had decided to rest his, as well. The rocking of the carriage and his fitful slumber the night before had likely contributed to his falling fast asleep. He had no idea how long he had been dozing.

He picked up the books he had brought along with him, but put them back down again, without so much as opening them. None of these books looked as though they were something he would enjoy reading at the moment. He decided, instead, to do some work and reached over for his satchel. He lowered his brows when he did not find it on the seat next to him.

He looked down at the floor of the carriage and shook his head. It was not there.

He suddenly pounded on the top of the carriage, startling his cousin.

"What in heaven's name?" Fitzwilliam looked about as if trying to orient himself. "What happened? Is something wrong?"

"I believe I left my satchel back at Rosings."

The driver drew the horses to a halt, and a footman came to the door, opening it with haste.

Darcy stepped out and gave closer scrutiny to the inside of the carriage, having Fitzwilliam stand up and look under his belongings. "It is not here. I need to return to get it."

Fitzwilliam slowly climbed out after him as his valet came over from the other carriage. "Is there a problem, sir?" his valet asked.

"Jenkins, do you recall if you put my satchel in either your carriage or mine, possibly with the other luggage?"

"I am sorry, sir, but the last I saw of it, you had it in your hands."

Darcy raked his fingers through his hair, his eyes widening. "You are correct! I carried it into Rosings when I went to check on the post." He looked down and shook his head. "I need to return for it." There were papers in there he would not wish for the wrong person to see. And the letter... he shuddered, just thinking about it getting into someone's hands.

"Shall I send someone back for it?" Jenkins asked.

"No!" Darcy practically barked his reply, and then softly added, "Thank you, no. I shall go."

Jenkins nodded. "Yes, sir. Shall we accompany you or wait at the next post station?"

Darcy waved his hand through the air. "No, go on ahead to London. That way you can have the carriage unloaded and everything in readiness when we arrive."

"Yes, sir."

Fitzwilliam tugged at Darcy's sleeve. "Must we go back? Send our aunt a quick missive and have a messenger bring it to London."

Darcy's insides tightened as he considered his letter inside the satchel and chided himself for not burning it. He could not risk someone finding it − if they had not already. "No. I need to retrieve it."

"How long have we been on the road?" Fitzwilliam asked as he stretched out his arms.

Darcy pulled out his pocket watch and was surprised to see how little time had passed. He felt as though he had slept for several hours, at least. "Less than forty minutes. If we can get in and out of Rosings without delay, we ought to arrive in town by dusk. I believe there is an early rising full moon tonight, so there should be no difficulty." He turned to his valet. "We shall see you this evening."

"Yes, sir."

Jenkins returned to the other carriage. Darcy waited while the driver of his carriage pulled ahead and found a place to turn around. The footman opened the door, and the two gentlemen climbed back in.

"You could not send for someone to bring it to you? You cannot have pressing work to do. At least you cannot have work needing your attention immediately."

Darcy rested his elbow on the window sill and rubbed his forehead with his fingers. He closed his eyes and said, "That is true. I am merely concerned some items I have in that satchel might get into the wrong hands."

"Like Rickland's?"

Darcy shook his head. "Anyone!" He blew out a puff of air and turned to look out the window. His fingers nervously tapped the sill as he considered his cousin had no idea how right he was.

The colonel shook his head. "I have never seen you so altered in the whole of my life, but at least I now know why."

Darcy turned to him. "Whatever do you mean altered?"

Fitzwilliam let out a hearty chuckle. "While I cannot say you are normally gregarious, at least you are clever enough to share in the conversation, often adding some well-timed wit. You were a blasted bore the whole time we were at Rosings, and yet we were in the company of one of the liveliest young ladies I have ever met." He leaned in towards his cousin. "But now I know you were in love with her, well, that explains everything." He gave his head a toss from side to side. "I cannot claim to understand it, but I suppose I can attribute it to love."

Darcy turned his face to the window. "I assure you, there is no more of that." He drew in a breath and began tapping his fingers again, but looked at his cousin and stopped. He promptly picked up the biography and opened it, setting his eyes to the page.

Fitzwilliam laughed again. "You cannot fool me, Darcy. I know you too well. But I am grateful you did not make a fool of yourself by asking for Miss Bennet's hand. I can guarantee it would not have ended well."

Darcy's brows lowered, but he kept his eyes in the book.

"Wake me when we are back at Rosings," Fitzwilliam said as he stretched out his legs and closed his eyes. "I can see you are still not going to be much of a conversationalist."

~~*

Elizabeth walked hurriedly as she carefully folded up the letter, holding it tightly for fear the wind might snatch it away. Her heart pounded as she speculated what was in this missive, but she was too near Rosings and the parsonage to read it without the possibility of someone seeing her. She would wait until she reached the woods.

As she finally entered the wide expanse of the forest, she stepped under the canopy of towering trees. She looked around, and once confident no one was near, she unfolded the letter with shaking fingers. She walked slowly as she began reading it again, only looking up to stay on the small path that wound its way through.

She felt a resurgence of the anger she had felt yesterday as Mr. Darcy attempted to justify separating Mr. Bingley from Jane. She let out a disgusted grunt as she began to read his excuses.

"If he only knew how much Jane loved... still loves Mr. Bingley!"

She had a fleeting recollection about a conversation she once had with Charlotte about Jane needing to display her feelings more, but she shoved that thought aside. Whether or not he believed her sister to be indifferent, it was not his responsibility to interfere as he had.

When she read his accusation about her family's unsuitability, she dropped her hands to her sides and marched on, unable to read for several moments. She paid no attention to the dark, ominous clouds overhead or the raindrops that had begun to fall.

At length, her curiosity as to the contents of the remainder of the letter prevailed over her anger at Mr. Darcy's words, and she continued reading.

She looked down, found her place in the letter, and as she read he had a third reason for separating Mr. Bingley from Jane, she said indignantly, "Oh, I can imagine you have several reasons, none of which..."

She gasped and came to a stop as she read, *I came to ardently admire and love you.*

She read the sentence over several times, as if she may have misread it. Was that what he meant to say? Were those truly his feelings? She kept her eyes adhered to the missive, reading the subsequent sentences slowly, trying to comprehend how this could possibly be. How could she not have realized this? And how could he love *her*?

She walked on; her steps quickened as did the beating of her heart. She glanced up and looked about her for the path, but did not see it. She turned, hoping to return in the direction she believed she had just come, as she tried to comprehend such an astonishing revelation. Mr. Darcy declaring his love and admiration for her was assuredly not what she had ever expected – or hoped for. She shook her head as she realized Charlotte had once more been proven correct.

The inducement to finish the letter overcame her desire to get back onto the path. Her feet moved aimlessly as she continued reading. A few drops of rain had already hit the missive, causing the ink to run slightly. She needed to finish reading it before the rain began in earnest and the letter became indecipherable. As she looked up, a few patches of clear sky allowed the sun to peer through, but the wind rose and the air cooled.

As she read, her jaw dropped in awe at another surprise. She could not fathom that while she had teased him with mean-spirited and even resentful motives, he had enjoyed their repartee! Little had she known while she had hoped to stir him to feel affronted, she was stirring him in other ways!

Her mind whirred with disbelief that Mr. Darcy had actually noticed the colour of her dress when he saw her the first day he came to the parsonage, claiming it made her eyes sparkle and her skin glow. She shook her head in complete amazement. She had hoped Mr. Rickland would notice something like this, but never imagined Mr. Darcy would!

But she came to an abrupt halt and felt her cheeks flush as she read he had been about to propose to her the other day when they met in the grove, and he had on more than one occasion wished to pull her into a warm embrace and kiss her lips.

She stopped again and looked about her. Her hand covered her pounding heart as she tried to get her bearings – and control the countless feelings she was experiencing – when she read his words. She stopped and took a couple of deep breaths. She let out a half-hearted laugh as she realized she was just as lost in these woods as she was in comprehending how he could feel this way and how she had not once suspected it.

"Even Charlotte suspected something!" she said with exasperation.

Her head began to spin, and she groaned as she pounded her hands down to her sides. How could *she* have been so blind? How could *he* have behaved so rudely when he supposedly loved her?

She quickly raised the letter and looked for the place she had last read, barely able to breathe. She was almost to the end of the letter, but she realized too late she was walking down an incline. She lifted her eyes as she attempted to catch her balance, but there was nothing to be done as she tripped over a large rock and fell forward down a small hill. Her ankle twisted beneath her, and she crashed down hard on her shoulder.

Elizabeth slowly opened her eyes. She looked around her and then up the slopes of the small ravine into which she had fallen.

"How could I have been so clumsy?" she chided herself. She took in a deep breath and tried to move. "Ohh!" Pain from her left foot and her right shoulder prevented her from manoeuvring much at all. She leaned her head back down as it began to ache.

"What am I to do now?" she said as much to herself as to the trees swaying tauntingly above her.

She decided she would rest a bit and then try to move again. If she could climb up to the top of the ravine, perhaps she could call out and someone might hear her. She shook her head. She had not seen nor heard anyone for quite some time. They would have to be out looking for her in order to hear her or be out walking in the woods as she was. She winced from the pain and the realization she was in a dire predicament.

Elizabeth laid her head back down on the ground, but suddenly recollected the letter, which was no longer in her hands. She looked around her for it and slowly lifted her head, hoping not to exacerbate the dull ache. She looked to her left and then right, spotting the letter just out of her reach.

She attempted to stretch out her right hand, but the pain in her shoulder was too great. She could barely lift her arm, yet she could not allow the letter to blow away. A sudden wave of guilt flooded her, chastising her for reading it when it had not been written for her eyes to see, but she quickly shook it off. The last of the sunlight was blocked by the merging clouds, and a few more raindrops fell, adding to her determination to retrieve it.

She studied the location of the letter and the position of her body, finally deciding to try to use her right foot, which did not seem to be injured. She managed to shift her body a little, so she could move her leg to catch the letter with her foot and drag it closer so she could then try to reach it with her right hand or stretch out and reach over with her left.

It was not easy, but slowly and carefully she placed her foot on the letter and pulled it a little closer. It was still too far for her right arm to grasp without a great deal of pain, so she reached over with her left hand and stretched it out as far as she could. Her fingers barely touched the edge of the letter, and when a small gust of wind began to lift it up, she came down on it with her foot to secure it. With one more stretch, she was finally able to capture it between two of her fingers.

She looked down at the letter to find where she had left off reading, and her eyes widened at the mention of Mr. Wickham. The rain began to pelt down harder as she held it close and bent her head to try to shelter the missive from getting too wet. Her eyes narrowed as she read his brief explanation, which actually prompted more questions about Wickham than gave her answers. It did give her pause to wonder about both of the men's stories, however, and she determined she would somehow seek to discover the truth.

She felt another wave of anger as she read Mr. Darcy's brief, uninformative warning about Mr. Rickland. She wondered what his concern about him was, but determined she would decide his suitability for herself – if he even wished to further their acquaintance beyond Kent. With her injuries, she determined she would likely be leaving sooner than later.

She read the last paragraph and slowly lowered the letter onto her lap, folding it up carefully. "His love for me will be for all eternity? How could I have not seen this?" She shook her head. "Not that it would have made any difference." She took in a deep breath, and her voice trailed off in a sigh.

"Hello!" she called out as she folded the letter and slipped it securely down into the front of her dress. She rolled onto her side as much as she could so if the rain continued, the letter would hopefully remain dry. She needed to read it again when she could fully concentrate on every word.

"Hello!" she called out again, looking anxiously about her.

There was no response, which did not surprise her. She wondered how long it would be before she was found. The wind seemed to be the only response as it hummed through the trees, causing the branches to wave down at her. As she lay on the ground, the sky darkened, the winds picked up, the temperature dropped, and the menacing clouds above taunted her.

~~*

It was not long before the carriage carrying Darcy and Fitzwilliam passed the parsonage and they were crossing the lane to Rosings. When the carriage pulled up and stopped, Darcy was surprised to see people gathered about and saddled horses nearby. Two men had just galloped away towards the grove.

"I wonder what has occurred," he said.

Wha… what?" Fitzwilliam asked, shaking his head. He groggily looked out the window. "Certainly more activity than we saw the whole of our visit."

As they stepped out, Darcy said to Fitzwilliam. "I am going to retrieve my satchel. You see if you can find out what is going on."

Darcy briskly took the steps up to the front of Rosings and nodded at the butler who was standing by the door.

"You have returned, Mr. Darcy? Shall I inform Lady Catherine?"

"No need. I fear I left my satchel here," he said. "I believe I put it just inside the door. We shall be leaving again immediately, so please refrain from announcing us."

When he walked in, he felt a tremendous weight lift as he saw the satchel exactly where he had left it. It did not look as though it had been touched. He walked back and asked the butler why everyone was standing around outside.

"Apparently Miss Bennet, the guest of Mr. and Mrs. Collins, went for a walk this morning and has not yet returned. Mrs. Collins was quite concerned due to the rain we received, and several men have gone out looking for her."

Darcy's heart raced as he pondered what may have occurred, although knowing Elizabeth as he did, she might have taken a lengthy stroll.

"Thank you." He walked out to join the others. Charlotte and Maria were there.

Darcy nodded to Charlotte. "I heard about Miss Bennet. I assume people have set out looking for her?"

Charlotte nodded. "Yes, Mr. Rickland and a few others have gone to the grove. These men were going to ride around the park." She shook her head. "I know Elizabeth may be taking a longer walk than normal, but she said she would be back within the hour. It has been almost two hours, and we have already had some rain, with more storm clouds approaching. I know she would not intentionally stay out in this." She wrung her hands together and seemed to be holding back tears.

"Mrs. Collins, I encountered Miss Bennet several times while out walking, and I might be able to find her. Allow me to put this in the carriage, and I shall set off at once."

"Do you want me to go with you?" Fitzwilliam asked.

Darcy shook his head. "No, wait here. If someone returns with her, come find me in the woods. You know where we once almost got lost when we were younger?"

Fitzwilliam shook his head. "*Almost* got lost? We *did* get lost, and I am quite certain I would likely get lost again if I were to set out for those woods. But yes, I believe I can find my way there – but only if I urgently need to."

Darcy rushed to the carriage and threw his satchel inside. He quickly grabbed his coat, throwing it over his shoulder. He walked to one of the horses that had been saddled, and grabbing the reins, he mounted. He then rode over to Charlotte. "Say a prayer, Mrs. Collins, that one of us finds her and she is all right."

Charlotte nodded. "I have already. And if nothing terrible has befallen her, I have prayed she will not be angry with me for worrying so and causing everyone such alarm."

Darcy rode off, not knowing what he might find or what state Elizabeth would be in if he did find her. His only hope was she would indeed be safe.

Chapter 14

Darcy kicked the horse's flanks, urging it into a gallop, and directed it towards the woods. He did not know if anyone else had thought to set out this way, but he knew where he had often seen Elizabeth and the path she had identified as her favourite walk. Hopefully she had not ventured far from there. The knot in his stomach told him it would be easy to get lost in these woods, as he and his cousin had long-ago discovered.

As he approached the woods, he slowed the horse. He wanted to be able to hear Elizabeth if she called out. He turned his head to the right and left, as much to see as to hear anything. The woods were so dense in some areas even if she were out here walking, he might not see her.

"Miss Bennet!" he called out as loudly as he could. "Are you here?" He pulled the horse's reins to bring it to a halt. Looking out into the vast woods, he realized she could be anywhere.

He nudged the horse along slowly, keeping a watchful eye out for any movement, anything that looked out of the ordinary. A flash of light off to his right drew his attention, but as he heard the following clap of thunder, he knew what had been the cause of it.

Unfortunately, the storm was moving towards him and would likely bring a deluge of rain. He called out again, wishing he had thought to bring his shotgun. The sound of the shotgun would travel further than his voice. It would be worse when the storm was on top of them.

"Miss Bennet!" he called out again as raindrops began to pelt him. He had to find her as soon as possible.

"Hello?"

Darcy quickly turned his head. He was certain he had heard her call out, but could not see her! His heart pounded in a mixture of hope and fear. "Miss Bennet, where are you?"

~~*

Elizabeth had stirred at the crack of lightning and boom of thunder, followed by rain pelting her like tiny pebbles. She had to get herself out of the ravine. She lifted her head and steeled herself for the pain that would surely assault her as she struggled to pull herself up. Perhaps she would be successful using her one good leg and one good arm.

As she attempted to move, she realized it would be slow progress, but she knew soon the ravine would be full of mud and she would not have any sort of footing. She took in a deep breath and pushed with her good foot and pulled with her uninjured arm. She felt a wave of discouragement threaten to overwhelm her when she made little progress.

"Miss Bennet!"

Elizabeth stopped and looked up. Did she really hear her name? "Hello?" she called out.

"Miss Bennet, where are you?"

Elizabeth smiled. Someone had found her. Or at least they would soon find her!

"I am here, down in a ravine!"

The voice had been too far away to tell who it was, although she was certain it was not Mr. Rickland. She was grateful someone had discovered her.

She kept her eyes adhered to the top of the ravine, occasionally calling out. The voice did not answer her, and she hoped he was finding his way to her. She feared there was no answer because he had not heard her and had gone on his way. The rain fell hard now, and she touched her fingers to her bodice to make certain the letter was not peeking out and was remaining dry beneath her spencer and stays.

She saw the head of the horse first and then heard, rather than saw, a man dismount.

"Oh, I am so grateful you found me! I wondered whether anyone..." Elizabeth stopped as she saw it was Mr. Darcy. "What are *you* doing here?" she cried out in surprise.

"Rescuing you, I believe. But if you would rather me not..."

Elizabeth waved her hand through the air, feeling a blush tint her cheeks. "Pray, forgive me. I did not mean it that way. I thought you had already departed Rosings." She felt terribly confused and wondered how she could ever face him now having read his letter. His words confessing his ardent love for her was prominent in her mind.

Darcy took several steps down into the ravine, his boots digging into the dirt, which was quickly becoming slippery mud. He was soon by her side, towering over her. "We had to return to Rosings as I had forgotten something and needed to reclaim it." He stooped down. "Are you hurt?"

She looked up at him and could not help but see the compassion and concern in his eyes. "Yes. My left leg and ankle and my right shoulder. I tried to pull myself up, but found it too painful. I was about to make another attempt when I heard you call."

"Do you think anything is broken?"

Elizabeth shook her head. "No bone is protruding, but I cannot say for certain."

"I shall need to remove you from here before it gets too muddy. The rain is increasing." He bit his lip. "The only way for me to do that is to carry you. I fear there is no other way."

Elizabeth blew out a puff of air, feeling the same warmth she felt as she read his declaration of love in the letter. She absently brought her hand up to the bodice of her dress. She looked into his eyes, which for the first time ever, seemed kind and caring. "I... it must be done."

"Tell me if I hurt you," he said, as he slid his arms underneath her and carefully and slowly began lifting her up. Once he was standing with her in his arms, he looked down at her, and she felt his muscles tense. A still moment hung between the two of them, and Elizabeth thought for a moment he was going to lean down and kiss her.

Taking in a deep breath, he said, "I shall attempt to make it up the bank without too much jostling."

She felt secure in his arms and did not feel any pain, but when he took a step up and the mud caused his foot to slip, she flung her good arm about his neck.

"Sorry!" they both said at the same time.

Elizabeth softly laughed, but then as Darcy took several forceful steps to get them out of the ravine, she held on tighter. They reached the top, and Darcy stole a glance down at her. "Are you all right?"

Elizabeth nodded. "Yes, thank you. I am greatly indebted to you."

Darcy shook his head. "There is no debt, and we are not yet finished. Do you feel steady enough to ride the horse on your own? I shall be by your side, of course."

Elizabeth's brows came together as she looked up at the horse. "I am certainly not a horsewoman."

"Allow me to lift you up onto the saddle, and we shall take it slow." He gently placed her onto the saddle so her legs draped over one side. "Hold on to the reins with your good hand." He placed them in her hand and then looked up. He took his coat and swung it over her shoulders.

She looked down at him, and their eyes met. She noticed him take in a quick gasp of air. He turned his eyes away and then looked back up at her. "Do you... do you feel steady?"

Elizabeth winced. "I am not used to riding horses, even when I am perfectly well. I feel slightly..."

She began to wobble, and Darcy moved quickly towards her, preparing to catch her if she began to fall.

"Take care, Miss Bennet."

Before she knew what was happening, Darcy slid his foot into the stirrup and was up and over the horse. As he came down, he lifted her slightly so he was able to slide down into the saddle behind her, and she found herself coming to rest on his legs. "Now, I fear to give better balance to you and enable me to see, I need you to lean your head against my chest."

Elizabeth was grateful he could not see her face as she pressed her head against his chest, for she knew he would see her brightly flushed cheeks. She wondered if he could feel her heart beating wildly. If only she had not read his letter! It was certainly making it much more difficult to maintain her dislike! Knowing he desired to hold her in his arms and kiss her... she could only imagine how he felt.

But perhaps he had already pushed her out of his heart because of her angry words to him yesterday. She determined she would concentrate on the anger he evoked in her rather than the sentiment she had only recently discovered. It would make this intimate closeness to him more bearable.

They rode in silence for a while, Elizabeth occasionally feeling a shot of pain in her leg due to the movement of the horse, despite Darcy's attempt to keep the pace slow and smooth. As the horse had to traverse a small slope, she felt his free arm go about her waist. His palm pressed into her side.

Elizabeth was frustratingly aware of his every touch. If it had not been for the letter, she would have been able to view this quite objectively. She wondered whether Mr. Darcy felt the same. Had he put aside those feelings he had so recently harboured for her?

They soon came out of the woods, and she felt him tense and shift beneath her. A few moments later, she heard him call out, "Over here! I have Miss Bennet!"

Elizabeth heard the sound of voices and horses' hooves drawing near. She peeked out from the coat and saw Mr. Rickland. She gave him a weak smile.

"Miss Bennet! Are you all right? We were so worried!"

She nodded. "I believe I shall survive, but I doubt I will be doing any dancing at the soiree tomorrow evening."

"Where did you find her?" Rickland's voice sounded almost accusatory.

"In the woods. She had fallen into a shallow ravine."

"A most inelegant manoeuvre," Elizabeth said, slightly embarrassed.

"I am taking her to the parsonage, but someone ought to summon the doctor."

Rickland looked at the man next to him and bid him fetch the doctor.

"I shall accompany you." Elizabeth did not miss the look Rickland shot Darcy as he said this.

Elizabeth turned her head back into Mr. Darcy's chest as she grimaced. She was now as angry at herself for reading his letter as she was for joining Mr. Rickland yesterday in enumerating Mr. Darcy's faults. But now, coupled with knowledge of Darcy's admiration, she could not help but wonder what it was he wanted to tell her about Mr. Rickland.

They rode in silence, with Mr. Rickland only occasionally inquiring after Elizabeth's well-being. When they reached the parsonage, Darcy gently steadied Elizabeth with his hand on her uninjured shoulder.

"I am going to get off first and then help you down."

Elizabeth nodded, and as he lifted himself in the stirrups, she slid off his lap, back onto the saddle.

"I can take care of her from here, Darcy," Mr. Rickland said in a severe tone indicating he would brook no opposition.

Darcy looked at him and then up at Elizabeth. He pursed his lips and rubbed his jaw. "Be careful."

He stood off to the side, but close enough, Elizabeth assumed, to step in if needed. Elizabeth stared down at the two. Rickland was neither as tall nor as muscular as Mr. Darcy, but she knew she had a light figure and he should not have any trouble carrying her. It was getting her down from the horse that had her concerned.

He held up his arms. "Lean down into my arms, and I shall catch you."

"Catch me?" she asked. Elizabeth looked pleadingly at Mr. Darcy, who stepped up next to Rickland.

"No, Darcy," Rickland said, waving his hand as Darcy drew near. "I know what I am doing!"

"Rickland, she is injured, and there is too much of a risk she might be dropped." Before Rickland could reply, Darcy had taken her in his arms and brought her easily down. "Run ahead to the house and find out where they wish me to take her."

Rickland paused for only a moment as if to say something, his face contorting with anger and frustration. He then turned and ran up to the door. It opened just before he knocked, and soon Mr. Collins, Charlotte, and Maria rushed out.

"Come! Bring her here! Is she all right?" Charlotte cried out.

"I am well, Charlotte, only a few minor injuries."

"We shall send for a doctor!" Mr. Collins announced, clasping his hands.

"It has already been done," Darcy said. "She twisted her ankle and injured her shoulder." He looked to Charlotte. "Where shall I take her?"

Charlotte directed him to the sitting room. "All of our bedrooms are upstairs, so this is best. We can close the doors to give her some privacy."

Darcy nodded and placed her gently down on the sofa after Charlotte placed a coverlet over it.

"Oh, Lizzy," Charlotte said, carefully removing her shoes and pulling the edges of the coverlet over her clothes to warm her. "I was so worried! What can I do for you?"

Elizabeth smiled wearily. "As soon as everyone leaves, I shall need some assistance getting out of these wet clothes." She shivered and then said, "I would like to write to my Uncle Gardiner. I must see if he can send his carriage for me. Jane is in town with them..." She unwittingly glanced at Mr. Darcy. "I can stay with them until I am well, and then she and I can travel together back home to Hertfordshire."

Darcy stood at the back of the room near the door, rubbing his chin.

"Miss Bennet..."

Everyone turned to Darcy. "Yes?" Elizabeth replied.

"I... my cousin and I will not be leaving today. It is too late. We will leave tomorrow. If I can secure a traveling companion for you, it would not be inconvenient if you were to accompany us to London. As long as travel is permitted by the doctor." He paused, and his jaw tightened. "You would be most welcome and would get to town much sooner."

Rickland stepped forward. "Miss Bennet would most certainly *not* wish to do that." Turning to Elizabeth he asked, "And why do you even have to leave? The doctor here will take good care of you."

Elizabeth watched Rickland turn back to Darcy, and the two men glared at each other. She lifted her hand. "Shall we wait and see what the doctor says? He may not wish for me to travel." She saw Rickland flash a triumphant smile at Darcy. "Or, he may feel I need to get to London as soon as possible." Rickland's smile faded, and Darcy's lips slightly curved up.

Charlotte turned to the two men. "Let us allow Elizabeth some rest, and she can make the decision about what to do once the doctor has seen her. We shall let you know. And now, I insist all the men leave immediately!" She practically pushed the two men out the door. "Tell your aunt we are grateful for everyone's assistance today."

Charlotte closed the door and stood in front of it. "Lizzy, I may be mistaken, but those two men…"

Elizabeth put up a hand to stop her, but her sore shoulder made her wince. "Oh!" She smiled weakly and added, "I should have lifted the other arm."

"You are in pain!"

"Just a little."

"So what have you to say now, Lizzy? If I were to put forth a guess, I would say there was a little jealous rivalry displayed there." Charlotte gave her a pointed look, almost daring her to say she was incorrect.

Elizabeth shook her head. She could not say anything to her friend about Mr. Darcy's letter or apparent admiration. "Charlotte, do not be absurd. They were both merely attempting to be of assistance."

Charlotte sat down on the sofa and smoothed the coverlet. "Believe what you wish, my good friend, but judging by the behaviour of both those men, I hold fast to what I said the other day."

"They are both merely interested in my well-being." She hoped she sounded convincing. "Now, dear friend, would you help me get out of these clothes? I hope we can do it without too much pain."

~~*

Darcy walked the horse back to Rosings, keeping two strides ahead of Rickland.

"You know how she feels about you, Darcy," Rickland said in a raised, irritated voice. "Do not force her to spend half a day in your company when you are the last man she wants to be with. Was it not enough she had to endure you holding her as you brought her back on the horse?"

Darcy stopped abruptly and spun around. "She knew, as well as I did, there was no other way. I believe she was grateful. That is all there is to it."

Darcy turned and began walking at a brisker pace. His long legs soon took him far enough away he could hear his rival no longer. Darcy shook his head. *He is not a rival,* he thought. *Elizabeth has no interest whatsoever in me!* He let out a huff. *If he were a rival, we would both have a chance to win her affection.*

When he reached Rosings, he asked the butler where he could find his aunt.

"She is in the parlour with her daughter and Colonel Fitzwilliam."

"Thank you."

He walked to the parlour and stepped in, greeting his aunt and cousins. "We have found Miss Bennet, and a doctor is on the way to check her injuries. She is in a great deal of pain, but I do not think it is anything serious."

"Good. You must be hungry, Nephew. There is some food on the sideboard."

"Thank you, Aunt. But I need to discuss something with Fitzwilliam, if you do not mind, and then clean up."

"You are not leaving today, are you? It is far too late."

"No, we shall leave on the morrow."

Fitzwilliam stood up, and the two men walked out. "How is Miss Bennet?"

They stopped in the hallway. "She was injured in a fall. Her ankle is hopefully merely sprained, and her shoulder suffered an injury. I do not think anything is broken, but she wishes to get to London as soon as possible. She was going to write to her uncle and have his carriage brought here, but that would take a few days, if he is even able to send it."

Fitzwilliam gave Darcy a knowing look. "You want her to join us?"

Darcy drew in a long breath and let it out slowly. "I have offered. I have no idea if she will agree."

"After yesterday, I doubt it. But Darcy, she certainly cannot travel with just the two of us."

"No, I have already thought of that. I was going to ask our aunt if she can part with Mrs. Beckett. Her son works at Suncrest House, and I am quite certain she would enjoy seeing him."

"Mrs. Beckett? You mean the little old lady whose hearing is as good as an ear of corn?"

Darcy laughed. "Yes, she is the one. I shall arrange it contingent on what the doctor says and what Miss Bennet wishes."

Fitzwilliam laughed. "You do realize if Miss Bennet accompanies us, you are likely to get an earful from her for the duration of the trip. Remember, she is not particularly fond of you."

Darcy nodded and lowered his eyes. "Do you have any other objections?"

Fitzwilliam shook his head. "None. I am at your disposal, Cousin. But I wonder if you are doing this to punish yourself. I cannot imagine it will be a pleasant journey."

"I am doing this for her, Fitzwilliam, not for myself."

"Then, my good cousin," he said, slapping Darcy on the back, "we shall have to make the best of it."

Chapter 15

As they awaited the doctor's arrival, Charlotte made certain her friend had something to eat and drink within reach, and brought her the book she had been reading prior to her eventful walk.

Once Charlotte stepped out of the room, Elizabeth pulled out the letter and slipped it between the pages of the book for safe keeping. She knew she ought to throw it away, but something compelled her to keep it. She wanted time to read it again more slowly.

The doctor arrived shortly thereafter and gave a thorough examination of Elizabeth's injuries. He determined there was no breakage, but she had twisted her ankle and possibly pulled a muscle in her leg if the swelling and discolouration was any indication. She would need to keep weight off of her foot until the swelling lessened and she was no longer in pain. He told her to keep her ankle raised as much as she could.

The worst of the injuries was her shoulder, which had been jarred out of alignment. The doctor was able to manoeuvre it back into place, but not without causing Elizabeth a great deal of pain. He then wrapped her arm and put it in a sling to ensure as little movement as possible while it healed.

He gave her some laudanum, and as he prepared to leave, he gave Charlotte instructions to give her more if needed for the pain. He also advised Elizabeth if she went to London, she ought to stay off her foot and avoid moving her shoulder for at least a week, if not longer. He saw no harm in traveling.

When he left, Charlotte sat down on the sofa next to Elizabeth. "I would be glad to have you stay here. I know we could take good care of you, but I understand you want to be with your family."

"Thank you, Charlotte. I do wish to be with my aunt and uncle and Jane."

"I thought as much. So what will it be, Elizabeth? Do we send a missive to your uncle to send his carriage for you, or do I send a note to Rosings informing Mr. Darcy that if he can secure a companion to accompany you, you will be joining them?"

"I should like to send an express to my uncle."

"Oh," Charlotte said, her smile fading. "I thought you would surely accept Mr. Darcy's offer. His carriage is quite luxurious, so I understand."

Elizabeth smiled despite the pain. "I am quite certain it is. That is why I will be writing to my uncle telling him to expect me late tomorrow afternoon, arriving in a carriage provided by Lady Catherine de Bourgh."

Charlotte clasped her hands together. "Wonderful! But you do not wish to mention it is Mr. Darcy's carriage?"

"Not in the letter. They shall discover whom I travelled with soon enough. No need for speculation until I arrive and can explain things."

"Very prudent, indeed! I shall get the stationery, quill, and ink, and while you are writing your letter, I will send a note to Rosings to inform Mr. Darcy of your decision."

Elizabeth struggled to write the simple letter, realizing the laudanum was affecting her ability to formulate the correct words and to hold the quill steady. She hoped it had not adversely affected her judgment in deciding to ride to London with Mr. Darcy and his cousin. She shook her head. No, she had made that decision earlier, before she had begun to feel the effects of the medicine. She merely wished to get to London as soon as possible, and the fact his carriage would be a much more comfortable ride certainly held an advantage.

Once the letters were written, Charlotte gave them to a servant to dispatch. She then returned to Elizabeth's side. Her eyes were closed, and she was very still. "Lizzy, are you asleep?" she whispered.

A smile formed on her lips. "No. I am trying not to think of the pain."

"Is it unbearable?"

"I ache from head to toe. I doubt I will be able to get comfortable enough to sleep tonight."

"And that is where the laudanum ought to help."

Elizabeth pursed her lips and nodded, her eyes still closed. "I hope you are correct, Charlotte."

~~*

Darcy stepped into the parlour where his aunt, cousins, and Rickland were sitting.

"Where have you been?" Lady Catherine asked impatiently. "I have been waiting most anxiously for you."

"I regret I had business that needed my attention."

"I am glad you are finally here. You must sit and visit. If I am fortunate to have another evening with you, I insist you favour us with your presence." She motioned to a chair and then continued to speak to the others, almost as if he were not there.

He remained silent, though almost restless, whilst the others talked animatedly amongst themselves. Anne sat still, at times appearing interested in what was being said, but at other times intent on her writing.

Lady Catherine suddenly turned back to him. "Are you still unwell, Nephew?" she asked, interrupting Rickland with her question. "You are unusually quiet this evening."

Darcy lifted his eyes to his aunt. "It has merely been a taxing day." He could not believe all that had occurred in the past four and twenty hours.

Before she could reply, there was a tap at the door, and the butler stepped in with a letter on a salver. "A letter for Mr. Darcy from the parsonage."

"What is the meaning of this?" demanded Lady Catherine.

"Most likely news about Miss Bennet," Colonel Fitzwilliam said.

Darcy gave the appearance of calm as he read the missive, but his heart began to beat rapidly as he comprehended Elizabeth would be joining them on the morrow. He looked up to see all eyes upon him.

"It seems Miss Bennet has accepted my offer to travel with us to London." He turned to his aunt, ignoring the short protest Mr. Rickland uttered. "I have already spoken with Mrs. Beckett about accompanying us as her chaperone. If you permit it, Aunt, she will travel to London with us to see her son, and then return in about a week's time."

"Mrs. Beckett? Can I even manage without her?" Lady Catherine groaned. She tossed her head back and forth. "I find this highly improper, having Miss Bennet travel with you. I shall send her and Mrs. Beckett in my carriage. You have no need to importune yourselves in this matter."

Mr. Rickland began to protest, as well, but Darcy interjected. "I would prefer the two ladies travel with us. It shall be no inconvenience. You will permit Mrs. Beckett to accompany us?"

She let out a long moan. "I do not know how I shall manage without her. Mrs. Beckett has agreed, I assume?"

"Yes, and I shall go inform her now that the plans are settled."

Darcy stood and walked out of the room as his aunt called out his name in irritation. He was eager to get away from Rickland's accusing glare and savour a few moments to himself as he contemplated what the morrow might bring, despite knowing it could prove to be most unpleasant for him.

After speaking with Mrs. Beckett, Darcy's heart was too full of hope to face the scrutiny of Rickland and his aunt. He knew there was little hope in securing Elizabeth's affections, but he would certainly entertain hopes of having her opinion of him at least slightly improved by the culmination of their journey. He sent a note back to the parsonage, informing them if Miss Bennet agreed, he had secured Mrs. Beckett as a traveling companion for her.

~~*

The laudanum soon took effect, and Elizabeth quickly fell asleep, despite its still being afternoon. Unfortunately, the drug gave her quite dreadful dreams. While they all seemed to run together, she remembered constantly being assaulted by tall leafless trees, whose branches waved about like angry arms and murmured taunting threats in the wind.

She awoke early in the evening in a state of confusion, and it took Charlotte some time to calm her. When asked if she wanted more laudanum, she vehemently declined fearing the return of the nightmares.

She was unable to go back to sleep when the rest of the household repaired to their rooms for the night. She wondered whether she had made a wise decision in refusing any more of the medication. She was in pain but wanted no more of those dreams. She also wished to be clear-headed in the carriage and not say anything she would regret. She would endure the pain.

The next morning Charlotte came to the parlour with a tray full of food and drink. Elizabeth was just waking.

"How are you this morning, Lizzy? Did you sleep well?"

"My ankle and shoulder are still causing quite a bit of pain, and I believe I fell into a rather fitful sleep only hours before dawn."

"I hope you have an appetite," Charlotte said, walking towards the sofa. "Our cook has outdone herself!" She placed the tray on a side table and looked down at her friend with a mischievous smile. "Do you feel well enough to travel today?"

Elizabeth smiled weakly. "I believe I do." As she moved to accommodate the tray on her lap, she winced in pain.

"Perhaps you ought to take more laudanum," Charlotte suggested.

Elizabeth closed her eyes and shook her head. "No, thank you, Charlotte." She winced slightly from the pain. "I wish to have a clear head when I travel with these two men."

She opened her eyes to see Charlotte scolding her with a look.

Maria stood next to her sister. "Are you truly leaving, Lizzy? I do not think I can face Lady Catherine without you by my side."

"You shall bear up admirably, Maria, I am quite sure."

"Please, Lizzy," Charlotte said. "Do take some more. I hate to think of you travelling in pain."

"I told you last night the laudanum makes me confused. You would not wish for me to suddenly declare my love to one of the men without knowing what I was doing, would you?" She laughed, which caused her shoulder to hurt.

"Oh my! Do you truly think you would? That would be quite scandalous!" Maria said, eyes widening with shock.

Charlotte smiled. "Well, I think it might be fun to see what their reactions would be!"

Elizabeth brought her hand up and rubbed her sore shoulder. "You might find me lying out on the road, having been unceremoniously pushed out!"

"That would not do, at all!" Charlotte laughed. "You would likely end up with both your shoulders and legs in dreadful shape."

"And that is why," Elizabeth said with a smile, "I refuse to take any more laudanum."

~~*

Elizabeth was grateful Mr. Collins paid his respects to her and took his leave early. He was polite, hoped she would give her family his deepest apologies for the calamitous event that caused her injuries, and wished her God speed on her travels. She was thankful he would be gone when it was time to depart. She did not want him to feel it was his duty to carry her to the carriage. She likely would end up in a heap on the ground.

But that made Elizabeth ponder who would carry her out. She felt certain she could walk, despite being told to stay off her foot as much as possible. She did not wish to be the object of an argument between any of the men, particularly Mr. Rickland and Mr. Darcy. She smiled as she thought she could suggest Colonel Fitzwilliam carry her. That would solve any possible dispute.

Elizabeth had no need to worry, however, for when the carriage came from Rosings, the doctor arrived, as well. He was a large man, and while she was not certain who may have asked him to come, she was grateful. He brought with him a pair of crutches for her to use.

He checked her shoulder and ankle and admonished her to take more laudanum as it would certainly help alleviate the pain. When she refused, he silently shook his head, but then proceeded to give her instructions on how to use the crutches.

"I am giving you the pair of crutches, but I believe with your sore shoulder, it will be difficult to use that arm. So I would beseech you to have someone walk with you, giving assistance on that side. When you walk, use the crutch to keep from putting full pressure on your left foot. You may touch the foot to the ground to assist in balance, but try not to put much weight on it."

Elizabeth nodded and thanked him. "What do I owe you for your excellent care?"

He shook his head and waved his hand through the air. "It is all taken care of. You need not worry about any fee, since you are the guest of Lady Catherine's clergyman."

Elizabeth was grateful. "Again, I thank you."

"Now, I shall assist you in getting up and see how well you do using the single crutch."

Elizabeth had seen crutches before but had never seen them being used. She closed her eyes and clenched her teeth when the pain was unbearable, but she soon felt confident and comfortable using it.

"Keep both crutches in case you find the pain in your shoulder tolerable enough to use both. But not before. Keep off of the one foot until the swelling goes down and the pain lessens."

Elizabeth thanked him again.

"Shall we attempt to walk out to the carriage? I shall assist you on this side and will do my best not to hurt you."

"Thank you," Elizabeth said and then turned to Charlotte, who had been joined by Maria. "Before we step out, I wish to thank you so much for everything, dear friend. I thoroughly enjoyed myself." She smiled at her friend. "I would hug you if I was not in so much discomfort."

Charlotte smiled. "But I can certainly hug you!" Charlotte reached her arms about Elizabeth. "I am so sorry you have to leave early and will miss the soiree. But most of all, I will miss having my dearest friend nearby."

"I shall miss you, as well. And please, enjoy the soiree for me."

"I doubt it will be the same without you."

Maria leaned over and gave her a hug. "And I shall miss you, Lizzy. I do not know what I shall do without you."

"As I said before, you shall fare admirably." Elizabeth smiled at them both, and they stepped out, coming to a halt at the front door, just before the steps.

"Allow me to carry you down the stairs, Miss Bennet."

The doctor easily picked her up and brought her down. He gently released her, helped her position the crutch, and then walked alongside, only giving assistance as needed. The three gentlemen from Rosings were waiting by the carriage. Mr. Rickland rushed up to her.

"It is good to see you up. I hardly slept at all worrying about you." He leaned forward and asked in a fervent whisper, "Are you certain you wish to do this? I hate to think of you riding all day with those men."

Elizabeth tilted her head and looked up at him. "Those *men*? I would have thought only one was of concern to you. Certainly you have nothing against Colonel Fitzwilliam."

Rickland shook his head. "No, I am certain you comprehend my meaning." He took in a deep breath, crossing his arms in front of him.

Elizabeth smiled and looked over at Mr. Darcy, who was watching the two of them. "I shall be perfectly all right. You have no need to worry." She gave him a reassuring smile. "Perhaps it is Mr. Darcy you need to worry about. I might give him a good set down that lasts all the way to town."

Rickland laughed. "Please do! I only wish I was along to hear you abuse him to his face!"

"I did a fair job of it two days ago."

Elizabeth pursed her lips together, realizing she had always enjoyed teasing Mr. Darcy in a rather impertinent manner. Now, on this journey to London, she hoped to find out who this man — whom she was so intent on disliking – truly was.

"I should like to stop in London to see how you are faring, if you are still there when I leave here." Mr. Rickland looked at her with pleading eyes.

"I would like that. How long will you remain here?"

"That depends on my aunt. Now that her other two nephews are leaving, she might require me to stay longer."

Elizabeth was about to say something about his being at his aunt's disposal, as Colonel Fitzwilliam had claimed to be at his cousin's disposal, but Darcy stepped up.

"If you are ready, Miss Bennet, we shall be off, but first I would like to introduce you to Mrs. Beckett, your travelling companion."

Elizabeth turned back to Mr. Rickland. "Perhaps I shall see you in London, then."

"I look forward to it! Make sure you get all the rest you need. I still want that dance you promised me."

Elizabeth smiled. "I shall hold you to that."

She turned back to Mr. Darcy, whose lips were pressed tightly together. She surmised it was either in anger at Mr. Rickland for expressing his hope to dance with her, or to prevent himself from saying something to him. Probably both.

Mr. Rickland left, and Elizabeth used the crutch to limp to the carriage with Mr. Darcy in attendance at her elbow. Mrs. Beckett was sitting inside.

As they approached the carriage, Darcy said, "Mrs. Beckett's son is one of the man servants in Suncrest House, my London home. She was once my aunt's personal lady's maid, but age and her hearing now preclude her from those duties."

"Is she still in your aunt's employ?"

"Yes, but I am trying to convince my aunt to allow her to leave so she can be closer to her son. My aunt likes to think she still needs her, but I think it is just a long-time attachment."

Elizabeth smiled and looked away.

After a pause, Darcy said, "Yes, I would agree with you."

Elizabeth turned back quickly. "What do you mean?"

"I saw that look. You were likely thinking my aunt enjoys having someone she can complain to all day even though Mrs. Beckett cannot hear her." A tentative smile appeared. "A mutual benefit, I think."

Elizabeth let out a surprised laugh. "Indeed, you are correct, Mr. Darcy." Her gaze lifted to Darcy's face, and she was struck by the fact he was smiling. She had seen that smile on a few rare occasions, but had never attributed it to being because of her. A blush warmed her cheeks. She quickly looked down, regret flooding her that she had read his letter. How could she look at him from now on without hearing those words of admiration he had for her? She was grateful Colonel Fitzwilliam joined them.

"Everything is packed, Darcy, as to your specifications."

"Good. I was going to introduce Miss Bennet to Mrs. Beckett, and then I shall speak with the driver."

"I shall introduce her. You can go ahead."

"Thank you."

Colonel Fitzwilliam assisted Elizabeth the remaining distance to the carriage. The door was open, and he leaned in. "Mrs. Beckett!" he called out in a loud voice. "May I introduce you to Miss

Elizabeth Bennet?"

Mrs. Beckett nodded repeatedly. A broad, but crooked smile lit her face, and her eyes twinkled with mirth. Elizabeth was believed the lady likely had been pretty when she was younger. She beckoned Elizabeth to join her with a wave of her bony hand.

"We thought it would be best to have you sit with your back against the side of the carriage and stretch your legs along the seat. We can prop up your ankle with a pillow." He extended his hand towards the interior of the carriage but gave Elizabeth a teasing smile. "I believe the carriage is wide enough that you will not have to rest your legs on Mrs. Beckett's lap."

"I would hope not," Elizabeth said with a laugh. "Mrs. Beckett would likely change her mind about chaperoning me if she was required to hold my feet for the duration of the trip."

The colonel smiled at Elizabeth. "We have several pillows and blankets if you have need of them."

"Thank you."

"I shall have the doctor assist you in boarding the carriage. Unfortunately, I have a minor war injury preventing me from being able to readily lift you up. So it shall fall to my cousin to take care of that pleasant duty at our stops." He leaned towards her, and with a conspiratorial whisper said, "Just giving you an advance warning, Miss Bennet, although he is truly not the beast some believe him to be." He gave her a quick wink.

"I thank you for the caution, Colonel Fitzwilliam. I am quite certain I shall bear up admirably."

The colonel waved for the doctor to lift Elizabeth in. Darcy returned, and the doctor instructed the two men on how best to assist her and cause as little aggravation to her injuries as possible.

Once Elizabeth was settled, the two men stepped into the carriage to find Mrs. Beckett tucking a pillow behind Elizabeth's head and arranging a blanket over her. Fitzwilliam sat across from Mrs. Beckett, and Darcy took the seat across from Elizabeth. Once they were settled, Darcy tapped on the top of the carriage. They were finally on their way to London.

Chapter 16

Elizabeth was grateful for Mrs. Beckett's attention to her comfort, but the woman need not have worried. Elizabeth had never ridden in such a luxurious carriage, with or without the pillows, blankets, and attentive care. She had enough room to stretch out her legs along the seat as she sat with her back against the side.

Mr. Darcy inquired whether she had need of anything, pointing to a basket filled with food and drink. She assured him all she needed at the moment was a nap, as she had not slept well the previous night.

She hoped she could close her eyes and listen in on the conversation he and his cousin might have. Perhaps it might provide a clue as to the real man behind the arrogant façade.

~~*

The jarring of the carriage wakened Elizabeth. She opened her eyes and met Mr. Darcy's gaze, which had been upon her. He quickly looked away and shifted in his seat. She had no idea how long she had been asleep, but she could not recall hearing any conversation.

A noise from the other side of the carriage drew her attention, and she saw Colonel Fitzwilliam suddenly jerk and make a garbling noise deep in his throat. She smiled and looked at Mr. Darcy, who smiled back at her. A more delicate sound came from Mrs. Beckett, who had also fallen asleep.

"I hope I did not make such sounds!" Elizabeth whispered.

"You did not. You slept peacefully," Darcy assured her softly.

His voice resonated with warmth and seemed to wrap around her. She shivered in spite of it. "How long did I sleep?"

"About an hour. The three of you fell asleep within minutes of each other." He shrugged his shoulders. "I can only assume it is the company you all found tiresome."

"I cannot speak for the other two, but I fell asleep because I did not sleep well last night."

"Did the doctor not give you anything for the pain? Laudanum?"

"Yes, he certainly did. I took some yesterday afternoon and slept like a baby for several hours. It did, however, cause frightfully vivid dreams and confusion when I awoke." She shook her head with the memory of it. "Therefore, I refused to take any more, and because of the pain, I slept poorly." She looked up and smiled. "But at least during the little I did slumber, I suffered no dreadful dreams."

Elizabeth drew a hand up to rub the tight knot in her neck. "I must have slept at a bad angle."

"Is there anything I can get for you? Do you have need of another pillow or blanket?"

She wiggled her toes under the blanket. "Thank you, no." She smiled. "As you may have surmised, it is not always easy for me to remain still for any length of time." She looked up and felt a mischievous smile appear. "I can be quite the fearsome creature when forced into idleness, as my sisters can attest."

Darcy's lips curved into a smile, which quickly disappeared when he brought his hand up and rubbed his jaw. "We shall make as many stops as you need, and you may take the opportunity to move around as much as you are able… with help, of course. Are you now in much pain?"

"Not as much as yesterday and last night. My shoulder feels worse than my ankle at the moment."

"I hope you will let me know if there is anything I can do for your relief. I would not have you in discomfort, especially if it is within my power to ease it."

Elizabeth was touched by his concern. "Thank you," she said softly.

There was silence for several moments, and then Darcy took in a breath as if he were about to say something. Elizabeth looked at him, nodding her head as if to encourage him to go on.

"I… yesterday, I fear I ought to have apologized."

"Apologized? For what? Rescuing me?"

Darcy shook his head and turned his gaze to the floor. "No, I do not mean I should have apologized for something I did yesterday, but I should have taken the time to apologize yesterday for interfering where I ought not to have based on unsound judgement. I regret... I deeply regret separating Bingley from your sister. It was wrong and presumptuous of me." His brow pinched and he added, "I regret I am the cause of your sister's grief." He cast his eyes down. "And I assume Bingley's, as well."

Elizabeth watched him struggle to get the words out. She inwardly smiled as she thought this man most likely rarely had to apologize. "Thank you."

She turned her gaze down to her linked hands in her lap. Looking back up, she said, "I appreciate you accepted as truth my assertion of Jane's admiration for Mr. Bingley over your own observation."

"Observation? What observation?" Colonel Fitzwilliam stirred from his sleep.

Elizabeth smiled. "We were discussing that as Mr. Darcy had observed my sister, he saw little evidence of her feelings for Mr. Bingley, yet he has now taken my word for it she does, indeed, feel a strong regard for him, and loves him even."

Colonel Fitzwilliam looked at his cousin with wide eyes. "How good of you, Cousin!"

Darcy forced a smile.

As he sat up and stretched, he looked over at Mrs. Beckett, who was still making dainty noises in her sleep.

"I was not aware women snored."

"I would hardly call that a snore," Darcy began, "after listening to you for a full hour."

Fitzwilliam let out an embarrassed laugh and looked at Elizabeth. "He always claims I snore, but I have never heard it. *You* did not hear anything from me, did you?"

"I cannot say I heard a full hour's worth of snoring, but yes, I did hear you."

"Heavens!" He hung his head in mock dismay. "All I can do is apologize for any and all offensive noises I may have unwittingly made."

"So now you have both apologized..." began Elizabeth.

"Both?" Fitzwilliam exclaimed. He turned to Darcy. "You apologized?"

Darcy silently nodded.

"For your interference?"

Again he nodded.

"Well, I am pleased to hear that. Surprised, but pleased."

Darcy's brows narrowed, but again he said nothing.

Fitzwilliam leaned towards Elizabeth. "What about the other offence?"

Both Elizabeth and Darcy raised their brows. "The other offence?" Darcy asked.

"You need to apologize for your comments about her family."

"I... er..."

"I think there may be a limit to Mr. Darcy's apologies," Elizabeth said with a teasing smile, but felt in all truth, he had every reason to think ill of them. "They do at times display a most..."

"I was wrong to speak in such a manner," he interjected. "Again, accept my apologies."

Elizabeth took in a deep breath. "As much as it hurts to hear someone say anything against my family, I am fully aware their behaviour is not always what it ought to be."

Elizabeth noticed Fitzwilliam look back and forth between her and Mr. Darcy. She began to wonder if he was aware of the feelings his cousin had for her.

Elizabeth thought the subject was dropped when suddenly Fitzwilliam asked, "Darcy, do you believe Bingley deeply loved Miss Bennet's sister?"

Darcy drew in a long breath. "Yes, he did speak of his admiration for her." Here he rubbed his jaw and looked out the window. He turned back to Elizabeth. "But I have seen him fall in love many times before."

"Yes, so you said," she remarked.

Darcy started. "I did? When?"

Elizabeth stifled a gasp as she realized she had read that in his letter. Her heart pounded as she determined what to say. "I... oh, perhaps it was Miss Bingley. Yes, when I was at Netherfield Miss Bingley made a comment to that effect." She tried to smile, but was inwardly chiding herself for speaking without thinking.

"Why would she have told you that?"

"I believe, Mr. Darcy, she said it as a means to discourage my sister from forming an attachment with her brother." Elizabeth tightly fisted her hands under the cover of the blanket. "The two of you were obviously of like minds." She could not keep the resentment from her voice and stole a glance up at him. She saw a look of resignation in his eyes.

"For myself," Fitzwilliam began, as he turned away to gaze out the window, "I doubt I shall ever fall in love. It does strange things to men."

Elizabeth noticed a slight smile. "Whatever do you mean, Colonel Fitzwilliam?"

"It alters their behaviour. I have seen many a good man do the most unspeakable things when in love." Here he looked at Darcy, who was glaring back at him. But that did not stop him. "Yes, love can turn a most amiable, intelligent person into a stiff, arrogant bore!"

"You cannot mean that!" Elizabeth said. "Why, Mr. Bingley was most amiable the whole of the time he was in Hertfordshire."

"You are being absurd, Fitzwilliam. No more of that."

The look Darcy sent his cousin was unmistakable. He did not like the direction in which his cousin was taking the conversation. Elizabeth believed his cousin *was* aware of his feelings for her and perhaps justifying his cousin's odd behaviour, even though they could have no way of knowing she was aware of his deep regard for her.

"I only speak of what I have observed. But it is particularly true when one is doing all one can to fight the attraction."

A slight tightening of his jaw and his pursed lips indicated to Elizabeth that Darcy wanted this conversation to end.

Elizabeth also wished to change the subject. She wanted to inquire about Mr. Wickham. When she and Mr. Darcy last spoke of him as they danced at the Netherfield Ball, it provoked him greatly. But she was determined to find out all she could because his letter had been so vague.

She finally said, in as casual an air as she could manage, "Pray, Mr. Darcy, what can you tell me about Mr. Wickham? He claimed he grew up with you." She held her breath as she watched him rein in his initial shock and anger at the mere mention of the man's name.

Colonel Fitzwilliam, however, made no attempt to disguise his reaction. "Wickham is a liar and a cheat!" he exclaimed." And worse!"

Darcy turned slowly to his cousin. "I believe I informed you Mr. Wickham was part of the militia in Meryton, the small village near the Bennets' home. He was received quite enthusiastically by some of the ladies."

Elizabeth bit her lip, knowing to which ladies he referred. She was one of them, and from the angry expression of both men, she now regretted how she had allowed herself to be deceived by Wickham. But she still did not know the extent of his deception. What had he done to provoke such animosity in these gentlemen?

Darcy looked from Elizabeth to Mrs. Beckett, who was still asleep, and then to his cousin, who gave a slight nod of his head.

Darcy leaned forward, clasping his hands together. "Miss Bennet," he said softly, as if fearing Mrs. Beckett might overhear. "I will tell you briefly about my association… our association with that man, and Colonel Fitzwilliam will verify all I have to say." He looked to his cousin for affirmation and then turned back to Elizabeth.

"He was the son of my father's steward, as you may know. We grew up together, being close in age, and spent a good amount of time together when we were young. He had a wild side to him as a child, but it was when he went to Cambridge, the education provided for him by my own father, that I saw a side of him that was… despicable."

"Dissolute!" exclaimed Fitzwilliam at the same time.

"Miss Bennet, my good father had promised him a living when it became available, but he died before that occurred." He took in a deep breath and looked down.

Fitzwilliam continued. "In time Wickham decided he did not wish to become a clergyman, which is probably the only decent decision the man has ever made in his life! No man could be more ill-suited for the clergy than he!"

Darcy looked up. Elizabeth could readily see how it pained him to speak of this.

"He asked to be compensated instead and received three thousand pounds. I did not believe he would use it wisely, but I hoped he would prove me wrong."

"But he did not," Colonel Fitzwilliam added. "He squandered that money and then came back demanding the living, which had then become available. Darcy refused and sent him on his way."

The two men then looked at each other.

"Miss Bennet, what I have to say now, I say in complete confidentiality." Darcy looked at Mrs. Beckett again, and then turned back to Elizabeth. "Our paths crossed again under most distressing circumstances. I shall not go into detail, but suffice it to say he attempted to… to…" His voice cracked, and he sighed deeply.

"He deceived a young lady, a member of the family, into thinking he loved her and she, in turn, loved him. He convinced her to elope." Colonel Fitzwilliam finished for him.

"She was but fifteen," Darcy added, "Fortunately, I found them before any damage done was irreparable." He spoke between gritted teeth and shuddered.

Elizabeth dropped her gaze, feeling all the shame of believing Wickham's lies and a sudden, gripping concern for her younger sisters. That man was still in Meryton, and her sisters would be susceptible to his deceptive charms.

There was silence for a moment, and Darcy finally said, "I believe he most likely told you a different story?" He gave her a questioning look.

Elizabeth slowly nodded. "Yes. He claimed you refused to honour your father's promise of providing a living for him."

"If you believe me, Miss Bennet, if you believe my cousin and me, you comprehend this partial falsehood. He was compensated for it at his request, squandered it, and then when he came back demanding the living, I did refuse him."

Mrs. Beckett awakened with a start, and there was no more talk of Wickham. Darcy opened the basket of food, and she readily took some fresh bread and fruit, enjoying it immensely. The others took little, as they were not inclined to eat after having suffered through the revealing conversation.

Neither man was inclined to talk, so Elizabeth made every effort, despite her grave emotions, to engage the woman in conversation. Although not being able to hear, Mrs. Becket enjoyed answering Elizabeth's questions, which were shouted rather than asked. And she answered the questions just as loudly.

At length, the carriage slowed down as it came into a small village and stopped at an inn to allow everyone to refresh themselves. The two gentlemen assisted Mrs. Beckett out of the carriage, and then Fitzwilliam waited while his cousin prepared to lift Elizabeth out. Darcy handed his cousin the one crutch and then turned to Elizabeth.

He leaned over and smiled warmly. "I find myself apologizing again, Miss Bennet, for having to be the one to carry you. With Fitzwilliam's injured shoulder, you must put up with me, yet again."

Elizabeth nodded. "There is no need to apologize, sir. It is needed, and I greatly appreciate your service."

Darcy stopped and clenched his jaw, and his nose flared as he breathed in deeply. He slipped his arms beneath her and lifted her up, although his height required him to keep his knees bent. As he stooped even lower to step out of the carriage, he paused.

"It was my sister, Miss Bennet. It was Georgiana with whom Mr. Wickham attempted to elope."

Elizabeth's jaw dropped. She felt all the heartbreak Mr. Darcy must have felt for his sister having been deceived by Wickham. At the same time, she felt the honour of being considered worthy of his confidence in this matter.

Chapter 17

Instead of feeling any sort of regret for confiding in Elizabeth it was his sister whom George Wickham had attempted to seduce, Darcy felt a reassuring warmth flood through him. It may have been due to the fact he was presently holding her in his arms, but he felt strongly she could be trusted with the information.

He knew deep in his heart the time he spent with Elizabeth today would likely sear his heart even more, especially if it passed as it had so far. She had been more than civil to him; he might even call it endearingly pleasant. He stifled a groan, however, as he considered when they parted later today in London, it might be the last time he would ever see her.

As he began to take the step down, his arms tightened about her. It was as much to indulge his desire to hold her as it was to steady her. And heaven forbid, he would not wish to drop her. They made the descent with little difficulty, and he reluctantly set her down. Making sure she was steady, he kept his hand on her good shoulder.

"Thank you, Mr. Darcy," Mrs. Beckett said with a nod. "I shall see to her now." The older lady was tall and thin, and in recent years had begun to lean forward slightly when she walked. She was more than willing to assist, however, and perform her duties as chaperone and companion.

Darcy and Colonel Fitzwilliam walked behind the ladies as they made their way towards the inn.

"I saw the look on your face back there, Darcy. You are not doing yourself any favours, you know," the colonel said in a fervent whisper.

"I have no idea to what you are referring."

The colonel shook his head and let out a mocking huff. "You most certainly do know! Be careful! That is all I will say."

Darcy kept his gaze straight ahead and remained silent. Finally, he said, "You can see why, though, can you not? I am not a fool."

Fitzwilliam shook his head slowly. "No, you are not. You have allowed yourself to fall in love with a remarkable woman. If only I could find such a woman." He then laughed. "Although I would have made sure she did not despise me, first, before I committed my heart."

Darcy turned and glared at his cousin.

"It appears our assistance is needed." Fitzwilliam nodded ahead at the ladies, grateful for the distraction.

The men hurried to catch up with them. They had reached the inn and had stopped, as Elizabeth was required to take two steps up.

"I was not quite sure how to help her get up the steps," Mrs. Beckett said.

"It will be easier if I lift her," Darcy said, almost as if Elizabeth were not there. He easily picked her up while Fitzwilliam went ahead and opened the door for them.

When they stepped inside, Darcy lowered her gently. The proprietor rushed over to greet his guests, addressing Mr. Darcy by name.

"Mr. Clarendon, we shall need a room for the ladies to use to freshen up," he said. "We shall also require a table for the four of us to have lunch."

The proprietor gave a short bow." Yes, sir. Always a pleasure to serve you."

"Thank you. And please have someone see to the needs of my servants outside as they tend the horses."

The ladies were shown to their room, while the men merely used a common room off the eating area. Later, as they waited at their table for the ladies to return, Colonel Fitzwilliam leaned forward, his hands clasped together.

"If I did not know any better, I would have surmised you planned this whole affair."

"What affair?" Darcy asked, his brows lowered.

"Miss Bennet falling and getting hurt. Our having to return to Rosings in time for you to rescue her so now she rides to London with us." He shook his head. "I knew I was at your beck and call, but it makes me wonder if you have some grander influence over the course of human events."

Darcy let out a huff. "I could not have orchestrated this had I tried." He turned his head to look in the direction of the ladies' room, and then clasped his fingers, bringing them up to his chin.

"No, you could not," Fitzwilliam laughed. "You have little imagination for this kind of thing."

When Darcy saw the ladies step out, he stood up and walked over. Colonel Fitzwilliam remained standing at the table.

"We are over here," he said, pointing with his hand towards his cousin. "Was everything to your satisfaction?"

Elizabeth nodded and smiled. "It was more than suitable, thank you."

"I am sorry it is not one of the finer inns. We would have to travel another hour before we reached a more superior one."

Elizabeth shook her head and waved a hand through the air. "No need to worry."

"There is another reason why we stopped here. You shall see."

The ladies walked to the table, where a pot of tea had been brought out and poured into the teacups. Darcy ordered soup for everyone, as it had cooled considerably outside. They also enjoyed fresh bread and cheese.

Elizabeth sat across from Darcy, which afforded him a pleasant view. He found himself looking in her direction often, and save for an occasional kick in his shin when his cousin thought he was staring or lost in thought, it was quite an enjoyable lunch.

As they were finishing their meal, Darcy looked at Elizabeth. "I told you there was another reason we stopped here. I seldom pass up an opportunity to partake of their sweet apple cakes. I have never tasted anything finer. May I order a slice for each of you?"

It took Elizabeth several times asking Mrs. Beckett before she finally understood, and a fervent nod of her head indicated she would certainly like to have one. Elizabeth happily agreed, as well.

"I have often tried to talk the cook here into coming to Pemberley so I could have her apple cakes for special occasions, which would be whenever I want one."

Elizabeth pursed her lips, trying to hide her smile. "She will not come?" she asked, tilting her head.

"No. It seems she is married to the proprietor and does not

wish to leave him." Darcy's lips twitched in a slight smile.

Colonel Fitzwilliam began laughing and coughing at the same time. Shaking his head, he said, "I cannot believe people these days! They have no concern for those who own elegant manors and require only the finest staff. This woman certainly needs a set down."

"She could not come with her husband?" Elizabeth asked.

"I have no need of a proprietor at Pemberley."

Mr. Clarendon arrived with slices of cake on a silver platter.

"Thank you. And thanks to Mrs. Clarendon, as well."

"You are welcome, sir. I shall indeed let her know." He nodded and left.

Darcy watched as everyone took a bite, but mostly his eyes were on Elizabeth. He was rewarded with a wide smile.

"This is certainly delicious. Perhaps we can kidnap her." Colonel Fitzwilliam took his last bite. "I think there is room in the carriage, Darcy. I should like to have her at Pemberley!"

Darcy shook his head. "It will not do. Her husband would likely send the authorities after us. If they stopped the carriage, we could all run away, but I fear you, Miss Bennet, with your injured leg, would certainly be apprehended."

Elizabeth looked at him archly. "With my injury, I might as easily convince them *I* had been kidnapped, as well!"

Darcy noticed his cousin looking back and forth between him and Elizabeth with a twinkle in his eyes. When they had finished their meal, and the ladies returned to their room one last time before setting out, he gave a tug on Darcy's sleeve.

"Now *that* is the Darcy I know. Where have you been? You were certainly not at all like this in Kent."

Darcy looked at the ladies as they disappeared into their room. He had missed the repartee he had had with Elizabeth in Hertfordshire. "I think it was Rickland. I spent more time thinking critically about him than how I might engage Miss Bennet in conversation."

"Well you had best put the time we have left to good use, if you wish to change her opinion of you!"

~~*

Mrs. Beckett gently assisted Elizabeth as they walked towards the door and stepped out. Mr. Darcy carried her down the stairs and then lifted her again into the carriage.

Once Elizabeth was settled back in her seat and they were on their way again, she came to a sudden realization she had never before had such an enjoyable time in Mr. Darcy's presence. But as she considered this, several instances at Netherfield when he had been teasing came to her mind. She had been so disgusted with him, she had given little thought to it at the time.

She suddenly looked up at him. When she and Miss Bingley had been taking a turn about the room at Netherfield, his words to them were teasing, but could he also have been flirting with her? A blush covered her cheeks, and she was grateful he was looking down.

She thought back to other interactions with him and began to see things differently. His asking her to dance should have been considered an honour. Instead, she wished only to make him miserable. As he stirred, she quickly looked away, reaching for the book she had brought along. She pinched her brows as she attempted to determine whether or not it would have made a difference if she had known then how fond he was of her.

She also could not stop thinking about what Mr. Darcy had confided to her about Mr. Wickham and his sister. There had been no need for him to tell her with whom Mr. Wickham had become involved. She knew that must have been difficult for him to admit.

Elizabeth picked up her book and opened it, quickly snatching Mr. Darcy's folded letter as it began to slip out from within the pages. Her heart pounded as she furtively stuffed it back in place. She quickly glanced up at Mr. Darcy and let out a sigh of relief when she saw his eyes were turned to the papers in front of him.

Her hands were still shaking, however, when she returned her eyes to the page.

"Still reading the novel by that woman?" Colonel Fitzwilliam asked.

She quickly looked up. "Yes, but I should have thought to bring along another book as I shall be finished with this one shortly." She hoped her voice was not quavering as much as she felt.

Darcy looked up. "I have some books here if you would like to read one. I doubt I will get to them. I am stymied over some numbers my steward sent me."

"Thank you. I will take a look at them when I am finished with this one."

Mrs. Beckett, unaware of the conversation, had begun to knit. Colonel Fitzwilliam was gazing out the window. Occasionally his head would nod, and Elizabeth was quite certain he would soon be asleep again.

They rode in silence for almost an hour, save for the occasional snort from the colonel, who indeed had nodded off. Elizabeth finished her book and set it aside.

"You said you brought along some books, Mr. Darcy?"

Mr. Darcy lifted his coat, which was lying on the seat, and pulled out the books. "That is odd. I thought I only brought along two books, but here are three." He shrugged. "I know not whether any will be of interest to you, but you are welcome to read one of your choosing."

"And if I do not finish it before we arrive in London?"

Mr. Darcy looked at her as he picked up the stack. "You may keep it. I have enough books to keep me occupied, both in London and at Pemberley."

Elizabeth smiled and reached for the books with her good arm.

Mr. Darcy shook his head. "No, these are too heavy. Allow me to place them on your lap for your perusal."

"Thank you."

She picked up the top one. "Hmm… a history of the House of Plantagenet." She looked over at Mr. Darcy and smiled. "It is quite thick, and I am certain it is interesting, but I think it is not what I want to read at the moment."

The next book was a biography of seventeenth century English poets and poetry. "Do you think there are some women poets included in this book?" she asked teasingly.

"I would assume there are. Women enjoy writing poetry."

Elizabeth cocked her head. "And reading it, but most of all, I think a woman enjoys being read poetry by her beloved."

Mr. Darcy set his paperwork aside, and Elizabeth noticed him take in a small breath. He regarded her with a tender look, and suddenly her thoughts revisited the letter and the words of love and admiration he had written about her. She felt her cheeks warm and hoped he did not notice the blush likely tinting her cheeks.

In a moment, he seemed to collect himself, casting his eyes down briefly. He looked up and said, "I believe I heard you once speak about the efficacy of a poem in driving away love."

Elizabeth's eyes widened and she smiled as she looked up at him. "You have an astonishingly good memory, Mr. Darcy. I did say that, but I said further it may drive away a weak love. A strong, stout love will be quite nourished by a good poem."

They studied each other for a moment, and Elizabeth wondered whether Darcy was going to say anything more. When he did not, she turned her attention to the third book.

She looked at the title and smiled. *Ah*, she thought to herself. *A Peculiar Engagement. This sounds interesting.* But when she noticed the author, N. D. Berg, she let out a gasp.

Elizabeth turned sharply and looked at Darcy, her eyes widened in surprise.

"Is there something wrong?" Darcy asked.

"No, no." She did not think she could speak. *How could he have this book, and did he know his cousin had written it?*

"What is the name of that book?" Darcy asked.

"*A Peculiar Engagement*," Elizabeth said softly, watching him closely for any indication he knew about this book.

"I do not recall putting this book in the carriage, let alone even seeing it." He took the book from Elizabeth, turning it over in his hands. "I suppose I somehow picked it up with my other belongings. It probably belongs to our aunt."

"Could Colonel Fitzwilliam have brought it?" she asked, as he handed it back to her.

Darcy looked at his cousin and gave his head an adamant shake. "Heavens, no! Not a book like this!" He looked back at Elizabeth. "Are you familiar with the book?"

Elizabeth shook her head. "No, not the book, but the author... I have heard of..."

Darcy's brows pinched together, and he leaned forward. "Who is it, again?"

Elizabeth began to speak, but then stopped. She did not dare speak the name herself, for fear it would come out sounding like 'Anne de Bourgh.' Instead, she held out the book to him so he could see for himself.

"N. D. Berg. I have never heard of him." He looked up at her. "Is he supposed to be a good writer?"

Elizabeth's hands were shaking as she returned the book to her lap. "I have not read anything by… this author, but I have wished to."

"Well, I hope you enjoy it, then. I am not certain how the book came to be in the carriage, but you are certainly welcome to read it."

Colonel Fitzwilliam straightened and looked over at his cousin with a smirk. Apparently he had been awake for some time and had been listening. "Confess, Darcy! I am convinced you were perusing the library at Rosings last night while Aunt Catherine was waiting impatiently for you to join us. You must have chosen that book then."

"No," Darcy said in a long drawn out manner. "I was not in the library; I was meeting with her steward."

"Again?" Fitzwilliam asked, shaking his head. "Is there a problem?"

"Something he wished to discuss with me." Darcy pointed to the papers on his lap. "These numbers…"

Elizabeth slowly opened the book. It appeared to never have been read; the pages were tightly bound. It was not a large book, and she was eager to begin reading.

She settled back against the side of the carriage and looked again at the author's name, N. D. Berg. If she had not read Mr. Darcy's letter, she knew she would be smiling at the irony of her reading a book written by his intended. But she could not smile; knowing now how he felt about *her*!

She turned to the first chapter and began reading.

Annabelle Drake distinctly recollected the first time she had perceived Fitzpatrick Danbury as the attractive young man he was. It was an inexplicable, sudden sensibility of his presence, his person, and the prominence he would have in her life. It moved something within her she had never before experienced. She trembled, despite the warmth of the room.

Instead of being the young boy who would occasionally stumble over his own two feet, he was now tall of stature and walked with an easy manner. His former tendency to jump from being open and conversant to exhibiting a formidable shyness in a moment's notice seemed to have found an easy balance of a more confident reserve. He no longer spoke in a voice that cracked and faltered when he was particularly anxious, but he now had a pleasant sounding, smooth voice.

Annabelle had known Fitzpatrick her whole life. His mother and her mother were sisters. He was her cousin, and they had been promised to each other in marriage since their birth. They had what might be called a peculiar engagement.

Elizabeth gasped and turned her head abruptly towards Mr. Darcy.

He slowly looked up. "Is the book already that good, or is it that bad?" He reached out his hand. "Here, allow me to read it."

She hugged the book tightly against her. "No, I... I just thought of something I... forgot..." Her heart pounded as she realized this was a book about Miss de Bourgh and Mr. Darcy, although the names were obviously changed.

She saw a look of distress quickly pass across Darcy's face. "Do we need to return?"

"Oh, no!" Elizabeth said, wishing to dismiss his concern. She waved her fingers slightly, even though her hand was mostly covered by the sling. She made a grimace when pain shot through her sore shoulder. "I... I merely forgot to *tell* Charlotte something."

"Are you certain?"

Elizabeth smiled. "I would not have us turn back now. I can send her a missive when I get to my aunt and uncle's."

Darcy nodded, and Elizabeth turned back to the book. She read and reread the first few paragraphs.

She turned to him again. "Where did you say you got this book?"

"I have no idea. It was in the carriage. One of us must have unknowingly picked it up."

Elizabeth bit her lip, wondering if Miss de Bourgh had placed the book here for him to find. She speculated whether the young lady had hopes he would read it and comprehend how much she loved him. "I see."

Elizabeth turned back to the book, eager to read more, as she was certain it would enlighten her about Mr. Darcy. Miss de Bourgh certainly would have a unique perspective of him.

Elizabeth could feel Mr. Darcy's eyes on her. Her breath caught, and her heart pounded within her chest as she wondered what revealing insights the young lady would have about the incomprehensible man sitting across from her.

Chapter 18

Elizabeth was soon completely entranced by Anne's words as she described how she and her cousin grew up under their mothers' constant reminders they would one day marry.

Elizabeth brought a finger up to her mouth and slowly tapped her smiling lips as she read about the young boy who was now the handsome man sitting across from her in the carriage.

Fitzpatrick was small, and his legs – too short to reach the floor – dangled over the edge of the large chair. He held himself perfectly still, except for what seemed to be a nervous twitch in his foot. Annabelle watched it curiously, her head tilting one way and then another, wondering if he possibly had ants in his shoes. His chubby little fingers incessantly drummed the arm of the chair. Fortunately the chair was thickly padded, so there was little sound to annoy their mothers.

Elizabeth could not prevent herself from turning her eyes to Mr. Darcy. She smiled as she noticed his foot tapping softly on the floor of the carriage. He was not drumming his fingers, but as he looked down at the papers in front of him, he tapped them with the pencil he held. Apparently, he had not outgrown these habits.

She turned her attention back to the book, reminding herself not to outwardly react to anything she read.

Most of the first chapter was about Anne – Annabelle in the book – and her home, parents, and some early memories of Fitzpatrick, the name she had given Mr. Darcy in her novel.

As she continued to read, she began to ponder the childhood they had shared together. It must have become difficult for them as they grew older, realizing the expectations their parents had for them.

She was amused by the typical antics of the young cousins that filled the pages. They spent a good amount of time playing together in the nursery. Elizabeth smiled as she read about the argument they had when Annabelle pretended they were going to a ball.

"You are too young to go to a ball, Annabelle."

She gave him a sidelong glance. "But I can dress up so pretty, and everyone will tell me I am the most beautiful lady there." She looked longingly at her doll and then reached up to smooth her wiry hair. "I think it would be so much fun to dance." She bit her lip and then added archly, "And I do not care who I dance with!"

Fitzpatrick let out a huff. "You should not say that."

Annabelle tilted her head. "Do you not wish to dance at a ball?"

Fitzpatrick shook his head decisively. "I think it would be more fun to go outside and kick a ball." He then turned back to play with his soldiers.

Elizabeth softly chuckled, as she recollected Mr. Darcy expressing his decided opinion that, "Every savage can dance."

"You must be enjoying that book."

Elizabeth was startled from her reverie and turned to Darcy. "Excuse me?"

Darcy leaned forward in his seat. "You have not stopped smiling since you began reading. Is it that entertaining?"

Elizabeth closed the book and placed it in her lap. She brushed aside a loose strand of hair that tickled her cheek. "It is a book that sheds light on some things that were heretofore unknown to me." She tilted her head. "I think when I am finished with it, there might be some things I understand more fully."

Darcy nodded. "Good. I am glad you are enjoying it." He began to tap his fingers on his satchel. "Perhaps once you have read it, I might be able to retrieve it from you so I can read it."

Elizabeth pinched her brows together. "I fear you would not enjoy it as much as I do."

"How can you be so sure?"

In her mind, she made a long list of reasons why he would not enjoy reading his cousin's novel. "Mr. Darcy, I can almost guarantee it." She flashed him a smile and then found her place in the book and continued reading.

She had compassion for a young Annabelle who overheard her

aunt and uncle speak about the supposed engagement between her and their son. She listened outside the door and discovered Fitzpatrick's father was not wholeheartedly in favour of it. His mother believed Annabelle's sweet disposition would make her a good wife for their son, but his father was not convinced, and wanted him to love his wife as he and his wife loved each other.

...Annabelle had heard enough to realize they did not feel as strongly as her mother did about Fitzpatrick marrying her. She slowly lowered her eyes to her dress and wondered if they felt she had not looked good enough for them today, as her mother had complained.

She could barely take in a breath, as her chest seemed to be so tight. Her uncle made it sound as if Fitzpatrick could choose whether or not to marry her. What had she done to disappoint them, and what could she do to make sure Fitzpatrick liked her enough to agree to the marriage their mothers desired?

Elizabeth lifted her eyes from her book and looked out the window.

"Is everything all right?"

"Oh, yes. I am merely pondering some things in the story." Elizabeth was eager to read more to see how much Miss de Bourgh loved the man sitting across from her, and she wondered if that love had survived all the years she had waited for him to ask for her hand.

She drew in a long breath as she considered how different he seemed today than from their time in Hertfordshire *and* Rosings. She had seen him thoughtful, teasing, even laughing. She was torn whether to read about him from Miss de Bourgh's point of view or converse with him directly.

She looked at Colonel Fitzwilliam and Mrs. Beckett, who had both fallen asleep again. Pursing her lips and lowering her brows, she said softly, "Do you think parents always know what is best for their children?"

Darcy looked pensive, and Elizabeth wondered where his thoughts were taking him. "I think... I would hope... a parent's intentions would be pure, but I would conjecture they might occasionally be wrong. Why do you ask?"

"Do you think one ought to obey a parent's wishes if they do not believe it is in their best interest?"

Darcy looked down and shook his head. "You are certainly asking some difficult questions, Miss Bennet. Did either of your parents ask you to do something you did not feel was right?"

Elizabeth began to shake her head, but stopped. She opened her mouth and quickly closed it.

Darcy looked at her with questioning eyes.

She finally said, "My mother, yes, on several occasions." She cast her eyes down and felt her cheeks warm as she recollected her mother's insistence she marry Mr. Collins. She wondered whether she ought to tell Mr. Darcy, but considered that since he had confided in her, she ought to do the same.

Darcy sat still, as if waiting for her to explain what she had just said.

She wondered what he would think of her if he knew. Perhaps he already did. She knew it would likely cement his feelings about the unsuitability of her parents, or at least her mother.

"Last November I received an offer of marriage."

Darcy put his pencil down and clasped his hands. "While we were in Hertfordshire?"

Elizabeth shook her head. "No, it was after you departed." She looked down at her hands, glanced up, and then swallowed deeply. "It was Mr. Collins." She could not prevent the blush that covered her face. "My mother insisted I marry him. Fortunately my father had the good sense to see it would have been a most imprudent marriage."

She was surprised Mr. Darcy showed no visible reaction. He merely nodded his head slowly.

Elizabeth turned to look fully at him. "You knew. You knew he proposed to me before securing Charlotte's hand."

Darcy skewed his mouth. "My aunt informed us."

"Us? You mean she informed you and your cousin and Mr. Rickland?"

He nodded, and Elizabeth shuddered. "And yet none of you said anything."

"It would have been highly improper to discuss it in front of Mr. Collins and his wife."

"No, I suppose you could not, although Charlotte and I are quite at ease with each other about it now. At first, it was awkward as I could not understand how she could agree to marry him."

"It is good you had your father to stand behind you in your decision. He seems to understand you."

"My father knows me quite well, and we are similar in many ways."

Darcy opened his mouth, but then quickly closed it. When he said no more, Elizabeth turned back to her book.

She had only read a few sentences when Darcy spoke again. "There are times, even though both my parents are gone, when their influence seems to affect my decisions, despite my wishing wholeheartedly to do otherwise."

Elizabeth wondered whether he was speaking of herself, Miss de Bourgh, or something altogether different. He said no more, and she wondered if he was about to tell her of his and his cousin's intended marriage, and then decided against it.

She stared out the window for some time contemplating this when Mr. Darcy spoke again. "Miss Bennet, I would have you know even though I spoke harshly about your family, I felt you and your elder sister always exhibited the most proper behaviour."

When she turned to look at him, their eyes met and locked. He then looked down briefly and then lifted his eyes. "I never intended to hurt or offend you. I... we both have members in our families that at times behave imprudently."

She felt a sudden warmth pass through her at this unexpected acknowledgement. She nervously adjusted the sling on her arm and shifted her body. Darcy noticed.

"Are you in discomfort?" he asked as he reached out his hand towards her. "Is there anything I can do for you?"

Elizabeth shook her head. "It hurts a little, but as I mentioned before, I find it difficult to remain still for extended periods of time." She wiggled her toes and said, "I fear I make a terrible patient. It will not be easy staying off my foot."

"Sometimes we must do things we do not like for our own good."

"I suppose that is true."

Darcy's eyes narrowed. "I would imagine you would have

preferred not to ride in the carriage with me after what transpired the other day."

Elizabeth looked levelly at him and weighed her words carefully before she spoke. "I admit I was angry with you. I felt you had no right to do what you did." She paused and took in a breath.

Colonel Fitzwilliam suddenly sat upright and clicked his tongue. "I wish to know what other offences he committed while he was in Hertfordshire. He would not tell me, you know, but I wonder if he is even aware of them all."

Darcy shook his head, blinking several times as he looked at his cousin. His eyes narrowed while Elizabeth widened hers in surprise.

"I thought you were asleep," Darcy said to him.

"I would not think of sleeping through a thorough recitation of your forays into misconduct!"

Elizabeth stole a glance at Mr. Darcy. "I do not know if I..."

The colonel leaned forward. "Miss Bennet, you must realize his close friends and family all consider this man perfect, above reproach. Most people think highly of my cousin. Well, at least the *women* of his acquaintance do." He let out a chuckle. "Until you. His close family and friends love to hear about anything he does that shows he might be as imperfect as the rest of us."

Elizabeth pondered Colonel Fitzwilliam's account of his cousin's character as she considered her own opinion.

The colonel poked his finger into Darcy's arm. "Now you pay attention, man. You might learn a thing or two."

Elizabeth wondered what to say. She thought it interesting she was being given this opportunity to speak her mind openly about all Mr. Darcy had done.

"Well, first..."

"Ah!" Colonel Fitzwilliam exclaimed. "I believe this is going to be a long list." He clicked his tongue again, settled back, and clasped his hands, as if he were about to watch a play presented on a theatre stage. "Do not leave a single one out."

Elizabeth looked back at Mr. Darcy, who clenched his jaw as a shade of pink worked its way up from his neck to his cheeks. He was about to be assaulted by two people. The first would offer the incriminating evidence; the second would likely verbally berate him. Oddly, Elizabeth was uncertain whether she was going to enjoy this, or not.

She began by telling Colonel Fitzwilliam how his cousin had referred to her, within her hearing, as only being tolerable, spoke to few people when in the neighbourhood, frequently stood silently at the window or fireplace mantel as he looked down at those beneath him, as well as a few other minor offences. When she had finished, she realized much of her dislike stemmed from Mr. Wickham's account of being abused by him, which she now knew was false.

"Darcy, by this account," Fitzwilliam cried, "you have dropped two notches in my estimation of your character. Now I know how you behave when around those you do not know." He directed his gaze to Elizabeth and smiled. "I hardly ever see him behave rudely, but I always enjoy hearing about it when he does." He clicked his tongue again twice.

Elizabeth readily noticed Mr. Darcy's discomfort.

"How shall we make him atone for his sins?" Colonel Fitzwilliam suddenly asked.

Elizabeth shook her head. She actually felt sorry for Mr. Darcy. If nothing more came from this ride into town, he would realize how his behaviour was regarded by others. "From all appearances, I believe Mr. Darcy regrets his actions."

Colonel Fitzwilliam tossed his head from side to side. "Or at least he regrets being called out on his behaviour." He let out a huff. "He never got in trouble as a child."

"Save for the times *you* got me in trouble," Darcy said with teasing reproach.

Fitzwilliam cocked his head. "Guilty."

Darcy suddenly hung his head. He raised his eyes slowly to look at Elizabeth. "There is one more…" He took in a deep breath, and his hands clenched into tight fists. "I am ashamed to admit this, but I… I knew your sister was in town and conspired with Miss Bingley to keep that information from Bingley." He shook his head. "He was unaware she had come to visit his sisters."

Elizabeth gasped and shuddered.

Colonel Fitzwilliam exclaimed, "You did what?" He lowered his head, shaking it slowly. His face, which had previously seemed to reflect great enjoyment in hearing about his cousin's offences, was now clouded with strong irritation.

Elizabeth stared wide-eyed at him. "But why would you do such a thing?" She took in a raspy breath. "Did you not believe your friend was capable of making a decision regarding his affections himself? Did you and Miss Bingley feel the need to throw aside all manners of decorum when the proper thing to do was to at least inform him of my sister's visit?" She crossed her arms in front of her and looked away. All thoughts of the cute little boy who nervously tapped his feet and fingers vanished.

Darcy clasped his hands together, and his shoulders slumped. He let out a long sigh and slowly looked up. "I…"

"Go ahead, Darcy!" Colonel Fitzwilliam spit out. "She is waiting to hear what you have to say… not that it will make any difference."

Elizabeth watched silently as he began to massage the side of his forehead with his fingers. "I am not proud of what I have done, Miss Bennet. But there was another reason I acted so injudiciously. I am not in a position to say what that was, but I do apologize."

"Another reason?" Fitzwilliam leaned back and looked away.

Mrs. Beckett stirred at the sound of Fitzwilliam's raised voice. She opened her eyes and smiled at the others. "Are we almost there?"

Darcy looked out the window. "Yes, we shall be arriving within the hour," he answered loudly so she could hear, but his voice cracked as he did so.

Mrs. Beckett smiled and thanked him, completely unaware of the tension amongst the others inside the carriage with her. She then picked up her yarn and knitting needles and began to knit something that, at the moment, merely looked like a tumbled mass of black, grey, and white.

There was little additional talk amongst Elizabeth and the men for the duration of the journey; however, Mrs. Beckett offered several morsels of information as the carriage entered the busy streets of London. It suited Elizabeth, as she was no longer in the mood to talk, and was actually disinclined to read any more of Anne's book.

What he just confessed had rightfully upset her, but she was fairly certain she knew what that other reason was, as he had mentioned it in his letter. He would have been thrown into her company if Mr. Bingley and Jane married, and he was fighting with everything in his power to rid himself of the feelings he had towards her.

If she had not found the letter and read it, she would understandably be more than ready to be out of his presence forever. But knowing more about him and the love he had for her gave her pause to consider the reason he committed this offense made it – perhaps – just a little bit less unforgiveable.

Chapter 19

The noisy, bustling streets of London precluded any additional conversation that might have taken place had it not been for Mr. Darcy's latest confession. Elizabeth and his cousin sat silently, both likely contemplating all he had told them.

Elizabeth turned her eyes back to the book but was unable to comprehend a single word, so tangled were her emotions. Her thoughts were accusatory again as she recounted every offence committed by Mr. Darcy. There was no excuse for his actions! This last transgression he had confessed to her was, on its face, an egregious breach of the most basic civilities expected of a gentleman.

Colonel Fitzwilliam sat rigidly beside Darcy. His arms were crossed over his chest, and he looked away from him, staring out the window, as if wishing to avoid even minor contact with his cousin.

Darcy kept his eyes intently fixed on his hands as he nervously twisted his signet ring. An occasional frown darkened his features.

Completely oblivious to the tension permeating the coach, Mrs. Beckett seemed content to cheerfully work on her knitting.

Elizabeth finally turned her eyes back to the book. She began reading about Annabelle's discovery that Fitzpatrick did not like to be teased and he disliked even more getting into trouble. She recollected Colonel Fitzwilliam's words in the carriage that his cousin rarely got into trouble except when the colonel instigated it.

She read about the incident in the turret Mr. Rickland had alluded to, when as a young boy, Darcy climbed up with both his cousins without first asking permission, and when they were discovered, they all were punished.

She kept her eyes on the page in front of her, but suddenly had a thought about her encounter with him in the turret. When she had looked through the telescope, it was aimed at the parsonage garden, which was where she had been walking before Mr. Rickland arrived. Her heart hitched as she suddenly realized he had likely been watching her!

She dared not turn her eyes to Mr. Darcy, as her heart pounded and she felt her cheeks colour. No wonder Mr. Rickland had been so accusatory towards him. He must have suspected that was what he had been doing, but at the time, she had no reason to even consider that.

Elizabeth noticed Darcy suddenly start, and turned to see him begin searching frantically through his satchel. He went through every piece of paper in it and was getting more and more agitated. He bit his lip, and his eyes narrowed, as he impatiently pulled out the contents, depositing various papers into an untidy heap beside him.

He let out a huff.

Colonel Fitzwilliam turned to him. "Did you lose something?" he asked tersely.

Darcy tapped his fingers nervously on the satchel. "I thought I had placed something of a personal nature in here. Now I cannot find it. I wish I had thought to look for it last evening, but I had other things on my mind."

"It may have blown away after you dropped your satchel yesterday. The wind did a good job of whipping everything up. It is likely floating around Hunsford as we speak."

"I would hope not," he said with urgency.

Darcy lifted his gaze to Elizabeth, and when his eyes met hers, she quickly averted hers. Looking down at her lap, she wondered if he was looking for the letter. That would explain why she had found it amongst the bushes. She took in slow breaths so as not to arouse suspicion she knew what he was talking about. Her cheeks warmed as she thought about the letter and what he would think if he knew she had read it.

He displayed a restless and slightly ill-humoured manner for the remainder of the trip, exasperated by the ruts in the road that jarred the carriage. Elizabeth had never ridden in a more well-sprung carriage and thought the ride quite superior to anything she had ever experienced. Obviously Mr. Darcy was so accustomed to his whole life being well ordered and smooth running that any slight bump caused him turmoil.

Yet she knew how disconcerting it would be not knowing if that letter might be found by someone. She only briefly considered telling him she had it, but then decided it might not ease any discomfiture he was feeling, as he would know she now ascertained the depths of his feelings towards her.

Elizabeth was increasingly eager to get to her aunt and uncle's home. She glanced out the window and was grateful to see they were passing familiar landmarks. They would soon enter Gracechurch Street, and she would be in the pleasant company of her favourite relations. She looked forward to seeing Jane again and putting some distance between herself and Mr. Darcy. She needed time away from him to think clearly.

Despite looking out the window, her attention was drawn to the sound of fingers tapping on the window sill. Unlike the chair in Anne's story, however, it was not padded, and therefore made a clicking noise with each tap.

"Would you stop that confounded drumming?" Everyone in the carriage, including Mrs. Beckett, jumped at Fitzwilliam's outburst.

Elizabeth directed Darcy a sidelong glance as he quickly drew his hands together, clasping them tightly. She looked down again, feeling a sense of helpless frustration. She knew not how to reconcile this man. On the one hand, he had blatantly insulted her the first evening they met, had acted more than once in a most unbecoming manner, and arrogantly tries to control others' lives. On the other, he had come to fall in love with her and had, on occasion, acted most chivalrous, gentlemanly, and caring in her presence. She gave her head a slight shake. Despite his inclination to behave in a most unbefitting manner, she felt motivated to at least attempt to finish the sketch of his character which she had earlier begun, rather than leave the portrait half-finished.

~~*

The carriage finally came to a stop in front of the Gardiners' modest home Elizabeth knew and cherished. Just seeing it again warmed her heart with tender memories of the aunt and uncle she loved so dearly. A meticulously tended garden with newly blossoming flowers showed how much they cared for it.

Elizabeth's heart was about to burst in anticipation of seeing the Gardiners and Jane again.

As the horses were tethered and the passengers waited for the door to open, Darcy turned to Elizabeth, looking uncomfortable. "Would you prefer your uncle carry you down from the carriage?"

Elizabeth heard the distress in his voice. It was apparent he assumed she wanted nothing more to do with him and was giving her the option to allow someone else to carry her.

"My uncle is a man with a big heart but, I fear, a rather small stature. I shall only need to be lifted out, and then I can use the crutch."

Darcy nodded and turned to the door as it opened. Jane and her aunt and uncle rushed towards them.

Darcy stepped out and offered a short bow. "Hello, Miss Bennet. It is good to see you again."

Jane smiled. "Hello, Mr. Darcy. May I present our aunt and uncle, Mr. and Mrs. Gardiner?"

"It is a pleasure to meet you," Darcy said.

"The pleasure is all ours," Mr. Gardiner replied. "I trust you had a good, uneventful journey."

"Yes, thank you," Darcy said with a slight nod.

"And how is Elizabeth?" asked Mrs. Gardiner, pressing her hand against her heart. "We have been so concerned since we received her letter."

"She is doing well. She needs some assistance getting out of the carriage, so I shall lift her out. She has a crutch she is using to keep her weight off her foot. She actually has a pair of crutches, but with her shoulder injury, presently she can make use of only one."

"We are so grateful for all you did, sir," Mr. Gardiner said warmly.

"It was no trouble. We were on our way to London as it was."

"Everyone is invited to come in. I am sure you would all enjoy some refreshment and a chance to stretch your legs."

"Thank you kindly, Mr. Gardiner."

Darcy stepped back into the carriage and faced his cousin and Mrs. Beckett. "Mr. Gardiner has invited us all in. Allow me to take

Miss Elizabeth out first, and then you can follow." He then turned to Elizabeth. "Are you ready, Miss Elizabeth?"

"I am, thank you," she said.

Colonel Fitzwilliam leaned forward, looking intently at Elizabeth. "What my cousin means to ask is whether you have steeled yourself to be carried in his arms, knowing how much you dislike him right now."

Elizabeth stole a glance at Mr. Darcy. The reaction to his cousin's words was evidenced by a heightened colour to his face and a tightening of his jaw. He lifted his eyes and met hers; then he quickly looked down again. Despite his staid countenance, she had been able to get a glimpse of the pain – and possibly regret – etched in his face.

As he leaned down to reach under her, he muttered an apology for having to carry her again, and she responded with a faint, "No need for that, Mr. Darcy."

She realized she actually did not mind being in his arms. She had enjoyed it the day before as he carried her up out of the ravine and held her on the ride back to the parsonage. This was another thing she had difficulty reconciling. Since he rescued her, she found she was – for the first time since meeting him – attracted to him. He was handsome, that was undeniable, and his tall stature was appealing. She had held, however, so strong a dislike of him in their earliest acquaintance she had been blinded to those remarkable traits. And she suddenly realized she felt perfectly safe and secure in his arms.

Elizabeth wondered what had changed. She was still angry with him, and while some of her accusations had proved false – mainly those due to Wickham's lies – he had still behaved abominably and perhaps unforgivably. Knowing how he felt about her, however, had begun to bring about a slight change in her. She gave her head an infinitesimal shake. Knowing he loved her – or had loved her – was certainly not a reason to give weight to any attraction she might now feel.

Darcy looked straight ahead as he stepped down carefully from the carriage.

"Thank you," Elizabeth said as he walked up to her family members who were eagerly waiting. "I think I can make it from here."

"No, I shall take you up the steps."

He turned her so she could greet her aunt and uncle and Jane, and she felt the awkwardness of being in his arms and being unable to address the questions on their faces as to how she came to be in Mr. Darcy's carriage.

As he carried her further up the walkway, Elizabeth felt Jane's hand upon her. She knew her sister must have the most questions and she had seen the slight hope on Jane's face that somehow this might lead to a reunion with Mr. Bingley.

Mr. Gardiner rushed ahead to open the door for the gentleman. "We have a small guest room on this floor you can put her in so she does not have to take the stairs," he said, extending his hand towards the door to the room. "Elizabeth, would you like to be settled on the sofa or on the chair?"

As Mr. Darcy brought her into the room, Elizabeth noticed a rather large chair in the corner of the room. "I think the chair will suffice for now," she said.

Mrs. Gardiner followed them in and said to her husband, "Dear, once she is seated, pull over the ottoman so she can rest her feet on it."

Mr. Darcy gently lowered and released her, taking care to keep his eyes averted from her face. He straightened up and moved aside so Mr. Gardiner could slide the ottoman over.

Once Elizabeth had settled into the chair and lifted her feet up, Mrs. Gardiner covered her with a blanket.

Mr. Gardiner turned and faced Mr. Darcy. "Sir, we owe you a great deal. I know you must have taken extremely good care of my niece, and we appreciate it."

Mr. Darcy appeared a bit uneasy with the praise. He bowed slightly and said, "It was no trouble, at all, I assure you."

Mrs. Gardiner came up and stood next to her husband, taking his arm. "Mr. Darcy, I have known of your family for many years, as I grew up in Lambton. I know your good father was always a generous and compassionate man, and I can see you have followed in his ways."

Darcy swallowed hard. "You grew up in Lambton, Mrs. Gardiner? So near to Pemberley. I... thank you for your kind words about my father. I fear I do not always live up to his good name." He took in a short breath and gave a quick nod of his head. "If you will excuse me, I shall take my leave."

"Do you not care for something to eat or drink?"

Darcy shook his head. "No, I thank you. We are almost to Suncrest House."

"Another day, then."

Mr. Darcy nodded.

Darcy turned around and faced Elizabeth. Drawing his shoulders back, he said, "God speed, Miss Elizabeth. I do pray your injuries heal quickly and completely."

"Thank you, Mr. Darcy, and I also appreciate all you... what you did for me."

He gave a short bow and walked to the door with Mr. Gardiner following behind.

Mrs. Beckett came over to say goodbye to Elizabeth.

She bent down and grasped her hand. "I pray you soon return to good health. It has been a pleasure getting to know you."

Elizabeth smiled and thanked her, but silently wondered how the woman could know her well at all.

Mrs. Beckett leaned in close to Elizabeth. She gave her hand a squeeze and said, "I have known Mr. Darcy his whole life, and I have never met a more excellent man." She quickly straightened and nodded a farewell to Elizabeth.

"Mrs. Beckett..." Elizabeth began, startled at the woman's words. Mrs. Beckett turned, however, apparently not hearing her name called, and stepped out the door.

It was then Colonel Fitzwilliam's opportunity to take his leave of Elizabeth. "My dear Miss Elizabeth, it has certainly been a pleasure, and I do hope, with all my heart, our paths cross sometime in the near future."

"Thank you, Colonel. I would truly enjoy seeing you again."

Once the guests had stepped out, Mrs. Gardiner and Jane excitedly rushed over to Elizabeth.

"Lizzy," Mrs. Gardiner began, "we had no idea when you said you would be coming in a carriage from Rosings it was going to be Mr. Darcy's carriage! What a surprise this was! How did you come to be with him?"

Elizabeth took a deep breath. "He was visiting his aunt, Lady Catherine de Bourgh, while I was there. Lady Catherine is our cousin's patroness and lives across the lane from the parsonage."

"His cousin seems pleasant," Jane said softly. "He expressed his hope for your quick and complete recovery and seemed to think my being here would help."

Elizabeth chuckled. "I spoke a great deal about how much I looked forward to seeing and being with you both again!"

"Mr. Darcy seems such a handsome and kind man," her aunt said with a smile. "You must tell us everything!"

Elizabeth took in a deep breath and closed her eyes. She nodded and smiled. "It is a long story. Please sit, and I shall, indeed, tell you a great deal!" She let out a long sigh. *But I cannot tell you all.*

~~*

Mr. Darcy extended his hand to Mr. Gardiner and expressed his pleasure in meeting him and his wife, as well as his confidence his niece would do well in their care. He was rather stunned at how fashionable and gracious the couple was. He had expected them to be more like Mr. and Mrs. Bennet. This was a pleasant surprise.

Colonel Fitzwilliam and Mrs. Beckett joined him shortly, and they climbed into the carriage. Darcy gave a sharp tap at the front of the carriage to indicate they were ready to depart.

He dreaded arriving at Suncrest House, for he was certain his cousin would chastise him once Mrs. Beckett left them to join her son. Colonel Fitzwilliam was leaning back in the seat looking out the window. One hand rubbed his jaw vigorously, as if he was contemplating all he was going to say to him.

He grimaced as he considered the whereabouts of his letter, which he had assumed was still in his satchel. He had been about to look for it the evening before, but he was interrupted by his aunt's steward, who wished to speak with him. He had been so occupied with what he had been told by him, that later he completely forgot about it.

He never thought of the letter again until they were coming into London. A surge of dread swept through him when he could

178

not find it, and he wondered whether anyone might chance upon it and read it. He could not recollect everything he had written, but he recalled enough to know he would hate to have someone discover it.

As they settled in for the short ride, Mrs. Beckett picked up her knitting but then looked directly at Darcy and pointed her bony finger at him.

"Miss Bennet is no fool. You must do something to atone for your offences."

As soon as she finished speaking, she returned her attention to her knitting. Darcy and Fitzwilliam turned to look at each other. His cousin gave a slight shrug of his shoulders and wore a genuinely blank look on his face. Darcy had to assume he had not enlightened Mrs. Beckett as to what had recently taken place. Perhaps she was not as deaf as everyone assumed.

Mrs. Beckett looked up again and gave him a piercing look. Her voice was loud but shaky as she admonished him, "You must *show* her the good man you are."

He and his cousin exchanged glances again, perplexed by her words.

Darcy wished to make things right with Elizabeth. He wished to apologize to her. Again. He lowered his head and slowly shook it as he tried to count how many times he had already apologized. Would his doing anything more make a difference in how she felt about him? He had no idea, but he already knew of two things he would do.

There was one additional thing he truly wished to do, but he could never do it. He wanted to confess his love for her. He absently shook his head. No, she would not welcome *that* at all.

Chapter 20

Elizabeth was grateful to be at the Gardiners' home, a place she had always considered her second home. Her aunt and uncle's modest dwelling had always been a welcoming respite to her. And having Jane there made everything nearly perfect.

For the first few days, her aunt and Jane nursed her with love and affection, good food and drink, shared laughter, and delightful conversation. They gave her assistance when she needed help getting around and admonished her lovingly when she insisted on doing things herself that would best have been left to others. Their main task was to ensure Elizabeth's comfort and improvement.

Elizabeth had written to inform her family about her fall, that she was now in London, and she would remain with her aunt and uncle until she was able to walk without assistance. She told them how much she missed them, but did not tell them how much she preferred this arrangement. She knew her mother's nerves would do nothing to aid in her healing, let alone Lydia's and Kitty's clamorous effusions.

Elizabeth was also certain Jane was not yet ready to return home, wishing to remain in London with the hope of seeing Mr. Bingley. They did not discuss him, but it was evident to her Jane often thought about him.

She wrote a letter to Charlotte, thanking her for all she had done during her stay and for her willingness to care for her when she was injured. She informed her she would likely remain in London for a while, that she was recovering nicely, and hoped they were all well. Finally, she told her she wished to hear all about the soiree. She had the letter sent immediately.

Elizabeth had not picked up Anne's book since arriving at her aunt and uncle's home. Her indignation towards Mr. Darcy was still fresh and strong. If only he could see the grief on her sister's face, he would know how wrong he had been. There were times she felt so angry she wanted to toss the book away.

The letter, however, was another matter. That, she read again and again.

She had to take care when reading it so no one would discover it. She kept the letter secured in an inner pocket in her valise, which was kept under the bed. She would waken early in the morning and reach down to pull it out, trying to comprehend, as her eyes devoured each word, exactly how Mr. Darcy could have come to love her. She was astonished he did, but was almost as surprised she never once had suspected it!

Her greatest struggle was settling upon who this inimitable man truly was. She had once tried to sketch his character, but now she realized she had been completely unsuccessful. What she thought she knew about him was not necessarily true, and there was still so much more to him she had not uncovered. He was certainly a complex individual.

As she lay in bed, cloaked in darkness on her third night in London, she considered what she knew about him. She weighed both his faults and commendable attributes, something she had done repeatedly in the past few days.

Elizabeth let out a soft moan. Perhaps she ought to read more of Miss de Bourgh's book. It might shed some light as to who this man truly was. She was too fatigued now. She would read more in the morning.

~~*

At first light, Elizabeth awakened. She wiggled her foot and rubbed her shoulder as she did each day, hoping to feel a bit less pain. She smiled, thinking she was finally on her way to recovery.

She reached under the bed and pulled out Anne's book. Up until now, she had read little other than when Mr. Darcy and Anne were young children, and she was anxious for them to grow up.

She was most interested in the next chapter, which had Miss de Bourgh travelling to Pemberley, called Pelbrook in her story.

As the carriage rambled into the dense woods, a sudden darkness overtook them. Tall trees canopied high over them, blocking the sun.

Annabelle suddenly felt cooler, despite the warmth of the day, as they traversed the shaded road.

A light caught her eyes, and she saw several rays of sunlight streak through the trees. She watched the streams of light play on the ripples in the river running alongside the road and found herself entranced as the twists and turns of the road followed those of the river.

She let out a gasp, however, when there, in full view out her window, stood a magnificent manor. What made it so striking was the mirror image of it in the perfectly still, blue lake in front of it. The carriage came to a stop.

"That," Lady Candace began, "will one day be your home." She extended her arm towards the house and swept it across from the woods to the lake to the gardens and beyond.

"You shall be the envy of ladies everywhere, Annabelle," her mother continued. "You shall be Mistress here at Pelbrook, at Rollings Manor, and at your home in town."

Pelbrook was different from Rollins Manor. Instead of the many tall spires, chimneys, pointed gables and roof lines, it had a flatter roof with lower chimneys. It was larger than Rollins, and she immediately noticed it was a more natural aspect. A higher expanse between the lake and the manor was populated with shrubberies and trees, none of which seemed pruned, as were all the plants at Rollins.

Rather than a straight road leading up to the front door, a nicely curved drive wound its way around the lake and to the front. She thought the whole prospect was delightful.

She was stirred from her admiration and reverie by her mother. "Now, Annabelle, once you are mistress, you must have the gardeners prune those wildish shrubs and overgrown trees. It is quite horrid, and I cannot believe it has been allowed to grow so wild!"

"No!" Elizabeth said aloud, practically slamming the book down. "Do not allow her to have her way in this! She shall ruin Pemberley!"

Elizabeth winced. She had no say in how Pemberley ought to be managed. She likely would never see it. "But I would hate to see Lady Catherine turn it into another Rosings!"

She continued reading, and her eyes widened as she read Miss de Bourgh's account of her first meeting with a young George Wickham, whom she called Gregory.

"Well, if it isn't Miss Annabelle Drake. Are you pining for your true love?" Annabelle turned to see Gregory Winston standing there, a long blade of grass protruding from his mouth. His eyes seemed even darker than when she first had been introduced to him.

Even reading something that happened years ago involving Mr. Wickham made Elizabeth shudder.

Gregory turned to Annabelle. "So is it true?"
She clasped her hands tightly together. "Is what true?"
"Are you supposed to marry him? Fitzpatrick?"
Annabelle swallowed, her mouth suddenly dry. "I think so. At least, our mothers desire it."
Gregory let out a laugh. "Ha! He does not love you, you know."
Annabelle wished to defend herself, or at least come to Fitzpatrick's defence. She looked away, fighting back tears. "We are still too young to be in love."
"How could anyone love a mousey creature like you?" He pointed at her and stood up, doubling over in laughter.
Gregory looked up, and his laughter stopped abruptly. Annabelle turned to see Fitzpatrick approaching. Gregory pointed at him and began laughing even louder than before. "Well, if it isn't Annabelle's intended! Have you come to kiss your bride?"
"Gregory!" Fitzpatrick said firmly. "Leave, right now!"
"Ooh, I am so afraid of you!" Gregory mockingly placed his hands on his cheeks and shook his head. "I am so glad I am not you!" He looked at Fitzpatrick and then Annabelle, before letting out another cruel laugh. He abruptly turned and hurried away.
Annabelle looked down as she rubbed her fingers together. She could barely bring herself to look at her cousin.
Fitzpatrick came and sat down next to her, handing her a small leather pouch.
"Here are some chestnuts. Robert and I took some into the kitchen, where they are going to roast them. We will eat those when they are done.

You can take these back to Rollings to enjoy later."

"Thank you, Fitzpatrick."

She looked at the small pouch she now clutched in her hand.

"Do not listen to what Gregory Winston says. His object in life is to make everyone he meets miserable. I think it is the only way he can make himself feel more important than he is."

Annabelle fought back the tears threatening to spill, but she could only contain them for a short while. At length, her shoulders began to heave as she took in gasps of air.

When Fitzpatrick reached out and took her hand in his, she suddenly felt a wash of calm flood through her. She looked up at him and smiled. Despite the look of concern on his face, he smiled back at her, and she felt all was right in the world.

Elizabeth put the book down slowly as she considered this aspect of Mr. Wickham. He had been tormenting Mr. Darcy since childhood. She shuddered as she realized how readily she had believed his lies and fallen for his deceptive charm.

~~*

The following day, Elizabeth wished to get out and walk, convinced she would feel better if she could get some fresh air. Jane and her aunt agreed they would allow her to join them on a short stroll up and down the street. She had been walking around the house using the crutches and they felt she would manage nicely.

They set a slow pace for Elizabeth's sake. She used the crutches, stepping gingerly on her sore foot, aware of every step. Her shoulder hurt more than her foot, but not enough to check her progress. They turned at the end of the street and were returning when they saw a carriage pull up in front of the Gardiners' home.

"It is Mr. Darcy's carriage, Lizzy," her aunt said. "Why do you suppose he has come?"

"I cannot imagine." Elizabeth bit her lip, pondering why he would be here.

The carriage door opened, and they watched Mr. Darcy step out and then turn back while another gentleman exited.

Jane suddenly gasped, gripping her sister's arm tightly. "No, it cannot be! It is Mr. Bingley! I do not think I am prepared to see him!" Her hand nervously drew a strand of hair from her face and then she lowered it to press against her heart.

Elizabeth smiled at her. "Jane, take a few deep breaths."

Mrs. Gardiner smiled, as well. "You have been waiting far too long for this moment, my dear Jane, to let vanity or fear keep you from seeing him." She took Jane's other arm and began walking. "Let us hurry before they are sent away, thinking we are from home."

Elizabeth reached for Jane's hand and gave it a reassuring squeeze. She felt it shaking within her own and noticed her sister's face had paled. She glanced at her aunt with concern.

"Aunt, perhaps you can hurry on ahead and invite them in. We shall walk more slowly to allow Jane time to gather her composure."

"An excellent idea, Lizzy. You need to walk slowly at any rate. Take all the time you need." Mrs. Gardiner began walking briskly towards the house.

Jane took in a much needed deep breath. "Thank you." She shook her head. "I feel like a child! I shall go in there and treat him as an old friend."

Elizabeth stroked her sister's hand. "Jane, you have nothing to worry about. You look lovely, and I know Mr. Bingley is as eager to see you as you are to see him."

Jane closed her eyes and took in another breath, letting it out slowly. "I hope so, Lizzy. It has been so long."

They watched Mrs. Gardiner reach the two gentlemen as they walked up to the house. The three then disappeared inside.

"Now, Jane, there is no need to rush; yet, let us not tarry too long, for we do not want Mr. Bingley to believe you do not wish to see him."

"No, no," she said, her eyes glistening. "If I only knew why he has not come the whole time I have been here." She stopped and looked at Elizabeth. "And why has he come now?"

Elizabeth pursed her lips together, knowing why he had not

come before, and beginning to suspect why he had come now. "Perhaps he shall explain, Jane."

"Do you suppose it is because Mr. Darcy told him he saw me?"

Elizabeth opened her mouth to answer, but the realization it was in all likelihood due to Mr. Darcy struck her forcibly. There was no other reasonable explanation. She swallowed hard. At the moment, she was so happy for Jane – whatever the outcome –she could not comprehend how she felt about Mr. Darcy, his being here and being the reason Mr. Bingley was here.

When Jane and Elizabeth entered the drawing room, the two gentlemen stood. A sense of awkwardness seemed to fall over the group, and Jane attempted to introduce Mr. Bingley to her aunt. She was told Mr. Darcy had already done so. A deafening silence followed. Fortunately, Mrs. Gardiner was enough in control of her faculties – unlike her two nieces –she invited everyone to sit down and asked a servant to bring in some refreshment.

Jane looked at everyone and everything save Mr. Bingley. She had difficulty meeting his hopeful gaze. Neither of them seemed to know what to say.

Elizabeth finally spoke. "Are you and your family well, Mr. Bingley? It has been many months since we have seen you."

His eyes lit up. "Yes, yes we are. It has been at least five months, I believe. The twenty-sixth of November."

"I believe you are correct," Elizabeth said with a smile. "At the Netherfield Ball."

Mr. Bingley rubbed his hands together and glanced at Jane. "It has been far too long. It was a cold winter, but spring offers new hope, does it not?"

Elizabeth stole a glance at Jane, who was staring at her hands, folded in her lap. Jane slowly lifted her eyes to Mr. Bingley. "Yes, it oftentimes does," she said softly.

Elizabeth turned to see if Mr. Darcy might now comprehend the depth of her sister's affections as he observed them. When his eyes met hers, she lifted a single brow and then looked away.

He shifted in his chair and then asked quietly, "How are your injuries, Miss Elizabeth? I see you are able to walk fairly well with the crutches."

She looked back at him and suddenly felt something she had

never before felt. Her breath caught in her throat, and her heartbeat sped up. She could only attribute it to the tender expression in his eyes. "I am... I am mindful of each step I take, but the swelling has gone down and it is not as painful. My shoulder still hurts on occasion."

"I am grateful you are recovering well and were not hurt more seriously."

"Thank you. I am grateful, as well." Something deep inside caused Elizabeth to shiver, and she thought back to one of the first sentences in Miss de Bourgh's book. *She trembled, despite the warmth of the room.* It was when Anne first discovered, in her teen years, she was attracted to this man, after knowing him all her life.

She turned and smiled at Jane, who was now speaking with Mr. Bingley. She did not want Mr. Darcy to see what might be on her face. She was not even certain *what* she felt was truly *how* she felt towards the man. For the first time in their acquaintance, however, she recognized him as the attractive man he was, and she readily saw in his face the depth of feeling he had for her.

The refreshments were brought in, and conversation ceased until everyone was served. Elizabeth was grateful for the brief distraction and attempted to still her rapidly beating heart and the thoughts that were now so different than what they had been previously.

Jane and Mr. Bingley were silent as they partook of the cake that had been brought out. Their attention seemed to be more on the refreshment than each other. Elizabeth was about to say something, but Mr. Darcy spoke first.

"Mrs. Gardiner, I hope you will forgive us for calling unannounced and uninvited this morning. I had to leave London the day after I arrived and only saw Bingley for the first time late last night. When I told him I had seen Miss Bennet, he was eager to pay a call immediately."

Elizabeth noticed Jane had an attractive blush on her cheeks, while Mr. Bingley gave an embarrassed laugh.

"I am delighted – we are delighted – you chose to do so," Mrs. Gardiner reassured both men.

"How long will you remain in town?" Mr. Bingley asked, looking from Jane to Elizabeth and then back to Jane.

Elizabeth noticed Mr. Darcy lean forward, as if anticipating an answer. If it meant Jane seeing Mr. Bingley again, she would remain in town as long as needed.

"I do not know..." Jane began.

"I want to make certain I am completely well before we return home..." Elizabeth paused, searching for an excuse to remain as long as they could. "But even then, I so much wish to see some sights around London before leaving."

"I know your parents are eager for your return."

Elizabeth turned to Mr. Darcy, thinking it an odd thing to say, as if he knew it as a fact. "Yes, I am certain they are. Our poor father has little patience with our three younger sisters, who, he claims, have almost no sense amongst them."

"Well, I for one, hope you remain for a few more weeks, at least," Mr. Bingley said, hope lighting his face. "I plan to return to Hertfordshire in the middle of May. Business keeps me in town until then."

Jane smiled, and her eyes lit up. Elizabeth readily noticed how content she looked, as if a great burden had been lifted.

"We look forward to your return, Mr. Bingley," Elizabeth said. "The neighbourhood was not the same once you left."

Mr. Bingley looked down briefly and then lifted his head. "I have greatly missed being there, as well."

After a few minutes of genial conversation, Mr. Darcy turned to Elizabeth. "I just received a letter from my aunt, who informed me the soiree we had all planned to attend was postponed due to heavy rains."

"How unfortunate!" Elizabeth said. "I wrote to Charlotte and asked her about it, but I have not yet heard back from her. I imagine there was a great deal of disappointment."

"I cannot say how strongly the disappointment was felt by all those concerned, but at least we did not miss anything noteworthy."

The men remained for about an hour, making plans to return on the following day.

Once they had left, Jane inexplicably burst into tears.

Elizabeth drew her into an embrace. "Jane, are these tears of joy we see?"

Jane nodded and mumbled something unintelligible. Mrs. Gardiner handed her a handkerchief.

After a moment, Jane collected herself. "He told me he has desired to see me ever since he left Netherfield. He had no idea I was in town until Mr. Darcy told him last evening." She reached out and grasped Elizabeth's hand. "I am so grateful he informed him."

"Yes, that was good of him." Elizabeth squeezed Jane's hand. "Mr. Bingley cares for you deeply, Jane. I could readily see it."

"Lizzy, I know you were not disposed to like Mr. Darcy when he was in Hertfordshire," Mrs. Gardiner said. "From all I have seen of him, he seems to be a likeable gentleman."

"Perhaps," Elizabeth said softly. She then turned to her aunt with a raised brow. "Indeed it was gracious of him to bring Mr. Bingley here to see Jane. And I certainly recognize how good it was of him to rescue me and convey me here. In Hertfordshire, however, he continually gave offense by his words and deeds, and I cannot be certain these few good acts can erase all those others." She let out a sigh. "But it is a start."

Chapter 21

Later that day, after the physical and emotional exertion of the morning, Elizabeth repaired to her bedchamber to rest. Unfortunately, her mind was in turmoil, and she found herself mulling over Mr. Darcy's actions.

It was highly possible he had brought Mr. Bingley to see Jane in an attempt to right a wrong; to finally do something he ought to have done when he discovered Jane had come to town. Knowing Mr. Darcy had such ardent feelings for her, she surmised he likely wished to make amends for those actions that had so angered her.

She had to admit it was generous of him, knowing how he felt about her family. At least she was confident he now understood Jane's feelings for his friend. That was likely no longer a matter with which he took issue.

But would there be other things with which he would find fault, when so many of his actions stemmed from his pride and arrogance? She had just begun to comprehend the honour of being loved by such a man, but she wondered whether she could fall in love with someone who had such faults. She shook her head. She was no closer to understanding him than when she had departed Rosings.

She pulled out *A Peculiar Engagement*, thinking – and hoping – it might provide answers.

She read of the death of twelve year-old Fitzpatrick's mother, who died following complications in childbirth. His father was so grief stricken he lost all interest in his affairs and seldom ventured from his estate.

The following year, Annabelle lost her dear father. When he died, she lost the one person who truly cared for her and loved her. Her mother became more authoritative, demanding, and was never pleased with anything she did. This aggravated Annabelle's breathing difficulties and caused her to draw even further away from her mother.

Fitzpatrick and his father finally came to Rollings again when she was sixteen and Fitzpatrick was seventeen years old. It had been several years since they had seen each other. The young girl's feelings were suddenly awakened, and for the first time, she finally came to understand the power of true love as she experienced a real attraction towards her cousin.

On the day they were expected to arrive, Annabelle watched, as she normally did, from the drawing room window. This time, however, she was more than simply curious about the changes she would see in her cousin. She had changed in the four years since last seeing him. Annabelle looked down at herself and wondered if he would be pleased – would even notice – her slightly blossoming figure. She waited with eager expectation for that first glimpse of him.

When Fitzpatrick finally stepped out of the carriage, Annabelle took in a deep breath, and her hand went over her rapidly beating heart. He was much taller than the last time she saw him, and as he walked to the house, she noticed he strode with a youthful confidence, tempered slightly by his reserve.

She suddenly found herself blushing at the mere thought of being in the same room with him. Even greater than that was the thought of being married to him. She raised both hands to her cheeks, feeling the warmth that permeated them.

Elizabeth thought it must have been rather awkward for both of them, now that they were of an age where attraction and a greater knowledge of what was expected of them were better understood.

She continued to read and was surprised – and yet not – as she read about Annabelle's mother's advice to her concerning her cousin once he departed.

Annabelle watched from the drawing room window as the carriage finally pulled away. When her mother returned to the room, Annabelle looked at her. "I do not believe he loves me, Mother. He is kind and generous, and most polite, but I do not believe he loves me." She lowered her head and slowly shook it. "I do not think he ever will."

"And why should he?" Lady Candace's voice was harsh. "One does not need love in marriage. That is for made up stories and fables. Love will only cause heartbreak. You must guard your heart so you do not fall in love with him. Then no matter what occurs once you are married, you will not be hurt."

Annabelle felt a wave of disappointment flood through her. She looked up at her mother and almost asked her what she should do if she was already in love with him. She knew what the answer would be, however, and decided not to ask. She did not want to feel the lash of her mother's wrath for being so foolish.

Not noticing her daughter's despondency, Lady Candace continued. "Fitzpatrick has a great sense of the duty he owes his family, and with the added wish of his beloved mother, how can he do otherwise but marry you to honour her memory? You have no reason to fear. Despite his not loving you, he shall indeed wed you."

Annabelle held back the tears threatening to spill. She felt certain, after the time she spent with him, that she already loved him and wanted nothing more than to receive his love in return.

She slowly walked away. Her heart had soared with the knowledge that this man, who was so kind and generous, good-natured and tender, was to be her husband. Now she had come to learn the harsh truth. He likely would never love her as she had come to love him.

She returned to her room and picked up her journal. If she could not experience love, at least she could write about it. When she had written stories in the past, it was almost as if she lived them. In writing her stories, she would hopefully come to know what it would be like to be loved by a man.

Elizabeth felt sorry for the young girl. It must have been difficult knowing although he was expected to ask for her hand, he did not feel for her as she felt for him. All these years of loving him and waiting…

A soft tap at the door stirred Elizabeth from her reading.

"Lizzy, are you awake?" It was Jane.

"Come in," she said, closing the book. "I was reading."

Jane walked in carrying a letter. "This just arrived. It is from Papa and was addressed to the two of us. I have read it and think you will be most interested in what he has to say. I was quite taken by surprise."

Elizabeth lifted her brows with curiosity and reached for the letter.

My dearest daughters,

I hope you are well, and Lizzy, that you are recovering splendidly. We were grieved to hear of your fall, but grateful your injuries were not what they might have been. We are certain you are in excellent hands. Your aunt and uncle and Jane are most likely smothering you with attention.

We so look forward to you both returning; especially me. Over the past month, on numerous occasions I have almost pulled my hair out — what little is left — due to the silliness of your sisters and your mother.

I shall not bore you with my troubles, but I wish to tell you of a most remarkable visitor we had at Longbourn. We had only just received your letter from town when but an hour later there was a knock on the door. I assumed it was likely a few of the militia come to visit Kitty and Lydia, and hoped they would not be too boisterous, for I wished some peace and quiet in my library.

Before I had barely entertained that thought, there was a knock upon the library door. I must confess I was rather perturbed but stood up and opened it. And who do you suppose was standing on the other side of the door? You shall never guess, so I shall tell you. It was Mr. Darcy! Mr. Darcy, of all people!

I invited him in, quite curious as to what had brought this gentleman to our residence. I suspected it was to apologize for what happened to you and give us an account of how you were doing. I was only partially correct, however.

This gentleman came expressly to warn us of Mr. Wickham. He informed me of his past with him, how Wickham has deceived everyone into believing he was ill-used by Darcy, and he told me a little of the man's vices.

This intelligence came at the right time, as Mr. Wickham had become engaged to Miss Mary King. Can you even comprehend how grateful I was he had not ensnared Kitty or Lydia, who both seemed so fond of him? Knowing him as I now do, however, I am convinced he would never have settled for anyone worth less than ten thousand pounds.

I went to speak with Miss King's uncle, while Mr. Darcy went to speak with Colonel Forster. It was discovered Mr. Wickham had run up many debts in and around Meryton, and when word quickly spread, Miss King was spared and Wickham was confronted. It is no surprise to many he has disappeared. I know not whether he resigned his regiment or if he has deserted, but I am thankful he is gone.

Is this not extraordinary?

Your mother wishes me to express to you how she always knew Wickham was not to be trusted and how much she enjoyed having the excellent Mr. Darcy dine with us. Did I tell you he dined with us?

A more intelligent fellow I have never met with. He also gave us a detailed account of your accident. I know somehow he was involved in your rescue, but he was too modest to take any credit for it.

I would have you know in addition to dining with us, your mother also invited him to lodge with us. She was prepared to put him up in your room, Lizzy, knowing Netherfield had not been opened since late last year. (The two rooms we normally use for guests had leaks from all the recent rains we suffered, and consequently she felt your room would be most suitable.) He professed himself most grateful for the offer, but politely declined, saying he had already secured a room at the inn in Meryton.

I cannot wait to see the two of you, but I think Mr. Darcy's visit will keep me quite at leisure to endure any silliness that occurs at Longbourn for some time.

Your loving father

Elizabeth looked up at Jane. "This is extraordinary, indeed!"

"That is what I thought, as well." Jane bit her lip. "Come, our aunt is waiting to hear what you think about this."

Elizabeth and Jane returned to the drawing room. Their aunt glanced up.

"What do you think of this astonishing news, Lizzy?"

Elizabeth let out a long sigh and shook her head. "Words elude me."

Mrs. Gardiner gave her a knowing smile. "I think perhaps we do not know all there is to know about Mr. Darcy." She raised an inquisitive brow. "Would you agree?"

Elizabeth felt her cheeks warm with a blush, and she turned away. Her hand went to the back of her neck as she pondered what to say. She had been thinking the same thing.

"I am surprised he went so far as to travel to Longbourn." She slowly turned back and with a nervous laugh said, "I am grateful, however, he did not agree to stay at our home. How mortifying it would have been to know he had to sleep… he took up lodging in my room."

Jane shook her head. "Oh, Lizzy, how could Mother have suggested such a thing? But I suppose that is why Mr. Darcy said 'I know your parents are eager for your return.' He truly knew that for a fact because he had seen them."

Elizabeth let out a breathy laugh. "Yes, I suppose he did. I did not suspect his having seen them when he said that. I thought he merely conjectured they would be eager."

"Lizzy," her aunt began, "are you at liberty to tell us about Mr. Wickham? He seemed a most friendly young man, although I was rather surprised at how freely he spoke of his past with Mr. Darcy." She clicked her tongue. "Now we know why he spoke as he did, as I assume it was all a falsehood."

"I cannot share all I know, but I will tell you what I can."

Elizabeth sat between her aunt and sister. She still held the letter from her father, occasionally looking down at it.

"We were all quite deceived by Mr. Wickham, and I cannot believe I did not see him for who he truly was." She bit her lip and pinched her brows, chastising herself for being taken in by him. Elizabeth gave a brief account of Wickham's dealings with Mr. Darcy and how he had asked for money instead of the living the late Mr. Darcy had promised him, and then returned several times asking for more. He lived a life of impropriety in more ways than gambling.

Elizabeth withheld from them his dealings with Mr. Darcy's sister. She knew it was told to her in confidence, and she would not betray that.

As the ladies marvelled over this, Elizabeth could not help thinking about those other secrets she was keeping from her dear sister and aunt.

She was unsure whether she ought to share her knowledge of the ardent feelings Mr. Darcy had for her. She knew she would certainly not tell Jane, for even though she trusted her implicitly, she felt her sister might inadvertently reveal that to Mr. Bingley. She considered, however, informing her aunt when they had some time alone. His generous actions had by now aroused her aunt's suspicions, and Elizabeth felt she might already be convinced of his admiration for her.

She could not tell Jane about Mr. Darcy's part in separating her and Mr. Bingley. She dared not do anything that might destroy the friendship the two men shared, even though Mr. Darcy had not always acted in his friend's best interests. She shook her head slightly as she reasoned Mr. Bingley ought to hear it from his friend's own lips. She smiled as she thought Jane, as sweet as she was, would likely forgive Mr. Darcy for his interference with no questions asked.

Jane seemed happier than she had been in months, which delighted Elizabeth more than anything. Her sister was especially pleased Mr. Bingley expressed a wish to return to Netherfield soon, yet she was still unsure of the extent of his affections.

The expression on Jane's face was one of *expectant* joy, tempered however, with caution that it all might come to naught. She shook her head, as if to remove any hopeful fancies. "The gentlemen said they would return on the morrow, yet they may not come at all."

Elizabeth and her aunt both began to laugh. "Oh, Jane," Elizabeth said, as she took her sister's hand. "You have nothing to fear. He shall be here. I am certain of it."

Before retiring for the night, Elizabeth eagerly picked up Miss de Bourgh's book. She read several more chapters, anxious to reach the end and see how she concluded it.

Years passed quickly in the book, as Fitzpatrick's visits became less frequent. Going to Cambridge and the death of his father made it a span of several years. Through all those years, the young girl waited with uncertainty for an offer of marriage which never came.

Elizabeth was tired, but there were only a few chapters left. Her curiosity overrode her fatigue, and she decided to read one more before dousing the candle. As she read it, she realized this chapter was different. All the others began with something that occurred when Fitzpatrick had visited Annabelle in their twenty-seventh year. The others chapters would then recount something from the past. This one, however, continued with the current visit. It was the year Georgiana went to Ramsgate and nearly eloped with Mr. Wickham.

Fitzpatrick received a letter from his sister while he was at Rollings telling him she was travelling to Ramsgate with her companion. Elizabeth had to bite her tongue not to cry out, "No!" When Fitzpatrick puts the letter away, she whispered, "You must go to her!"

Elizabeth lifted her eyes from the page. She doubted Miss de Bourgh knew what had occurred once Mr. Darcy departed that year to surprise his sister at the seaside town. She imagined he would not have told his cousin or his aunt his sister had almost eloped with Mr. Wickham.

She continued reading. Annabelle poignantly realized Fitzpatrick would never ask for her hand, and she did something Elizabeth found quite compelling. Annabelle made a list of the qualities she believed her cousin must be looking for in a woman and she wondered why he had not yet found that woman. Elizabeth practically held her breath as she read.

Exactly what was Fitzpatrick looking for in a wife? It pained her to think about this, but she must.

She sat down and began making a list. Fitzpatrick is looking for a woman who... *She stopped, tilted her head, and closed her eyes as if envisioning someone. She started with what she knew would be the obvious traits. She is intelligent, loves to read, enjoys going for walks, is generous, is compassionate, and is accomplished in playing and singing.*

She read the list and pondered what else he might find appealing. Annabelle smiled. She is witty and makes him laugh, stimulates him in conversation, does not always agree with him, does not concern herself with the trappings of society, is pretty, but not exceptionally beautiful... Truly? There were times she wondered where her words came from.

She looked at the list again, satisfied with it, but then something else came to her. Her brows suddenly furrowed as she contemplated it. She was not certain whether she ought to add it to her list, for it was quite surprising to her. But she decided she must add it anyway.

She will be a woman quite different from the type of women others would expect him to marry. Her eyes widened. She may not even have the fortune and connections equal to his!

Annabelle sighed deeply and bit her lip. She was not this woman and could never be. But she suddenly realized she loved him enough to release him from her heart so he could be free to find this woman he had long been looking for.

Elizabeth closed the book and blew out the candle. She was amazed at how insightful this young lady was. Elizabeth had always considered herself a good studier of character, but Annabelle – Miss de Bourgh – was truly an expert. Finishing the book would have to wait.

In the darkness, Elizabeth suddenly saw Mr. Darcy's face. His eyes looked at her with tenderness and care. "How could he have come to love me," she asked herself softly, "when all I ever did was try to find fault with him?"

She pulled up the coverlet and rolled over, causing pain in her shoulder that reminded her of her injury. She blew out a puff of air as it also reminded her of how gallant Mr. Darcy had been in rescuing her.

She suspected she would not sleep well. What she had read would likely occupy her thoughts for most of the night.

Chapter 22

Elizabeth woke up the next morning with a severe headache. Her fingers lightly massaged her forehead in little circles between her brows. She squinted at the sun's rays which poured through the window, flooding the room with light. She quickly closed her eyes again.

Rolling away from the window, she sighed. Her sleep had been restless as she pondered Miss de Bourgh's words describing the type of woman Mr. Darcy would likely marry. While she could not claim with certainty she filled *all* of the traits, she knew several could be attributed to her.

She realized Miss de Bourgh must be perceptive. She likely studied people to such a degree she knew more about them than they knew about themselves. Elizabeth surmised when the young lady was writing in her journal, she was either working on her story or taking notes on the others in the room.

Her head hurt too much to read more of the book. She would wait until later.

~~*

Elizabeth was grateful by late morning she was feeling much improved and so joined her aunt and sister in the drawing room. Just before two o'clock, the ladies heard a knock at the door, and they all looked at each other. Jane's hand went over her heart, and her face paled.

"Dearest Jane," began Elizabeth, "if you do not cease having an attack of your nerves every time Mr. Bingley arrives – or you even suspect he has come – your poor heart may fail before he ever has the opportunity to ask for your hand!"

"Oh, Lizzy, it is far too early to even consider that!" Jane said in a hushed voice, looking towards the door in case he stepped in.

"I think we can be quite certain *you* have considered it!"

Jane blushed and began knitting her fingers together. "Please, do not tease me in such a manner, Lizzy."

"I am sorry, Jane. I do not mean to make you uneasy."

A maid appeared at the door and announced the caller.

"A Mr. Rickland is here to pay a call on Miss Elizabeth."

Elizabeth's aunt and sister looked at her with unspoken questions on their faces.

"This is a surprise." She turned to her aunt. "I believe I told you about Mr. Rickland, Lady Catherine's other nephew who was there while I was visiting Charlotte." What surprised Elizabeth even more than his paying a call was she had barely thought of him over the past few days.

"Please invite him in," Mrs. Gardiner said as she looked curiously at Elizabeth. In a whisper, she said, "You certainly seem to be quite popular with the gentlemen, Lizzy. And did you tell us about him? I do not recall."

Elizabeth shook her head. "I fear he has quite been out of my thoughts since arriving here. He is a most amiable gentleman, but he is likely here solely to see how I am faring, just as Mr. Darcy did."

A knowing nod from her aunt was interrupted by Mr. Rickland's appearance.

"Good afternoon," he said with a bow. "I thank you for admitting me with no advance notice of my coming."

"It is good to see you again, Mr. Rickland. May I present my aunt, Mrs. Gardiner, and my sister, Miss Jane Bennet?"

He stepped forward and greeted them. "It is my pleasure. I hope you were not otherwise engaged."

"We were not. Please come in," Mrs. Gardiner bid him sit with a motion of her hand.

"Thank you. I am only arrived from Kent. Mrs. Collins advised me where you were staying in London, Miss Elizabeth, and when I realized I would pass close by, I thought I would stop." He reached out and took her hand. "I have been anxious about your recovery." He looked down at her foot. "I see you are walking without the aid of crutches."

"Yes, I am doing quite well. I have even taken some short

walks outside."

"Good. I have been so concerned." He shook his head. "Such an unfortunate accident." He paused and leaned in towards her, clasping his hands. "I hope the journey here was not too wretched." He let out a short laugh.

Elizabeth knew he was referring to having to endure Mr. Darcy's company. "I was quite comfortable, thank you. It passed without any agitation."

He almost seemed disappointed, but expressed the opposite. "Good. I am glad to hear it."

"How were the Collinses and Miss Lucas when you left them?" Elizabeth asked.

"I believe they were all quite well. They came to dine at Rosings on Sunday. Unfortunately, the soiree on Saturday had to be put off because of heavy rains."

"Oh, yes! Mr. Darcy informed me of that. He had just heard from his aunt."

"Mr. Darcy?" Mr. Rickland looked rather surprised. "Has he been here since Saturday, then?"

"Yes, yesterday he came by. He brought his friend, Mr. Bingley."

Mr. Rickland pinched his brows. "I see."

Elizabeth was irritated she had felt the need to justify Mr. Darcy's visit to Mr. Rickland. She began to wonder – and fret just a little – whether he knew Mr. Bingley was the gentleman Mr. Darcy had kept from her sister. She could not recollect if his name had been mentioned that morning she discovered what Mr. Darcy had done. She hoped he would not mention anything about it if he knew.

Elizabeth breathed a sigh of relief when Mr. Rickland smiled and said, "I have a splendid plan to make up for having to miss the soiree. A close acquaintance of my family is hosting a ball this coming Saturday. It is one reason I have returned to London and why I called on you today." He looked down at his hands, pursed his lips, and then looked back up. "While it is not a public ball, I am at liberty to invite you and your family, as I am the godson of the hosts. All of you would be most welcome as my particular guests."

Elizabeth looked at her aunt. "I am not certain if we have any plans."

Mrs. Gardiner shook her head. "We have no plans. A ball sounds like the perfect diversion for our nieces during their stay in London. This is generous of you, Mr. Rickland."

"Splendid! I shall speak with Mr. and Mrs. Underwood and inform them you are planning to attend." He looked at Elizabeth expectantly. "Do you think you shall be able to dance?"

"I believe by Saturday I should be much improved," Elizabeth said with a smile. "I am only experiencing a little pain. Perhaps I can manage at least one dance."

"I am glad to hear that." He turned to Elizabeth's aunt. "Mrs. Gardiner, simply give your names at the door."

He had finished giving them the location and time of the ball when there was a knock on the front door.

The maid appeared again, this time announcing Mr. Bingley, Mr. Darcy, and Miss Georgiana Darcy.

Elizabeth did not miss the scowl that appeared on Mr. Rickland's face. She knew she had a look of surprise written on hers. It was not unexpected Mr. Darcy would arrive with his friend, but that he would bring his sister was quite unforeseen.

When the three walked in, Elizabeth met Mr. Darcy's gaze. He smiled, but it quickly faded when he noticed Rickland. He gave a brief nod, but then turned back to his sister, his smile returning.

"How good it is to see you again," Mrs. Gardiner said. "And you have brought a new guest."

Darcy nodded. "I hope you do not mind. We found ourselves in the neighbourhood."

"Not at all!" she exclaimed.

"May I introduce my sister, Miss Georgiana Darcy?" He turned to his sister, "This is Mrs. Gardiner, Miss Jane Bennet, and Miss Elizabeth Bennet." After a pause, he added, "And Georgiana, I believe you remember Lady Catherine's nephew, Mr. Matthew Rickland?"

A hint of shyness touched her features, but she smiled and curtseyed to the ladies. "It is a pleasure to make your acquaintance." She turned to Mr. Rickland. "Hello, Mr. Rickland. It has been a long time since we have been in company."

Elizabeth readily noticed the admiration in Mr. Darcy's eyes for his young sister, despite his apparent discomfiture in finding Mr. Rickland there. Brother and sister were quite different from each other, save for the same reticent personality. She had blond hair and a slender build. Mr. Darcy had been correct. He had mentioned at Netherfield his sister was about as tall as she was, and Elizabeth believed they were about the same height.

Mrs. Gardiner stepped forward. "I do not know if your brother informed you, Miss Darcy, but I grew up in Lambton and knew of your late father. Everyone who knew him spoke so highly of him."

"Yes, my brother did inform me of that. It is always good to hear from people who knew him and to know he was well liked." She looked up to her brother and then back to Mrs. Gardiner.

Miss Darcy then turned to Jane and Elizabeth. "May I inquire which one of you had to be rescued?"

Everyone looked at or pointed to Elizabeth. She extended her hands in resignation. "I am the one who was not watching where I was going and clumsily tripped over my own two feet."

Miss Darcy laughed softly. "I am thankful you were not hurt worse than you were."

"As am I," Elizabeth said.

"Shall we all sit down?" Mrs. Gardiner asked.

"I fear I must take my leave," Mr. Rickland said. "Thank you, Mrs. Gardiner, for extending me such warm hospitality."

"You are very welcome, sir."

On his way to the door, he stopped in front of Elizabeth. "It was good to see you again, Miss Elizabeth. I hope I shall finally get my dance with you at the ball."

"Certainly!" she said. "I look forward to it."

He cast a brief sidelong glance at Darcy and then stepped from the room.

As the men took their seats, Elizabeth could almost hear the question Mr. Darcy wished to ask her. She could see it in his face and even in his posture. But it was Mr. Bingley who inquired.

"Are you going to a ball?"

The ladies all nodded. "One given by a family acquaintance of Mr. Rickland," Mrs. Gardiner said. "On Saturday."

Miss Darcy looked up at her brother. "That would be the ball being given by Mr. and Mrs. Underwood, I believe."

"Yes!" said Mrs. Gardiner. "Are you acquainted with them?"

"I am," Mr. Darcy said curtly. "We received an invitation, as well."

"But we cannot attend," Georgiana added, looking nervously at her brother, as if perhaps she should not have volunteered that information.

Elizabeth noticed Mr. Darcy take in a deep breath and begin to tap his fingers on the arm of the chair. He was not happy, and she wondered if it was because Mr. Rickland had paid her a call or because he had invited them to a ball. Most likely both.

He shifted slightly in the chair and then seemed to make a determined effort to strike Mr. Rickland from his mind and concentrate on making his sister comfortable.

Elizabeth was determined to do the same, although the vague warning in Mr. Darcy's letter about Mr. Rickland prompted questions she wished he would answer, but she could not ask. She also realized she ought to thank him for going to Longbourn and warning her father and Colonel Forster about Wickham, but with Miss Darcy there, she dared not mention Wickham's name.

She was curious about this young girl, recollecting Mr. Wickham said she was proud. However, Elizabeth knew now his words could not be trusted. If any fault were to be found in her, it was that she seemed shy.

Miss Darcy looked at Elizabeth and finally said, "My brother told me when you fell, you could not get up and walk." She bit her lip. "I would have been so frightened, not knowing whether anyone would find me."

"I own I was afraid, just a little. I had wandered into the woods and I was aware no one knew exactly where I was."

"Were you lost very long?" Miss Darcy asked.

"I lost all track of time, but I know I was gone several hours."

"I am glad my brother happened upon you."

"Yes, I… I was grateful to be found." She glanced quickly in Mr. Darcy's direction, feeling her cheeks warm. He was leaning back in his chair, his head down, but he lifted his eyes to meet hers.

Elizabeth asked Georgiana what she enjoyed doing while she

was in London, and they talked about her love of music and the theatre.

"Tell me, Miss Darcy, will you be in London long?"

"I expect to be in town until early May, when we return to Pemberley."

"Do you look forward to returning to the country?"

"Oh yes. I do love it there." Her face and eyes lit up as she spoke. She looked down at her folded hands and then back up to Elizabeth. "Are you in town much longer?"

"I am not certain when we shall be returning home." Elizabeth paused and then added, "I do hope, however, our paths cross again."

Georgiana turned first to her brother and then back to Elizabeth. "Yes, I should like that very much."

They talked at length, and finally Mr. Darcy apologized and announced they had another engagement and must leave.

After their guests departed, Mrs. Gardiner clasped her hands excitedly and began talking about the ball. "I would never have imagined being invited to such an elegant ball as this likely will be. The two of you must wear your finest attire."

Jane and Elizabeth stole a glance at each other.

"I fear, Aunt, even our finest would not be fine enough."

She lifted her brows with an accompanying smile. "Then you must come with me, for I have just the thing!"

Mrs. Gardiner invited her nieces to look in her closet at the three ball gowns she owned. She invited them to choose the ones they wanted to wear, and she would wear the third one. The ladies were all of similar size, but she knew they would likely require some alterations, as well as some further embellishments such as ribbon and lace the young ladies might desire.

Elizabeth chose a sapphire blue silk gown, a little deeper in colour than the dress Mr. Darcy mentioned liking in his letter. She decided she would like to add ivory lace to the neckline and sleeves. Mrs. Gardiner promised Elizabeth she could borrow her sapphire pendant for the evening.

Jane chose a rose silk gown already adorned with white lace and a lighter pink ribbon tie. Mrs. Gardiner told her she could choose either a small ruby pendant or a pearl necklace from her jewellery box.

Their aunt deemed it prudent to go immediately to a friend's dressmaker shop. The two gowns each required some minor alterations to fit them perfectly. Mrs. Nason, the seamstress, promised to have them ready to try on by Thursday of that week.

On the way home, Elizabeth leaned back in the carriage and looked out the window as Jane and her aunt talked excitedly about the ball. It had certainly been a day of surprises with Mr. Rickland inviting them to the ball and Mr. Darcy bringing his sister to meet them.

She knew she ought to feel a sense of anticipation about attending the ball, but she was disappointed Mr. Darcy would not be there. She shook her head slightly as she again pondered Mr. Darcy's letter. What was it he wished to warn her about regarding Mr. Rickland? If she only knew, it might ease her unsettled feelings.

Chapter 23

Later that day, Jane went into the nursery to play with the children. This gave Elizabeth some time alone with her aunt.

"Ever since the men left, you have seemed quite inattentive, Elizabeth. Actually, both you and Jane have provided me with poor company. I can understand Jane. She thinks of nothing but Mr. Bingley." Mrs. Gardiner looked pointedly at Elizabeth. "But I am rather perplexed by your peculiar behaviour." She laughed softly. "Although I have my suspicions."

Elizabeth shook her head. "I knew you had your suspicions, Aunt, and there is something I have not told you. But I believe it will be beyond anything you suspect."

Mrs. Gardiner sat back in her chair and smiled. "I am all anticipation."

"Aunt, what I am about to tell you can go no further. Not even to Jane. At least not yet." She lifted her brows as she waited for her aunt to agree.

"I promise to tell no one, although now I am not only suspicious, I am curious."

Elizabeth pursed her lips together. "I must get something, first."

Elizabeth went to her room to get Mr. Darcy's letter. She pulled it out and started to make her way towards the door, then stopped. She turned and picked up the book, as well.

She returned to the drawing room, looking down at the letter as she sat beside her aunt. She slowly lifted her eyes to meet her aunt's intent gaze.

"I found this letter the afternoon I fell. It is actually the reason I fell. I was rather…" Elizabeth shook her head. "I was rather distracted by its contents."

Mrs. Gardiner held out her hand. "You were reading a letter you found?" Her brows lowered. "You ought not to have read a letter meant for someone else."

Elizabeth turned her face away, feeling a blush warm her cheeks. "It is not that I read someone else's letter. It was actually written to me."

"Oh!" Mrs. Gardiner bit her lip. "Who is it from?"

Elizabeth looked down and then lifted her eyes to her aunt. "It is from Mr. Darcy."

Mrs. Gardiner's eyes widened. "Mr. Darcy wrote a letter to you?" She began shaking her head. "Lizzy, you know that is most improper. I cannot believe a man of his consequence would risk your reputation by presenting you with a letter."

Elizabeth put up her hand to stay her aunt. "He did not intend for me to see it. He was not going to give it to me."

"I fear I do not understand."

"Apparently he lost it when he dropped his satchel and its contents blew around. The letter must have disappeared from his view. I happened upon it."

"I see. What does it say?"

Elizabeth slowly unfolded the letter. "He... I..." Elizabeth drew in a breath. "Here," she said as she handed the letter to her aunt. "You can read it yourself."

Elizabeth intently watched her aunt's expressions as she read the letter. Mrs. Gardiner uttered a few words of surprise, glanced up with shock, and occasionally smiled.

When she finished reading it, she dropped both hands in her lap. She was silent for a moment, as if collecting her thoughts. Finally she spoke. "Elizabeth, this is serious. Has he spoken to you of his feelings? Does he know you have read his letter?"

Elizabeth shook her head. "No. I certainly cannot tell him I am in possession of his letter and I read it. I suppose I could have left it in his carriage on our journey here, but I was so concerned about keeping it hidden from him that leaving it did not cross my mind until we had arrived and they had departed."

"So Mr. Darcy admires you, whether you wish it or not. What are your feelings towards the man? I know you disliked him when he was in Hertfordshire." She looked again at the letter in her hands. "How did you find his behaviour in Kent?"

"Occasionally I enjoyed his company; yet, at other times I was quite perturbed or simply perplexed by him." Elizabeth looked at her aunt, feeling a great deal of distress. "There are things he has done which have angered me greatly. In addition to what he mentioned in the letter, on our way to town he confessed something else he had done. It incited my anger even more."

Mrs. Gardiner lifted her brows. "What was that?"

Elizabeth's shoulders rose as she took in a slow breath. She let it out in a huff. "He kept Jane's presence in town from Mr. Bingley. He knew she was here, that she had visited Mr. Bingley's sisters, and yet he, in complicity with Miss Bingley, did not tell his friend."

"Hm. Serious, indeed."

"To own the truth, Aunt, my feelings have changed – are changing – but I certainly left him in no doubt of what my feelings have been towards him. I told him what I thought of his officious interference while we were in Kent and again in the carriage as we travelled here." She blew out a puff of air. "Yet now... he has been so gracious in bringing Mr. Bingley here, and even going to my family to warn them about Mr. Wickham. I have come to realize he is, in his essentials, a good and generous man, but I have no idea how to let him know I have begun to realize that."

After a moment, Elizabeth let out a chuckle.

"What is it, dear?"

She gave her head a quick shake. "Mrs. Beckett said something to me that I found most surprising. She is supposedly deaf, or at least hard of hearing; she slept almost the whole way here, yet she seemed to know I was angry with Mr. Darcy. Before she bid me farewell, she leaned over and whispered, 'I have known him all his life, and I have never seen a more excellent man.'" Elizabeth shrugged. "I do not know why she said that to me, unless..."

Mrs. Gardiner gave Elizabeth an encouraging smile. "Yes?"

"Unless she knew how he felt about me and how I felt about him!"

"Well, my dear Lizzy, if it is any help to you in sorting out your feelings, his family was highly esteemed by all who knew them. I heard nothing but good spoken about his father from those I knew in Lambton." Mrs. Gardiner gave her a teasing smile. "He is also wealthy. I am quite certain, Lizzy, if you were to see

Pemberley, you would fall in love with him if only for that!"

Elizabeth laughed. "Then it is a good thing I have not seen Pemberley!" She gave her head a shake. "Although, he did talk to me about it quite often. It sounds lovely."

"If I may be so bold, Lizzy, I do believe he is still very much in love with you."

"I do not know why he would be."

Mrs. Gardiner grew serious and looked down at the letter, pointing to his vague warning about Mr. Rickland. "Do you know to what this refers?"

Elizabeth shook her head. "It could be anything. It is possible he did not appreciate having a rival for my attentions."

"Or he truly knows Mr. Rickland's character is lacking."

"Perhaps. I do not think I can trust my judgment anymore regarding someone's character." She looked down at the book in her hands. "Then there is this."

Mrs. Gardiner reached for the book. "*A Peculiar Engagement* by N. D. Berg. I have never heard of it nor the author."

"While I was at Rosings, I learned Miss de Bourgh, Lady Catherine's daughter, is an author and has two novels published, although no one in her family knows. This is one of them."

Mrs. Gardiner's eyes widened. "Is it really?"

Elizabeth nodded. "Anne de Bourgh is writing under the name N. D. Berg. This novel is the story of her engagement, since her birth, to Mr. Darcy, as expressed and hoped for by their mothers." She glanced up at her aunt, biting the corner of her lip. "It was in the carriage when we set out for London. No one knew where it came from."

"Perhaps she wished for you to read it."

"Or perhaps she hoped Mr. Darcy would. From what I have read so far, Miss de Bourgh is in love with him and still hopes he will make her an offer."

Her aunt shook her head. "By no means does that mean a marriage between them is going to occur."

"No, but everyone expects it." Elizabeth let out a long sigh.

"Have you finished the novel?"

Elizabeth chuckled. "No. There were times I was so angry I did not want to have anything to do with him, let alone read about him."

"Do you suppose the book ends with her still waiting? That is not normally the expected ending of a novel."

"That is true. I hope to finish it tonight."

"Yes, please do! I want to hear how this *peculiar engagement* ends. At least in the mind of Miss de Bourgh." She let out a soft chuckle. "Oh, but Lizzy, I do hope she does not intend to make this a novel in three volumes. We shall have to wait forever to see how it all unfolds!"

~~*

That night, Elizabeth settled in bed to read more of Miss de Bourgh's book. Annabelle had finished writing her first novel, "The Girl in the Turret," and her companion, Mrs. Adamson, had begun talking about it to her son, who owned a small publishing company in London.

Because of Annabelle's difficulty breathing the London air, Mrs. Adamson arranged for her son, John, to come for a visit while Lady Candace was away from home. Mrs. Adamson, while not one to defy the woman, believed Annabelle was old enough to make her own decisions and live her own life. She felt, however, it would be much easier for her if her mother was not there to dash all of Annabelle's hopes and dreams.

The afternoon Mr. Adamson was to arrive, Annabelle waited in the drawing room, tightly gripping the heavily padded journal that contained her novel. While she was certainly nervous, she was also confident Mr. Adamson would truly like the story.

When the sound of a carriage was heard, Annabelle's hand went to her heart. Her face paled as she realized she was about to present her completed book to a publisher.

As they waited for him to be brought in, Annabelle considered she had never before done anything like this without her mother's knowledge. In addition to being nervous, she felt a slight wave of guilt that she was doing all this while her mother was in London. But any remorse disappeared quickly at the prospect of getting her novel published.

When Mr. Adamson stepped into the room, the younger lady felt a sudden wave of disbelief that this was about to happen. Mr. Adamson approached them with a wide grin, and Annabelle's heart began to beat thunderously.

Mrs. Adamson introduced her son to Annabelle.

"Miss Drake, it is a pleasure to finally meet you. I feel as though I already know you. My mother often speaks about you with such great delight when she visits me in London."

Finally, before her was the man she had come to know through his mother. He was quite tall, and while not exceptionally handsome, he had warm brown eyes and a smile that seemed to never leave his face.

"Thank you, Mr. Adamson." Annabelle replied with a soft, nervous laugh. "I feel very much the same."

Now Mrs. Adamson laughed. "As the two of you are my favourite people, how can I not talk to the one about the other?"

Elizabeth feverishly read more and then looked up from the page. A suspicion was forming that there was a mutual fondness between Annabelle and the young gentleman. It was obvious Annabelle felt as though she could honestly talk with him about her life, her struggles with breathing, and to her dismay, having to cease all visits to London because she struggled with breathing.

She quickly turned back to the book.

"There are things we sometimes are forced to give up to improve our lives," he told her. "Do not regret what you cannot do. You must allow yourself to fully enjoy those things you can do and be thankful for those blessings."

Annabelle smiled, but deep inside, she felt a wave of regret. Mr. Adamson lived and worked in London. The thought crossed her mind — foreign and unbidden — that she would like to marry someone like him. But that could never be, as she would not be able to tolerate the air in London and would struggle almost constantly to take a single breath. No, their lives would always be separate.

At least she was able to write. It gave her a sense of contentment and satisfaction nothing else could come close to providing. She may not ever be loved for herself, but she would be able to give her characters a deep and abiding love that would pour forth from her heart, as if it were her very own.

Elizabeth slowly put the book down. "Annabelle *has* fallen in love with Mr. Adamson," she said softly. "But is this merely fiction, or is it truth?" She bit her lip and narrowed her eyes as she pondered this. "Is Miss de Bourgh truly in love with her publisher?"

Elizabeth closed the book and cradled her chin in her hand. Whatever the outcome of the book, it either closes with a wedding that has never taken place or some other fictionalized ending. Miss de Bourgh could not end the book mirroring how things were in truth between her and Mr. Darcy or her and the fictional Mr. Adamson.

She continued to read, discovering not only did Annabelle fall in love with Mr. Adamson, but he fell in love with her. In the week he spent with her and his mother, he not only agreed to publish her book, but he confessed his admiration for her. As Lady Candace was still from home, Annabelle was free, with Mrs. Adamson's approval and presence, to spend a great deal of time with the young man.

Never had she felt such tenderness and care, except from her father, whose death had removed all displays of love and affection from her life. Her mother had often told her she need not worry about love when she married Fitzpatrick; there would be other rewards. But in the week she spent with Mr. Adamson, she found herself falling in love and realized she wanted to marry a man whom she loved — and who loved her in return.

Elizabeth had a sudden realization. *It appears Miss de Bourgh does not love Mr. Darcy and has no wish to marry him!* She wondered if this part of the book was true — whether Miss de Bourgh had fallen in love with her publisher, the son of her companion. But how could she ascertain whether that was the case? As she began to read more, her heart almost stopped when she realized there was possibly a way to find out.

She quickly flipped the pages of the book to the beginning, and she was shocked to see the words printed on the first page:

Jenkinson Publishing, Coleman Street, London.

It was indeed Mrs. Jenkinson's son who published this! Anne certainly would not have had a storyline such as this if it were not true. Elizabeth wondered if Mr. Darcy had any idea.

She decided she had to finish the book tonight. She was far too curious as to how Miss de Bourgh ended her novel. Since this was written as fiction, it was certainly conceivable it ended in a marriage to her publisher. Elizabeth was determined to know the truth.

Elizabeth finished reading the novel after midnight. She closed the book, her thoughts reeling with the ending. Annabelle's mother finally discovers her daughter's secret love and refuses to allow them to marry. Annabelle and Mr. Adamson consequently elope, without her mother's knowledge, to Gretna Green.

Elizabeth smiled as she read the last few paragraphs.

As the elated married couple journeyed back to England, their thoughts and conversation addressed what they would now do. Despite Annabelle's being the rightful heir, Lady Candace would likely forbid her daughter and new husband admittance to Rollings. Living in London would prove too difficult for Annabelle, due to her breathing difficulties. Occasionally she might be able to go, but she worried about what to do because of Mr. Adamson's publishing business.

Fortunately, Mr. Adamson had a small inheritance he had received from his father. He had put a portion of that inheritance into his publishing business.

Mr. Adamson had a business partner who did all the actual work to produce the books. Mr. Adamson read the submitted manuscripts and edited them. He could do that from anywhere, and he told Annabelle they could live in a small home he owned in the country north of London.

Annabelle was delighted with the solution, as long as her husband was content. When they arrived at his home, she loved everything about it. Annabelle knew she had come home to true happiness.

Elizabeth looked up from the page and shook her head. This could not possibly have happened as it was written. Lady Catherine did not seem to have any idea there was a Mr. Jenkinson in Miss de Bourgh's life, let alone that she wrote novels. Elizabeth doubted they could have secretly married in Gretna Green, even with the assistance of Mrs. Jenkinson, for she was so sheltered in her house. In addition, there was the fact that Miss de Bourgh resided by herself at Rosings.

Elizabeth lowered her head onto the pillow that night, her mind swirling with more questions than she had answers. If Miss de Bourgh still truly loved this young man, Elizabeth hoped she might somehow find the happiness she longed for and deserved.

Chapter 24

The next morning Elizabeth joined the Gardiners and Jane for breakfast. She knew her aunt was curious about the book; she questioned her with a single raised brow. Elizabeth answered with a slight nod. They would talk later.

The perfect opportunity arose when Mr. Bingley arrived. He came by himself, which disappointed Elizabeth, but as he wished to walk with Jane, it gave her and her aunt an opportunity to discuss the remainder of the book as they followed a short distance behind the besotted couple.

"I assume you finished the book?" Mrs. Gardiner asked when Jane and Mr. Bingley were out of hearing distance. The glimmer in her eyes convinced Elizabeth she was most eager to hear.

"I did. I must admit I was completely astounded," Elizabeth replied.

"Now I am even more curious! Please tell me what happened!"

Elizabeth gave her a sly smile. "Are you certain you do not wish to read it yourself? I would hate to spoil it for you."

"You will tell me right now, young lady!" A hint of a laugh belied Mrs. Gardiner's firm tone.

"All right, Aunt, if you insist. Miss de Bourgh, or Annabelle as she is in the story, falls in love with – and marries – her publisher, who happens to be the son of her companion."

"Now that is quite a fanciful story. So she has fictionalized the ending?"

Elizabeth raised her shoulders. "I am not able to discern how much is truth and how much is fiction, but the publisher of the book is Jenkinson Publishing. Her companion's name is Mrs. Jenkinson."

"My! It is completely plausible, certainly, for her to have fallen in love with someone else."

"It is, and if he is as attentive and caring towards her as he is portrayed to be in the book, then how could she not? But I do have my doubts they have actually married. In the book, they elope to Gretna Green and settle in a small country home he owns. I think that fortuitous circumstance is merely a device for the story to come to its proper conclusion. There is much that cannot have truly happened."

"You are probably right. Perhaps even now they are determining how to convince her mother to allow them to marry."

"And it is possible," added Elizabeth, "their love was not able to endure the hardship of a forbidden union. It may have already dissolved…"

"Poor girl," her aunt said. "If this is truly the case, I feel sorry for her."

"As do I," Elizabeth said.

~~*

When they returned to the house, Mr. Bingley remained for a short while and chatted with the ladies. As they conversed, a letter was brought in and delivered to Mrs. Gardiner.

She looked down at it and smiled. "It is from Mr. Rickland and is addressed to all of us. I imagine it concerns the ball."

She opened the letter and read it, a smile appearing on her face. "Well, Mr. Bingley, this is timely. He has assured us you are more than welcome to join us at the ball." She folded the letter and placed it in her lap. "Do you have plans this Saturday? We would be pleased for you to accompany us."

A smile lit Mr. Bingley's face. "I would be delighted! Please allow me to bring my carriage to convey us to the Underwoods' home."

"Thank you, very much!" Mrs. Gardiner said. "That is most generous of you."

Jane looked at Mr. Bingley, her wide smile evidence she could not be happier.

Elizabeth was pleased for her sister but was curious about Mr. Darcy. She dared not ask about him. Mrs. Gardiner, however, kindly inquired about both Mr. Darcy and his sister.

"I understand Darcy has returned to Kent," he said. "I do not believe Miss Darcy accompanied him."

"This sounds rather sudden. I do not recollect him mentioning anything about a trip back to Rosings. Do you expect him to return to London soon?" Elizabeth tried to ask as casually as she could.

"I am not certain. Apparently he had some business there requiring his immediate attention. He said it concerned something he ought to have settled years ago." He looked up and tapped his finger on his chin. "He claimed there was something he needed to finally make right."

Elizabeth felt all the blood drain from her face. Her insides tightened, and a tremor of fear passed through her. She could think of nothing but that he had finally gone to ask for his cousin's hand. And if that was the case, there would be four people who would likely be very unhappy. And, as odd as she found it to be, she was one of them.

Elizabeth looked to Mrs. Gardiner for help. Her aunt appeared more concerned for her than about the silence now permeating the room. She quickly turned back to Mr. Bingley. "We hope everything will work out for him as it ought."

Mr. Bingley smiled and nodded. "Oh, I am certain it shall. He is one of the most capable and determined men I know. If he sets his mind to something, it will happen."

Elizabeth made a concerted effort to engage in the conversation, silently berating herself for such a violent reaction that was completely the opposite of what she had felt only a few days before.

After a short while, Mr. Bingley left, and Elizabeth went to her room. A real pain gripped her, knowing now she would never have the opportunity to inform Mr. Darcy her feelings towards him had begun to change. She also felt a great sense of regret that any affection he once had felt for her likely no longer existed.

How could this have happened? How could she finally have felt the tender stirrings of love at the moment he decided to ask for his cousin's hand? She felt herself a fool to have berated such a man, especially to his face, only to discover he had such ardent feelings for her.

She buried her head in her pillow to console herself in her tears.

The first tears she had ever shed over Mr. Darcy – and they fell in tribute to her utter foolhardiness.

~~*

Elizabeth left her room a short time later only to encounter concerned looks from her aunt and Jane. "I am well, truly. I have no idea what came over me."

Jane rushed up to her, taking her arm. "Lizzy, you must tell me what has happened. Our aunt would tell me nothing; she said it was up to you to inform me of events that have occurred."

"I shall, Jane," she said as she took Jane's hand. Turning to her aunt, she asked, "May I have some tea?"

"Certainly." Mrs. Gardiner left the sisters together.

"Jane, several things happened in Kent I only recently shared with Aunt Gardiner." She shook her head, letting out a quick breath. "I would have told you, as well, but because of Mr. Bingley, I did not. I did not want you to accidentally tell him."

"Oh, Lizzy, you know I would not."

Elizabeth patted her hand. "Yes, I know you would never reveal a confidence intentionally, but even I have inadvertently said some things to Mr. Darcy I ought not to have said."

"But what?"

Mrs. Gardiner returned, followed by the maid bringing tea and biscuits.

Elizabeth took the teacup, wrapping her fingers around the cup for its warmth. "Mr. Darcy wrote me a letter, but he never intended for me to see it. He dropped some papers, and his missive blew away. I happened upon it on my walk one morning."

"He wrote you a letter? What did he say?" Jane's face displayed her confusion.

Elizabeth took a sip of the tea and then placed the teacup down. She pulled out the letter and began to slowly unfold it. "Allow me to read you a portion."

As Elizabeth read about Mr. Darcy's strong affection for her, Jane's reaction was much the same as hers and her aunt's had been. When she finished, Jane was slowly shaking her head.

"Mr. Darcy has been in love with you all this time?"

Elizabeth smiled weakly. "I do not know if it has been *all* this time, but apparently for some time." She continued by telling Jane about the innumerable feelings, from anger and dislike to admiration and respect, she had felt for Mr. Darcy. She also told her about Anne's book, and how it had helped her to begin to see him differently.

"But something in her book has me perplexed... and concerned."

"What?"

Elizabeth told her how in the book Miss de Bourgh's character, Annabelle, fell in love with her publisher, the son of her companion. A look of concern infused her features. "I cannot help but wonder if it is true."

"She and her publisher?"

Elizabeth slowly nodded "If Mr. Darcy is on his way to ask for his cousin's hand, as I assume he is doing, her mother will force Miss de Bourgh to agree to it, and they both will live a life of misery, I am sure of it."

She shook her head. "I cannot be certain this affection between Miss de Bourgh and her publisher is true. In the book she and her publisher marry. It may have been a fictionalized way for her to end the book happily, but in all truth, Jane, I never saw any love exhibited between her and Mr. Darcy."

"Is the publisher here in London?" Jane asked.

Elizabeth nodded. "Yes..."

"Then is there anything to prevent you from paying him a call? Perhaps if he is in love with Miss de Bourgh, as well, there might be something he can do."

Elizabeth looked at Jane incredulously. She could not believe her sister suggested this. "The publishing company is on Coleman Street, but going to him would appear too forward. I should feel awkward inquiring about his relationship with Miss de Bourgh."

"Coleman Street is reasonably close," Mrs. Gardiner said. "We could go there to perhaps... peruse his selection of books. Bring the book along with you, Lizzy, and merely let him know how much you enjoyed it. In due course, he may reveal the truth of the matter without you even having to ask."

"I do not know what seeing Mr. Jenkinson might reveal, if

anything," Elizabeth replied. "We have no business going there, and I doubt there is anything he could do." Her heart raced, one moment in dread that she would find out for a certainty Mr. Darcy had gone to offer his suit to Miss de Bourgh. The next moment she was fighting off the anger that rose up. The anger was no longer directed at Mr. Darcy for what he had done, however, but at herself for how blind she had been in regards to him. There was only a small ray of hope remaining she might get another chance with him.

"Well, there is no harm in trying." Mrs. Gardiner put her arm about Elizabeth's shoulders. "Besides, I am most interested in reading *The Girl in the Turret* by N. D. Berg. Perhaps he can provide us with a copy."

Elizabeth reluctantly gave in, and the three ladies set out within the hour. They took the carriage the few miles to Coleman Street and looked on both sides of the street for Jenkinson Publishing. Jane was the first one to see it, as did the carriage driver, who pulled over, bringing the equipage to a halt.

The ladies stepped from the carriage and walked up to the small business. Before they opened the door, Elizabeth stopped. "I am still not certain we should be doing this. Do you think we ought?"

Her aunt reassured her with a smile. "You have no need to even mention Mr. Darcy. Merely tell Mr. Jenkinson you enjoyed the book and see where it leads."

Elizabeth nodded her head. "Oh, Aunt, I hope you are right."

They walked into the bookstore, and Elizabeth looked around in delight. There were shelves and shelves filled with books, and she could readily smell the leather of the covers. A young man sat behind a desk, looking through a ledger as they walked in.

"Good afternoon, ladies," he said as he stood. "Is there anything I can help you with?"

Elizabeth stepped forward, smiling. "Is there a Mr. Jenkinson here?"

"Mr. Jenkinson is in the back. Is he expecting you?"

"No, but I should like to speak with him if he has a moment."

"Please have a seat. I shall see if he is available."

The three ladies began looking at the selection of books as the gentleman left the front office. Elizabeth turned to her aunt. "I hope he…"

At that moment, a taller man appeared and bowed. "I am Adam Jenkinson. How may I be of assistance to you?"

Elizabeth smiled. "My name is Elizabeth Bennet, and this is my aunt, Mrs. Gardiner, and my sister, Miss Jane Bennet."

"It is a pleasure. How may I help you?"

Elizabeth held out Miss de Bourgh's book to him. "Did you publish this book?"

Mr. Jenkinson looked down at it, and his face lit up with a smile. "I most certainly did. Have you read it?"

Elizabeth nodded. "I finished it. Miss de Bourgh wrote a wonderful and engaging novel. We wondered whether you had her first novel."

"*The Girl in the Turret?* We most certainly do," he said, nodding his head. He began walking towards a wall of books but suddenly stopped. His brows lowered. "You know about Miss de Bourgh?"

"I do," Elizabeth replied. "She told me herself she is the author."

"She must trust you implicitly," he said earnestly, pulling her novel off the shelf. "Are you an intimate friend?"

"Hardly," Elizabeth said with a nervous laugh. "We only just met while I was visiting a good friend of mine who is married to the Hunsford clergyman. We dined several times at Rosings, and while I spoke with Miss de Bourgh on occasion, I was surprised when she confided in me."

Mr. Jenkinson's eyes lit up as if he had a revelation of sorts, and he clasped his hands together. "You were just recently there?"

Elizabeth nodded.

"I understand Mr. Darcy also visited there recently. Did he happen to be there when you were staying with your friend?"

"Yes, he was." Elizabeth thought it odd he seemed to be pleased Mr. Darcy had been there while she was there. She had to bite her lip to keep from blurting out the question foremost on her mind.

Mr. Jenkinson silently regarded her for a moment and then pointed to the book in Elizabeth's hands. "I assume your visit here is related to that book somehow?"

Elizabeth pursed her lips together in disappointment. He

obviously was not going to reveal anything to her about Mr. Darcy, Miss de Bourgh, or himself. "Yes, it is. I was able to determine this is the story about the peculiar engagement between Mr. Darcy and Miss de Bourgh. I was able to piece together who the different characters were. It is all quite apparent if you know those involved."

"Yes, she felt it was best to at least change the names, although for the most part, everything else is true."

Mr. Jenkinson's cheeks grew flushed, and he looked down. "Well, almost everything. You are most likely wondering about the ending."

"Yes, I confess I am." Elizabeth said with a nervous laugh. "I assume you are Mrs. Jenkinson's son?"

Mr. Jenkinson slowly looked back up and glanced briefly at Mrs. Gardiner and Jane. He waved Elizabeth towards his desk, which was back in the corner of the room. In a hushed voice he said, "I am. And in case you are wondering, Miss de Bourgh and I have quite unexpectedly developed a strong mutual affection for each other." He took in a deep breath, letting it out slowly. "I only tell you this, as I know Anne must have trusted you implicitly."

"For some reason, she did," Elizabeth said softly.

He took another deep breath and let it out slowly. "We did not run away to Gretna Green and get married, however."

"I did not think that you had." Elizabeth paused and bit her lip. "Mr. Jenkinson, there is a particular reason why I have come today. There is something I must tell you about Miss de Bourgh."

Chapter 25

Mr. Jenkinson's eyes opened wide, and the colour drained from his face. He walked over to his desk and braced his hands upon it. "What is it? Has something happened to her?"

"We were informed Mr. Darcy left yesterday for Kent. His good friend told us he had some business to take care of... business he ought to have concluded years ago." Elizabeth's voice began to tremble, as much as she tried to appear composed. "Might he have gone to ask for Miss de Bourgh's hand?"

Mr. Jenkinson's face fell, and he brought his hand up slowly and rubbed his chin. Very softly he said, "We knew this might happen. We hoped it would not." He looked down and shook his head. "We never thought it would! She has never detected any admiration on his part."

Elizabeth looked at him entreatingly. "Has she told her mother of the feelings you have for each other?"

Mr. Jenkinson turned to gaze out at the busy street. "No." He was quiet for a moment and then let out a forced laugh. "Lady Catherine is not even aware of my existence." He turned around and braced his hands on his desk. "Miss de Bourgh loves her mother, but she also greatly fears what she would do if she knew."

"I can imagine," Elizabeth said softly.

"I want nothing more than to marry Miss de Bourgh, but we have yet to come up with a way to convince her mother to allow it." He turned away and hung his head, his shoulders slumping. "As you might imagine after reading her novel, Anne... Miss de Bourgh has a vivid imagination and fears being whisked away and locked up somewhere, hidden from sight." He let out a long sigh, glancing down at Anne's other novel he held in his hands. "Much like *The Girl in the Turret*." He looked at Elizabeth imploringly. "I assume I can trust you with this information as much as she seemed to trust you."

"You certainly can trust me, and I appreciate your telling me."

He rounded his desk and slowly sat down. Mr. Jenkinson motioned for Elizabeth to sit down on a nearby chair.

Elizabeth smiled. "Thank you."

Mr. Jenkinson's gaze turned to the book in his hands. Suddenly a faint smile appeared. "I received a letter from her last week. She wrote to tell me she suspects Mr. Darcy is in love with another." Mr. Jenkinson raised his brow. "A young lady who was there visiting her friend in the parsonage."

Elizabeth felt her cheeks warm in a blush.

He smiled weakly. "Observing her cousin with this young lady even provided the inspiration for a new novel."

"Truly?" Elizabeth asked. She brought one hand, now trembling, up to her throat.

"Yes, she wants to title it, *Love in the Drawing Room*. She said it is about the desperate love a handsome and wealthy gentleman has for a young lady, while the lady is completely oblivious to his admiration." He shook his head but looked at Elizabeth inquisitively. "She believes there was even some animosity on the young lady's part."

Elizabeth could barely breathe. *How could others have seen it and not her?*

"Perhaps I ought not to have said anything." He clasped his hands together and rested his chin on them. "Miss de Bourgh has never known for a certainty what Mr. Darcy's intentions were towards herself. He has never, as far as she knew, exhibited interest in her or any other woman, for that matter. As you read in her book, they got along splendidly when they were younger. She does highly esteem him."

"So what can be done?" Elizabeth asked. "If he proposes, nothing can undo it. His aunt will likely hold him and her daughter to it."

Mr. Jenkinson wrung his hands. "Perhaps Miss de Bourgh will turn him down and risk being on the receiving end of her mother's wrath." Despite speaking of that hope, his face betrayed his doubt.

"Do you believe she will?"

"She always wished she could speak her mind. She is a young lady filled with dreams and passions, but never allowed to do as she desired." He closed his eyes for a moment and rested his head on his hands.

"If Mr. Darcy goes to Lady Catherine first to inform her of his intention to ask for Miss de Bourgh's hand..." Elizabeth's voice trailed off as she fought to hold back the tears threatening to fall.

Mr. Jenkinson slowly shook his head. "I fear it is too late to do anything now. Whatever purpose took him there has likely already been accomplished."

Elizabeth felt as helpless as Mr. Jenkinson looked.

"May I be so bold as to inquire what your feelings are towards Mr. Darcy, if indeed you are the lady who inspired Miss de Bourgh to write a new story?"

Elizabeth turned her head slightly towards her aunt and sister, both of whom continued to peruse the bookshelves. She let out a long sigh. She could not tell him she loved Mr. Darcy, but she did wish to convey that her feelings were at present quite the opposite of what Miss de Bough had earlier observed. "I think... I believe... I would like more time to find out who he truly is, if it is not too late. He believes I despise him," she said with a resigned laugh. "Miss de Bourgh's book, however, has given me an insight into his character I would not have gleaned by my own misguided observations."

Mr. Jenkinson looked at Elizabeth intently. "Miss Bennet, if you have any doubts about Mr. Darcy's character, any concerns, I can tell you, there is no man finer than he! I have spent the past year wondering how I could ever win Miss de Bourgh's affections from such a man. How could I ever compete with such a rival? It is only because he exhibited little interest in her, nay, *no* interest in her, that I was able to secure her love and devotion."

He stood and walked again to the window, staring out. "There is nothing for us to do now but wait... and put our hope in a providential miracle." He let out a deep sigh. "I think, in a way, I had been resigned to the possibility of this happening. As much as I wished we would one day marry, I could not envision any conceivable way her mother would allow it."

Elizabeth smiled. "You could always elope. She does not need her mother's permission."

Mr. Jenkinson looked up and smiled. "We did talk about me

snatching her up one day and whisking her away to elope. My mother kindly offered her assistance."

"I believe your mother would," Elizabeth said with a brief smile.

"Lady Catherine keeps a close eye on Anne and barely lets her out of her sight. It would be difficult, especially with her respiratory difficulties." He shook his head. "She could never live in London. The foul air from London travels to Kent on occasion and aggravates her condition." Mr. Jenkinson lowered his eyes and shook his head. "It is even becoming difficult for her to live there."

"Is there any hope Miss de Bourgh might confide in Mr. Darcy she is in love with another?"

Mr. Jenkinson shook his head. "I doubt she would. She fears he would consider me lacking in consequence and wealth, despite my late father's decent connections and position in society. His eldest son by his first wife inherited the majority of his fortune at his death, leaving my mother to seek work as a companion and me to seek my own employment. Even though I own a small manor and have a slight inheritance, Miss de Bourgh is not certain where Mr. Darcy's loyalties lie. She knows not whether he would feel the match was beneath her and would, therefore, feel it his duty to inform her mother."

Elizabeth folded her arms. "I can understand that more than you know." She shook her head. "I will not take up any more of your time. It has been a pleasure making your acquaintance, Mr. Jenkinson. I hope everything works out for you."

"Thank you. And I hope the same for you." He gave her a knowing look.

She laughed nervously. "Thank you."

As they began to walk out, Elizabeth stopped. "Oh, Mr. Jenkinson, might we purchase a copy of *Girl in the Turret*? I would very much like to read it."

Mr. Jenkinson smiled and handed her the book. "Please consider this a gift."

Elizabeth took it from him. "Thank you."

~~*

Before returning to the Gardiners' home, the ladies stopped by the dressmaker's shop to try on the ball gowns that had been altered for them. As the travelled the short distance, Elizabeth made every attempt to put her conversation with Mr. Jenkinson out of her mind, but she could not. His words weighed heavily upon her.

It was not until she and Jane tried on their gowns and stepped out for their aunt to see, that she was able to genuinely smile. She felt beautiful and thought the colour complimented her complexion.

"You both look lovely!" her aunt said.

As Elizabeth stood before the mirror, looking at her reflection while the dressmaker made a few minor alterations, a wave of regret passed over her. Although Mr. Rickland would see her in it, Mr. Darcy would not. How she wished she knew why he had gone to Kent. Not knowing why he returned to Rosings was robbing her of almost all joyful anticipation in attending the ball.

It was silent in the carriage, and Elizabeth was lost in her thoughts. She would never have imagined feeling this way about Mr. Darcy. She was not certain that what she felt was love, as she needed to ascertain whether those faults she so disliked in him would rear their heads again, but she would like to have an opportunity to find out; she hoped she would.

When they arrived back at the house, a message was waiting for them. It was from Mr. Rickland, expressing his hope they were all still planning to attend the ball and informing them he anticipated seeing everyone there. He also reminded Elizabeth about their promised dance.

"Mr. Rickland seems a proper sort of gentleman. You said he was quite attentive to you in Kent, did you not?" asked Jane.

Elizabeth let out a sigh of resignation. "Yes, he was an amiable and proper gentleman. We did enjoy ourselves." Her brows furrowed. "There was an afternoon when I found myself terribly angry at Mr. Darcy, and Mr. Rickland was more than willing to escort me away from his presence as we shared our mutual dislike of the man."

"Do you know what his intentions towards you are?" her aunt

asked.

"We never specifically talked about it." Elizabeth smiled and shrugged. "He may have none at all."

"And he may have strong affection for you," Mrs. Gardiner said with a soft laugh. "What are your feelings for the gentleman?"

Elizabeth hung her head and then, taking a deep breath, raised it. "I did prefer his company to that of Mr. Darcy's while at Rosings." In a soft voice, she said, "He was most personable, and I greatly enjoyed getting to know him." She slowly shook her head.

"I am certainly not in love with him, and I cannot dismiss Mr. Darcy's warning."

She turned away, folding her arms tightly in front of her. "Mr. Darcy has just enough pride and even more reserve that would prevent him, I believe, from stepping in and thwarting the affections of someone he might consider his rival." She let out a long sigh. "But now, as incomprehensible as it may seem, I truly wish he would!"

~~*

The next day, Elizabeth and her sister and aunt spent the day quietly, deciding how they would wear their hair, and other matters pertaining to the ball. They spent the evening with the Gardiners' four children, who were invited to join them in the drawing room. The children each gave an account of their day, while the youngest, Harriet, sat on Elizabeth's lap.

A knock at the door brought the butler to the drawing room with a letter for Elizabeth.

"For me?" She looked at Harriet with a smile and a wink.

She took the letter and her eyes widened as she saw it was from Charlotte Collins.

"It is… it is from Charlotte. I wonder what she has to say." Her hands inexplicably trembled as she slowly opened the letter, wondering what news it might contain from Hunsford… or Rosings.

"Your hands are shaking," Harriet said. "Are you afraid?"

Elizabeth tried to smile. "Of course not. I merely wonder what my friend has to say."

She looked up to see her aunt and sister giving her concerned looks. Mrs. Gardiner stood and walked over to her. "Come, Harriet. Sit on my lap while Lizzy reads her letter."

Elizabeth swallowed as she read Charlotte's words.

Dear Lizzy,

How are you faring, dear friend? I would imagine you are recovering nicely. I expect Mr. Rickland stopped by. He looked forward to seeing you again. He is such a pleasant gentleman.

It has been a most unusual few days here. We were quite surprised when Mr. Darcy returned, and despite my husband's most cunning attempts to determine what was going on — for certainly something was going on — he was not successful. There were no invitations to dine or visit, and poor Mr. Collins felt completely ill-used.

But while we were waiting and wondering, little did we know something remarkable — and most unexpected, if you ask me — was taking place. Apparently, Mr. Darcy returned to Rosings to ask for Miss de Bourgh's hand in marriage. I knew this was expected of him, but may I say again — how unexpected it was for him to acquiesce to this most unusual arrangement.

Even more surprising than that, however, is instead of waiting to have a wedding performed at Hunsford Church by Mr. Collins, they have gone off to Gretna Green. I am not teasing you, Lizzy! They are eloping!

They were discovered gone this morning, with merely a note left behind. Mr. Darcy and Miss de Bourgh departed in secret some time before dawn, along with Mrs. Jenkinson. Lady Catherine is vexed one moment and ecstatic the next. She cannot believe they resorted to this secrecy, while at the same time she is elated that her greatest wish has come to pass. She is angered by their intention to elope, while delighted Mr. Darcy has finally fulfilled his duty. Do not think me silly, Elizabeth, but I believe she is actually surprised a wedding between the two is finally taking place!

My poor husband seems the most gravely affected. He deeply feels the loss of the honour he would have had in performing what certainly would have been a most elegant ceremony uniting two illustrious persons. He is seriously displeased.

I cannot help but feel quite foolish in my suspicions that Mr. Darcy's affections tended in a different direction, Lizzy, but I suppose if he had any

such inclination for you, his strict adherence to duty and family overruled it.
I so enjoyed our visit. Give my best to Jane and your aunt and uncle.
Yours, etc.,
Charlotte

Elizabeth looked up slowly, feeling somewhat faint.

"Lizzy, what is it? Your face is so pale." Jane stood up and came over to her.

Elizabeth drew in a slow breath and swallowed. She began shaking her head. "It appears Mr. Darcy and Miss de Bourgh intend to marry. Charlotte said they departed Rosings and have set off for Gretna Green."

Elizabeth directed a smile, albeit a half-hearted one, at the others. "I believe I shall go to my room if you do not mind."

Mrs. Gardiner reached out her hand and grasped Elizabeth's firmly. "Certainly, dear."

Elizabeth turned and hurriedly quit the room.

Elizabeth collapsed onto her bed, assaulted by such feelings of regret and despair it surprised even her. She no longer had any right to hope Mr. Darcy would continue in his affections for her. It grieved her that such a man had once loved her, yet she had treated him reprehensibly.

In her book, Miss de Bourgh had described him as a man of the utmost integrity and principles. Despite not being loved by him, Miss de Bourgh could readily appreciate his merit. Elizabeth hugged her arms tightly about her as she pondered this in the solitude of her room. Even Mr. Jenkinson spoke well of him! If only she had seen those attributes in him and taken the time to discover that side of him, her life could now be so different. But instead, she had been blinded by her vanity and deceived by her folly.

She rolled onto her stomach and buried her face into her pillow. She felt her body shudder as she began to cry. Tears streamed down her face as she realized how foolish she had been, what could have been, and what was now lost to her.

She knew not how long she wept, but at length she felt a gentle hand on her shoulder.

"Lizzy, what can I do for you?" Despite her anguish, her aunt's soft voice and touch soothed her. "I brought you a handkerchief."

Elizabeth took it and lifted her head. "Thank you." After dabbing her eyes, she said, "Oh, Aunt, I am so confused and do not understand why I feel this way. I never sought Mr. Darcy's attention. I had such a strong dislike of him, but now I cannot help feeling as though I behaved shamelessly." She choked on her next words. "He must consider me a fool."

Mrs. Gardiner patted her on her back. "I would not be so certain. He likely admires you for standing up for what you believed. You felt he committed an injustice..."

"Several injustices," Elizabeth interrupted with a forced laugh.

"Yes, but his fortune did not tempt you to overlook those things you believed were wrong." She began to stroke her niece's hair. "Lizzy, think of all the ladies who would do anything to secure his affections without giving any thought to who he is."

"But I have been so wrong." She rolled to face her aunt and began fingering the handkerchief lightly.

"Not about everything. Remember, he actually righted one of those wrongs, which is a good indication he felt you were justified in your anger. He did not have to reunite Mr. Bingley with Jane."

"That was good of him." Elizabeth took in a raspy breath. "I do not believe I have ever met a more excellent man."

"I know you feel a great deal of regret for what might have been, but remember there was a reason you disliked him in Hertfordshire. It is possible he still has all the pride and arrogance you found disagreeable."

"Trust me, Aunt, I have tried to convince myself of that, but it has not helped." She put her hand to the nape of her neck and rubbed it gently. She looked at her aunt and tried to smile. "My head is trying to tell me it is just as well he is marrying another, while my heart literally aches for what will never be." Elizabeth slowly sat up and wiped away another tear with the handkerchief. "When we went to see Mr. Jenkinson, I hoped with my whole heart he would give me the assurance Miss de Bourgh would not agree to marry Mr. Darcy. I could see in his eyes he wished the same, but he did not have that assurance himself."

Mrs. Gardiner leaned over and kissed the top of Elizabeth's head. "Try to get some sleep, dear. Tomorrow you may wake up and find the strength of feeling you now have for Mr. Darcy will have diminished somewhat."

"Thank you, Aunt. I hope so."

As she closed her eyes in an attempt to finally fall asleep, she decided she would make every effort to put Mr. Darcy out of her thoughts and heart. Her eyes filled with tears again as she considered while it would not be easy, it was something she desperately needed to do.

Chapter 26

When Elizabeth came out of her room the next morning, she joined her aunt in the sitting room. She sat down and rested her head in her hands.

"I assume you did not sleep well last night?" Mrs. Gardiner asked.

"Very little." Elizabeth blinked her eyes several times. "I am certain I look positively dreadful. I doubt even the beautiful dress I am wearing tonight will be of any help."

Mrs. Gardiner reached over and took Elizabeth's hand. "A little fresh air, sunshine, and an easy walk will work wonders."

"To improve my appearance or to clear my thoughts of Mr. Darcy?"

Her aunt smiled softly. "Perhaps you need to begin thinking of Mr. Rickland."

Elizabeth let out a long sigh and merely shook her head.

"I imagine you are still wondering about Mr. Darcy's warning in his letter."

Elizabeth turned to look out the window. "When I first read what little Mr. Darcy had written about him, I was angry he would attempt to discredit the man. Yet now it gives me pause to consider what his grievance against him might be."

"Well, your uncle and I shall keep a close eye on him tonight. You need not fear if his intentions towards you are not of the highest integrity." She smiled teasingly.

"I am not worried about that. I would suspect Mr. Darcy would object more to something about his family or his fortune." She laughed half-heartedly and cast her eyes down. "Or mine."

"Let us not worry now. Let us think about the ball this evening. I know the Underwoods are a highly esteemed family. We shall be pleased to find ourselves amidst pleasant company and be thankful for the honour of being invited."

Elizabeth looked up with a smile. "Yes, you are correct. I shall enjoy myself and try not to think about what may have been the greatest error of judgement of my life."

Mrs. Gardiner patted her niece on the shoulder. "Do not be so harsh on yourself, Lizzy. All shall be well." She let out a sigh. "Let us try to dwell on pleasant thoughts until it is time to get ready for the ball."

~~*

Throughout the day, Elizabeth was thankful for her aunt and sister. They were such an encouragement to her and helped her to dwell on things other than her regret over Mr. Darcy and her suspicions about Mr. Rickland. They took a leisurely walk outside, which brightened Elizabeth's spirits immensely. She felt as though she might be able to enjoy herself at the ball.

Later in the afternoon, the ladies went their separate ways to ready themselves for the evening's entertainment. Looking at herself in the mirror, Elizabeth had to own she had never looked as pretty as she did wearing the blue gown. One of the young maids assisted Elizabeth, weaving blue ribbons through her hair, and placing sprigs of small white flowers here and there. The maid fastened the sapphire necklace around her neck, and Elizabeth's hand immediately went up to touch it. She smiled at the young girl. "It is beautiful, is it not?"

The maid smiled. "*You* are beautiful, Miss Elizabeth."

Elizabeth thanked her and went to the drawing room to await the others. She realized being invited to this ball was an honour, and she looked forward to seeing the Underwoods' home and meeting those in attendance. She stretched out her foot and wiggled it, satisfied it had healed well enough to allow her to dance without too much difficulty. Her shoulder still hurt on occasion, but she was grateful the aches and pains were minimal. She was grateful her injuries would not hinder her enjoyment of the evening, although she wondered whether intruding thoughts of Mr. Darcy might.

Mr. and Mrs. Gardiner joined her, and they talked with so much animation about the upcoming evening Elizabeth could not help but eagerly look forward to it. She was delighted with her aunt and uncle's fashionable attire. They looked as though they could have stepped out of the most elegant home.

Mr. Bingley arrived soon after, looking as handsome as he had at the Netherfield Ball. He rubbed his hands together as he conversed with the three, and his attention was drawn to the door with every sound, in anticipation, Elizabeth assumed, of seeing Jane.

Jane finally stepped into the room. Her rose gown brought out the pink in her ivory cheeks, and a deep rose ribbon was woven through her golden locks, with a few tiny pink flowers added.

Mr. Bingley's response to seeing her was well worth the wait. He stopped speaking in midsentence; his eyes widened, and his jaw dropped.

Mr. Gardiner let out a hearty laugh. "My dear wife and nieces, you are stunningly beautiful tonight!" He poked Mr. Bingley in the ribs with his elbow. "What say you, Mr. Bingley?"

Mr. Bingley nodded enthusiastically. "Yes, yes. She is... They are... all beautiful."

"Well, let us not delay any longer. We have a ball to attend!" Mr. Gardiner took his wife's arm and led the way out of the room.

Mr. Bingley extended his arms for both Jane and Elizabeth to take, and they followed behind.

~~*

The ride to the Underwoods' home was not quite half an hour, but as they approached the house, the line of carriages prevented them from progressing the final distance in a timely manner. It took another fifteen minutes to reach the main walkway up to the house, where they were helped out.

The candlelight indoors shone radiantly through the many windows, and music could be heard as they walked up to the door. It was a beautiful, large, stately home, although Elizabeth had to smile, as its overly pruned gardens reminded her of Rosings.

Mr. and Mrs. Gardiner led the way, again, followed by their nieces on Mr. Bingley's arms. As they went up the steps, Mr. Bingley said, "Miss Bennet, I would be honoured if you would dance the first dance with me."

Jane's eyes were cast down, but a smile lit her face. "I would be delighted, Mr. Bingley."

A single nod of his head affirmed his gratitude. He then turned to Elizabeth. "Miss Elizabeth, would you do me the honour of dancing the second with me?"

She laughed. "It would be my pleasure, sir."

They waited in the line of guests to greet the Underwoods. Elizabeth peered ahead and saw a distinguished looking couple, slightly older than her aunt and uncle. They greeted each guest warmly.

She then looked around, hoping to see Mr. Rickland. He had told them he would watch for them to make the introductions.

"I do not see Mr. Rickland. I had hoped he would meet us here," she said.

"Yes, it would have been the proper thing to do," Mr. Gardiner said. "But as we do have an invitation, I suppose it will be left to us to introduce ourselves."

A few steps more brought them in front of Mr. and Mrs. Underwood.

Mr. Gardiner bowed. "Good evening, Mr. and Mrs. Underwood. We are the invited guests of Mr. Matthew Rickland." He then proceeded to introduce the party.

"Oh, yes!" exclaimed Mr. Underwood. "It is a pleasure to make your acquaintance. I am Alfred Underwood, and this is my lovely wife, Viola." He leaned forward with a sly smile. "I suppose Matthew is enjoying himself in the gaming room."

Mrs. Underwood smiled. "It is a pleasure to make your acquaintance. It is not often our godson requests a special favour for an invitation. In fact, he rarely attends the balls we give, but we were more than happy to oblige him."

"Thank you. We are honoured you extended the invitation to us," Mrs. Gardiner assured her.

Mrs. Underwood gave an acknowledging nod of her head. "If we see him, we shall certainly inform him of your arrival."

They each thanked the couple as they moved past and were soon in the large ballroom. It was laden with ornate carvings, immense paintings, and colourful tapestries. The light from the flickering candles held in the large chandeliers overhead and sconces around the room danced off the walls, much like the couples who had already begun dancing. A small orchestra provided the music.

"Lovely!" exclaimed Mrs. Gardiner clasping her hands.

Refreshments were being served, and Mr. Gardiner suggested, with a teasing laugh, that they do their due diligence as guests and see if anything looked good enough to sample. As they each partook of the offerings and commented on how delicious everything was, Elizabeth heard her name spoken behind her. She turned to see Mr. Rickland smiling broadly.

"I am so pleased you came. My godparents informed me you were here."

"We are grateful for the invitation, Mr. Rickland." While Elizabeth was sincere in her appreciation of the invitation, she could not help but wonder what Mr. Darcy wished to warn her about Mr. Rickland. She felt a knot in her stomach as she considered she had a greater wish to be with the gentleman she once despised than the one standing before her, whom she had once so freely admired.

Mr. Rickland and his guests conversed as they watched the dancers move across the ballroom floor. Despite the animation of the others in her party, however, Elizabeth felt little inclination to join in. She did her best to hide those concerns that plagued her, but she knew her aunt could readily see it. A look and a slightly raised brow was all she needed to convey to Elizabeth she was troubled.

The next dance was about to begin, and Mr. Bingley escorted Jane to the floor. Mr. Rickland turned to Elizabeth and with a bow asked, "May I have this dance, Miss Elizabeth?"

She nodded. "Certainly."

They walked to the dance floor, followed by Mr. and Mrs. Gardiner.

Fortunately, it was an easy dance, and Elizabeth was grateful her feet obeyed with nary a stumble. At one point, when they had to grasp hands, her shoulder and arm ached, but other than that, she felt well.

Mr. Rickland was an excellent dancer and most attentive to

Elizabeth. He wore a smile on his face throughout the dance. When the music stopped, and the dance ended, his smile quickly turned to a mock frown. "Our dance cannot be over. It seems as though we just began!"

Elizabeth chuckled. "I must confess I am fatigued."

"How careless of me not to inquire earlier! Are you still in much discomfort?" He extended his arm for Elizabeth to take, and they walked over to join the Gardiners.

Elizabeth shook her head. "There were only a few times my shoulder hurt, but that can be expected in the exertion of a dance."

"Pray, do take care!"

When Jane and Mr. Bingley joined them, Mr. Rickland called to some people who were standing nearby. They were introduced to a striking young lady and her family. Elizabeth did not think she had ever seen such a beautiful woman. She had flawless porcelain skin, honeycomb-coloured hair, and bright blue eyes.

Miss Grace Strathern was the young lady's name, and she smiled sweetly as the introductions were made, but even though she observed every courtesy required, her eyes travelled about the room. Elizabeth's eyes, however, were focused on the jewellery Miss Strathern wore. A beautiful necklace of diamonds and sapphires draped her neck, reflecting the light from the candles with each move she made.

Her parents spoke with Mr. and Mrs. Gardiner, while she turned to Mr. Rickland and Elizabeth.

"And how have you been, Miss Strathern?" Mr. Rickland asked. "Are you enjoying yourself tonight?"

"I would be, if only your cousin would arrive. I thought you said he would be here."

Mr. Rickland raised his brows and wagged his finger. "No, I said he was invited." He brushed his hands together as if wanting to wipe something off of them. "And Mr. Darcy is *not* my cousin."

Elizabeth was unable to stifle a slight gasp at Rickland's words. She looked from him to the young lady. She could not help but wonder whether Mr. Darcy would, indeed, attend the ball, and who this lady was who wished him to be here.

"I shall be most displeased if he does not come."

"Come, Grace." Mrs. Strathern waved for her daughter to follow them.

She turned back to Mr. Rickland. "Pray, tell your cousin he is invited to our home any time." She dipped a curtsey, smiled at Elizabeth, and left.

Mr. Rickland watched her leave and then faced Elizabeth. "There has been much speculation about Miss Strathern and Mr. Darcy. I believe if he does not offer for her soon, she shall be quite heartbroken."

Elizabeth tried to smile, if only to convince Mr. Rickland it was of no interest to her, but it was almost too great an effort. Despite feeling Miss Strathern was the least of her worries, she now wished she had not come. But as she was here, she was obliged to do her best to find pleasure in the evening. She certainly would not allow her disappointment to hinder the enjoyment of her family, especially Jane.

When the musicians signalled the beginning of the next dance, Mr. Bingley claimed Elizabeth's hand, and Mr. Rickland bowed to Jane. The Gardiners chose to sit this one out as they continued to converse with some new acquaintances.

When the last notes sounded, Elizabeth returned to her aunt and uncle. She did not wish to exert herself too greatly and risk further injury.

Her aunt extended her hand as she came near. "Dearest Lizzy, you look to be in pain. Come, sit for a while."

"Yes. I think I would like that. My poor foot and shoulder have begun screaming that I have used them quite ill this evening." She gave a weak smile.

"Let me get you something to drink," Mr. Gardiner said. He did not wait for a reply, but promptly stood and walked away.

As Elizabeth and her aunt talked, Elizabeth looked about the room. She noticed Jane and Mr. Bingley standing off in a corner of the room talking. It reminded her of the times in Hertfordshire when they first met. She was truly pleased for her; Jane's happiness was of utmost importance to her. She would try not to regret what might have been with Mr. Darcy. It would not be easy, however.

She glanced around the room again, but did not see Mr. Rickland. She surmised he must have returned to the gaming room. She noticed Miss Strathern dancing with a rather handsome gentleman. Perhaps she had forgotten about Mr. Darcy, as well.

Mr. Gardiner returned, handing Elizabeth a glass of punch. "I think, my dear Lizzy, when you have finished your drink, we ought to depart. Do you mind leaving early?"

Elizabeth shook her head. "No. Mr. Rickland is off somewhere, although I suppose we ought to find him to properly take our leave. I see the Underwoods on the dance floor."

Mrs. Gardiner nodded her head towards Jane and Mr. Bingley. "And those two can continue their conversation anywhere."

Elizabeth laughed. "I have no doubt of that, Aunt. I believe they have continued their conversations from almost six months ago as if it were yesterday!"

"I shall see if they are ready to take their leave." Mr. Gardiner walked over to the couple.

Elizabeth finished her drink and stood up. She heard her name again and turned to see Mr. Rickland, who came and stood beside her.

"I hope I can convince you to dance a second with me. I would not wish you to do so if you are in any pain, but I so enjoyed my time with you."

Elizabeth began to open her mouth to thank him and tell him they were about to leave, when she heard another voice behind her.

"I believe she still has a dance promised to me."

Elizabeth spun around to see Mr. Darcy standing there. Her heart suddenly felt as though it had jumped into her throat.

"What are *you* doing here?" both Elizabeth and Mr. Rickland asked at the same time.

Darcy gave a slight shrug of his shoulders. "I received an invitation. I only regret I was not able to arrive earlier."

Elizabeth's mouth was open, but she could not trust herself to say anything. When she felt the stinging of tears in her eyes threatening to spill, she steeled herself to breathe slowly and remain calm.

"I assume, Miss Bennet," he said, "you have already danced with Mr. Rickland?"

She nodded mutely, wondering why she could not think of a

single word to say.

"Did you not promise me a dance when we were at Rosings?"

Again she nodded.

The music began, and Mr. Darcy extended his elbow. "Shall we?"

Elizabeth took his arm, hoping he would not notice her shaking, and she soon found herself facing him on the dance floor. She needed to say something, but all that came to mind was, again, "What *are* you doing here?"

They stepped forward at the start of the dance and grasped hands. "Must you always greet me in that manner?" He gave a slight smile and shook his head. "Shall you ever be able to greet me properly? A simple 'Good evening' would suffice."

Elizabeth felt both mortified and elated as they turned to spin with their neighbouring partners, which gave her a few moments to think.

They came back together. "Pray forgive me. Good evening, Mr. Darcy, but are you not here with Miss de Bourgh?"

"Anne?" He was obviously taken aback.

"I... we understood you had gone off to Gretna Green with her."

Darcy's jaw dropped, and he raised his brows. "Truly?" He shook his head. "Rumours travel ridiculously fast and... quite erroneously."

Elizabeth almost laughed in relief. "Charlotte... Mrs. Collins wrote to me."

"Ah, that would certainly account for it."

They took a few more turns with different partners, but when they came back together, he merely replied, "As you can see, I am here and not in Gretna Green."

Elizabeth felt a wave of joy flood her, but she still had so many questions.

As they took another turn together, he said softly, "You look lovely this evening, Miss Bennet."

"Thank you." Elizabeth felt her cheeks warm, and she gave her head a slight shake. "*What* are you doing here, Mr. Darcy?"

"We are back to that, I see." He looked in Rickland's direction. "Perhaps I have come to rescue you again."

Elizabeth eyed him suspiciously and then turned to look at the gentleman who was watching them closely. "What is it you have against Mr. Rickland? What is it you would wish to warn me about him?"

"What makes you think I wish to warn you about him?"

"Because you mentioned..." Elizabeth's eyes widened as she realized what she was about to say.

"I mentioned... what?"

"Nothing." She tightened her jaw so hard it hurt. She and Mr. Darcy parted again. When they came back together, she said, "I have seen something in you that looks like animosity towards him. Actually, from both of you."

Darcy's brows pinched together. "There is something I would tell you, but now is not the time, and this is not the place."

They grasped hands as they walked down the line of dancers. His hands felt warm and secure, making Elizabeth unable to determine if she wished more to pull her hands from his grasp or be drawn into his arms.

"Will you promise me something?" Darcy asked, a pleading look on his face.

"I shall first have to hear what it is you would have me promise."

He gently squeezed her hands, causing her to feel slightly dizzy. "If Mr. Rickland asks to see you tomorrow, would you tell him you have a previous engagement? I wish to come and speak with you." He looked at her pointedly. "It is imperative."

There was something in his look that told her he still cared and wanted nothing more than to ensure her well-being.

She wanted to tell him about the letter, the book, and the change in her feelings towards him. She smiled to herself, however, as she thought of Mr. Darcy's earlier words: *Now is not the time, and this is not the place.*

She still did not know what had happened with Miss de Bourgh, but she knew she would likely find out the next day. It seemed quite evident he was not engaged, and certainly not married, which gave her heart a reason to leap with great joy.

The dance continued with little additional conversation, but as it was about to end, Elizabeth noticed Darcy start. She followed the direction of his gaze and saw Miss Strathern on the other side of the room. She suddenly felt a stab of jealousy, wondering what truly was between Mr. Darcy and the beautiful young lady.

He seemed somewhat disconcerted, but politely escorted Elizabeth back to her party. Just before they reached them, she looked up at him and gave him an encouraging smile. "You asked me to promise not to see Mr. Rickland before seeing you again. Mr. Darcy. I promise I will not."

Chapter 27

After escorting Elizabeth to her aunt and uncle, Mr. Darcy spoke briefly with them, gave a short bow, and then thanked her again for the dance. He stepped away, and she did not see him again for the remainder of the evening. Mr. Rickland, however, would not leave her side, pleading for permission to call on her the following day. When she told him that would be impossible, as they already had plans, he pleaded for the next. She said she would likely be available to see him then.

Mrs. Gardiner overheard the conversation and sent her niece a questioning look. Elizabeth could readily see her aunt musing that perhaps Mr. Darcy played a part in this unknown 'engagement' that had prompted her to offer such an excuse. She knew her aunt would wait to inquire until they had some time alone together.

They took their leave soon after, thanking the Underwoods for the delightful evening. Mr. Bingley expressed to the others how pleased and surprised he was to see his good friend make an appearance at the ball. He had been able to speak with him for a few minutes before he departed. Bingley then inquired whether the two men could pay a call on the morrow. Mrs. Gardiner looked to Elizabeth to see if those plans she mentioned to Mr. Rickland would preclude this visit.

"I know of no pressing engagements," Elizabeth said with a smile. She was glad both men would come. She was pleased for Jane, and eager to find out what Mr. Darcy would say about Anne, Mr. Rickland, and especially, himself.

~~*

Elizabeth had no idea what to expect the next day. She had told her aunt what Mr. Darcy had said as they danced, and how he gave her another vague warning regarding Mr. Rickland. While she was curious about what he had to say concerning him, she was more interested in hearing about Anne de Bourgh. That they were not married was certain, but Elizabeth's greatest concern was whether he still possessed the love for herself she had for him. Yes, she had come to love him.

She could not think of him without her pulse quickening, her cheeks warming, and a slight feeling of breathlessness. She had never known what it was to be in love, but she felt these were some of the indications. In addition to those physical signs, she could not stop thinking about him. She had slept more soundly that night. While she still had questions, she did not have the pressing anguish she had the night before.

The men arrived promptly at ten o'clock. They chatted with the ladies and Mr. Gardiner, and then Mr. Bingley suggested they take a stroll about the neighbourhood, as the weather was so lovely.

Mr. and Mrs. Gardiner approved his suggestion, saying it was a delightful idea, but declined to go themselves. Elizabeth hoped Mr. Darcy had not seen the quick wink Mr. Gardiner sent in her direction.

As they walked out, Mr. Darcy seemed overly concerned about Elizabeth's foot. She assured him she was feeling quite well, even after all the dancing the night before.

"If you need a slower pace, please tell me. Mr. Bingley and your sister might wish to walk more quickly."

"We do not mind walking slowly," Jane offered.

Elizabeth realized what Mr. Darcy was trying to accomplish. "No, please do not feel you must wait on us. I believe I ought to take a bit more care as I walk."

It had not been necessary for Mr. Darcy to make that suggestion, as Mr. Bingley and Jane soon forgot their companions as they strode briskly up the street.

Darcy walked with his hands casually clasped behind him. Elizabeth clasped her hands in front, her fingers nervously knitting together. She stole a glance up at him; the sunlight danced on his fine features. Despite not being able to read his countenance, she was struck anew with how handsome he was. It almost took her breath away.

Once Bingley and Jane were a good distance ahead of them,

Mr. Darcy spoke. "I imagine you have some questions." He looked down at her with a smile, which helped calm her unsettled nerves.

Elizabeth nervously laughed. "I have many questions, but I know not where to even begin."

"Shall we begin with Anne?"

Elizabeth nodded. "Since you are here, I assume you did not set out for Gretna Green with her as everyone suspected."

He shook his head and chuckled. "It was not my intent to deceive anyone. In fact, I did not know a letter had been written and left behind. Anne must be to blame for that."

"She was eager to give the illusion the two of you were going to elope?"

He nodded. "She is in love with another," He gave her a pointed look and a knowing smile. "But you already knew that."

A shiver passed through Elizabeth at the look he bestowed upon her. "Yes."

"She was relieved I had not come to ask for her hand. I went to her first, so her mother was never aware of my real intent. Anne devised this plan. It kept me in Kent a day longer than I had anticipated, but Anne felt this was the only way. She knew if her mother believed we had run off to Gretna Green together, she would at first be angry, but would soon be pleased, thinking her daughter and I were finally going to marry."

"You left so abruptly…"

"I knew I had to settle the situation with her once and for all. I could not leave her waiting any longer. When I told her I could not marry her, you can imagine my surprise when she told me she loved another. I knew nothing about Mrs. Jenkinson's son." He looked down at her and smiled. "She told me about her book, as well, and that she had told you she was an author." He shook his head. "Little did I know as you were smiling and reading that book in the carriage, you were reading about Anne and me."

"Yes. It was quite diverting and enlightening." Elizabeth chuckled. "And in reading the book, I was able to deduce she loved Mr. Jenkinson."

Mr. Darcy smiled. "And we all wondered how that book appeared in the carriage. Anne placed it there the morning we departed."

"She is remarkably clever."

"She hoped either you or I would read it."

"I assume you brought her to London to meet Mr. Jenkinson? Did they truly go to Gretna Green?"

He let out a soft chuckle. "Yes, they left almost immediately with Mrs. Jenkinson. Despite being old enough to marry without her mother's consent, she and Mr. Jenkinson wished to marry quickly and not have to wait for the banns to be read. Anne feared someone might find them and try to stop them." He laughed softly. "She has finally made a decision of her own that went against her mother's wishes. It is about time she did. I shall be off in a few days to inform my aunt of the truth."

"I do not envy you. How do you suppose she will react to this news?"

Darcy gave a slight shrug of his shoulders. "I shall arm myself with my pistol in the event I need it." He smiled down at her. "No, I shall know how to handle my aunt. When they return, I will advise Anne and her new husband what *they* can expect from her mother."

Elizabeth raised a single brow. "You did not object to her marrying someone who was not quite her equal in rank?"

"I knew she would receive enough disapproval from her mother." His hand went up to rub his jaw. "His relations are not so decidedly beneath Anne's. His father was a gentleman with a manor and land in the country. It is only unfortunate Mr. Jenkinson was not the eldest son, thereby receiving only a moderate inheritance."

"Will that improve your aunt's opinion of the young man?"

"Hardly. She will likely despise everything about him and question his intentions, which at first I confess I did, but I do not now. I have known his mother for many years and do not believe she would allow Anne to marry someone who had scheming motives – even her own son."

Elizabeth smiled up at him. "Miss de Bourgh must be grateful for your approval."

"With or without my approval, it will not be easy for them. My aunt will do everything in her power to make things difficult for them." He gave his head a toss. "Of course, Anne has a rather large dowry and Rosings does belong to her."

"Would she wish to live there?"

"Not unless her mother makes some greatly needed changes, especially concerning the manner in which she treats Anne. Of course, when my aunt dies..." Darcy's voice trailed off.

Elizabeth finished his thought. "It will be hers to do as she wishes."

Darcy nodded and stopped at the corner. The street was filling up with merchants calling out their wares, people bustling to and fro, and horses conveying carriages at a hurried pace. Darcy extended his arm, and Elizabeth readily took it. Instead of continuing on, he turned. "There is a small park in this direction. I would feel more comfortable continuing our conversation where there are fewer people to eavesdrop. We can meet Bingley and your sister back at the house."

They continued on in silence until they reached the park. It was Darcy who spoke first.

"Now, unless you have more questions about Anne, I suppose you wish to hear what I have to say about Rickland and the purpose of my warning last evening."

Elizabeth bit her lip and closed her eyes for a moment. Her heart raced, but she knew now was the time for her admission. "Not quite yet. I have something I must tell you."

Mr. Darcy's face grew sombre. "What is it?"

"A confession, actually." Elizabeth drew in a long breath. "I... you see... on the day of my accident... you see... I...the reason I fell..."

"Miss Elizabeth, I have never seen you at such a loss for words. What can possibly account for this?"

Elizabeth shook her head. She withdrew her hand from his arm and opened her reticule, pulling out his letter, where she had placed it earlier. "I believe this is yours." She handed it to him, holding her breath as she did so, and feeling her face flush with warmth.

Darcy looked down and took it, slowly unfolding it. Elizabeth noticed only a slight faltering of his steps and a sharp intake of breath when he realized what it was.

When he did not look up or say anything, Elizabeth began to feel uneasy. "It was the reason I fell. I was paying more attention to your words than where my feet were taking me. I had no idea..." Her voice trailed off. "Pray, forgive me."

He rubbed his jaw as he continued to read, his eyes fixed to the stationery.

"I should never have read it. I saw my name..."

Darcy finally looked up. "I could not recall all I wrote, but I recollected enough to fear the implications if this fell into someone's hands. It was personal, particularly regarding the... attachment of my affections."

"As I said, it was so wrong of me to read it."

Darcy stopped and turned. "Miss Elizabeth, please do not berate yourself. If anyone was to find it, I am actually grateful it was you."

He rubbed his jaw, as he seemed to contemplate what this meant. Suddenly his eyes widened. "You had already read the letter, then, when we were on our way to London?"

She nodded silently. "I know you did not intend for me to see it."

Darcy shook his head and put up his hand. "Please, Miss Bennet. It is I who must apologize. It must have been excessively disconcerting for you to read... this." He waved the letter through the air. "I would never have wished you to feel uncomfortable."

Elizabeth was silent for a moment. "I did not feel uncomfortable. I was more astonished. I had not a single suspicion of your..." Her voice trailed off, and she let out a huff.

"Ardent admiration?"

Elizabeth came to a stop, and they looked at each other without saying a word. By the look in his eyes, Elizabeth felt if they were not in a public place, he would lean over and kiss her. Just as he had said he wished to do in the letter.

At length, a nanny rushed past them after her charge, breaking the spell of the moment. They turned and continued walking. Very softly, he asked, "May I inquire, other than astonishment, what else you thought as you read it?"

Suddenly her mouth was dry. She swallowed and licked her lips. "I began to wonder if I truly knew who you were." She let out a nervous laugh. "It may not have been immediate, but I began to look upon you quite differently, especially after your chivalrous rescue. It was also quite noble of you to make all the arrangements for me to accompany you and Colonel Fitzwilliam to London, knowing how I felt about you. Those circumstances helped me to see another side of you. That is, of course, until you confessed your final transgression to us in the carriage." She cast a slightly apologetic look up at him. "It angered me that you had kept my sister's presence in London from Mr. Bingley."

"I am not proud of that. It was wrong of me to interfere in such a way."

Elizabeth quickly reached out for the letter, snatching it from his fingers.

"What are you doing?"

"You wrote this letter to me. I am taking my rightful ownership of it." She challenged him with a smile, which he readily returned.

He began tapping the fingers of his hand against his leg. "And Anne's book? I have not read it, but she was glad you had begun reading it. She thought it might give you a better understanding of who I am."

Elizabeth chuckled. "Indeed, it has. Your cousin knows you well and admires you a great deal."

He came to a stop and looked down at her. "And what about yourself?"

There was a short silence in which Elizabeth felt she could pour her feelings out to him; feelings that had altered so dramatically. She bit her lip and breathed in deeply to try to calm her erratically beating heart. "I have come to realize how misguided I have been in my estimation of your character."

He took in a deep breath. "And...?"

"I... my feelings are now quite the opposite of what they had been."

He smiled and reached for her hand.

Elizabeth was not certain she could formulate another word. As she took in a breath, she trembled. Finally, she said, "In your letter you expressed a subtle warning about Mr. Rickland and then again during our dance last evening. I am now ready to hear about him."

Darcy drew himself erect. "Rickland and I had not seen each

other for several years, but I had heard nothing of him to cause me concern. Within the first few days of our having arrived at Rosings, my aunt's steward, Mr. Lowell, asked to speak with me about him. He informed me that he and Rickland had been in discussions about his manor. Rickland's steward had recently departed – quite abruptly – and he was left with no one to manage it. Lowell was concerned and was at a loss to know what precipitated this. On the day Fitzwilliam and I first departed Rosings, he received a letter from Rickland's former steward. He was told Rickland had gambled away a great deal of money and was being sought by creditors. His steward had left his position in anger over such recklessness. Lowell informed me of this when I met with him the evening we returned, after your fall."

"It is unfortunate many men get caught up in that vice."

"Yes," Darcy said, nodding his head slowly. "But there is more, and it grieves me to inform you of this."

Elizabeth stopped. "What is it?"

Darcy drew in a deep breath. "Apparently Rickland returned to London for several days after he had been at Rosings for a time. He returned the day before Fitzwilliam and I arrived."

"Yes, he said he had some business here."

"Well, the business was nothing more than a high stakes card game."

"Oh."

"Unfortunately, that is not all." He nudged her to begin walking again. "This news did not reach me until yesterday, when I returned from Rosings. It is the reason why I decided to make an appearance at the Underwoods' ball."

"You have me intrigued."

"That is an appropriate word, considering the circumstances."

Elizabeth could not imagine what had him so concerned. "Pray, continue."

"A friend of mine was also at this card game. He wrote me a letter describing the events that took place at his table. He sent the letter to Pemberley, and it only recently arrived at my home in town." Darcy paused for a moment and shook his head. "He heard my name mentioned by two men seated by him and listened closely to what they were saying."

"*Two* men?"

Darcy nodded. Elizabeth felt his body tense in anger. "Rickland and Wickham."

Elizabeth abruptly stopped. "They are acquainted?"

"I know not when they first met, but it was most likely owing to their mutual acquaintance of me... and their common interest in gambling."

Elizabeth could readily see the anger masked behind his features. "I see. What did your friend say they talked about?"

Darcy reached in his pocket for the letter and handed it to Elizabeth. "Now I have a letter I would ask you to read. I think it would be best for you to read his own words."

Chapter 28

Elizabeth released Darcy's arm and took the letter, looking from him down to the words.

Darcy~

I hope this letter finds you well, but more than that, I hope it comes into your hands in a timely manner. I overheard some men talking about you and thought it would be prudent of me to inform you of a scheme they became involved in. I was in a high stakes card game. (No need to rebuke me, I know my faults!) They were seated to my right, next to each other. Fortunately, they knew not who I was or that I was acquainted with you.

The two men were Rickland and Wickham. Rickland, it seemed, had been at the home of his (and your) aunt and was expecting your arrival any day. Wickham disparaged you to Rickland, claiming the two of you had been in the same neighbourhood this past autumn, much to his chagrin.

But it was the mention of another person – a lady – that drew my concern. A Miss Bennet, if I recollect correctly. Apparently, both were acquainted with her and agreed she was a lovely, lively, and delightfully engaging young lady.

Wickham seems to have an all-consuming dislike of you, Darcy, and encouraged Rickland to do all he could to secure this lady's affections, believing that you, Darcy, may have a particular interest in her.

Elizabeth was filled with anger as she read these words, chiding herself for being taken in by both of these men. She could not believe even George Wickham had seen Mr. Darcy's admiration for her, while she had not. She was at a loss to explain this odd turn of events and turned her eyes back down to the page.

Rickland was more than willing to do Wickham's bidding. He told Wickham he was already greatly enjoying her company, but he would do more to secure her affections, if needed, once you arrived.

I am well aware, good friend, if you have your heart set on this particular lady, she must be exceptional, as no lady has ever tempted you in the slightest – even Miss Strathern.

Elizabeth's heart warmed at the thought that it was she, and she alone, who had touched Mr. Darcy's heart. But she was also curious about what his feelings for this Miss Strathern might have been. She had not been able to dismiss the young lady's perfect features, exquisite dress, and golden hair, and she wondered about her relationship with Mr. Darcy, especially perceiving the beauty's keen interest when she had questioned Mr. Rickland about him. She looked up. "Miss Strathern? I believe she was at the ball last evening."

Darcy drew in a deep breath, and Elizabeth noticed a slight flush infuse his features. "Yes, I saw her. She is... merely an acquaintance. There was a lot of meaningless speculation earlier this year..."

"She is quite lovely. I do not think I have seen a more beautiful woman, even Jane." Elizabeth stole a glance up at Darcy. "She asked Mr. Rickland about you at the ball last evening, thinking you would attend."

Darcy brought up a fist and pounded his chin. "Did she? I wonder if Rickland put her up to it." He shook his head. "Not that she would willingly agree to participate in his scheme, but I would imagine he might have been able to orchestrate her coming to him with her question so you would hear her and believe there was something between us." He pinched his brows. "He likely led her to believe I was going to make an appearance, when he truly did not think I would."

"The man is incorrigible!" Elizabeth said, grasping tightly the letter in her hand.

"I did not stay long at the ball after I saw you. That was, after all, my reason for attending, and, I have to confess...." He slowly shook his head as he looked down. "I was able to make my exit without her being aware of my presence there."

Elizabeth turned away from him, for she could not prevent the smile from forming on her face.

When he said nothing more, Elizabeth looked back down to

the letter she nearly crumpled. Her hands began to tremble as she considered he had attached his affections to her when this seemingly perfect young lady obviously had hoped he would return her ardent feelings. She continued to read.

At the end of the game, Rickland had lost most of his money. Wickham decided to add a little incentive to his proposal by providing the man with more banknotes, either to pocket or to feed the pot. Wickham departed, as did I. What Rickland did, I have no idea.

I know not whether this information is even of interest to you, but I greatly dislike hearing someone I so respect being vilified. I hope these two men will do nothing more than plot and scheme, and their plans will come to naught.

Always~
Marshall Stalling

Elizabeth stopped and held out the letter to Mr. Darcy. He reached for it, and their fingers touched briefly. She felt a shiver that travelled down to her toes, and she glanced up at him. Mr. Darcy's eyes were upon her, regarding her with tenderness. She pressed her hand to her throat, feeling both the warmth of his gaze, as well as anger towards the two men.

She let out a long, mournful sigh. "How can men be so deceitful?"

"I assume you are including me in your question?"

"Mr. Darcy, I know you are not deceitful by nature, as these two men apparently are. I trust you would never resort to something like this." She was silent for a moment while she considered her next words. "You have actually been quite gracious towards me this morning, particularly after I admitted to reading your letter. You have been gracious *and* forthright. I know it cannot be easy – when I abused you so to your face – to acknowledge you... you..."

"Ardently admire and love you?"

Elizabeth's breath caught. To hear him speak those words was very different from reading them on paper. She did not trust herself to speak, so she merely nodded, encouraging him with a smile.

He looked down at Elizabeth, a rather sly look on his face. "You are surprised to hear me speak so freely about my feelings of admiration for you." He smiled. "There is a reason I would be so brave."

"And what is that, Mr. Darcy?"

"Some information I received yesterday." He took her hand and tucked it in his elbow. "I understand you paid Mr. Jenkinson a call."

"Yes." Elizabeth's heart began to race as she futilely attempted to recollect all she said to the publisher. "I thought he ought to know about you and Miss de Bourgh. As I thought you had gone to ask for her hand, I wanted him to know in case there was anything he could do."

"So he told us. I thought it odd you would have gone to the trouble to find him." Darcy paused, biting his lip. "I thought perhaps... Was that the only reason you sought him out?"

A rush of feelings flooded her, making it difficult for her to think clearly. She could barely consider anything other than the warm sensation his touch evoked.

Elizabeth felt her cheeks grow warm. She looked down. "I knew there would be several unhappy people if you proposed to your cousin."

"Yes?"

They continued walking silently for a moment, and then he added, "I had rather hoped..." Darcy swallowed hard and gave his head a shake. He turned and faced her. "Miss Bennet, I do not know if either Mr. Jenkinson or I misinterpreted some things you said to him when you visited him, but..." He drew in a deep breath. "I have to confess what he told me gave me hope when I had no other assurances whatsoever."

He looked down and began gently stroking her hand. "Tell me, did you truly say to him you would like more time to find out the nature of your feelings for me? Do I have reason to hope you are no longer resolute in your censure of me?"

Elizabeth could barely breathe. "I cannot recall all I said to him, but I believe I may have said something to that effect." She stopped and faced Mr. Darcy, her heart pounding so powerfully she felt her whole being shake with each beat. Smiling, she placed her free hand upon his for a brief moment, giving it a gentle squeeze. "I do know, however, when I said there would be several unhappy people if you proposed to Miss de Bourgh, I could readily count four: you, Miss de Bourgh, Mr. Jenkinson, and lastly, myself."

"You cannot know how grateful I am to hear that, but I must ask that you allow me to right the wrongs I committed."

"You have already done so much towards that end, Mr. Darcy."

He shook his head. "Not enough. In these past few days I have had time to deliberate on my behaviour. Whilst riding to and returning from Rosings, my mind worked incessantly. I was either berating myself for all I had done or reliving every moment with you and examining what I ought to have done differently."

"Perhaps we both needed to learn some things about ourselves and each other," Elizabeth said.

"I discovered that not only did I make no effort to display open and inviting manners to your family and friends in Hertfordshire, I was guilty of the very thing of which I accused your sister in her behaviour towards Bingley. I realized I displayed no outward signs of affection for you and was wrong to presume you were aware of my affections. I was even more mistaken to believe you welcomed them." He gave his head a shake.

Elizabeth raised her brows and pinched her lips together in a smile.

Darcy shook his head. "I know what you are thinking."

"Do you indeed?" she laughed.

With a nod, Darcy said, "You are thinking that even if my feelings had been displayed openly, you would not have welcomed them."

"You may be correct. I fear I was prejudiced against you; convinced you exhibited nothing but arrogance and pride. I could see nothing beyond that." She looked up at him with regret in her eyes. "I was very wrong."

Darcy smiled and drew in a breath. "Come, let us walk."

~~*

They continued to stroll quietly about the park. They had drawn so close to each other they touched from their shoulders down to the occasional brushing together of their legs as they walked.

Mr. Darcy felt a strong connection to Elizabeth even in the silence. He almost refrained from speaking, fearing it would break the spell. But there was something else he wished to tell her. "You asked last evening if I had gone to Rosings to finally offer for Anne."

Elizabeth looked up at him. Her brows were knit together. "I thought perhaps you had. I *feared* you had." She looked at him oddly. "Why did you suddenly decide to go?"

"My object in going to Anne served a different purpose. My feelings for you have remained as constant and strong as they were when I wrote the letter. By the time we arrived in London, I felt... I hoped your opinion of me had improved. I could not, however, in all good faith, make any attempt to secure your affections while I had the expected marriage between Anne and myself hovering over us. I needed to finally settle this matter with my cousin – and her mother. I had no idea how either would respond to my declaration, but I felt it had to be done before I could confess my feelings for you." He began to rub his chin. "I had no notion you already were aware of my feelings, and I also knew there was no guarantee of your ever returning them."

He watched as Elizabeth grasped the import of his words. Her mouth opened, but she remained silent. Finally, she sighed and whispered a soft, "Oh."

Darcy clenched his jaw. "When I saw Rickland with you at your aunt and uncle's home, gloating about his promised dance with you, I knew I had to do something, even if it was merely to warn you about him. I knew it might afford you no pleasure to hear such words against him from me, but I was determined to leave you in no doubt of his reckless living." Lowering his head, he said softly, "Yet I knew I had no right to do or say anything until I had spoken with Anne."

"I hardly know what to say. That was quite honourable of you, Mr. Darcy."

Shaking his head, he said, "No. The conversation with Anne should have been had years ago. Every year I determined to have that dreaded discussion, but I always left without saying anything."

He sombrely shook his head. "There was one time I came close to telling her…"

"In the turret!" exclaimed Elizabeth.

Darcy stopped and turned to look at her. "Yes! How did you know?"

A smile graced her lips. "Miss de Bourgh wrote about it in her book. If I remember correctly, she quickly changed the subject."

"That she did. I was aware she knew what I was going to say and she did not wish to hear it. That was last year. It made it more difficult this year for me to bring up the subject."

"She claims to have released you from the hold you had on her heart after that incident." Elizabeth said softly. "It was soon after that time she met Mr. Jenkinson and they fell in love."

As they continued to walk, Elizabeth suddenly said, "Mrs. Beckett!"

Darcy looked down at her and then around. "What? Do you see her?"

"No, no," Elizabeth said with a light laugh. "But I do not think she is as hard of hearing as we were led to believe."

"Why do you say that?"

"Because she said something to me before you departed my aunt and uncle's house."

Darcy stopped again, surprised, thinking of what Mrs. Beckett had said to him. "What did she say to you?"

"She said you were the most excellent man she has ever known." Elizabeth waved her hand through the air. "I thought it quite peculiar. It was so unexpected."

"I can see why you would think that, but she is a little biased, as I did hire her son. He is a little slow, and I do not think he would have secured a good position elsewhere. He likely would have been taken advantage of… or worse."

"That was so very kind of you."

Darcy shrugged. "It was the least I could do. She has had to put up with my aunt for these many years." He shook his head. "She is moving to London so she can be near her son."

"I am glad to hear that, but rest assured, Mr. Darcy, I did not think *what* she said was peculiar, but *that* she said it." Elizabeth laughed. "She must have heard us! Despite being deaf, she knew I was angry with you."

They were silent again until Darcy spoke. "She said something to me, as well."

Elizabeth looked up. "She did?"

Darcy nodded. "She told me I had to show you the good man I was by atoning for my offences." He squeezed Elizabeth's hand. "I had already decided I would bring Bingley to see your sister and would warn your father and Colonel Forster about Wickham. The third thing – going to Anne – came to me as a revelation when I saw Rickland with you. I was living a deception as bad as his, as long as I remained silent and did not let Anne know what my intentions were – or were not."

Elizabeth smiled up at him. "I cannot thank you enough for all you have done. I know it could not have been convenient or easy for you to ride to Hertfordshire to warn them about Mr. Wickham."

Now it was Darcy's turn to smile, for all he could think of was her mother offering him Elizabeth's room and the use of her bed. He did not dare mention that. "Your father and I had a pleasant discussion, and we enjoyed an excellent dinner. In addition your mother was well behaved."

"Yes," Elizabeth suddenly giggled. "My father most likely gave her a strict warning. I am certain you must have been quite appalled, however, when she offered to let you stay the night in my room!"

"You heard about that?"

"Oh, yes. Father told us in his letter."

"Well, I have to confess the offer did have some appeal to it." He kept looking straight ahead, but he noticed Elizabeth glance up at him. He also felt her arm shake and attributed it to another laugh, silent this time.

Elizabeth cast her gaze down. "I know you believed, when you wrote your warning about Mr. Rickland in your letter, that if you tried to caution me about him I would accuse you of interfering. I had no idea, of course, to what evils you were referring, but I would have you know I have thought about it a great deal since reading your letter. Your vague warning actually tempered any admiration I may have felt for the man."

"Did it?" He let out a satisfied sigh. "Of course when I read my friend's letter about how he and Wickham had schemed, I was even more determined to separate him from you. Needless to say when I left you at the dance, I was grateful you would not see him until after I talked with you."

Darcy began tapping his fingers on his leg again. "Will you... will you see him again?"

"He is to pay us a call on the morrow."

"Is he?"

"You have no need to worry he shall in any way deceive me again." She looked up at him intently. "I am grateful you informed me of his true nature and intentions." She then looked to the ground. "You know enough of my frankness – after abusing you so abominably to your face – that I am not averse to speaking my mind to someone, letting them know my decided opinion of them."

Darcy covered Elizabeth's fingers with his free hand. "Everything you said to me I deserved."

"No, not all." Elizabeth shook her head. "I was deceived both by my own perception of you and Mr. Wickham's claims."

There was silence as they continued to walk. At length, Elizabeth said, "I know Mr. Bingley is departing for Hertfordshire soon..." She paused and drew in a breath. "Will you remain in town long?"

Darcy entwined his fingers with hers and squeezed her hand gently. "No, unfortunately I cannot. I travel in the morning to speak with Colonel Fitzwilliam's family about Anne, and then will leave for Rosings in the next few days to speak with my aunt. I regret I must return directly to Pemberley once that is behind me. My steward has need of me there."

"I see." Elizabeth lowered her gaze.

Darcy stopped and turned to Elizabeth. "I shall likely be there a month. May I... would you...?" He searched her face as he sought the right words. His heart thundered in his chest as he gazed into Elizabeth's eyes, which no longer held contempt for him. "Bingley is likely asking your sister something of utmost importance as we speak and will probably return to Netherfield directly. If I came to Hertfordshire when my work at Pemberley is complete, what would you think…?"

"I would like that!" Elizabeth's voice cracked, and a smile lit her face.

Darcy felt a great sense of joy well up inside, and he returned her smile. "I am glad."

He gazed into Elizabeth's eyes. His heart swelled, knowing the smile on her face was for him. It was not mocking, teasing, or patronizing, but was a smile of genuine affection. He did not trust himself to move, fearing he might wake up to find all of this had been a dream.

He looked around and then brought both her hands up to his lips, kissing each one gently. He looked down into Elizabeth's lovely face and wished so much to kiss her trembling lips. "Perhaps we ought to return to your aunt and uncle's home. Bingley and your sister may have returned, and they will be wondering where we are."

Chapter 29

When Elizabeth and Mr. Darcy arrived back at the house, Bingley and Jane were sitting in the drawing room with Mr. and Mrs. Gardiner. Jane's face shone with blissful joy, and Mr. Bingley excitedly jumped out of his chair, followed by Mr. Gardiner.

"Ah! You have returned! Splendid!" Mr. Gardiner clasped his hands together and walked to Bingley's side. "These two have something they wish to tell you."

Mr. Bingley reached for Jane's hand and brought her to stand at his side. Elizabeth could not determine who had the widest smile, and she was certain hers was just as broad.

Mr. Bingley looked at Darcy and then back at Elizabeth. "I asked for Miss Bennet's... Jane's hand..."

"And I accepted his offer," Jane finished softly. A pleasing blush tinted her cheeks.

Elizabeth wrapped her sister in a hug, as Darcy gave his friend's hand a congratulatory shake.

"I am delighted!" Elizabeth said as she looked from one to the other.

"I wish you both the best," Darcy said with a smile.

They sat down and began to talk with a great deal of animation about the exciting news. Mr. Bingley had already sent word to have Netherfield opened and ready for his arrival on the morrow. Once there, he would speak with Mr. Bennet.

Jane turned to Elizabeth. "We shall leave in three days. I feel we ought to be there when Mother is told."

"That is an excellent idea, Jane." She lifted her brows knowingly. "For Papa's sake, we ought to return home as soon as we can."

"Yes, but Aunt and I have decided to visit the seamstress tomorrow about my wedding gown. Do you think Mother will mind that she had no say in it? She always likes to be involved in these types of decisions, but I would prefer not to have her with me." She reached for Elizabeth's hand. "Oh! I cannot believe this is happening!"

Elizabeth had to laugh at her sister's most unexpected loquaciousness. "Oh, Jane, I am so happy for you."

The two gentlemen readily accepted Mrs. Gardiner's invitation to stay for dinner. As they conversed for the remainder of the day, Elizabeth observed Mr. Darcy as he spoke with Mr. Gardiner. She was pleased he did not seem to consider her uncle to be beneath him. He appeared genuinely to enjoy his company.

Her aunt sent her questioning looks throughout the afternoon, which Elizabeth silently answered with a sly smile. She knew her aunt was curious about what had been said between her and Mr. Darcy while they were on their walk, but she would wait to discuss it with her in private. She knew, however, her aunt could discern the open and easy manners Mr. Darcy displayed with them – especially with her niece. That, in itself, likely spoke volumes to her.

Mr. Bingley and Jane gave a lively description of how he had asked for her hand. They each had their own perspectives, and Elizabeth had to smile as they kept remembering different things.

"It was busy on the street," Bingley said, "and I suggested we return to the house. My heart was so full, and I needed to think clearly so I could express the depth of my love and affection. I wanted so much to say the right words, but I could barely hear myself think."

"We returned to the house – we did not see you, Lizzy, as we walked back – and we came to the drawing room," Jane explained. "We were not aware Aunt and Uncle Gardiner had stepped out to take a stroll."

"I decided it was the perfect opportunity to get down on my knee and ask for her hand." Mr. Bingley smiled at Jane. "I was delighted she accepted."

"We returned shortly after," Mrs. Gardiner added. "We could not have planned that better had we tried!"

They talked for at least an hour about the proposal, while Elizabeth surmised with a smile the whole event likely lasted less than five minutes.

Elizabeth's joy was complete as she beheld the delight in Jane and Mr. Bingley's faces, as well as knowing Mr. Darcy had done so much for her. She felt the honour of Mr. Darcy's continued affection, as well as his conviction he had to make things right with his cousin before he could even warn her about Mr. Rickland, let alone confess his admiration for her.

It was late in the evening when the gentlemen reluctantly declared they had to take their leave. Mr. Bingley seemed torn between remaining with his betrothed and departing to take care of all that was required of him before returning to the country. Despite being eager to seek an audience with Mr. Bennet, he regretted leaving Jane. He expressed his fervent hope that he would see her soon at Longbourn.

Mr. Darcy remained silent about his own inclination to remain at the Gardiners' longer, but he gently encouraged his friend to linger a little more, assuring him he would have sufficient time on the morrow to arrange for his departure. Mrs. Gardiner stole glances at Elizabeth and gave a sly smile and a lifted brow each time that gentleman assured his friend he would still have plenty of time.

When the men rose to depart, the Gardiners said goodbye and remained in the drawing room. Elizabeth was quite certain it was to allow the two couples an opportunity to have some time alone before they separated.

Jane and Mr. Bingley walked directly to the waiting carriage and stopped, turning to talk quietly with each other. Mr. Darcy gently took Elizabeth's hand and caressed it as he tucked it in his arm. The darkness cloaked them as they stood in the small covered porch. His hand remained fixed on hers.

"I shall miss you, Miss Bennet," he said softly. "I hope you know how much I..." his voice faltered as he took in a breath. "...how much I admire and love you."

Elizabeth did not trust herself to speak, but placed her free hand over his. His hand, warm to the touch, turned and enveloped hers.

Elizabeth felt as if the world was whirling about her. She was grateful for Mr, Darcy's support as he stood next to her. She could feel his strength almost as a pillar, holding her upright.

She opened her mouth to speak, but he spoke again.

"I have spoken to Bingley about my feelings for you." He squeezed her hand again. "He was quite delighted." He paused for a moment. "My affections are seriously attached to you, and I must assure you my intentions are sincere."

Elizabeth's heart beat so forcefully she could barely hear herself think. She drew in a slow breath and said, "I appreciate how difficult it must be for you to speak so openly of the feelings and affections you have for me." She stole a sly glance up at him and smiled softly. "And then there was the letter." A quaver crept into Elizabeth's voice. "Pray, allow me to declare what my feelings are for you."

She felt him stiffen, but he quickly relaxed. He pressed his fingers to her lips. "Not now. I would not want you to rush your judgment of my character. I think there is still too much you may find wanting."

She could hear regret weighing down his words and knew he was feeling all the shame of his actions.

"Perhaps when you come to Hertfordshire in a month, we can begin anew," Elizabeth suggested with a smile. Her mouth was dry, but she needed to continue. . "I shall oblige you and wait, but I would have you know I look forward to beginning a new sketch of your character, having thrown out the first one."

Mr. Darcy chuckled. "Along with the letter, I hope."

Elizabeth tilted her head. "Oh, no, Mr. Darcy. I insist on keeping that letter. It had the greatest influence on several circumstances. I could never part with it."

"Truly?"

Elizabeth nodded. "Had you not written and lost it, I would not have found it. I would not have been reading it, which was the reason I fell. There would have been no rescue when you returned for your satchel and no ride together to London. That letter is the reason you and I are standing here together – most amicably – this very moment."

"Yes, and alone in the dark." His voice was husky, and he suddenly wrapped his hands about hers. He brought her hands to her lips. "We shall begin again in Hertfordshire, Miss Bennet, but I pray you would forgive me for this indulgence to keep you in my heart and thoughts while we are apart." He kissed both of her hands and then lowered them. He stood silently before her and then leaned down quickly and placed a warm, tender kiss on her cheek.

Elizabeth shivered as his lips touched her face, despite the warmth that flooded her.

When he pulled away, he looked at her as he continued to squeeze her hands within his. "Might I ask of you a favour, Miss Bennet?" he asked in almost a whisper.

"Of course," she said softly. Elizabeth was certain her heart pounded louder than her words.

"Other than your closest family, I would ask that you not speak of my feelings to anyone. I wish to speak with my sister, and I will not be seeing her for nearly a week."

"It shall remain our secret, Mr. Darcy." Elizabeth reassured him warmly. "As long as I can inform my aunt and uncle... and Jane, of course."

He gave a nod of approval.

"Would I be correct in assuming you would not have me inform Mr. Rickland, either?" She gave him a teasing smile.

He let out a low grumble. "He deserves to know this scheme he and Wickham concocted has failed, but he shall find out in due time." He shook his head. "No, if you can avoid mentioning it to him, I would appreciate it. I would not have you tell him an outright lie, however. If he asks a direct question, I suppose you must answer."

"I would enjoy seeing his reaction, but I shall not mention it."

"Good." He released her hands and gently touched her lips with his finger. "And I would ask you not be persuaded to believe anything that man may have to say to try to justify his action, or worse yet, make some sort of accusation about me."

"Fear not, Mr. Darcy. I shall know how to deal with him."

They both turned when they heard Mr. Bingley and Jane approach. "Are you ready, good friend?" Bingley asked.

"Yes," he said, gazing longingly at Elizabeth. "I look forward to seeing you soon."

Elizabeth nodded, feeling as though a part of her had been taken when he stepped away and walked towards the carriage.

The two gentlemen finally took their leave, and Jane joined Elizabeth on the portico, where they watched the carriage drive away until it was no longer in sight. Jane's hand rested on her heart, and she let out a long sigh.

"Oh, Lizzy! I am so happy! You cannot know how happy I am." She reached out and took Elizabeth's hand, squeezing it tightly. "I feel as though today has been a dream."

Elizabeth laughed softly. "I assure you, it was not."

Jane pulled Elizabeth back when she turned. "Mr. Bingley said he has not gone one day without thinking of me since he left Netherfield."

"And I would wager the same is true for you, too."

Jane nodded. "He told me he never knew I was in town. His sister never informed him I paid her a call. He said he always intended to return to Netherfield, but family issues prevented it." Jane took in a deep breath. "He said he has loved me all these months and greatly regrets any pain he caused."

Elizabeth smiled despite knowing Mr. Darcy had played a part in the deception. "I always knew he deeply cared for you." She drew Jane to her in a hug. "I am so happy for you. Now, let us go to our aunt and uncle before they retire for the evening."

They stepped back into the house, where they found the Gardiners in the drawing room.

"We wondered when you two ladies would decide to join us again," Mr. Gardiner said as he walked up to Jane and Elizabeth with a broad grin.

Mrs. Gardiner joined them. "We want to hear all the details now the men have departed, and Elizabeth, we are particularly interested in what you and Mr. Darcy talked about earlier." She raised her brows as she finished speaking.

Jane suddenly turned to Elizabeth. "Oh, Lizzy! I had not even thought about you and Mr. Darcy! You must tell us what happened! What did he say?" Jane grasped her sister's hand. "I am so sorry; I have been thinking only of myself."

"You need not concern yourself, Jane. You have had enough on your mind."

"Well, ladies, shall we sit down and hear what Lizzy has to say?" Mr. Gardiner gave his nieces a knowing smile. "Although judging by Mr. Darcy's behaviour tonight, I can certainly guess how it went."

Elizabeth felt her cheeks warm in a blush. "There is much to tell, and Uncle, you are correct. Mr. Darcy owned he still has feelings of affection for me. He leaves on the morrow to visit family before travelling to Pemberley and will then be joining us in Hertfordshire in about a month."

"Oh, Lizzy!" exclaimed Jane. "I am so pleased. Mr. Bingley admires him more than anyone else of his acquaintance."

"We have agreed to begin anew at that time, putting the past and our misunderstandings behind us."

Elizabeth smiled and then told them his reason for going to Rosings, as well as the news Miss de Bourgh and Mr. Jenkinson were travelling to Gretna Green to marry.

"Mr. Darcy is full of surprises," Mrs. Gardiner said.

Elizabeth nodded, absently touching her cheek where he had kissed her. "He is, but he has asked that we do not speak of his affection for me to anyone else until he shares this news with his sister."

Mrs. Gardiner clasped her hands together. "You have our word!"

All sense of joy and contentment departed, however, at the thought of Mr. Rickland. "But there is something else."

"What is it?" Jane asked, a touch of concern in her voice.

"It concerns Mr. Rickland, and why Mr. Darcy wished to warn me about him."

"We are listening." Mr. Gardiner leaned forward in his chair and clasped his hands.

Elizabeth explained how Mr. Darcy learned of Mr. Rickland's excessive gambling, the financial woes of his estate, and his steward leaving his position as a result.

"This is a shame," Mrs. Gardiner said. "The desire to increase one's wealth quickly and with little effort can certainly lead to this unfortunate circumstance."

Elizabeth lowered her head as she rubbed her fingers together. "But there is still more."

"Are you at liberty to tell us?" her uncle asked.

Elizabeth nodded and told them about the letter Mr. Darcy had received from his friend. She gave her shoulders a slight shrug. "Apparently, Mr. Wickham suspected Mr. Darcy had feelings for me and bribed Mr. Rickland to pay particular attention to me. For some reason, he hoped to keep my affections from Mr. Darcy." She pounded her fisted hands onto her lap. "That man!"

"Those *two* men!" Mr. Gardiner exclaimed.

Elizabeth nodded. "Both men!" She took in a breath. "I am so ashamed to think how Mr. Rickland and I enjoyed disparaging Mr. Darcy. We were both a little too eager to lay out his faults."

"Now, Lizzy, do not be too hard on yourself." Mrs. Gardiner patted Elizabeth's shoulder. "You had a prejudice against Mr. Darcy before Mr. Rickland came along."

Elizabeth dropped her head into her hands. "But I should have been more discreet in expressing my opinion of him to someone I hardly knew."

"But Lizzy..." Jane began, looking perplexed. "How did Mr. Wickham know Mr. Darcy had such feelings for you? He was in the company of the two of you but once, and that was only briefly, when we first met him on the streets in Meryton."

Elizabeth narrowed her brows as she looked at her sister. "Was he not...? No, I believe you are correct, Jane." She shook her head. "And I merely wondered how Mr. Wickham had been able to perceive Mr. Darcy's affection towards me when I could not. I can only presume someone else told him of their suspicions – one of his fellow soldiers, perhaps."

Mr. Gardiner stood up and folded his arms across his chest. "Well, however he came to know of it, what he and Rickland did was wrong."

"And I am grateful Mr. Darcy has taken measures to correct some of those grievances you had against him." Mrs. Gardiner smiled at her niece. "His family was always so respected in Lambton. They were kind and generous."

Elizabeth lifted her head. "Yes, it seems he is, as well."

"And am I correct in assuming Mr. Rickland is still to pay us a call tomorrow?" her aunt asked.

Elizabeth nodded.

"I shall send him a scathing note, telling him he is not welcome here and we shall not admit him. He is a disgrace!" Mr. Gardiner announced heatedly.

Elizabeth smiled. "There is no need to do that, Uncle. I wish to see him and tell him to his face what I came to learn of his wretched scheme. I shall enjoy hearing what he has to say and watching his reaction."

"Are you certain, Lizzy?" her aunt asked. "There is no need for you to see him."

"I want to make certain he never does anything like this to anyone again." Elizabeth smiled. "Besides, I need to give him a little dose of what the two of us heaped onto Mr. Darcy. At least allow me that consolation."

~~*

They talked well into the evening. Mr. and Mrs. Gardiner were not altogether certain it would be wise for Elizabeth to see Mr. Rickland, but they did not press her. She assured them she would only tell him what she knew and allow him to feel all the shame of it. She would suggest they go for a walk when he came, and the Gardiners and Jane could follow. That way, they could keep an eye on them.

Elizabeth smiled. "You can observe us, and if you believe Mr. Rickland is in danger of bodily harm, you may step up and suggest to Mr. Rickland it might be best if he were to take his leave."

Mrs. Gardiner gave her a stern warning, tempered by a mischievous smile. "I do not doubt you are angry enough at him to give him quite the verbal lashing, so take care."

"You need not worry, Aunt. Certainly, I was flattered by his attentions, but I never had any deep affection for him. I shall know how to act."

Chapter 30

The next morning, Mr. and Mrs. Gardiner made separate attempts to dissuade their niece from seeing Mr. Rickland, but it was to no avail. She was determined.

He was expected at ten o'clock that morning, which would still allow plenty of time for them to visit the seamstress in the afternoon. As Elizabeth readied herself for his visit, she could not help but recollect how much she had enjoyed spending time with him. She shuddered as she thought that if Mr. Darcy and his cousin had not returned to Rosings when they did, and if she had not fallen, she would have been in Mr. Rickland's company for another week. She might well have found herself in a fair way towards being in love with him.

Lizzy joined her aunt and uncle and sister in the drawing room to await Mr. Rickland's arrival, and Mr. Gardiner's eyes lit up when she walked in. "Ahh! You look lovely, Elizabeth. This young man will certainly regret his behaviour when he realizes he has no hope of securing the respect and affection of such a beautiful, intelligent, and gracious woman."

Elizabeth laughed. "Do not speak too hastily, Uncle. I may prove to be anything but gracious."

"I do not doubt that. I can see that glimmer of mischief in your eyes. And it is not a playful mischief."

The bell rang, interrupting their discussion, and her uncle looked at her. "That is likely the young man himself. I can still send him away, Lizzy."

Elizabeth shook her head. "I want to hear what he has to say for himself."

"All right," Mr. Gardiner said. "Remember, we shall be watching."

Mr. Rickland was shown into the drawing room. He entered, wearing a broad smile, and extended his hand to Mr. Gardiner.

"Good morning, Mr. Gardiner, Mrs. Gardiner." He then looked to Jane and Elizabeth. "It is a pleasure to see you again, Miss Bennet, Miss Elizabeth."

They all greeted Mr. Rickland, and Mrs. Gardiner invited him to sit down. Elizabeth almost laughed as she noted the stiff comportment and stern expressions of her family.

Mr. Rickland clasped his hands together. "I do hope you enjoyed yourselves at the ball. I was disappointed you had to depart so early."

Elizabeth forced a smile. "We did enjoy ourselves and thank you for the invitation. I was not inclined to dance any more, and as my foot was protesting vehemently, we deemed it best to leave."

He pinched his brows together. "I feared it may have been something Darcy said to you. He can be frustratingly critical sometimes." He let out a soft chuckle and looked at her as if he was waiting for a response.

Elizabeth forced a smile and shook her head. She looked down at her fingers, which she angrily knit together. "I cannot recall him being critical about anything, but I think perhaps it was the dance with him that made me realize I truly could not dance another."

Mr. Rickland appeared relieved, and they talked a bit more about the ball. Elizabeth made every attempt to be amiable when she felt anything but that. At length, she turned to Mr. Rickland. "It looks to be a lovely day; would you be inclined to take a stroll about the neighbourhood?"

Mr. Rickland's eyes lit up. "I would enjoy that immensely. It is quite pleasant outside."

As Elizabeth picked up her shawl, Mr. Gardiner said, "You two go on ahead. We shall follow in a moment after I take care of a few things."

"Certainly!" Mr. Rickland's smile and raised brows indicated he realized this would give him an opportunity to walk – and talk – with Elizabeth alone.

The two of them stepped outside, and Mr. Rickland stopped. "Do you have a preference as to which direction you would prefer to go?"

Elizabeth looked both ways, and then pointed to her right. "If we walk in this direction, the sun will not be in our eyes."

"Splendid, although it will be in our eyes on our return."

"Yes," she said, "but when we get to the end of the street, we can cross, and then we will be walking back in the shade." She thought to herself, however, they might return directly if things did not go well.

They walked silently at first. When Mr. Rickland extended his arm for Elizabeth to take, she barely touched it with her fingers, doing so more out of politeness than any desire to hold his arm. She found herself looking away from him, just the opposite of what she had done when she had walked with Mr. Darcy.

At length, he said, "I was surprised to see Darcy make an appearance at the ball. He has never before accepted an invitation from the Underwoods."

"Perhaps he has always had previous engagements and this was the first one he was able to attend. I would imagine he is a busy man."

"I felt it was quite impolitic of him and rude to my godparents for departing as quickly as he did. He left almost as soon as he had arrived."

"Well, as I said before, he likely has many demands on his time."

Rickland grumbled. "He did not even extend the most basic civilities! In addition, he did not pay his addresses to Miss Strathern and her family. They felt slighted when they discovered he had been there and had not sought them out."

Elizabeth noticed he had turned his eyes to her. She tilted her head up towards him. "Miss Strathern?" she asked feigning innocence. "She was the young lady I met, if I recollect correctly."

"Yes, the very one. I believe she even inquired of me about Darcy while I was with you."

"Yes, as a matter of fact, she did." Elizabeth pressed her lips together. She was now certain he somehow arranged it so Miss Strathern would ask about Mr. Darcy in her hearing. "Perhaps he was not aware she was there. After all, it was quite crowded."

Rickland shook his head. "The more I know about the man, the less I am impressed. Miss Strathern has been expecting him to offer for her."

"Truly?" She pinched her brows together. "How can that be

when I understood there was an expected engagement between Miss de Bourgh and him?" She stole a sly glance at him.

He pounded a fist through the air. "That is something else I have never understood about him. As far as I know, that man has never discussed his intentions with Anne, who has been waiting all these years for him to act on that promise. I doubt he will honour the wishes of both his aunt and mother."

Elizabeth wondered whether he knew of the rumours about Mr. Darcy and Miss de Bourgh going off to Gretna Green and asked, "Have you had any news from your aunt recently?"

He let out a laugh. "No. The only time I hear from her is when she has need of something. She often consults with me." He looked at her warmly. "I have to admit, I had not been looking forward to my visit to Rosings this year, but I certainly enjoyed it this time. If I may be so bold as to tell you, your presence was a delightful addition."

Elizabeth said nothing, and she could readily see Mr. Rickland's disappointment that she was not entering into a lively – and flirtatious – conversation. She could feel only shame that he would expect it. He waited a few moments and finally spoke again.

"I was glad to see Mr. Bingley came to the ball with your sister. It is apparent he takes great pleasure in her company."

"We are all delighted in what has transpired."

"He can ill afford to take any more advice from his *good* friend." Rickland let out a sarcastic laugh. "I know not how he calls him friend, and I was surprised to see the two of them conversing at the ball."

Elizabeth gave her shoulders a small shrug. "I believe Mr. Bingley values Mr. Darcy's good judgment, and I imagine he will have no qualms about soliciting his opinion again in the future."

Rickland shook his head. "Then my opinion of Bingley has been greatly diminished. A good friend does not take part in such officious interference, as Darcy did."

They came to the end of the street, and Rickland escorted her across. When they turned to walk back on the other side of the street, Elizabeth saw her aunt and uncle. Jane must have stayed at the house. She nodded her head and smiled at them, and then glanced back at Mr. Rickland.

"And do *you* have a good friend, Mr. Rickland?"

"I have several good friends." He looked at her with a smile. "I think you would enjoy meeting some of them." He began to tap his finger against his chin. "But unlike Bingley's friend, I believe a good friend would..." He paused and gave Elizabeth a meaningful look. "He would give me good advice, not based on false assumptions or his misguided and arrogant presumptions. He would support me in all I do but also be honest with me. Most importantly, he would not take life too seriously and would know how to have a good time."

Elizabeth silently nodded her head. She looked straight ahead and pursed her lips together.

He looked at her with a teasing smile. "Miss Bennet, you are rather serious this morning."

"Perhaps. But if you do not mind, I have another question." She stopped, her anger roused by his accusations. She turned to look up at Rickland with a single raised brow and drew her hand from his arm. "Would you consider Mr. George Wickham one of your good friends?"

Rickland stiffened and clenched his jaw; his smile quickly faded. "I..." He let out a puff of air. Shaking his head, he asked, "George Wickham?"

Elizabeth nodded and gave him a pointed look. "I understand the two of you are acquaintances."

Rickland rubbed his chin. "I... he... I know that he is a long-time acquaintance of Darcy."

"Mm, Yes. But I understand the two of you have a common interest."

Rickland swallowed hard. "I am at a loss to know of what you are speaking and why you even brought up the man's name."

"I heard the two of you participated in a high-stakes card game here in London." She glanced at his face as he averted his eyes. "That was the business that took you from Rosings those few days. Is that correct?"

His eyes darkened, and he replied with an edge to his voice. "I do not know how you became acquainted with such information, but I assure you, if Wickham happened to be there, it was not because we are particularly good friends."

"No, I would imagine not." She paused, more to collect herself than to end the conversation. She tightly fisted her hands as she felt her anger rising. Finally, she said, "But I would assume one would truly have to consider another a friend if they agreed to do something for that person, even if it went against everything that is civil and proper." She clenched her jaw after she pronounced these words.

Rickland was silent for a moment. "Miss Bennet, I..." He looked at her and smiled. "I see. My guess is Darcy has something to do with this line of questioning. Somehow he discovered I had been at a gaming table with Wickham, and he informed you of that fact." He shook his head. "I knew the two of them disliked each other, but I hope you will not think less of me for a mere card game."

"Certainly not." She turned, and they began walking again. This time she did not take his arm, and he did not offer it.

Rickland scowled, and his jaw tightened. After drawing in a breath, he said, "What I do with my money, Miss Bennet, is my business. It is certainly not Darcy's business to spread rumours and lies about me."

She felt her indignation rise at his accusation against Mr. Darcy. She stopped and folded her arms tightly in front of her "No, but perhaps it becomes his business when a plan is made to do something rather devious that would greatly affect him and his good name." Elizabeth could not conceal the heated trembling in her voice. She watched him carefully as she spoke.

He stopped and promptly crossed his arms in front of him. His brows and mouth twitched, and he looked away. When he turned back to Elizabeth, he brought a clenched fist up to his mouth, tapping it a few times. He then noticeably relaxed and finally asked, "What exactly did he tell you?"

"Oh, he had no need to tell me anything," Elizabeth said with a derisive laugh. "A gentleman with whom he is acquainted was sitting at the table with the two of you, and he overheard everything. He wrote Mr. Darcy a letter, detailing how Mr. Wickham agreed to compensate you if you would only flatter me with your attentions, as Wickham supposed Mr. Darcy had some feelings of affection for me." She laughed mockingly. "Can you imagine Mr. Darcy having such feelings for *me?*"

Mr. Rickland flushed and took in a deep breath, straightening his shoulders. "Miss Bennet, I know not what Mr. Darcy claimed this friend supposedly wrote…"

"As I said, Mr. Darcy did not claim anything; he merely showed me the letter. This gentleman overheard you agree to Wickham's scheme that you pay me particular attention in order to dissuade me from any inclination I might have for Mr. Darcy." Elizabeth shook her head. "How unfortunate for Mr. Wickham that he gave up a sum of money, and fortunate for you when you became aware of the intense dislike I had for Mr. Darcy."

Mr. Rickland seemed to relax. "For that, I am grateful." He looked at the ground and shook his head. "I am not proud of what I agreed to do. I have never done anything like this before. I imagine I allowed greed to rule my decision. It was wrong of me." He looked at her with an expression of regret. "I believed it to be a rather easy way to pocket some extra money, as I am actually quite fond of you."

Elizabeth forced a smile, but then her brows pinched together. "That is a poor excuse and, unfortunately, it is not sound. But there is something else I do not understand."

He nodded for her to continue, an expression of uncertainty clouding his features.

"You knew my opinion of Mr. Darcy. Why did you continue this charade in London and invite us to the ball?"

Mr. Rickland winced and drew in a deep breath. "I…" He paused, and his face grew flushed. "Wickham wrote to me after you departed Rosings, to inform me Darcy had made a trip to Hertfordshire to speak with his regiment's colonel about him. Wickham claimed Darcy spread some lies about him." Mr. Rickland swallowed hard.

"Mr. Darcy spread lies? This is indeed serious. I am not quite certain I can believe Mr. Wickham's claims, knowing his character as I do, but what has this to do with continuing this scheme here in London?"

"Wickham believed Darcy would not have done this if he had no intention of continuing to pursue you." He scuffed a foot across the ground. "He asked that I spend some time with you when I was in London just to make certain your feelings towards Darcy do not change."

"I see." She brought her fingers up to her forehead, rubbing it as if she were in pain. She looked across the street towards her aunt and uncle's home. "Mr. Rickland, I fear I am rather fatigued, and I have heard enough to convince me you and Mr. Wickham are two men of similar character."

Rickland's face was ashen as he looked at the ground. "I would hope not."

Elizabeth's face lit up. "Oh! So you are aware of his character!"

Rickland looked somewhat confused. "I…no, I mean…"

"There is no need to try to explain yourself, Mr. Rickland. Would you be so kind as to escort me across the street?"

He nodded, and when they came to the house, Elizabeth said firmly, "I think it would be best if you took your leave… immediately."

"I…" Rickland shook his head and looked down. "I can only ask for your forgiveness, but I know that to be asking a lot. I am not proud of what I have done."

"No, I would imagine you are not, and I can only hope you will never do anything of the sort again. Goodbye, Mr. Rickland." Elizabeth turned without saying another word.

Elizabeth heard Mr. Rickland give a rather curt order to his driver, and the carriage door was opened and quickly closed after he stepped in. She stopped and watched it pull away, knowing she would likely never see Mr. Rickland again and not regretting it for a moment.

The Gardiners soon came upon Elizabeth and joined her, observing the carriage as it ambled down the street.

"We had a watchful eye on you and were trying to determine what was being said between the two of you, but could discern little. We are certainly curious as to what happened," Mrs. Gardiner said as she took Elizabeth's hand.

Elizabeth pinched her brows together and shrugged her shoulders. "It did not go as I thought it would." She looked at her aunt and uncle with a resigned smile. "For some reason, I did not find as much enjoyment in berating him as he and I had found when we attacked Mr. Darcy with our words."

Mr. Gardiner rested his hand on Elizabeth's shoulder as they walked up to the house. "Perhaps it is because Mr. Rickland was a commiserating partner with you in the verbal assault on Mr. Darcy."

"More like a *conspiring* partner," Elizabeth said with a sarcastic laugh.

"I believe, dearest Lizzy, you have learned a hard lesson," her aunt said.

Elizabeth looked from her aunt to her uncle, and then back. "Yes, I believe you are correct." She squeezed her aunt's hand and reached for her uncle's. "And as much as I will miss you, I think it is time Jane and I return home."

Mrs. Gardiner smiled. "We have so enjoyed having you and Jane with us, and you know we will miss you, as well." She drew in a breath. "Your uncle and I would like you to join us on a tour of the Lake District this summer, as Jane accompanied us last year. Of course it will depend on when we can go, and the date of Jane's wedding, but please consider it."

Elizabeth's eyes brightened with delight. "You know I would love to! Let us see how events transpire once we return home."

"Certainly," her aunt replied with a knowing smile. "But I cannot help but think there is much that might happen which will be much more to your liking."

Chapter 31

Later that afternoon, Elizabeth was grateful for the diversion of doing something *other* than thinking about Mr. Rickland and their earlier conversation. She eagerly accompanied Jane and their aunt to the seamstress, where Jane selected the fabric for her wedding dress. She chose a white satin fabric for the dress, which would have an overlay of silver lace below the beaded bodice. A wide silver ribbon would tie in the back.

As Jane was having measurements taken, Elizabeth and Mrs. Gardiner looked through additional fabrics and illustrations of wedding gowns from which to choose. "And if you were to choose your wedding gown today, what would your preference be? And what fabric would you select?"

Elizabeth enjoyed looking through the various illustrated designs. "Oh, I do not think I could choose. They are all so beautiful." Suddenly she stopped and gasped. "But, oh my! I think this is exquisite!"

Mrs. Gardiner looked at it and then to her niece. "It is lovely!"

"I can imagine this in a shiny ivory satin with a hint of lace. Yes, please remind me of this in ten years when I marry an old widowed gentleman." She sent her aunt a teasing smile.

Her aunt walked away chuckling. "I highly doubt that, my dear."

Elizabeth smiled and continued looking through the array of fabrics.

At length, Mrs. Gardiner approached her nieces, her arms full of the sheerest pink fabric they had ever seen.

"What is that for?" Jane asked. "It is beautiful, but I think we have everything already selected for the wedding gown."

"Ahh!" Mrs. Gardiner said with the raise of her finger. "But this is for the wedding night. It will be perfect for your nightgown."

Jane's cheeks turned as rosy as the fabric her aunt held in her hands. She carefully slid her hand under the silk and was able to clearly see the outline of each slender finger. "I do not think I could wear something as transparent as this." She suddenly smiled. "Oh, there must be another fabric that will line it."

Mrs. Gardiner shook her head. "No, this is all you will need."

Jane bit her lip. "I am not certain…"

Her aunt would hear no more and assured Jane her husband would be delighted and she had better not plan to wear anything else. Then she chuckled and with a smile added, "It is highly likely you will not be wearing it long, anyway."

Jane was too embarrassed to formulate an intelligible response and watched as her aunt took the fabric to the seamstress.

On the ride home, Elizabeth and Jane discussed how their mother would likely respond once she discovered they had already started shopping for the wedding. They agreed she would likely be unhappy not to have been consulted about where to find the best shops. They knew, however, her displeasure would be short-lived, for it would be an even greater pleasure to ponder that her eldest daughter was to be married to Mr. Bingley of Netherfield.

~~*

The greeting Jane and Elizabeth received when they arrived at Longbourn three days later was warm and boisterous. Mr. Bennet welcomed his daughters with warm embraces, while Mrs. Bennet could not contain her effusive joy at the prospect of Jane and Mr. Bingley being engaged. The two sisters had decided they would wait until the following day to tell their mother of the shopping they had already undertaken in London.

Elizabeth noticed the apologetic glances Jane gave her as she was receiving all the attention while Elizabeth was being chiefly ignored. It seemed to be almost an afterthought when Mrs. Bennet finally addressed her second eldest daughter. "Oh, Lizzy! You seem to be doing quite well. I assume your injuries have healed?"

She nodded. "I am quite well. Thank you, Mama."

"Good! Now, we have so much to talk about! A wedding! I can scarce believe it! And Mr. Bingley is such a fine gentlemen, and

Netherfield is the perfect home for you!"

As Mrs. Bennet smothered Jane with her ebullience, Elizabeth sent her sister a sympathetic look.

The chatter continued as they entered Longbourn, where they were greeted by their sisters, who were looking at Jane in awe. Elizabeth smiled at the thought their sister was to be married. But more than that, Jane had never looked more beautiful, sweet, and completely happy.

"I have invited Mr. Bingley to dine with us tonight," Mrs. Bennet announced. "He shall be here in a little over an hour, so the two of you must get yourselves ready," she continued as she noticeably pushed them towards the stairs.

As the two sisters hurried to their rooms, Elizabeth gave a tug on Jane's sleeve. "I want you to know I am delighted for you, because I can see you are so happy." She leaned towards her conspiratorially. "And I can see everyone else is pleased, as well. You deserve, of all of us, to be the happiest in marriage."

"Oh, Lizzy, I am! I truly am!" She drew her sister into a hug. "But I know you will someday be just as happy!"

"On that, we shall have to wait and see."

If her family thought Jane looked happier than they had ever seen her when she and Elizabeth arrived home, they would soon change their minds. When Mr. Bingley arrived later that day, her face glowed with love and delight.

~~*

Elizabeth woke up the next morning, never having been more grateful for her own room and bed. She normally hopped out of bed at the first light, but this morning she lingered, thinking about all that had transpired – and changed – since the last time she woke up here.

The biggest change had been in her estimation of Mr. Darcy. Her feelings were now completely the opposite of what they had been previously, and she was rather ashamed at how mistaken she had been in his character. She shook her head and thought how long ago it seemed; yet, it had been a little more than a month since she had harboured such dislike for the gentleman.

She smiled. The dinner with Mr. Bingley had gone well. Each time Elizabeth saw him with Jane, she was even more convinced they were perfect for each other.

Elizabeth slid her feet out from underneath the coverlet and let them dangle over the side of the bed, while she wiggled her toes and stretched out her arms. She wondered if Mr. Darcy had talked to Lady Catherine yet, and what her response to her daughter's elopement had been. She could not imagine his aunt would take it well and regretted he was the one who would suffer as the bearer of such news.

She recollected he was going to Pemberley for a month immediately upon departing Rosings and felt a sense of despondency overtake her. She did not think she could patiently wait that long to see him again. She wrapped her arms about herself and swayed, thinking of how it had felt to be in his arms. Of course, he had only carried her after she had been injured, but she had enjoyed it. She tried to imagine what it would be like for him to wrap his arms tightly about her and draw her close for a kiss. She smiled at the thought and reached up to touch her cheek where he had kissed her, prompting a flood of warmth to envelope her. She would count the days until she was with him again.

~~*

Fortunately, there was much to do to keep Elizabeth's mind off waiting. There were many decisions about the wedding she helped Jane make, fabrics to select for additional gowns and fittings, and invitations to address and send out. Mrs. Bennet took the news well that Jane's dress was already being made. The Gardiners would bring it when they arrived before the wedding, and a seamstress in Meryton would make any additional alterations if needed. It would be a joyous time, and Elizabeth was grateful for the continued busyness, as it would help occupy her thoughts until Mr. Darcy came back to Hertfordshire.

Elizabeth smiled as she considered her new role as Charles and Jane's chaperone, one she quite enjoyed. She spent a great amount of time with them at Netherfield as the couple discussed the changes they might want to make it their home. Each was so insistent on pleasing the other that neither would express a personal thought or preference, but each wished to hear what the other wanted. Elizabeth had to chuckle, as it seemed difficult for them to make a final decision.

There were several times when Elizabeth had taken the opportunity to wander about the house and grounds as the two sat in the drawing room whispering. Mr. Bingley often took Jane's hand, stroking it as he looked into her eyes. It was those times Elizabeth quietly walked out, as she did not wish to intrude. And it made her miss Mr. Darcy even more.

Two weeks after they had returned home, Elizabeth heard Miss Bingley was to join her brother at Netherfield. Elizabeth knew that meant she would no longer be needed as a chaperone when Jane went to Netherfield to see Charles, as his sister would likely insist upon that duty herself. And Elizabeth was correct. She spent two days in their company before Miss Bingley informed her, most graciously, that she was certain Elizabeth was needed at home and she would take on the responsibility of chaperoning the couple herself.

Elizabeth was actually grateful, for it meant she would not have to endure Miss Bingley's accusatory looks and snide comments made under her breath. She wondered how the woman would treat Jane now she was engaged to Charles, as she had been instrumental in separating them.

Elizabeth did not escape Miss Bingley's company completely, however, for she accompanied her brother several times on visits to Longbourn. Fortunately, Elizabeth detected only the slightest disapproval in Miss Bingley's manner and occasionally in her tone of voice. Jane did not seem to notice it, but as Elizabeth was such an astute observer of character, she could readily detect it. She chose not to say anything to Jane, however, as to the common observer, Miss Bingley's behaviour could be deemed strictly proper.

Her only regret was that her sister seemed to suffer. Jane admitted to her having Caroline around was most vexing. She rarely left her and Charles alone, hovering near them like a hawk, as if she expected them to behave with impropriety if she turned her head for even a moment.

It was the following week Jane asked Elizabeth if she would accompany her to Netherfield, as Charles had informed her his sister had a gown fitting in Meryton. Elizabeth was thrilled with the opportunity to do so.

When they arrived, Mr. Bingley welcomed them cheerfully. He invited them into the drawing room, explaining someone had just arrived and he wanted to introduce them. As they walked in, Elizabeth was disappointed to see Miss Bingley had not yet left for her appointment.

The two ladies greeted Miss Bingley, who politely returned the greeting.

"Pray, forgive me, Miss Bingley. I understood you were from home, and had I known otherwise, I would not have come to chaperone Jane and Mr. Bingley."

Miss Bingley let out a huff. "A situation arose, and I had to change my plans."

"I see," Elizabeth said.

Jane turned to Charles. "You said there was someone you wished for us to meet?"

Miss Bingley shook her head. "Whatever are you talking about, Charles? There is no one here needing an introduction."

Charles wore a wide smile on his face. "Well, I am certain there is."

Footsteps were heard, and they all turned towards the door. Elizabeth let out a gasp when she beheld Mr. Darcy standing there. He bowed and approached the party as Elizabeth struggled to maintain an attitude of composure when she felt anything but.

"Come in, Mr. Darcy!" Bingley said cheerfully. "You are acquainted with Miss Jane Bennet, but please allow me to introduce to you Miss Elizabeth Bennet."

"Charles!" Miss Bingley cried. "You are quite mistaken! They are already well-acquainted!"

Despite Miss Bingley's protests, Mr. Darcy approached and bowed. "It is a pleasure to see you again Miss Bennet, and Miss Elizabeth, it is a pleasure to meet you."

Jane giggled and looked somewhat confused, but Elizabeth knew immediately what Mr. Darcy was doing. She smiled and curtseyed. "I assure you, the pleasure is all mine, Mr. Darcy."

"Come now!" Miss Bingley protested. "You cannot all be under the misapprehension that the two of you have never met!" She turned to her brother. "What is all this nonsense?"

Bingley shrugged his shoulders. "Caroline, I am only doing the bidding of my good friend. He is the one you must ask."

She turned to Mr. Darcy. The look on her face exhibited a curiosity mixed with a little dread of what he might answer. "Pray, Mr. Darcy, what is the meaning of this?"

Elizabeth watched Mr. Darcy as he pondered his answer and wondered what reason he might actually give Miss Bingley.

He let out a soft laugh. "I realized in all the time we were in Hertfordshire, I had never been properly introduced to Miss Elizabeth." He turned his head slightly and gave Elizabeth a quick wink only she was able to see.

Elizabeth's breath caught in her throat. To think a man such as Mr. Darcy would wink at her! Winking was... well, she had often noticed her father winking at her mother when they shared a secret between them, although she did not see him do it as often now as he used to.

She felt her face warm in a blush and hoped no one – especially Miss Bingley – would notice. She was certainly seeing a different side of him. When he had told her in London that perhaps they ought to begin anew, he had apparently been serious. A fresh introduction was a start!

She looked at Miss Bingley, who was eyeing them with a look of distrust and open resentment. She now understood why the woman had suddenly decided not to attend to her errand. She did not wish for Elizabeth to be here with Mr. Darcy while she was from home.

Bingley clasped his hands. "Well, now that all the formalities have been observed, shall we sit down?" He extended his hands towards the chairs and sofas.

Elizabeth followed Miss Bingley, and she knew – she could feel – Mr. Darcy was right behind her. She knew not what Miss Bingley would think if she discovered the extent of time they had spent together, but she would allow Mr. Darcy to be the one to divulge that information if he wished. For that matter, she might already know, for her brother could have informed her.

Miss Bingley walked to a chair on the far side of the room and turned. She extended her hand. "Miss Elizabeth, please have a seat."

Elizabeth smiled obligingly and sat down. She then watched as Miss Bingley manoeuvred the others in such a way that she was now seated beside Mr. Darcy on the sofa. Elizabeth would have been vexed had it not been for the look of desperation upon Mr. Darcy's face. It mattered not what Caroline Bingley said or did, she would not find herself in his favour.

As the party conversed, Elizabeth noticed Darcy's occasional glance at her. She surmised he wished to know her feelings. When she gave him encouraging smiles, they did not escape Miss Bingley's notice, and the woman would immediately draw Mr. Darcy's attention away.

Elizabeth was most curious about how his aunt had taken the news of Anne's elopement. She smiled and looked down as she thought that, judging from his appearance, his aunt had not inflicted any bodily harm on him. She was grateful for that!

Miss Bingley did everything in her power to draw Mr. Darcy's attention away from Elizabeth. It served only to confirm Elizabeth's original estimation of the woman. She thought only of herself and looked down on those who became obstacles to something she desired, and it was obvious that she desired Mr. Darcy.

When she and Jane departed later that day, Elizabeth felt quite downcast. She realized how much she had enjoyed conversing with Mr. Darcy while in London, and now with Miss Bingley in their midst, he did not seem much inclined to talk. Oh how she wished Miss Bingley had gone to her appointment. Elizabeth was certain she remained to keep an eye on Mr. Darcy – and her!

Jane appeared quite oblivious to her sister's plight. She had enjoyed her time with Charles, and Miss Bingley was treating her politely. Of all the people present, Elizabeth believed only she and Mr. Darcy were aware of Miss Bingley's scheming and the lack of civility she was exhibiting.

That evening, as the Bennets gathered around the table for their evening meal, Jane was lost in her pleasant thoughts; the two youngest daughters were characteristically boisterous, and Mary persistently gave the two looks of warning. Elizabeth was quiet, as she felt a heavy sense of disappointment in not being able to speak with Mr. Darcy.

As the family ate, Elizabeth began to notice Kitty and Lydia were whispering and giggling. This was not uncommon for them, but they were carrying on in such a fashion everyone became annoyed.

Elizabeth wiped her mouth with her napkin and then virtually threw it back onto her lap. Directing her gaze at them, she exclaimed, "If you two do not have anything to share with all of us, please refrain from this behaviour! You are displaying terribly rude manners!"

Lydia drew her head back and widened her eyes. "Well, I do have something to share with everyone, but even Kitty does not know. She only knows I have a secret and she has been trying to guess, but has been all wrong!"

"What?" Kitty asked. "What is it?"

Lydia looked rather proud and announced she had been invited to join Mrs. Forster and her husband in Brighton when the militia was transferred there in two weeks. She looked at each one around the table as she spoke, ending at Kitty. With an emphatic nod of her head, she added, "I have been invited as Mrs. Forster's particular friend."

Kitty's face grew red. "That is not fair! I am just as much a friend to her as you are!"

Lydia shook her head. "No, Kitty. She told me they can only take one of us, and she prefers me."

Elizabeth leaned in towards her sister. "Lydia, Father has not yet given his consent." She turned towards her father. "Certainly you do not intend to allow her to go."

"And why not?" Mrs. Bennet whined. "Oh, how I wish we could all go!"

Elizabeth looked incredulously at her mother and then back to her sister. "Well, for one thing, there is Jane's wedding."

"They are departing after the wedding. I shall be here for the wedding and then go off to Brighton. Oh! I cannot wait!"

Elizabeth sent her father a pleading look.

Mr. Bennet looked down at his plate of food slowly shaking his head. "I see no reason not to allow her to go. I would prefer to have her go rather than have her here moping about because I forbade it."

"Really, Father!" Elizabeth wished to speak to him, but she knew now was not the time. She would be more persuasive in a private conversation.

"This is not fair!" Kitty exclaimed. "I am older and should have been asked first."

Mr. Bennet picked up his napkin and wiped the corners of his mouth. "I will add, however, that I might change my mind if the two of you do not keep quiet while we eat."

Lydia promptly directed her attention back to her plate of food, while Kitty let out a disgruntled moan.

"Oh, I am so happy for you!" Mrs. Bennet said with a quick clasp of her hands. "Imagine! Lydia going to Brighton... and with all those handsome officers!"

Her husband, however, looked at her and lowered his brows, giving her the same ultimatum. She wiggled her shoulders in defiant delight.

Chapter 32

Elizabeth joined her sister when she left for Netherfield the following day, but Miss Bingley met her with the same treatment as she had experienced the day before. While appearing to be a most gracious and attentive hostess to all of her guests, she would not leave Mr. Darcy's side. Even when he made an attempt to step over to Elizabeth, she followed, as if she were attached to him with a cord.

As it was a pleasant day, Mr. Bingley suggested a walk outside, which was something Caroline never enjoyed. Elizabeth wondered if Mr. Darcy had asked him to propose the idea, for it seemed the perfect answer to their dilemma. The four of them joyfully agreed it would be a most pleasant way to spend the morning. Unfortunately, Miss Bingley also declared nothing would give her more pleasure.

At the end of the day, Miss Bingley found an opportunity to approach Elizabeth alone. "As I told you earlier, I know you must have much to occupy yourself with at home, having been away for so long a time. I believe I can do an adequate job of chaperoning Charles and Jane. As that is the only reason for you to come to Netherfield, I can assure you that your presence here, while certainly welcomed, is not necessary." She forced a smile.

Elizabeth knew not what to say. She was so angered she pursed her lips together to hold back any retort. She finally replied, "Thank you, Miss Bingley. I know you shall faithfully exercise your duty as a chaperone most rigorously." Elizabeth did not think they even needed one, and in truth, since Mr. Darcy's arrival, the couple would often disappear without Miss Bingley seeming to take notice at all, so focused was her attention on their guest.

The following day, Elizabeth found her mother did indeed need her help, and as much as she would have liked to go with Jane to Netherfield, she knew Miss Bingley's presence would serve only to irritate her.

Elizabeth was pleased when Mr. Bingley finally returned with Jane, but she was disappointed Mr. Darcy had not accompanied them. She knew it was due to the lateness of the hour, but she so wished to see him.

Once Mr. Bingley took his leave, Elizabeth immediately sought out Jane's company, intending to hear all about the events of her day. She also hoped to have news from Mr. Darcy. As they approached Lydia's room, they could hear her talking with Kitty quite loudly.

"But Mrs. Forster should have invited me, as well. It is not fair!"

"La! Kitty, I have already told you she could only take one of us!" They heard her giggle, and then in a softer voice she said, "But you shall have Mr. Wickham all to yourself!" Lydia began to giggle more.

Elizabeth felt a tremor of dread ripple through her at the mention of Wickham's name, and she rushed to Lydia's door. She braced her hands on the door jamb and looked in. "Lydia! Whatever do you mean she shall have Mr. Wickham all to herself?" She tightened her grip even more as she felt her hands begin to shake.

Lydia's hand went to her mouth, and her eyes widened. "Oh! You should not have been eavesdropping! It was supposed to be a secret!"

Elizabeth quickly moved across the room and stood in front of Lydia. She fisted her hands and tried to remain calm. "What was supposed to be a secret?"

Lydia tilted her head and smiled, as if she were party to the most delicious bit of gossip. "Mr. Wickham is here. We have seen him several times in Meryton."

Elizabeth's heart lurched, and she placed her hands squarely on her sister's shoulders. "Lydia! How can he be here? What is he doing here?"

Lydia gave her shoulders a slight shrug. "I suppose he came to visit all his friends." She lifted her eyes accusingly. "There are some here who are still his friends." She reached for one of Elizabeth's hands, removing it from her shoulder. "And do not ever grab me like that again."

Elizabeth wrapped her arms firmly about her and turned around with a stamp of her foot. She turned back to face Lydia. "If you only knew how contemptible that man is! If you only knew all the things he has done!"

Lydia stole a sly glance up. "I believe you once rather liked him."

Elizabeth felt her face heat with anger. "That was before I knew who he truly is." She looked at Jane. "Would you please bring Father here?"

Lydia stood up and faced Elizabeth. She was slightly taller than Elizabeth but raised herself even more by standing on her toes. "And what do you think Father will do?" She looked at her as if defying her to answer.

In truth, Elizabeth did not know. He had never taken much of a role in disciplining his daughters, especially the younger two.

She shook her head in frustration. "He shall have Mr. Wickham forcibly removed from the neighbourhood... if not arrested for unpaid debts."

"You are making too much of a fuss over this, Lizzy," Lydia huffed. "It is not as if he has done anything worse than every other man has done!"

Elizabeth drew in a breath to calm herself. "Oh, Lydia, that is not true in every respect." She brought her fingers up and rubbed her temple. "Where is he staying?" She looked at Lydia and then to Kitty.

Both girls shook their heads. "We do not know, Lizzy," Kitty said. "He is not staying with the militia, of course, but I do not think he is even in Meryton."

"Kitty!" Lydia gave her sister a warning look. "You do not have to say any more." She looked back at Elizabeth. "But it is true; we do not know where he is staying."

Mr. Bennet strode into the room. "What is this about Wickham being here?"

Elizabeth extended her hand, still shaking, towards her two younger sisters. "I hope you can get more information out of them than I was able to do."

Mr. Bennet braced his hands on his waist. "I insist you tell me where you have seen him and everything you know about him!"

By the end of their conversation, not much more was discovered. The girls did not know where he was staying, but confessed he had grown a beard and disguised his appearance before his return to Meryton. Apparently Mr. Denny had confided to the girls he had not even recognized Wickham when he first saw him. They assured their father Wickham had not divulged where he was staying.

Mr. Bennet left the girls with a warning they were to have nothing more to do with him. Furthermore, if they even so much as saw Wickham in Meryton or anywhere in the neighbourhood, they were to keep away from him and immediately send word to Longbourn, or contact their Uncle Phillips or Colonel Forster.

Still shaken after the conversation with her two sisters, Elizabeth returned downstairs with her father and joined him in his library.

"So what do you think, Lizzy? Has Wickham come to seduce another rich young lady or has he truly come to see his friends?"

Elizabeth bit her lip and looked at her father with a quick shake of her head. "That I do not know; the man seems always to have another scheme up his sleeve."

Mr. Bennet sat down and propped his elbows on his desk and clasped his hands. "I dare say his being here does surprise me."

"Father, why cannot Lydia and Kitty comprehend he is not to be trusted?"

"I wish I knew." He stood up and began to walk about the room, his hands clasped behind his back.

"People must be warned."

"Ah, yes. I shall spread word about the neighbourhood tomorrow. I doubt my method of getting news out will be as quick and effective as your mother's, but I do not trust her with all the details."

"Mr. Darcy ought to be informed. I wish it was proper for me to send him a letter so he is made aware of it."

"No, you cannot write to him, but *I* certainly can!" He reached for his pen and ink. "Now, off with you and try not to worry. There may yet be an acceptable reason for Wickham's presence." He shooed her away with his hand.

Elizabeth returned to her room, stopping at Jane's door on the way. She gave a light tap.

"Come in, Lizzy."

She opened the door and peeked in. "How did you know it was me?"

Jane smiled. "I expected you would come. What did Father say?"

"He will inform others in Meryton tomorrow and is now sending a letter to Netherfield to acquaint Mr. Darcy with the news."

"Good. But Lizzy, do you truly believe we need to be concerned?"

Elizabeth sat down on the bed next to Jane. She took Jane's hand and squeezed it. "I cannot be certain, but why would the man risk coming here when he knows he could be arrested for not paying his debts?"

Jane's face lit up. "Maybe that is why he came! If he had enough money to bribe Mr. Rickland, maybe he has come into some money and intends to honour his debts and reclaim his reputation."

Elizabeth's brows lowered. "If he came into money, I doubt he came into it in a proper manner." She looked down at their clasped hands. "And he would most likely *not* use it to pay his debts." Her shoulders sank. "Nor would he have reason to disguise himself if that was his intention."

"Oh, Lizzy, please do not worry."

"I cannot help but worry." She looked down as she ran her free hand over the coverlet on the bed. "I hope Mr. Wickham has not come to do anything despicable." She patted Jane's hand. "I will try not to think of it." A smile appeared. "How was your day with Mr. Bingley?"

A soft smile brightened Jane's face. "It was actually quite nice. Would you believe Caroline actually left us alone for several hours today? Mr. Darcy seemed not at all concerned to be with us all the time."

"I am glad." She reached out and placed her hand on Jane's shoulder. "Our aunt and uncle arrive tomorrow with your gown. I cannot wait to see it!" She laughed. "I cannot wait to see *you* in it!"

"I hope Charles will think me pretty in it. That is all I hope."

"Oh, Jane, he would think you were beautiful even if you were to wear a gown made from the sitting room curtains!"

"Lizzy, be serious!"

"Indeed, I am!" she said and leaned over to give Jane a hug. "Good night, dear sister."

"Lizzy?"

"Yes?"

"Mr. Wickham may be scheming and deceitful, but do you truly believe he would do anything malicious."

"I hope not, Jane. I sincerely hope not."

~~*

Darcy sat in the drawing room at Netherfield penning a letter to his sister. Miss Bingley lingered near him, speaking frequently about his penmanship and inquiring after Georgiana.

"As I said earlier, she is doing well. I am merely requesting she join us here at her earliest convenience. She…"

"Splendid!" Miss Bingley clasped her hands. "Such a sweet young lady. I cannot wait to see her. Tell her how much I anticipate seeing her." She turned to her brother. "We must have the green room made up for her."

"It is already done, Caroline." Bingley stood up and began to walk about the room. "I do not know how I shall manage not being able to see Jane tomorrow. Her aunt and uncle arrive with her wedding gown, and she will be going into Meryton for a fitting soon after they arrive. Oh, I cannot wait until all the wedding arrangements are completed."

With eyes still on the stationary, Darcy said, "I would think you could not wait until the wedding *ceremony* was completed!"

"Oh! Mr. Darcy! You tease him so!" Miss Bingley let out a tittering laugh.

"Well, that is true," Bingley said, his smile widening. After a moment's pause, he added, "Just the thought of having Jane by my side as my wife fills me with the greatest joy."

Miss Bingley turned back to Mr. Darcy. "And when shall your sister come?"

"I will send off this letter by early post and hope for either a reply or her arrival within the next few days."

"She is so sweet."

"Yes, you said that."

"Tell her I cannot wait to see her."

Darcy was growing more and more irritated with Miss Bingley, who hovered close to him at all times, but even closer when Elizabeth was present. Since arriving at Netherfield, he had not had a single opportunity to speak with Elizabeth alone and wondered when he would. Had her feelings towards him improved? Did he have a chance with her? Dare he even entertain hope she would welcome an offer of marriage?

He shook his head. He could not make an offer too hastily. While he would be delighted to ask her this very day, he needed to be certain she felt the same depth of love he felt for her. He let out a huff. And to think he almost blurted out a proposal to her in Kent. How foolish he was! He could only imagine how that would have ended, knowing now how she had felt about him then.

"Is anything amiss, Mr. Darcy?"

He quickly looked up, realizing he had been absently staring across the room. "No, I was... I was trying to recollect if there was anything else I needed to tell my sister."

"Perhaps you can tell her..."

Fortunately, Miss Bingley was interrupted by a knock at the front door. She turned her head in question. "I wonder who that could be." She then looked at Mr. Darcy, as if he would know.

"I would have no idea."

"Charles, are you expecting anyone?" Miss Bingley asked her brother.

"Not that I recall."

Miss Bingley widened her eyes and turned back to Darcy. "Perhaps it is your sister already here, surprising you with a visit!"

"I highly doubt that."

A servant entered the drawing room carrying a silver salver. "A letter for Mr. Darcy."

"Oh!" Miss Bingley exclaimed as she clapped her hands excitedly. "It is from your sister. I just know it is!"

Mr. Darcy took the letter and looked at it, but did not recognize the handwriting. The wax had been sealed with an initial, but it was quite smeared. He shook his head as he said, "No, it is not from my sister."

Miss Bingley approached Mr. Darcy and looked inquiringly at him. "Whoever could have sent it?"

He stepped away, opened the letter, and looked down at the signature, somewhat surprised to see it was from Mr. Bennet.

When his eyes went to the beginning of the letter, his breath caught.

Mr. Darcy,

Pray excuse this interruption of your evening activities, but I must inform you that this evening we discovered Wickham is in the neighbourhood. My two youngest daughters, Kitty and Lydia, informed us – somewhat reluctantly – they had both seen and talked to him.

Darcy felt the flames of anger ignite as he read these words.

"Is something wrong, Darcy?" Bingley asked. "You look quite ill."

"Nothing... yet," he replied.

"Is there anything we can do for you?" Miss Bingley inquired. She pointed to a chair. "Pray, you ought to sit down."

"No, thank you." Darcy waved her away with his hand and finished reading the letter.

They said he had grown a beard, was wearing some kind of a disguise, and was staying at an undisclosed location somewhere outside of Meryton. That is the extent of our knowledge. Elizabeth thought you should be told, and I agreed with her.

I shall be informing those in and around Meryton on the morrow, but Lizzy felt you ought to be informed this evening.

T. Bennet

Darcy drew in a slow breath and fisted his fingers about the letter, crushing it. He schooled his features, for he did not wish for Miss Bingley to know what the contents were or who the letter was from. If she caught so much as a whiff of distress, she would not be satisfied until she knew all.

"Bingley, I am rather fatigued and wish to retire to my chambers for the evening. Thank you again, and thank you, Miss Bingley, for your hospitality."

"Certainly," Bingley replied.

"Mr. Darcy, there is nothing better for fatigue than an evening spent with intimate friends at their leisure." She tilted her head with a smile. "Is it not peaceful and quiet here this evening?"

Darcy knew she was referring to the absence of the two eldest Bennet sisters, and he shook his head slightly at the thought he did not consider her an intimate friend and she produced more annoying clamour than almost anyone he knew.

"I thank you, no. Good night." As he walked away, he wished so much to tell her what he thought, but he was more intent on making sense of the news he just received.

He entered his chambers, closed the door, and sat in the chair at the desk to read the letter again. He rubbed his jaw as he contemplated what that man might be up to. He could not imagine why Wickham would return to the neighbourhood and risk getting caught. It did not make sense.

He shook his head. Even bribing Rickland had not made any sense to him. Obtaining money was the man's sole object in life, and his paying someone to keep Elizabeth away from him was most perplexing.

Unfortunately, the presence of Wickham meant his sister would not be able to come. He would not allow her anywhere near Hertfordshire until he was convinced that man was gone!

"Does he have some sinister plot?" Darcy whispered. "Is there something I do not see?" He raked his fingers through his hair and then dropped them down to the desk. He nervously began to tap, his trimmed nails clicking steadily, much like the tick of a clock. "I know he resents me and blames me for his lot in life..." Darcy stopped and closed his eyes. "No, *he* is to blame for his own misfortunes, and while he tries to convince others it is my fault, he knows he is in the wrong."

He leaned his head back in the chair. There had to be something else he was not seeing. And whatever that something else was, it had brought Wickham back to Meryton.

Chapter 33

Elizabeth did not sleep well, and the following morning she awoke early, a sense of unrest burrowing deep within. She tried to convince herself there was nothing to worry about, but she could not think of any reason why Wickham would have returned. At least they had been able to warn Mr. Darcy, since it was likely because of him Wickham was nearby.

Even though it was early and the house was quiet, Elizabeth knew her father would be awake, sequestered in his library. She slipped on her robe and slippers and walked down the stairs. The aroma of bread baking filled her nostrils, and she looked forward to having a slice topped with honey and butter.

She was rather surprised she could even think of eating, and she attributed it to needing something pleasant about which to think. She came to her father's door and tapped lightly.

"Come in, Lizzy," her father said softly.

She opened the door slowly and peered in. "I do hope you did not stay here all night, Father. Please tell me you went to bed and were able to sleep, for I certainly did not."

"Oh, I went to bed, and I confess I slept soundly." He shook his head. "But it was not until after I examined every possible reason why Wickham would have returned to the neighbourhood, and I cannot come up with anything that makes one ounce of sense." He rubbed his jaw. "But I assume if he has some ulterior motive, we shall likely discover it soon enough."

Elizabeth sank down into a chair. "I was unable to account for his presence here, either. I know he dislikes Mr. Darcy, but I cannot see Mr. Wickham as a man who would actually do him harm. From what I have seen of him, he merely likes to make Mr. Darcy's life as miserable as he can or pocket as much money by doing as little work as possible."

"Yes, but I suspect he is now here because Mr. Darcy has

come."

"Does he intend to spend his whole life following Mr. Darcy around, keeping him in suspense of what he might do?" Elizabeth asked with a frown, lowering her brows.

Mr. Bennet shrugged his shoulders. "It is possible, but it is difficult to determine the motives of those who do not live by the same values as the rest of us."

There was silence for a moment, and then Elizabeth asked, "Did you tell Mother?"

He nodded. "She said she is certain he has come to pay off his debts and believes him to be a good man as he was always so attentive to her daughters and so handsome." He lifted one eyebrow. "She said she has always liked him."

"As she likes anyone until she finds a reason to dislike them."

"Mm," her father agreed. After a moment of silence, he continued. "I not only sent a note to Mr. Darcy last night as we discussed, but I decided to send one to Colonel Forster, as well. If his men do not know where Wickham is staying, as Kitty and Lydia claim, there is not much he can do, other than issue a stern admonition if the man is seen, they are to report him." He glanced up at Elizabeth with a hopeful look. "Perhaps he shall depart the neighbourhood as quietly as he entered it."

Elizabeth stayed and talked with her father a little longer, but neither could guess with certainty whether Wickham's presence would result in some trouble. Mr. Bennet assured his daughter if Mr. Wickham was still in the neighbourhood, he would be discovered.

~~*

Later that morning, a letter from Charlotte was delivered to Elizabeth. She had written to Charlotte to inform her she and Jane were home. Elizabeth did not mention Mr. Darcy, nor did she ask about Lady Catherine. She was anxious to see what her friend had to say and opened the letter quickly, hoping there would be information about Lady Catherine's reaction to the news about her daughter.

Dear Friend,

I have to confess the surprise I expressed in my previous letter when we all believed Mr. Darcy had eloped with Miss de Bourgh has quite been exceeded. For Mr. Darcy recently returned but without a bride. He did not marry his cousin and never had any intention to do so. He came solely to inform his aunt Miss de Bourgh was marrying Mrs Jenkinson's son. The couple travelled to Gretna Green and there was nothing to be done as they were likely already married.

I know I do not need to tell you, Lizzy, the upheaval this has caused. While Lady Catherine will despise all her relations one moment, she will deeply feel the loss of her daughter the next. My poor husband knows not what to do or say, but prepares himself with encouraging words for her before each visit. I fear he is running out of them.

I cannot say this to my husband, but I confess I am delighted Miss de Bourgh has found happiness. I would have never thought her to be the romantic or adventurous young lady who would do something like this. But I have never had the opportunity to get to know her well.

Pray, do not despise me, but I own I have also found myself exceedingly interested in the gossip this news has raised in the neighbourhood. I know Mr. Collins would be quite displeased with me if he knew the extent to which I sought out the discussion of this subject, but to those who are spreading the tales, I can appear quite disinterested. I have also been able to give a few ladies a gentle set-down for spreading such news amongst themselves.

Lizzy, I am glad you are home and healing well. My mother informed me Mr. Bingley returned to Netherfield, so I assume Mr. Darcy will come back into the neighbourhood to visit his friend. If you happen to see him (and may I add my hopes and suspicions you might), perhaps you can get some information about his cousin from him. I would so love to hear his side of the events that transpired.

I miss you, dear friend.

Yours, Charlotte

Elizabeth folded up the letter and smiled. Charlotte had been correct in her suspicions about Mr. Darcy, but she could not write to her friend until she knew for certain his feelings had not changed.

It was after noon when the Gardiners arrived. Hugs and kisses and enthusiastic greetings welcomed them. The children gave generous hugs and then immediately ran off to find some amusement, as they were eager to run about after having had to sit still for the lengthy journey. The Bennet ladies waited as patiently as was possible for the wedding gown to be brought out.

"In due time," Mrs. Gardiner said, with a wag of her finger. "We would not wish to bring it out here and have it soiled." She grasped Jane's hand. "It is beautiful. I cannot wait for you to see it!"

Jane decided she did not wish to see the gown or try it on until they were at the dressmaker's shop in Meryton, so the ladies set out immediately to the seamstress for the dress fitting.

Lydia, however, begged to remain at home, as she had much to do in preparation for her journey to Brighton. Elizabeth could not imagine what she had to do so far in advance but actually was grateful she chose not to accompany them, for all they would have heard about was her upcoming travels with the Forsters and the officers.

They went into the dressmaker's shop, and Jane's gown was brought out. The seamstress, who made most of the local wedding gowns, gently ran her fingers over the dress. Looking up at Jane, she whispered, "It is beautiful!"

"Oh, Jane, you will look so lovely in this. Mr. Bingley will not be able to take his eyes off of you, I am certain." Elizabeth gave her sister a hug. "Now, go try it on!"

"I am almost afraid to," she said softly.

"There is no need to fear," the dressmaker said. "I can see it has been lovingly and meticulously sewn." She leaned in and smiled. "We *all* cannot wait to see you in it."

Elizabeth had been correct. When Jane stepped out, she looked lovely, and everyone expressed their pleasure, especially Mrs. Bennet.

"Oh, my dearest Jane! I knew you would be the most beautiful bride! I confess I was so disappointed when I was not able to accompany you to select your dress and fabric, but it is beautiful!"

Mrs. Gardiner leaned in toward her niece. "Do you like it, my dear? Are you pleased?"

Jane nodded mutely, her eyes dancing with delight.

Some minor adjustments were made as everyone looked on. Fortunately, there were only a few alterations needed, and they soon after left the shop.

The ladies decided to walk to the Phillips's home, and as they passed people on the street, Mrs. Bennet proudly declared to almost everyone they met that her beautiful daughter was about to marry Mr. Bingley of Netherfield.

As they passed a milliner's shop, Kitty begged to stop and look at the bonnets and purchase some ribbon to add to one of hers.

"Well, do not dawdle!" Mrs. Bennet ordered. "We will not be long at my sister's. If you are not there when I am ready to leave, you will have to walk home."

"Yes, Mama."

Mrs. Phillips was delighted to see everyone and eager to hear all about the dress, which Jane was willing to describe to her. While Jane was modest with her description, Mrs. Bennet was effusive.

Clasping her hands in jubilation, Mrs. Bennet exclaimed, "Oh, sister! You will agree, I am certain, when you see Jane walk down the aisle, that you will have never seen a more beautiful bride!"

Mrs. Phillips nodded politely, and Jane's cheeks reddened in a blush.

Later, when Mrs. Bennet and Mrs. Phillips began to discuss the latest fashions in London with Mrs. Gardiner, Jane and Elizabeth excused themselves. They wondered at Kitty's extended absence and thought to go fetch her.

Mrs. Bennet agreed it was a splendid idea. "I hope to depart soon, so tell Kitty if she wants to ride in the carriage, to come directly."

"We will, Mother," Jane replied.

Once outside their aunt's home, Elizabeth looked at her sister and smiled. "I know she hopes to depart soon, but that will likely depend on how much gossip there is to hear!"

As they walked the short distance to the shop, Elizabeth took Jane's arm. "Oh, Jane, can you believe your wedding is almost here?" She felt Jane's arm tighten about hers.

"Lizzy, there are times when I feel like pinching myself to make sure this is not a dream."

"Trust me, Jane. It is not a dream."

As they turned the corner, Elizabeth pointed up ahead. "There is Kitty over there by that carriage. It appears she is speaking to the passenger inside.

At that moment, a gentleman stepped out from behind the open door.

Elizabeth suddenly stopped. "Jane! I think it is Mr. Wickham!" Her heart plummeted as she realized what was happening. She wrapped her fingers tightly about Jane's arm. "Oh, no! They are getting into the carriage together! Come, we must hurry!" As they rushed down street, they watched in horror as the carriage drove off down the street.

"Kitty!" Elizabeth screamed, but she knew it was highly unlikely their sister heard her. They watched the carriage disappear as it turned a corner. "Oh, Jane! What has Kitty done? What was she thinking?"

"I do not know!" Jane's voice trembled. "Do you think he forced her to get into the carriage with him?"

"I know not what just occurred." She grabbed Jane's hand and looked about for someone on horseback who could give chase, but there was no one nearby. She drew in a shaky breath. "Come, it is critical we inform Mother and our aunt and uncle. Perhaps Uncle Phillips can notify the authorities and begin a search, and Father must be told." As they hurried back to their aunt and uncle's home, she added, almost completely spent of breath, "Jane, you and I must go to Netherfield! We must also tell Mr. Darcy directly!"

Mrs. Bennet received the news with much wailing and crying for her smelling salts. She vacillated between optimism that he must have good intentions towards her second youngest daughter and great fear that harm might befall her. "But he is basically a good man," she tried to reassure herself. "So handsome in his red coat. Perhaps he is in love with her and has asked for her hand! Yes, he must be on his way to get Mr. Bennet's approval."

"Even if he was, which I highly doubt, it is not likely Father would give his approval, Mother," Elizabeth said. "But we must leave immediately to inform him."

"Yes! We must go, but I am certain they are on their way to

Longbourn this very moment!"

Mr. Phillips assured them he would begin a search, while he helped the ladies into the carriage.

The carriage took Jane and Elizabeth to within a mile of Netherfield, where the sisters stepped out to walk the remainder of the distance so their mother and Mrs. Gardiner could reach Longbourn as soon as possible. Elizabeth was weary of hearing her mother make excuses for Wickham, conveniently forgetting how they had been warned about him.

Once out of the carriage, the quiet of the countryside eased Elizabeth's concerns, if only because her father and Mr. Darcy would soon know.

It was an easy walk, and with quickened steps, they soon arrived at Netherfield Manor.

~~*

They were shown into the sitting room where Mr. Bingley jumped to his feet, a wide smile on his face when the two ladies were announced.

"Jane! Miss Elizabeth! What a pleasant surprise!" His smile faded when he noticed their sombre expressions. "Is something wrong?"

Elizabeth nodded. "Something dreadful has happened!"

Darcy rushed to them, his eyes searching Elizabeth's face. "What is it?" Without thinking, Darcy began to reach his hand out to her.

He was prevented from doing so, however, when Miss Bingley hurried over and stood between them. "Yes, please tell us what has happened?"

"It may be nothing," Elizabeth said as she tried to catch her breath. "We were in Meryton, and Kitty wanted to go into one of the shops, while Jane and I accompanied our mother and Aunt Gardiner to visit our Aunt and Uncle Phillips. Later, Jane and I saw Kitty get into a carriage with a gentleman." Her brows pinched together as she turned to Mr. Darcy. "We believe it was Mr. Wickham."

The heat of anger surged through Darcy. "Heavens! She got

into the carriage with him? Did it look as though he forced her to get in?"

Elizabeth's eyes filled with tears. "I could not tell, but she was warned to stay away from Mr. Wickham, and I do not believe she would have gone with him voluntarily. The carriage drove off as soon as he stepped in behind her." She looked at Darcy with pleading eyes. "They must be found as soon as possible. If he has taken her against her will…"

Caroline shook her head and began wringing her hands. "No! No! He would never do such a thing! Certainly nothing so blatantly wicked." Caroline's face grew flushed. "I am certain this must be a… a misunderstanding!"

"I hope so, but knowing him as I do, I cannot help but wonder what he may be up to." Elizabeth's lips began to tremble, and she turned back to Darcy.

Caroline quietly stepped back, and Darcy immediately took the opportunity to move closer to Elizabeth. He wanted so much to reassure and comfort her with words, but he was not as optimistic as Caroline when it came to Wickham. He glanced at Bingley, who had drawn Jane into his arms, quietly consoling her. How he wished he could do the same with Elizabeth!

He gently took her hand, enfolding it within his. "I spent the whole of the morning searching for him, but to no avail. Can you give us a description of him and of the carriage?" He found himself stroking the palm of her hand and had to force himself to stop when he noticed Elizabeth looking down, her cheeks the most delightful rose colour. He shook his head to concentrate on what she was saying.

"He… he has grown a short beard, and his hair was a little longer." She looked up and met his gaze. "I was not close enough to see if there were any distinguishing markings on the carriage."

Darcy spoke to a nearby servant. "Please have the carriage brought around to the front and have someone ready my horse."

"Of course, sir."

Darcy turned to his friend. "Bingley, would you escort the ladies back to Longbourn so they can await news with their family? I shall go see if there is anything I can discover."

Elizabeth looked at him with a smile of gratitude. "We thank you, sir." She bit her lip, and he felt her give his hand a squeeze. "Please take care. I would not have you do anything that might prove dangerous to you."

Darcy placed his other hand atop hers. Her hand felt so soft in his, and he was tempted to stand and hold it, gazing into her eyes. It took his every ounce of determination to release it. "I will do everything in my power to ensure your sister's safety."

Chapter 34

As Bingley's carriage rambled towards Longbourn, Elizabeth could barely remain calm. She now worried not only about Kitty, but also Mr. Darcy. Exactly what *was* Mr. Wickham capable of? And why was he so determined to cause such distress to Mr. Darcy and now to her family, as well?

She pinched her eyes closed as she tried to figure out what his motive might be. Why would he have taken Kitty? Had she gone with him by her own volition or had he taken her by force? She shook her head and shuddered.

Mr. Bingley was doing his best to console the two ladies, reassuring them everything was being done to find Kitty and he hoped it would all turn out to be a misunderstanding. Jane seemed to be soothed by his words; Elizabeth knew too much about Mr. Wickham to believe there was not something menacing afoot.

Jane could see the concern on her sister's face. She reached out for her hand. "Lizzy, perhaps we will find Kitty has returned. When we get home, all shall be well and our worry for naught."

"I hope so, Jane, but I still do not understand why the man returned. He resigned the militia but departed without paying off his debts in Meryton." She rubbed her fingers nervously. "He is being sought by too many people that he should risk coming back unless he had some incentive, which translates into money."

Bingley held Jane's hand, stroking it gently. "Darcy has told me a little about Wickham over the years. It is difficult to believe someone you have known all your life would resort to something like this." He quickly patted Jane's hand. "Not that it is anything we need to worry about." He tried to smile, but it quickly faded. "I am certain everything will be all right."

When they arrived at Longbourn, they rushed into the house.

"Mama?" Elizabeth cried out as she took off her bonnet. She heard a moan coming from the sitting room, and the three hurried to it.

Mrs. Bennet sat in a chair dabbing her forehead with a handkerchief. She sat up abruptly when her daughters and Mr. Bingley stepped in. "Do you have some news? Has Kitty been found?"

"Not that we know," Elizabeth said. She looked at her aunt, who was holding one of her mother's hands.

"Your father and uncle have gone to Meryton to see what they can find out. We are hoping to hear something soon."

Elizabeth sat down next to her aunt. "Mr. Darcy has gone out to look for them, as well." She looked down at her hands, clasped in her lap. "If only we had been with her, this would not have happened!"

Jane stepped over to her sister. "Lizzy, you cannot blame yourself for this! We had no idea something like this was going to happen. Kitty must take some of the blame, do you not think?"

Elizabeth pressed her lips tightly and lowered her brows. "But it is not like Kitty." She suddenly looked up. "Has anyone talked to Lydia?"

Her aunt nodded slightly. "Yes, before your father left, he demanded to know what she knew. She did not have much information to give him."

"She has to know something!" Elizabeth said indignantly. She stood up and walked to the door. "I am going to pester her until she gives me some answers or until Kitty returns!"

She took the stairs hurriedly and came to Lydia's door, which was closed. She tapped on it a few times.

"What now?" Lydia moaned.

"Lydia, it is Elizabeth. I need to talk to you."

Lydia opened the door and then turned and walked to her bed. She fell down upon it as she complained, "I told Father everything I know!"

Elizabeth fisted her hands as she attempted to remain calm. "Yes, Lydia, I know. But maybe there is something you feel is not even important. Something that might shed some light on why Mr. Wickham is here or why he took Kitty. Did he say anything that might indicate what he was about?"

Lydia shook her head. "No! And I am so tired of hearing about

Wickham and Kitty!" She pounded her fists down upon the bed. "He preferred me! Even when he became engaged to Mary King, he told me he preferred me over any other lady!"

Elizabeth shook her head. "Lydia, a man ought not talk like that when he is engaged."

"Well, that is all I know. The day we saw him, we visited briefly, and then he left to see someone."

"See someone? Do you know who?"

Lydia shook her head. "No, he didn't say."

Elizabeth pressed her fingers to her forehead and moved them in a circular motion. "Can you think of anything else he said? Did he ask about anyone?"

"He asked whether Mr. Darcy had returned with his friend to Netherfield."

"He did? What did you say?"

"I said he had. Should I have not told the truth?"

"Of course," Elizabeth closed her eyes for a moment. "Did he ask about anyone else?"

"Yes." Lydia looked at Elizabeth. "He asked whether you had returned home from London."

"And, of course, you said I had."

Lydia nodded. "Then he said there was someone he had to see, and he left."

Elizabeth sat silently for a moment. When she said nothing more, Lydia finally asked, "Are we done?"

Elizabeth nodded. "I think so. Thank you, Lydia."

She returned to the sitting room pondering all Lydia had told her. There were two things her sister had said that struck her as possibly important. One was Wickham did not have any interest in Kitty. Although that could have been Lydia's vanity speaking, Elizabeth knew Kitty was not as flirtatious and fun as her youngest sister. Someone like Wickham would prefer Lydia over Kitty. And the other thing was once Wickham heard that both she and Darcy had returned, he said he had to see someone. But who?

Elizabeth shook her head. She was not certain, but it now seemed probable someone else was behind this scheme and was paying him to carry it out!

She stopped outside the sitting room door. If Wickham was

being paid to prevent any sort of attachment between Darcy and herself, that would not be worth his risking jail or even death by committing a crime as severe as kidnapping. And what purpose would that achieve in bringing that objective about? There was something she was not seeing, and she desperately hoped they would have some answers soon.

~~*

After seeing Bingley and the ladies into the carriage, Darcy set out for the stables. He heard the brisk clip clop of a horse, and turned to see Miss Bingley drive away in a phaeton that had been brought to the far side of the house. He shook his head in disbelief. He knew she occasionally drove one by herself, but he was surprised she chose to do so now.

He watched with curiosity as the phaeton set off in the opposite direction from Meryton, which was where he assumed she was going. He could understand her having an appointment in the small village, but could not account for her driving in the opposite direction.

He hurried his steps and met the stable boy as he brought out the saddled horse.

"Thank you!" he said, more brusquely than he intended. He clenched his jaw tightly as he mounted. He drew in a breath. "Thank you, young man."

He gave the horse a kick and set out, but not for Meryton. He was not certain, but Miss Bingley's behaviour earlier when Wickham was mentioned was quite peculiar. He was not sure why, but she seemed more unnerved by it than he would have expected. And why did she depart suddenly without properly taking her leave. But more importantly, where was she going?

He brought the horse to within sight of the phaeton as it began to travel into a heavily wooded area. She had no acquaintances in this part of the neighbourhood, and he suspected she would never wish to be seen with any of the people who might live out here, as the homes were mere cottages and the residents mostly farmers.

The road she took was one Darcy had never travelled, and he looked from one side to the other as he took in the occasional tenant dwelling. The farther from Netherfield Miss Bingley travelled, the greater his suspicions grew.

The phaeton slowed and turned down a narrow road. When he came to the road, he looked ahead and saw it led to a small, rather derelict cottage. Shutters hung askew at the window, and the hand railing up the front steps had splintered into two useless pieces.

There was no noticeable landscape; weeds had overtaken the lawn, and unpruned foliage filled the garden beds. Darcy looked incredulously at the sight before him, wondering what Miss Bingley was doing here.

He had no idea how she might be involved, but he was certain her coming here had something to do with Mr. Wickham!

While making sure he remained concealed in the thick trees, he guided the horse off the road and drew near the cottage, where he reined it in. After tethering the horse, he walked stealthily towards the cottage, coming around the far side, so he would not be seen. He stayed hidden but peered out to see Miss Bingley step out of her phaeton.

He suddenly heard a door slam shut and saw a man hurry towards her. He quickly drew his head back and fisted his hands. His heart lurched in his chest, and he closed his eyes. The man walking towards Miss Bingley was none other than George Wickham!

Darcy's heart pounded with anger as he watched Miss Bingley and Wickham, but before he confronted the two, he hoped to hear some news about Miss Kitty.

"What are you doing here?" Wickham demanded as he marched towards Miss Bingley. "You were never to come here!"

Miss Bingley braced her hands on her hips. "I have come to find out what reckless act you have perpetrated! Whatever were you thinking?" Miss Bingley demanded in a high-pitched squeal. "I did not expect you to commit such a crime as abduction! I can ill afford to be associated with such behaviour!"

"Abduction?" Wickham exclaimed. "I did not abduct anyone!"

"You mean Miss Kitty Bennet went with you voluntarily?"

"Well, not quite voluntarily…"

Darcy could barely maintain his control, but he remained steadfastly out of sight until he knew more.

"I did not pay you to break the law! You are a fool and have made a mess of this whole affair, first with that young man at Rosings and now with Miss Kitty!"

Darcy's eyes widened, and his heart lurched at the news his best friend's sister was not only involved in this affair, but was likely the instigator!

He watched Wickham lean into her. "The scheme was working quite successfully with Rickland, and he felt he was making good progress. Besides, he claimed Miss Elizabeth harboured a great deal of animosity towards Darcy. She told him so to his face!" He braced his hands on his hips. "How do you know she does not still feel the same? What makes you think anything has changed?"

Caroline shook her head. "I can readily discern when a woman has the intention of securing a gentleman's affections, and I recognized it immediately when I saw the two of them together. And for some inexplicable reason, Mr. Darcy still seems to take obvious pleasure in her society."

Despite his shock in discovering Miss Bingley's involvement in Wickham's scheme, he could not help but wonder if she was correct about Elizabeth's feelings. He remained still, straining to hear every word.

Wickham laughed. "Ha! If she is seeking his attentions, it has to be due solely for his fortune. She likely has given thought to what she could do with all his money!" He let out a huff. "That man does not know how to charm a woman as I do. In fact, she was quite partial to me when I first came into the neighbourhood."

"I do not care whether her affection leans to him or his money; I paid you to do something to make *him* realize what a misplaced affection this is!" Caroline brought her hand up to her forehead. "You will not receive a single shilling more until I am convinced there will be no wedding between them!"

Wickham began arguing with her, and Darcy closed his eyes and leaned his head back. He pinched his brows together as he attempted to push back the thought that Elizabeth had been receiving his attentions solely for his fortune. Could that be true?

He did not care! He loved her and would shower her with anything she wanted. His heart sank, however, as he knew he wanted nothing more than for her to love him for himself alone.

He listened intently, hearing nothing but silence for a few moments. He was about to step out when he heard Miss Bingley.

"You must tell me where the girl is!"

"She is probably home by now. I professed my undying love to her and tried to persuade her to accompany me to Gretna Greene to be married, but she would have none of it. After several attempts to get her to agree, she insisted we let her out, so we obliged." Wickham directed a glare at her. "I did nothing wrong, and Mrs. Younge, who was with me, will vouch for everything I have said."

Darcy was shocked Wickham was still bringing Mrs. Younge into his schemes. But he was relieved Miss Kitty had not been taken against her will – if Wickham was being truthful.

Miss Bingley's face contorted in anger. "What do you think marrying that silly girl would do?"

Wickham arrogantly crossed his arms in front of him. "I had my reasons. Unfortunately, I believe I would have been more successful had it had been her sister Lydia. I am certain she would have left with me, and then my scheme would have worked. When I was unsuccessful in coming upon Lydia alone, I hoped, but actually strongly doubted, that Kitty would agree to elope."

"I still do not understand," Caroline said. "What would eloping with that foolish girl have accomplished?"

Wickham smiled and began stroking his beard. "Do you not see? If I married one of the Bennet sisters, Darcy would likely want nothing to do with Miss Elizabeth." He leaned in towards her. "He would not wish to marry her because he would then be forced to acknowledge me as his brother!"

"Why do you have such a haughty look on your face? I see nothing intelligent in this idea of yours. There is no guarantee he would choose not to marry her!"

"Ahh," said Wickham, pointing a finger at her. "That is where this was such a brilliant plan. For if I married Kitty or Lydia, and he married Elizabeth, I would be his brother, and he would be forced to provide for me." He let out a sinister laugh. "I would not need your trifling money."

"You are a fool!" Caroline declared.

"You both are fools!" Darcy said in a formidable voice as he marched around the corner of the house towards them.

Caroline's face drained of its colour and then grew flushed. "Mr. Darcy, I... How long have you..."

Darcy put up his hand. "We shall speak of this later, Miss Bingley. Right now, Wickham, tell me exactly where Miss Kitty is!"

He gave a slight shrug of his shoulders. "She is not here."

Darcy took a few steps closer and glared at him. "Tell me where she is!"

"She is likely home by now. She asked to be let out, so we let her out. There is a road about a mile back that she said leads to Longbourn."

Darcy rubbed his jaw. "I am not leaving this place until I am certain she is not here, and I plan to check with Mrs. Younge to see if her story corroborates yours." He gave Wickham a menacing glare. "I assume Mrs. Younge is inside?"

Wickham tilted his head and raised a single brow. "She is, but I am rather disappointed, Darcy, that you do not believe me."

"I can rarely believe anything you say, Wickham."

"You think me so vile I would kidnap a young lady?"

Darcy drew himself erect, and Wickham did the same. They stood about the same height, so their eyes locked.

"I know when it concerns women or money, nothing is beneath you!" Darcy stated gruffly.

Wickham smiled. "I see you still have not forgiven me for capturing your sister's heart. She was such a sweet thing... and so trusting."

Darcy's fist clenched as tightly as his jaw. "You will not speak of my sister again! Now, you will wait here while I verify your story."

Wickham extended his hand towards the front door. "Be my guest."

Darcy glanced at Miss Bingley, who had barely moved; a look of fear glazed her face. "Wait in the phaeton until I know for a certainty Miss Kitty is not here. If she is here, she will need to ride back with you."

Caroline gave a resigned nod of her head, barely looking up as she did.

Darcy had to walk away from Wickham to avoid striking him.

He was furious but would not lower himself to violence, as much as he felt inclined to act on it. He walked towards the front door with Wickham on his heels.

"You will find I am telling the truth. She is not here."

Darcy stopped abruptly and turned. He pushed his index finger into Wickham's chest. "I need to see for myself, and if I find that you so much as touched her, I shall make sure you spend the rest of your life in prison!"

Wickham straightened his shoulders. "You shall see, Darcy. I have done nothing wrong."

"Wait here while I speak with Mrs. Younge."

Darcy looked around as he walked through the house. He could barely breathe, as the odours emanating throughout were nauseating. "Hello!" he said loudly. A moan came from a back room, and he rushed to it, his heart racing. "Miss Kitty?"

"Who is it?" the voice cried.

When he came to the small room, he saw Mrs. Younge. Her eyes, drooping from sleep and most likely an excess of drink, widened when she saw him.

"Mr. Darcy!" she gasped.

"Mrs. Younge," he said in acknowledgment.

"I... um... what a pleasant surprise!"

"Mrs. Younge, I am not here to be social, nor am I here to be civil. I demand to know what happened to Miss Kitty!"

"Oh," she said, slowly rising from her chair. She rubbed her forehead with a few fingers and promptly sat back down. "Miss Kitty. I believe she intended to walk home. She refused Mr. Wickham's offer of marriage." She slowly shook her head. "I cannot imagine why she would not want to marry him, such a charming gentleman he is." She let out a long sigh. "Once she said she would not have him, we let her out of the carriage."

As Mrs. Younge spoke, Darcy looked about him. The cottage was in great disorder, but he opened the closet doors and cupboards to make certain Kitty was not there. He called out her name several times.

"Mr. Darcy, she is not here."

He looked around a bit longer before he was satisfied. "I know it is not worth my effort to tell you and Wickham to remain here for the authorities to come for you, but I warn you if I find any harm has come upon the girl, I shall seek you both out and make sure you will never walk free again!"

Mrs. Young smiled. "No harm has befallen her. I am not a violent person, Mr. Darcy, only one who looks to come into some money, and this seemed a good plan… at first."

Darcy stepped out of the house and walked over to Wickham. He issued the same stern warning to him as he had to Mrs Younge. He did not wait for a response before he walked over to Caroline. He could tell she had been crying, and she would not meet his eyes.

"We shall take the road towards Meryton to look for the path Miss Kitty may have taken, and then set out in the direction of Longbourn. She may be tired and need a ride, so you must go with me. I will follow behind you."

Miss Bingley nodded, and he turned to retrieve his horse.

"Mr. Darcy," her shaky voice called out.

"Yes?"

"I am… I am sorry. I do not know what came over me to do such a thing."

Darcy did not reply and began to walk again.

"You are not going to say anything to Charles about this, are you?"

Darcy stopped and turned back. "He has every right to know. Miss Bennet's sisters will soon be his sisters. He bears every responsibility towards them as he has towards you." Darcy looked down and kicked the dirt. Taking in a breath between clenched teeth, he then added, "Yes, Miss Bingley, I most certainly am going to tell him!"

Chapter 35

As Darcy followed the phaeton, he suddenly felt a wave of fatigue sweep over him. He was emotionally spent after having gone through all the uncertainty throughout the day. When he first heard Wickham was in the area, he could not help but wonder what the man was up to, and since hearing what he had done, he had been anxious about Elizabeth's sister. Once they determined Miss Kitty was safe, he would feel a degree of relief over that matter; however, he was now faced with another uncertainty. Did Elizabeth only care about him for his money?

He tried to think back to the time when she seemed to change in her regard. Had he said anything about his wealth? He blew out a puff of air as he recollected telling her all about Pemberley as they walked at Rosings. And he knew that knowledge of his fortune seemed to follow him everywhere. He recollected even hearing it discussed at the Meryton Assembly. He shuddered at the thought. But more than that, he wondered about the possibility Elizabeth may have decided it would not be so disagreeable after all to be married to someone as wealthy as he.

He shook his head. Wickham may have merely been speaking wishfully, rather than with any certainty. And yet, he could not help wondering. After all, she had for quite some time truly despised him.

Although Darcy kept an eye out for a road that might lead to Longbourn, in truth he saw little of the land they passed. The image of Elizabeth's smiling face, sparkling eyes, lively laugh, and intelligent conversation was all he could think of. And he felt real pain deep within as he pondered whether any of it had been truly for him.

He brought the horse to a halt as he suddenly realized the phaeton had stopped. He pulled up alongside and looked at Caroline. "Is there a problem?"

She drew in a shaky breath. "I think we have travelled about a mile, and this little road to our right seems to lead to that small hill, which I believe is Oakham Mount. I remember Miss Elizabeth saying she would often walk to it from Longbourn."

Darcy followed Caroline's gaze, realizing she was probably correct.

"If it is, Longbourn is still a good distance. I hope Miss Kitty is all right if she has had to walk that far."

Caroline's face paled, and she gripped the reins tightly to mask her trembling. "As do I, Mr. Darcy." She stole a glance up at him. "I truly do."

The road they turned down was empty. There were no homesteads, so if Kitty had needed assistance, there would have been no one around to help her. Darcy pinched his brows together, looking on both sides of the road for any sign of her. Perhaps she was familiar with the area and knew of a shortcut to get home.

After travelling for about fifteen minutes, he noticed a figure slumped on the side of the road ahead. His heart pounded, and he kicked the horse, bringing it to a gallop. He rode around the phaeton, and as he drew near, he saw it was a young lady.

"Hello there!" he called out. "Are you all right?"

When the young lady slowly lifted her head, Darcy saw it was indeed Kitty, and he brought the horse to a stop. He quickly slid off and rushed to her side.

"Miss Kitty!" He hurried over to her. "Are you hurt?"

Kitty slowly shook her head, looking somewhat confused. "No, but I am tired." Tears began streaming down her face. "How did you find me? I thought no one would." When she looked over and saw Caroline Bingley driving a phaeton towards her, she crinkled her nose and pinched her brows together in disbelief. "And Miss Bingley, too!"

"Never mind that now; we must get you home. Everyone is so worried about you." Darcy reached down to help her. "Can you stand, or shall I lift you?"

Kitty looked up into his face and bit her lip. "I think... I believe I could use your assistance."

"If you would allow me to carry you to the phaeton, Miss

Bingley will drive you back to Longbourn."

As he lifted her, Kitty smiled. "I have never been carried by a gentleman before... at least not since I grew up."

"I am honoured to be the first."

Kitty inhaled deeply. "I am not at all like Lizzy, who can walk for hours on end and find herself barely out of breath."

Darcy nodded, a smile appearing as he thought of all his walks with Elizabeth. "Your sister does enjoy walking."

He set Kitty down next to Caroline and then stood back, rubbing his jaw. "Tell me, Miss Kitty, did Wickham do anything – anything at all – improper when you were in the carriage with him?"

Kitty looked down and shook her head. "I never should have entered that carriage with him, but no, he did nothing inappropriate."

Darcy felt a wave of relief wash over him.

"Can you tell me what happened?"

Kitty clasped her hands tightly together. "When the carriage stopped, and he stepped out, I was startled to see him. But he told me there was a lady in the carriage who greatly wished to meet me."

"So you stepped in to meet her?"

Kitty silently nodded. After a moment, she continued, "Mr. Wickham immediately stepped in after me and the door closed. When the carriage started to move, he began to profess his love and admiration for me. He told me he could think of no one other than me."

Darcy rubbed his jaw. "I am certain that is something any lady would enjoy hearing from a gentleman."

A blush tinted Kitty's cheeks. "Then he told me he wanted to elope with me. The lady with him, Mrs. Younge, assured me I was all he talked about because he cared for me so deeply."

"And you believed both of them?"

"At first."

"Then what happened?"

"Mr. Darcy, you must think me a simple-minded, foolish girl! But you see, I was flattered he was singling me out. It was hard not to be. Most men adore Lydia and only pay attention to me because

I am with her. I thought… I hoped… it was true, although I knew we had been warned about him."

"And then?"

"I told him I did not want to elope. I want a lovely wedding with my family and friends. He became rather desperate in his pleas, even angry. I began to suspect something else was behind his declaration of love." She looked up and a tear trickled down her cheek. "Fortunately, I came to my senses and asked to be let out."

"I am glad you did."

Kitty nodded. "I was actually becoming quite frightened of his behaviour by then. I think Mrs. Younge began to worry. She told him if he did not release me, they might both be arrested. She insisted he let me out."

"Thank you, Miss Bennet. I know this has not been easy. I am grateful no harm befell you." He turned to Caroline. "Miss Bingley, I shall escort you until we are in sight of Longbourn, then I shall set off for Meryton to advise anyone there who still might be looking for Miss Kitty that she has been found." He turned his head back in the direction of the cottage. "And I shall advise the authorities where Wickham is." He paused and said, "Or at least where he was when I last saw him." He let out a huff. "I do not know whether he has actually committed a crime, but I know there are people looking for him who want to be paid back what he owes them."

Miss Bingley drove the phaeton towards Longbourn, and Darcy followed behind. He watched, noticing that neither lady spoke to the other, and he thought both likely felt a great deal of shame. He shook his head and wondered how Bingley would feel when he discovered what his sister had done. He would not worry about that now. He knew however Bingley chose to handle the situation, *he* would no longer tolerate his sister's company. If she remained at Netherfield until the wedding, he would find suitable lodgings in which to stay. A smile formed on his lips as he considered he might inquire whether Mrs. Bennet's offer for a particular room still stood.

He nudged the horse with his heels, causing it to raise its head and begin to gallop. He gently pulled the reins and patted its neck as he reprimanded himself. He had to cease such thoughts. He could not torment himself with what might never be with Elizabeth.

He hoped he and Elizabeth would finally have some time to themselves. He needed to find out once and for all if she cared for him. Since leaving Kent, he felt she had been amiable towards him and seemed to welcome his attentions. He let out a huff. At least she had not rebuffed him when he kissed her hand and even more so, when he kissed her cheek.

He shook his head. Now that the concerns that had weighed him down since last evening were alleviated, he could not stop thinking about Elizabeth. Oh, how he hoped beyond hope she had come to love him as much as he loved her.

~~*

At the sound of Longbourn's front door being opened and voices in the hallway, the family all jumped up. Kitty stepped into the sitting room alone.

"Kitty!" exclaimed Mrs. Bennet. "You are safe! I knew how it would be! But where is that fine Mr. Wickham?"

Elizabeth rushed over and hugged her as Lydia bounded down the stairs. "Has Kitty returned?" Lydia asked.

"Yes," replied Elizabeth. "Kitty, we are so happy to see you! You must tell us what happened. How did you get home?"

Kitty walked to a chair and fell into it. "Miss Bingley brought me. She wished to return directly to Netherfield."

Elizabeth jerked her head back. "Miss Bingley?"

Charles and Jane rushed over. "My sister found you?" Charles's eyes narrowed in confusion.

She nodded and leaned her head back. "I am so tired and thirsty."

Mrs. Bennet turned to Elizabeth. "Ring the bell for Hill, Lizzy."

Elizabeth walked over to ring for a servant, but saw Hill outside the door. "Please bring Miss Kitty something to drink."

She came back and sat down in front of her sister. "Tell us what happened, Kitty. We have been so concerned."

Kitty looked down at her fingers, which she nervously entwined together. "I saw Mr. Wickham, and he was so friendly and seemed delighted to see me. He said there was a lady in the carriage who wished to meet me." She pursed her lips together and her eyes filled with tears. "He said it was providential he encountered me, as he had been speaking to this lady, a Mrs. Younge, about me." Her brows pinched, and she cast a remorseful look at Elizabeth. "I was more curious than anything else, and stepped in the carriage to meet this woman. I had no idea Mr. Wickham would also get in, and then, before I realized what was happening, the carriage began moving."

"Kitty! We told you Mr. Wickham cannot be trusted!"

"I know that now." She glanced up quickly and then cast her gaze back down. "He began to tell me how deeply he had fallen in love with me and had been talking endlessly about me to Mrs. Younge." She gazed up at Elizabeth with a look of regret. "I was more flattered than wise, and it was when he began insisting we elope that I realized something was not quite right." She shook her head. "I still do not know why he wished to elope with me, but I told them to let me out of the carriage at once."

Lydia's expression seemed to indicate she doubted the truth of Kitty's version of the events that transpired, but she said nothing.

Mrs. Hill brought in some tea and biscuits, and Kitty took several sips of the warm liquid.

"Mr. Wickham tapped for the carriage to stop and I stepped out. I could see Oakham Mount and began walking towards it, but I grew so weary, I had to finally sit down by the side of the road. There was no one around, and I thought I would die out there."

"And how did Caroline happen to come by?" Charles asked.

"She and Mr. Darcy both happened by."

"Mr. Darcy?" exclaimed Elizabeth. "What was he doing there with Miss Bingley?"

Kitty shrugged her shoulders. "I do not know. He was riding his horse while Miss Bingley drove a phaeton. He made certain I was all right and helped me into the phaeton. He followed us to within sight of Longbourn, and then set off to Meryton to inform them I had been found and to tell them where Mr. Wickham was."

"You mean they found Mr. Wickham's whereabouts?"

Kitty nodded. "I assume. I was not in the mood to talk to Miss

Bingley, and she did not seem at all inclined to talk to me. All I know is what Mr. Darcy said before we set off for Longbourn." She finished her tea. "Oh, I am so glad to be home!"

As the rest of the family talked with Kitty about how grateful they were no harm had befallen her, Elizabeth noticed Lydia remained uncharacteristically silent. She was certain Lydia felt a great deal of jealousy as well as curiosity about what happened and why. She was certain Lydia would want to hear every detail of Kitty's dealings with Mr. Wickham once they were alone in their room tonight. She hoped Lydia would come to realize how much of a scoundrel he was.

But Elizabeth could not help but wonder how Mr. Darcy had found Mr. Wickham. And why was he with Miss Bingley? Oh, the questions she had for Mr. Darcy continued to increase. She would barely know where to begin once she had time alone with him. Most of all, she hoped to assure him of her feelings for him – as long as his had not changed. Her insides fluttered at the mere thought of spending time alone with him, but she knew not when that might be!

Kitty had little additional information to give, and Elizabeth realized she would have to wait until they heard from either Mr. Darcy or Miss Bingley. Whatever the circumstances, she was grateful Kitty was safe and out of Mr. Wickham's hands.

As dusk fell, Mr. Bingley thought it best to take his leave. As they all walked to the door, Mr. Bennet returned.

"Oh, Mr. Bennet! Is this not the best news? Kitty has returned home!" Mrs. Bennet rushed up to her husband, a wide smile on her face.

"Yes, it is." He took off his hat, and a servant helped him out of his coat. "I do not wish to discuss it now." He directed a glare at Kitty. "I shall have a word with you in the morning." He walked into his study, closing the door behind him.

"Well, it has all turned out as we hoped," Jane said. "Please express our deepest appreciation to Caroline for bringing her back."

"I shall!" Bingley replied, looking at Jane with a smile of adoration.

"And please do the same for Mr. Darcy," Elizabeth said.

"Whatever his involvement was, we appreciate it."

"Certainly!"

Jane walked with Bingley to the carriage, while Elizabeth waited for her sister outside the front door. She could not imagine the events that took place, but as she thought about it, she recollected Miss Bingley had disappeared soon after she and Jane had arrived and told them what had happened regarding Kitty and Mr. Wickham.

Elizabeth pinched her brows. She could not imagine Miss Bingley feeling the inclination to look for Kitty herself. She shook her head. No, she would not be concerned enough for one of the younger Bennet sisters that she would do something like that. Elizabeth looked back towards the window of her father's study, which glowed from the light of the candles inside.

"Certainly, he must know!"

She bit her lip as she pondered whether he would allow her in to speak with him. She looked back at Jane and Charles, who seemed completely oblivious to her presence. Smiling, she opened the front door and entered, walking directly to the study.

She gave a slight tap onto the closed door and waited for a reply.

"Come in," Mr. Bennet said. When he looked up and saw it was Elizabeth, he closed the book he had been reading. "I wondered how long it would be before you came to see me."

"Do you mind, Father?" When he waved for her to come in, she walked in and sat down. "Thank you."

"So, Lizzy, what do you want to know. I am certain you have questions."

"I would have you tell me everything, for I do not even know what to ask."

"I shall tell you, my dear, but you must promise me something."

The look on her father's face told her it was rather alarming. "Of course!"

"You must not tell anyone in the family yet, especially Jane. It is imperative you do not mention this to her because Charles will want to tell her himself."

"They are outside at this moment. Might he be informing her

now?"

Mr. Bennet shook his head. "He is not yet aware of this information."

Elizabeth pinched her brows in confusion. "I fear I do not understand."

Mr. Bennet rubbed his chin, and when he spoke, his voice was sombre. "What I found out tonight concerns his sister. Miss Bingley has acted quite shamelessly, and Mr. Darcy feels it should be up to Mr. Bingley to tell Jane. He will be informed once he returns to Netherfield."

Elizabeth's thoughts swirled with every possibility. "Father, I cannot imagine what she could have done."

Mr. Bennet stood up and clasped his hands behind his back. He began pacing about the room. "Apparently, it was Miss Bingley who concocted this whole scheme with Mr. Wickham."

"Miss Bingley was behind it?" Elizabeth's eyes widened, and her jaw dropped.

Mr. Bennet nodded and then leaned against the wall. "It would seem, dearest Lizzy, that Miss Bingley perceived Mr. Darcy had a strong affection for you!" A wry smile appeared. "Can you imagine? Mr. Darcy bestowing his affections on my Lizzy?"

Elizabeth could think of nothing to say, she was in such shock.

"I see you are speechless, as well. Of course, Miss Bingley was of the opinion it was a rather misplaced affection!" He leaned in towards Elizabeth with a wide smile. "I suppose she was hoping he would fall in love with *her*."

Elizabeth shook her head, her thoughts still trying to comprehend Miss Bingley's actions. "I cannot believe she would resort to such a scheme."

"Apparently, she encountered Wickham in London several months ago and paid him to discourage Mr. Darcy from this partiality he seems to have for you." He let out a laugh. "I still find it astonishing Mr. Darcy is in love with you!"

Elizabeth felt her cheeks warm in a blush.

He shrugged his shoulders. "Somehow this Rickland character was brought into it." He walked over and leaned against his desk next to Elizabeth. "I can see you find this as astonishing as I did."

"Yes, it is all so surprising, but what did Miss Bingley do this evening? She is the one who brought Kitty back."

"Mr. Darcy saw her leaving Netherfield after she heard you say Kitty had disappeared with Wickham. Darcy was suspicious because she was not heading in the direction of Meryton, but out where she would not have known anyone who lived there."

"She knew where Mr. Wickham was and went to see him?"

Mr. Bennet nodded. "Now, rest assured, Lizzy, she was not involved in Wickham's latest scheme to kidnap my daughter, which I am not certain he actually did. When she heard your suspicions he had abducted Kitty, she went to confront him. She led Mr. Darcy directly to him, as he followed her on horseback without her knowing."

"But Miss Bingley! Oh, I wonder how Charles will take this news. I am certain it will cast a serious pall over the upcoming wedding festivities." Elizabeth pressed her lips together in irritation and dropped her head.

"It may, indeed, but we shan't worry about that, shall we? As long as they are married at the end of the ceremony, I shall be quite delighted." Mr. Bennet gently lifted Elizabeth's head up with his fingers under her chin. "But tell me, dearest Lizzy, how could you keep this news about Mr. Darcy from me? He told me himself Miss Bingley had been correct in her suspicions and you were aware of his feelings!"

Elizabeth smiled weakly. "Yes, I knew, and I was as surprised as you, but it is a long story." She stood up and drew in a deep breath. "It has been a tiring day, and I think I will retire for the night." She leaned over and kissed him on the cheek. "Good night, Papa"

"Good night, Lizzy. And do not worry about Jane. She and Charles both have such a generous opinion of people I am certain it shall be forgotten in no time."

A small smile appeared on Elizabeth's face. "I believe you may be correct, Father."

Chapter 36

The next morning, the three eldest Bennet sisters sat together in the drawing room, carefully applying their needles to the handkerchiefs they were embroidering with Jane's new initials. Kitty had not yet come out of her room, and Lydia had hurried down to eat, only to return upstairs directly. Mary had opined at length about the incident, and Elizabeth finally feigned a headache and politely informed her she was in great need of silence. Mary must have felt it would have been too difficult a task to comply with her sister's wish, so she abruptly left the room.

In truth, Elizabeth did prefer silence, for it would guarantee she would not say anything to Jane about Miss Bingley. She wondered how Charles had taken the news and what he would do about it. She could not believe the amiable Mr. Bingley had been born of the same parents as such a despicable sister. She looked at Jane and gave a slight shake of her head. How would *she* receive the news?

A knock at the door caused Elizabeth to start. Her hand went over her heart, and she looked at Jane with wide eyes.

"What is it, Lizzy?" Jane asked, a wry smile appearing. "I suppose you hope Charles has brought Mr. Darcy with him?"

At least she could admit to Jane she was correct, for she did hope Mr. Darcy had come. And if he had, it was almost certain Miss Bingley would *not* be accompanying them. She wondered if she was even still in residence at Netherfield.

"You know me quite well, Jane. I feel as though I have not been able to talk to him since he arrived."

Jane reached for her hand. "If Miss Bingley has joined them, I shall do my best to distract her from you and Mr. Darcy."

"Yes, you do that, Jane. I shall be most grateful!" She laughed, but her smile quickly faded. She wondered what had happened after Mr. Darcy returned to Netherfield and informed his friend of the events that had transpired.

Hill came to the room and announced Mr. Bingley and Mr. Darcy had arrived. Jane stole a quick look at Elizabeth and smiled with a single raised brow and a knowing nod.

The two men stepped in and at once inquired of their health. Mrs. Bennet entered on the men's heels. "We are quite well, thank you, now Kitty is safe. What a harrowing time it was when we knew not of her whereabouts, but it has all turned out perfectly well."

Both men offered her a polite smile. Mr. Darcy's was brief, and he seemed unable to hide the disgust he felt. Mr. Bingley seemed embarrassed, but rallied enough to offer his agreement.

"But I cannot imagine why Kitty did not believe Mr. Wickham earnest in his declaration of love! It is all so vexing to me!" She shook her head and picked at a piece of lint on the arm of the chair. "He seems a most amiable young man!"

"Mama!" Elizabeth cried. "We know for a fact he was a most deceitful man!"

"But oh, so handsome," she sighed. "Especially in his red coat!"

Mr. Bingley cast a nervous glance at Mr. Darcy, and then back to Mrs. Bennet. "Mrs. Bennet, it is a lovely day outside, and we were hoping to walk out. Would that be acceptable?"

Mrs. Bennet clasped her hands jubilantly. "You certainly may," she said with a nod. "Mr. Bennet and I used to take long walks in our younger years, and I was surprised to discover instead of feeling fatigued at the end, I felt quite rejuvenated."

The foursome stepped out, grateful that none of the younger sisters were near enough to express a wish to accompany them. Jane walked alongside her sister as they took the steps down. The men followed, and Jane took Mr. Bingley's arm as soon as he came up to her. Elizabeth could readily see he wished to hurry ahead and have some time with his betrothed alone. Without saying a word, the party set off towards Oakham Mount.

When the couple was a good distance ahead, Mr. Darcy took Elizabeth's hand and tucked it in the crook of his elbow. She noticed him look down at her and then straight ahead.

After a few moments of silence, she said softly, "My father

informed me about Miss Bingley." She took in a deep breath and then added, "I did not say anything to Jane, as you requested."

"Thank you. Last night was difficult for Charles when he heard all his sister had done."

"I can imagine."

Darcy rubbed his chin with his free hand. "Miss Bingley locked herself in her room and refused to talk to anyone. That was fine with me, but Charles would have none of it. He demanded she open the door so he could hear what she had to say for herself."

"I wonder if she thought she would get away with this without its being discovered."

Darcy came to a halt and looked down. He scuffed the dirt with his boot and replied in a gruff voice, "She behaved recklessly, especially in paying Wickham to participate in this scheme. Had she really known that man, she would have realized he would likely reveal the plot one day... when he needed more money, and he would not hesitate to reveal her complicity in it if she did not pay for his silence."

His shoulders rose and fell as he took in a breath. "I believe she is suffering the great shame of what she has done."

Elizabeth lifted a brow. "And of being found out, I would imagine."

"Very much so."

"Does Mr. Bingley know how this all came about in the first place?"

Darcy pressed his lips tightly together. "Apparently earlier this spring Miss Bingley encountered Wickham in town when a few of the officers were on leave. Somehow the conversation turned to me. Apparently he knew, either from his own observation or that of his friends, she had a strong inclination to be Mistress of Pemberley." He kicked a rock on the path and sent it flying into the shrubbery. "He taunted her about whether or not she had been successful, and your name was mentioned. Wickham most likely used that opportunity to convince her that for a nice sum of money, he would do what he could to ensure my affections towards you would cease."

"And then he brought Mr. Rickland into it?"

Darcy nodded his head. "I believe it was a coincidence they ran into each other. I imagine Wickham paid Rickland only a portion of what Miss Bingley promised him in payment. Having Rickland do the work, he was able to return to Meryton and to Miss Mary King, to whom he had already become engaged." Darcy pounded his walking stick into the dirt. "Even when he thought he would marry her and receive her fortune, he was not satisfied and was greedy for more."

"How did Mr. Bingley receive this news about his sister?"

Darcy's expression was solemn. "It was the first time I had ever heard Bingley raise his voice in anger in all the years I have known him. He was angry… and ashamed. Later, when he told me what she had told him, I tried to reassure him her actions would not affect our friendship." He was silent for a moment and then added, "Charles was worried even more what Miss Bennet would think when she was told."

Elizabeth smiled "Then he does not truly know Jane's heart. She will be more concerned for him and do everything she can to assure him there is no need for him to worry about it."

"I thought she might."

"And what of Miss Bingley now?"

"She left for London early this morning. She shall return the day before the wedding and depart the day after." He let out a huff. "It will likely be a long time before Charles is able to understand how she could have done such a thing, let alone forgive her."

She looked up to him and noticed him clench his jaw. "Shall you forgive her?"

"I doubt we shall be much in each other's company, but I believe I can treat her with the basic civilities when we are." He was silent for a moment and then added, "When Georgiana and Mrs. Annesley come for the wedding, we will stay at the inn in Meryton. I have already made arrangements for the rooms. Bingley decided he would tell no one but the Hursts what their sister did, as it would only raise questions amongst his other family members and guests if Miss Bingley did not stay at Netherfield."

"And what happened with Mr. Wickham?"

"He and Mrs. Younge left the house quickly, but they were soon overtaken. Colonel Forster had nothing to do with him as he had already resigned from the militia, but his unpaid debts will likely result in time spent in prison. I cannot imagine he will be able to pay them off."

"And Mrs. Younge?" Elizabeth asked.

"No charges are likely to be brought against her. Her presence in the carriage was actually beneficial to Miss Kitty, as it prevented any claim of Wickham compromising her by being alone in the carriage with her."

"I suppose we can be grateful for that. It gives me great peace of mind to know he will no longer be in the neighbourhood." Elizabeth let out a long sigh. "I have missed our conversations. We have not had the opportunity to talk since you arrived in Meryton, thanks to Miss Bingley's hovering presence."

"Yes, she made it quite difficult."

Elizabeth stole another glance at him. "I have been wondering about the visit with your aunt." Elizabeth laughed softly. "I received a letter from Charlotte describing the aftermath of Lady Catherine's receiving the news about her daughter and Mr. Jenkinson, but I wondered what you had to say."

"I would be most curious to hear from Mrs. Collins how my aunt is now doing. When I went to her, she would not listen to reason. She was possibly angrier at Anne and me than she was at Mrs. Jenkinson and her son. They went to Gretna Green so they could marry quickly. He would not have been able to obtain a special license, and if they waited the three weeks to marry, Anne was afraid her mother would find her and somehow prevent the marriage from taking place."

"Will Anne be able to return to Rosings? Will her mother allow it?"

Darcy smiled. "Rosings is hers. Her mother cannot keep her out, but Anne will not return home as long as her mother remains angry with her. As I informed my aunt when I departed, she will not be allowed at my home in town or at Pemberley until she accepts Anne and her new husband."

"Did that seem to persuade her at all?"

Darcy tossed his head slightly. "Somewhat, but I hope the stronger argument was in assuring her Mr. Jenkinson is of noble birth. It is only unfortunate his older brother received the greater inheritance. Mrs. Jenkinson was the second wife of old Mr. Jenkinson and received little, as did her son. That was why she became Anne's companion and he started a book publishing business."

"Does she still consider Anne to be married well beneath her?"

Darcy nodded. "Unfortunately, yes, despite the fact he owns a manor in the country and can continue his business from there, only travelling to London on occasion." He patted Elizabeth's hand. "Anne finds the air in London aggravates her breathing."

"I am glad she was able to achieve happiness."

They walked on silently for a bit. Elizabeth wondered how she would ever bring up the subject of how her feelings for him had greatly improved.

"Mr. Darcy…"

"Miss Bennet…"

They both chuckled softly. "Go ahead, Miss Bennet," Darcy said with a nod of his head.

Elizabeth's heart pounded, and she felt her cheeks warm. She had no idea where to begin. "No, please, Mr. Darcy. You first."

"As you wish." Darcy drew in a long breath. "We have spoken about Charles and his sister, my aunt and cousin, your sister, and Wickham and Rickland, but we have yet to speak about…" He paused and squeezed her hand. He cast his eyes down at her. "When we last saw each other in London, I asked you to wait to form an opinion of me." He turned and nodded his head to begin walking again. "We have yet to speak about what your feelings are for me at present."

Elizabeth was not certain whether he was stroking and squeezing her hand on purpose or due to nervousness he might feel, but she could barely form a cohesive thought. She looked up at him and smiled, hoping to reassure him while she determined what to say.

Darcy met her gaze, and their eyes locked for several moments. While it may have encouraged him about the strength of her feelings, it also had the adverse effect of causing her to stumble over a large rock in the path. As she flew forward, Darcy quickly reached out for her and quickly swept her up in his arms. He held her exactly as he had when she had injured her ankle.

He took a few steps without releasing her, and Elizabeth let out a soft laugh. "Mr. Darcy, you can set me down, now. I promise I will heed my steps."

Darcy shook his head with a smile. "No, I think this is best." He looked at her with a single lifted brow. "Now, what were you going to say?"

Elizabeth was not certain she could think rationally while being carried in his arms. "Mr. Darcy, I am perfectly able to walk. What if someone sees us?"

"I shall tell them you stumbled and injured your foot."

Elizabeth's eyes widened. "You shall lie? I am truly surprised. I had come to believe you a man of utmost integrity."

"Had you?" he asked, with a wide smile. "Well, it is not so much a lie, as you did stumble and injure your foot." He shrugged his shoulders. "They do not have to know it was some time ago."

Elizabeth stifled a chuckle and then suddenly felt awkward. She did not know what to do with her arms, so she merely rested them on her lap and clasped her fingers together. "If I had fallen, I believe most people would assume we would be walking back *down* Oakham Mount."

Darcy gave his shoulders a slight shrug, and he looked down at her with a smile. The smile quickly left his face, however, and was replaced with a serious expression. "Do you know, Miss Bennet, when I carried you after you had fallen, I... I almost kissed you?"

Elizabeth's whole body warmed at his admission. She believed her cheeks were flaming red in a blush. Her voice quavered when she softly replied, "I know."

Darcy came to an abrupt stop. "You knew I wanted to kiss you?"

Elizabeth slowly nodded her head. Her mouth was dry, and she swallowed hard. "I had just read your letter, and in it, you... you confessed how there had been several times when you wanted to kiss me." Elizabeth looked up into his eyes. "The look on your face – it was much like how you look now – made me think you were going to lean down and kiss me."

Darcy's gaze remained on her face. He pressed his lips together and then asked, "What would you have done if I had?"

Elizabeth felt her emotions swirling through her. She could

barely think, but she knew she had to be honest. With a nervous laugh she replied, "I believe I would have slapped you."

Darcy chuckled. "Good! I would have deserved it!" His expression grew serious again, and he asked softly, "What would you do if I kissed you now?"

Elizabeth's breath hitched, and she unwittingly licked her lips, "I think... I believe that would depend on what your intentions towards me are."

"Miss Bennet, my intentions are strictly honourable. I still admire and love you more than life itself."

They were silent for a moment. Despite barely being able to take a breath, Elizabeth said, "I am glad." She could not keep her eyes from resting on his lips as he lowered them to meet hers.

His kiss was tentative at first, only lightly brushing his lips against hers before he began to pull away. She was uncertain whether he changed his mind, but their lips were soon joined again, more firmly this time. She closed her eyes, savouring the moment, but wondered, had he lowered his lips or had she lifted her head to continue the kiss? Perhaps it was both.

Elizabeth suddenly knew what to do with her arms. She wrapped them tightly about his neck and, when she did, she felt his arms tighten about her.

She had not expected anything like this. Any fantasies she may have had about her first kiss were nothing like what she was experiencing. The kiss deepened and lengthened, and she felt completely lost and yet safe in his arms. Her body trembled. At length, Darcy slowly lifted his head.

Their eyes locked, and he gently released her from his grasp. Despite her feet now touching the ground, she felt as if she were floating. Her arms were still about his neck, and she felt so unsteady she was certain if she let go, she would topple onto the ground.

She leaned her head against his chest and heard him groan against the thundering of his beating heart.

"I suppose it would have been more proper for me to have allowed you to express your opinion of me before I kissed you." His voice resonated throughout her.

Elizabeth pulled her head away from his chest and looked up at him with a mischievous grin. "Could you not ascertain my feelings from our kiss?"

Darcy smiled. "I fear my hopes have been too strong for me to speculate reasonably. I have fed my hopes with your warm smiles, dancing eyes, and most amiable manner towards me. What I discerned from *kissing* your lips was you welcomed it, but..." He drew in a breath and exhaled with a low moan. "I would prefer to *hear* from your lips your opinion of me." He drew himself erect and straightened his shoulders. "I am now ready to hear whatever you would tell me."

Elizabeth could not prevent the giggle. "My affections are..." Elizabeth bit her lip and tilted her head. "I believe, Mr. Darcy, I am a fair way towards being in love with you." A warmth flooded through her as she proclaimed her admiration.

A smile appeared. Darcy swallowed hard and blew out a long puff of air as if he had been holding his breath. "You know not how I have longed to hear you say that." He took each of her hands in his. "I do not deserve your affection; I have erred in so many ways."

"Let us not examine our faults, for we are both guilty."

Darcy pulled her close and wrapped his arms tightly about her again. He looked down and released her to cup her face with his hands. "Elizabeth, nothing would make me happier than having you by my side as my wife. I am violently in love with you and, although you have every reason to refuse me, I ask if you would consent to be my wife." He drew in a breath, and Elizabeth was quite certain he held it.

Rather than keep him in suspense, and quite certain he would collapse from lack of air if she delayed too long, she immediately replied, "I would be delighted and honoured to be your wife." She nodded her head enthusiastically. "Yes, I consent!"

Darcy leaned down and kissed her again. She felt him tremble this time as he pulled her even closer. They were so close Elizabeth could feel their hearts thunder in union.

When he finally pulled away, he gently kissed her forehead and then took her arm and placed it in the crook of his elbow. "I shall have the banns published immediately, but we shall have to wait three weeks to marry." He suddenly looked at her. "Will that be enough time to make all the arrangements?"

Elizabeth tilted her head so it rested against his arm as they walked. "The wedding gown will require the most time, but I am certain a simple dress could be sewn quickly."

"I would marry you no matter what you wore, but I want you to be pleased with the gown."

"And I am certain I shall!" *Somehow*, she added to herself.

At length, Elizabeth looked about her and let out a sigh. "I cannot believe how many people were able to see you had ardent admiration for me. Even Miss Bingley readily discerned your feelings." She shook her head and looked down. "I was quite blinded by my own folly."

Darcy stopped and clasped her hand. "Miss Bingley, I fear, had an advantage over you."

Elizabeth's eyes widened. "And pray, what was that, Mr. Darcy?"

He pressed his lips together and rubbed his jaw. "First of all, do you think you can call me Fitzwilliam?"

Elizabeth smiled. "Certainly, Fitzwilliam."

"That is better... Elizabeth," he said with a smile. "What I did was to foolishly admit to Miss Bingley one evening that I admired your fine eyes."

Elizabeth felt her cheeks warm in a blush. "My... my fine eyes?"

"Certainly! Your eyes dance with joy and laughter, intelligence and liveliness." He cradled her hand in his. "I ought never to have confided in her. I know not what I was thinking, except... I was lost in my admiration for you and felt – at least, in part I hoped – owning my admiration for you would discourage any inclination she might have for me."

"I hope you do not blame yourself for her actions. I still cannot believe what she did."

"Neither can I." Darcy let out a disgusted huff. "I knew she had every hope of my sister marrying her brother, but I was blind to her aspirations to become the Mistress of Pemberley."

He stopped and put his arms about Elizabeth's waist. "Here again, I was guilty of not perceiving what was before my very eyes. I did not see Miss Bennet's admiration for Charles, I did not see

Miss Bingley's interest in me, and I did not see your loathing of me."

Elizabeth rested her hands on his arms, her fingers circling around them. "As I said before, we are equally guilty, and while your guilt was in not perceiving something, part of my guilt was in speaking my mind to you in a most disrespectful manner."

"I would not have you argue that you bear the greater guilt, for much of what you said I deserved."

Suddenly Elizabeth laughed. "I think we have both forgotten something, Fitzwilliam. We began anew when you returned to Netherfield. I sincerely hope we can forget all that transpired before then."

Darcy leaned down and briefly touched his lips to hers. He lifted his head and smiled. "You are correct, Elizabeth. But I do hope when we are married, you will feel the freedom to speak your mind if you see me do anything that displeases you."

Elizabeth gave her head a firm shake. "Oh, no, Fitzwilliam, that will never do! For you know I am not afraid of speaking my mind, and if you give me leave to do it whenever I feel you are wrong, you shall grow quite impatient with me. No, I shall reserve it for your most grave offences."

Darcy gave her an obliging nod. He looked up and down the path. "I do not see Charles and your sister, but I believe we ought to return to Longbourn so I can speak with your father. Shall we?"

Chapter 37

When the newly engaged couple arrived at Longbourn, Mr. Darcy proceeded directly to Mr. Bennet's study, and Elizabeth went in search of her mother. She was grateful to find her with both her aunt and uncle in the sitting room.

Elizabeth greeted them and sat down next to her mother, folding her hands in her lap.

"Did you have a pleasant walk, Lizzy?" Mrs. Gardiner asked. "You look as though you did. Your face is glowing." She raised her brows in the knowing look Elizabeth had so often seen over the years.

"I did," she replied. Her heart pounded again, not so much in fear of telling them, but for what she suspected her mother's reaction might be. She hoped it would not be so excessively exuberant Mr. Darcy would hear. She reached over and took her mother's hand. "There is something I wish to tell you." She paused and drew in a breath. "While we were out walking, just now, Mr. Darcy asked me something of great import."

Mrs. Bennet's eyes narrowed, while Mr. and Mrs. Gardiner looked at each other with wide smiles.

"Is he not pleased with some detail about Jane's wedding?" Mrs. Bennet asked, tightly gripping her daughter's hand.

Elizabeth shook her head reassuringly. "No, Mother. It is nothing like that. As a matter of fact, he made me an offer to be his wife, and I have accepted. He is talking to Father at this moment."

Mrs. Bennet's jaw dropped, and her shoulders wobbled slightly. She was speechless for a few moments, as if her mind could not grasp the meaning of her daughter's words. Finally, with eyes rapidly blinking, she uttered, "You... you are to be Mrs. Darcy... of Pemberley?"

Elizabeth nodded, but was soon fetching her mother's smelling salts while Mr. and Mrs. Gardiner made a futile attempt to calm her down.

"Oh! Another wedding! How are we to do it? But it is wonderful! It will be the talk of all Hertfordshire, I am certain!" Mrs. Bennet could barely put two coherent thoughts together. "But when shall you be married? I suppose he will want to get a special license and get married quickly. I do not know how we will manage!"

Elizabeth stroked her mother's hand. "No, Mother. We shall have the banns read for two weeks and marry in three. We shall have a small, simple wedding. There is nothing to worry about."

"Oh, but certainly he would want the finest wedding in all of England. He will want to invite all..."

"No, Mother. He would not."

Elizabeth bit her lip and looked at her aunt. "Aunt, I would so love to go to town and visit your seamstress again to have them sew my gown. Jane's turned out beautifully. But I do not believe I can go until after Jane's wedding. Do you think that would give them enough time to make it?"

Mrs. Gardiner gave her a satisfied smile. "You have no need to go to town, Lizzy. My seamstress has your measurements, and while we were in the shop, if you recollect, you pointed out the gown and the fabric you would have chosen for your wedding gown. If your preference has not changed, I left all the information with her, and I shall write directly to have her begin making it."

Elizabeth's eyes widened in astonishment. "Do you mean to tell me you suspected Mr. Darcy would ask for my hand?"

Her aunt nodded. "Oh, my dearest Lizzy, I have lived many more years than you, and I certainly can recognize when a man has fallen deeply in love with the lady of his dreams." She reached over and grasped her hand. "It was only a matter of time." She lowered her head, smiled, and lifted her eyes to her niece. "What do you say, Lizzy? Shall I write? When we return for your wedding, we can bring it along with us so you can have any alterations made here, as we did for Jane."

Elizabeth's hand went over her heart. "Oh, my dear Aunt! Please do write to her! It will be perfect!"

~~*

When Mr. Bingley and Jane returned, she could not stop smiling and hugging Elizabeth. She was delighted with news of her sister's engagement. But later, when they met in Jane's room, her expression became more sombre.

"Oh, Lizzy! I am so happy for you, but I feel such distress over Caroline's actions. And poor Charles is not only angry at her, but embarrassed for himself." She looked down and knitted her hands together. "I tried to assure him it does not affect my feelings for him, but he is still in such agony."

"It was wrong of her, and I know Mr. Darcy is quite perturbed, being as it was all done in her pursuit of him."

"She feels a great deal of mortification, of course," Jane added. "She did not even want to come back for the wedding, but Charles assured her he would tell no one but their sister of her actions." Jane reached out and grabbed Elizabeth's hands. "He is such a good man, Lizzy, and it was difficult for him to see such shameless behaviour exhibited by his sister."

Elizabeth slowly nodded. "She will likely suffer the consequences of her actions for a long time." She cast her eyes down and then looked back up. "Even though only a few people know about it, she will have to live with the knowledge that those closest to her are well aware of what she did."

Jane let out a long sigh. "I hope she has learned a lesson from this and never attempts anything like it again."

Elizabeth smiled. "Yes, dearest Jane. We can only hope."

~~*

The days that followed would have been nearly too much for Mrs. Bennet to bear, if not for the presence of Mr. and Mrs. Gardiner. As final preparations were made for Jane's wedding, in addition to the plans beginning for her own wedding, Elizabeth occasionally thought it would almost be preferable if one of the couples eloped. And she was inclined to think it ought to be her and Fitzwilliam.

Darcy was also a great help to Elizabeth, as he continually

assured her he desired only the simplest ceremony. He would have been pleased with just the two of them at the altar being married by a clergyman. She teasingly asked whether Gretna Green would suffice, but he would not hear of it and felt that was taking things a bit too far. One family member doing that was more than enough.

In the late afternoon a few days before Jane's wedding, Elizabeth and her sister were at Netherfield. Guests were arriving, and Jane was kept busy meeting the family and friends Charles had invited.

Elizabeth stepped away from talking with a cousin of the Bingleys' and she looked about the room for Darcy. She finally found him, looking as uncomfortable as she had ever seen him, in the midst of three ladies and a gentleman. She thought back to the first time she met him, and realized what she had attributed to arrogance was most likely due to a sense of discomfiture and reserve. She hurriedly walked over to him to see if she could ease his distress.

A smile lit his face when she walked up to him, and he eagerly introduced her to the four that stood about him. Elizabeth felt a warm flood of gratitude at the joy in which he proclaimed her soon to be his wife.

Elizabeth thanked them for the wishes of joy they offered and then turned to Darcy. "Fitzwilliam, I fear you are needed elsewhere." She looked at the party and said, "If you will excuse us, please?"

As they walked away, he looked down with a concerned look. "What is it?"

"A rather urgent matter, actually. You are needed outside."

"Outside?" He looked at her oddly.

When they stepped outside, Darcy breathed in deeply and looked about him. "I see no one."

Elizabeth looked up at him with a smile. "Exactly." Despite looking straight ahead, she knew he had glanced down at her with a questioning look. "I thought perhaps you might want to get away from the multitude that has descended upon Netherfield."

Darcy stopped and brought his fingers under Elizabeth's chin. "You have no idea how much this means to me. I felt as though I could not breathe in there."

"I had no idea Charles had such a large family and so many close friends." Elizabeth looked up and tilted her head as they began walking again.

"He makes friends easily; however, I am not certain how close he is to them." He let out a soft laugh. "I promise you I will not invite even half as many family and friends to our wedding."

Elizabeth smiled up at him. "You can invite whomever you choose, but I do look forward to meeting those family and friends who are near and dear to you."

Darcy smiled. "And you shall."

Elizabeth drew in a deep breath, raising her shoulders as she did. "When the Hursts arrived earlier, I believe they felt terribly awkward around us since they are aware of Miss Bingley's actions."

"After our initial greeting, it was apparent they did not know what to say and, I confess, neither did I." After letting out a groan, he added, "I am actually grateful Charles chose not to tell anyone else. His family does not need to be tainted by such a scandal."

Elizabeth silently nodded.

Soon they were out of sight of the house, and Darcy drew Elizabeth nearer. "Thank you so much for rescuing me."

She leaned her head against his shoulder as they walked. "Now we are even," She looked up and smiled. "You rescued me once; how could I not have done the same?"

"You were in great distress when I rescued you; I was merely suffering from unease."

"Well, to own the truth, I had selfish motives."

"Truly? And what could those selfish motives be?" Darcy raised a brow.

"With your sister arriving tomorrow, she will be much in our company. I thought this might be our last opportunity to be alone for a while."

Darcy tilted his head and whispered in her ear, "Mm. I believe I rather like your selfish motives."

Their walk was suspended as Darcy drew Elizabeth close to him. As he gazed into her upturned face, he smiled and cupped it with his hands. His thumbs drew circles around her cheekbones, causing Elizabeth to close her eyes and sigh.

His kiss was tentative at first, but soon deepened as Elizabeth slipped her arms about his waist. She was certain their hearts pounded to the same rhythm and at the same intensity. She did not wish for it to end.

At length, he raised his head, kissing her once, very briefly, on her forehead. "I shall miss being alone with you." Darcy traced a finger around her lips. "Perhaps we ought to walk."

They ambled silently for a while, enjoying their closeness as they did.

Finally, Darcy said, "I am looking forward to your deepening your acquaintance with Georgiana. She is delighted she will finally have a sister – and one she admires."

"I look forward to getting to know her better, as well."

"I think she has greatly feared who the lady might be to whom I would declare my affections. She confided to me that if I had married one particular lady, she did not know what she would have done." He looked down at Elizabeth and sighed. "I do not have to tell you which lady she had in mind."

"I do believe I know." Elizabeth said ruefully.

"I have no idea what to expect from her when she arrives."

"I imagine she will try to avoid you… and me. She cannot feel proud of what she did."

"No, no she cannot."

As they continued on, Darcy began talking about Pemberley. Elizabeth had already heard about the paths that wound through the woods, the stream that fed the large lake situated in front of the manor, the large grassy knolls that were splayed about the grounds, and the extensive library. This time, however, she could hear in his description his eagerness for her to see it and be a part of it with him.

They stopped and sat down next to each other on a fallen log. She leaned against his chest, and he wrapped his arms about her. "Do you know, Fitzwilliam, when you spoke to me of Pemberley as we walked about the grounds at Rosings, I believed you were merely boasting to me about your home. I had no way of knowing you wished for me to be there with you."

"I should not have assumed you would want to be there with

me."

"You made it sound beautiful. If I had not been so stubborn, I might have easily fallen in love with it by your mere description."

Darcy pulled her closer. "In truth, what I wished for even more than that, was for you to fall in love with me. In a way, I am glad you have not seen it."

Elizabeth turned her head and looked at him incredulously. "Why? Fitzwilliam Darcy, were you afraid I would fall in love with your Pemberley instead of you?"

He was silent; his brows lowered.

Elizabeth's eyes widened. "You were!"

Darcy's cheeks coloured. "Only briefly. I had some doubts when I overheard Wickham claim to Miss Bingley the only reason you were interested in me was because of my fortune."

"That man! You cannot trust a thing he says!"

Darcy shook his head. "No, he was correct in one area. He claimed I do not have the charms he does."

Elizabeth let out a huff. "A woman ought always to avoid *his* kind of charms!" She placed her hand over his. "Fitzwilliam, if I had been interested solely in your fortune, I would not have behaved so impertinently around you when we first met!"

"I know. And you would have continued to harbour your anger against me, and I am quite certain your kisses would certainly not be as warm and inviting as they have been." His arms tightened about her.

"Inviting? Mr. Darcy! Are you implying I invited you to kiss me?"

He lowered his head to the back of her neck and tenderly kissed it. His breath tickled and warmed her. She tilted her head away from him and closed her eyes as he continued to press his lips to her. "Yes, Miss Bennet, I would say *that* definitely was an invitation."

She was at a loss to defend herself. All she could do was let out a long sigh as he continued to kiss her neck down to her shoulder.

When she shuddered, his arms swept her up, and he placed her across his lap. "But as lovely as it is to kiss your neck and shoulders, I would much prefer to kiss your lips."

Elizabeth slowly opened her eyes. Her breath hitched when she saw his face so near to hers. He lifted his brows, as if seeking her approval.

She smiled mischievously and then ever so slowly lifted her head and met his lips, wrapping her arms tightly about him.

When he finally drew away, he tilted his head and touched her forehead with his. They both took a few moments to catch their breaths.

"My loveliest Elizabeth, you have no idea how happy you have made me," he said in a breathy whisper.

"I suspect," Elizabeth began, as she stroked his cheek with her fingers, "my happiness quite equals – or even exceeds – yours."

Darcy grasped her fingers and brought them to his lips. "*That*, my dearest Elizabeth, makes me even happier."

They took advantage of their time alone and remained outside until the sun had set. They would walk and then stop to kiss, talk and then be silent, and hold hands and then draw together in a close embrace. It was with great reluctance, but mutual resolve, they thought it best to return to Netherfield before it grew dark.

~~*

Georgiana and Mrs. Annesley arrived the following afternoon.

When the carriage in which they were riding pulled up in front of Netherfield, Darcy could not contain his eagerness to see her. He immediately took Elizabeth's hand, and they stepped outside to greet his sister.

When Georgiana was helped out of the carriage, Elizabeth released Darcy's hand and urged him to go to his sister. The joyous reunion between them made Elizabeth's heart swell with delight. It was apparent the two of them held each other in the deepest esteem. He turned and motioned for Elizabeth to approach.

She was welcomed into their intimate circle, and Darcy spoke in a soft voice to his sister. "Georgiana, you remember Elizabeth, who is now to be your sister."

The sweetest smile appeared on Georgiana's face, and Elizabeth believed tears had pooled in the young girl's eyes.

"I am so delighted, Miss Bennet. "I cannot tell you how pleased

I was when Fitzwilliam wrote to me and told me the news."

Elizabeth took her hand and gave it a gentle squeeze. "Thank you. I had every hope you would be pleased, but would you call me Elizabeth?"

Georgiana fervently nodded her head. "Oh, yes, and please call me Georgiana." She tentatively looked up at her brother and then back to Elizabeth. "I have always longed for a sister, and I could not ask for a finer one or a more perfect wife for my brother."

"You are too kind, Georgiana. Come inside and let us visit."

~~*

In the time they spent together, Elizabeth and Georgiana grew as close as any lifelong sisters could be, just like Jane and Elizabeth. They spent every free moment together and found each other's company genuinely amiable and enjoyable. Elizabeth readily encouraged the young lady and drew her out when she occasionally seemed overtaken by shyness. As the days passed, Elizabeth saw her exhibit less reserve and more confidence.

Georgiana provided a diversion in her willingness to share stories about her brother, notwithstanding his teasing threats she best not. They laughed a great deal, and despite not having time alone with Darcy, Elizabeth would not have changed anything in those days for the world.

It helped that Darcy and his sister were residing at the inn in Meryton, for they were able to avoid the press of people at Netherfield, in particular Miss Bingley, who was to arrive in two days. Due to Miss Darcy's reserve and her brother's discomfiture in being around people he did not know well, it suited them well.

There was much to do for both of the weddings, so Elizabeth could not spend all her time with them. She wished to do as much as she could for Jane's wedding so her sister could be at ease and spend time with family and friends coming for the wedding. With everyone's help, Mrs. Bennet was free from almost all vexations and able to share in the excitement with everyone.

Except Kitty and Lydia. Lydia had been dealt a disappointing blow when Elizabeth became engaged and a second wedding was planned, for Mr. Bennet changed his mind about her trip to

Brighton. She was no longer permitted to go and she reminded Lizzy of her great dissatisfaction each time she saw her.

Kitty still suffered the shame of what she had done. She made an attempt to feel the joy of both her sisters' weddings, but it was difficult, especially after realizing how greatly she had disappointed her father. She confided in Elizabeth it would have been easier if he had been angry at her, but his displeasure in her actions grieved her more than she thought possible.

Elizabeth was delighted to visit with Charlotte, who had come alone to attend Jane's wedding. It was with great joy Elizabeth shared the news of her engagement with her friend.

"Lizzy!" she said as she grasped Elizabeth's hands. "I knew it! Did I not tell you?" She suddenly pressed her fingers to her face. "Oh, dear, now I must lengthen my stay in Hertfordshire. I cannot return until after your wedding! Perhaps I need to stay even a month or two longer!"

"That long?" asked Elizabeth.

"Oh, yes!" Charlotte replied with a firm nod of her head. "For Lady Catherine cannot be pleased, and if she is not pleased, my husband shall not be pleased!"

Elizabeth smiled. "I would suggest you stay as long as you deem necessary."

Elizabeth particularly missed Jane's company in those days before her wedding and cherished the late evenings with her when they gathered in one or the other's room and sat on the bed talking about the day. They knew after their weddings, they would be separated for an indefinite amount of time and a great distance.

~~*

The wedding of Mr. Charles Bingley and Miss Jane Bennet was a joyous occasion. Elizabeth attended her sister, and Mr. Darcy stood up for his friend. If they heard nothing the clergyman said, it was because their eyes were fixed on each other and their thoughts on another wedding ceremony that could not come soon enough.

At the wedding breakfast, Elizabeth, Darcy, and Georgiana did their best to avoid Miss Bingley. As she was also trying to stay away from them, there were only a few unexpected encounters.

Elizabeth actually felt rather sorry for her, as she appeared quite mortified. She did not have the style of walking and the air of poise that had earlier been so pronounced in her. Elizabeth wondered how much of her anguish was also due to the great disappointment of losing the man she had cunningly tried to ensnare for herself.

After the newly married couple departed for a short wedding journey, Darcy, Georgiana, and Elizabeth took a stroll towards Oakham Mount.

"Do you know," Georgiana asked, "this was the most pleasant experience I have ever had in Miss Bingley's presence?" A mischievous smile appeared. "If only she had behaved in such a manner all the other times I was in her company."

Darcy laughed, putting his hand on her shoulder. "Do you mean how she avoided you?"

Georgiana nodded. "I believe I would have liked her so much better if she had not smothered me with her praises." She looked down and shook her head. "I always knew it was an act, solely for the purpose of trying to look good in your eyes." She glanced up at her brother with a brief smile.

"I am sorry you had to endure such treatment," Darcy replied, wrapping his arm about her shoulder and drawing her in for a quick hug.

Georgiana then turned to Elizabeth. "I know I already told you how delighted I am you are marrying Fitzwilliam. I feel as though the more I get to know you, the more I am convinced you will not only make him a wonderful wife, but will be an exceptional sister to me."

Elizabeth smiled at Georgiana and then looked up at Darcy, who had a wide grin on his face. She placed her hand over Darcy's, which still rested on his sister's shoulder. "And I cannot wait to marry your brother and call *you* my sister."

Very softly, Darcy replied, "Neither can I."

Chapter 38

When one has to wait three weeks for something one is looking forward to more than anything, the time usually passes far too slowly or, if one is fortunate, it passes quickly. The latter was the case for Darcy and Elizabeth.

Because they had to begin thinking of another wedding as soon as the first one was over, it was quite chaotic. The busyness kept their minds off the passing days, hours, minutes, and seconds.

Before they knew it, their wedding was over, and they had spent a week in Darcy's townhouse, where Elizabeth was introduced to the staff and the stately home.

They were finally on their way to Pemberley. Elizabeth enjoyed listening to her husband talk about it, and she felt as though she knew it as well as if she had actually visited. Of course she had the added descriptions of the manor from Anne's book as well as from her aunt, who had grown up in the nearby village of Lambton and had seen the house and grounds several times.

Elizabeth brought along Anne's book and had entertained her husband by reading portions of it on the long, slow journey.

"It was good to see Anne so happy when she and Mr. Jenkinson came to the wedding," Elizabeth said as she looked down at the book.

"She is happy, but I could see the regret in her eyes over her mother's refusal to acknowledge her husband or their wedding."

"Do you think your aunt will ever come to welcome Mr. Jenkinson into the family?" Elizabeth asked.

"I believe once she realizes she no longer has any family who is in agreement with her, she will be obliged to reconsider. Even her brother has sanctioned Anne's marriage." Darcy rubbed his jaw. "Anne faithfully writes to her mother as if nothing is wrong between them. It is now up to my aunt to decide if she is going to accept their marriage."

Elizabeth sighed. "I would imagine she will not accept ours as long as she does not accept Anne's."

"True." Darcy squeezed Elizabeth's hand. "I heard from my aunt's steward the other day." He smiled down at her. "He sends along his wishes for our greatest happiness, but that is not why he wrote to me."

Elizabeth looked up at him. "Was it about Mr. Rickland?"

Darcy nodded. "The man is in greater debt than what Jenkins originally thought. He is almost to the point of losing his manor unless he makes some critical decisions – both about the home and his lifestyle."

Elizabeth leaned her head against Darcy's shoulder. "I suppose any decisions he makes will reflect what he feels is important to him."

Darcy took her hand and squeezed it. "But I do not wish to discuss Rickland. Have I told you how beautiful you looked as you walked down the aisle towards me? I had to keep telling myself to stand still and not rush up to snatch you from your father's arm?"

"Several times," Elizabeth laughed. "Did you truly like the dress?"

"Were *you* pleased with it?" Darcy asked.

"Oh, yes! I thought it was lovely?"

"Then I did, too! You were stunning."

Elizabeth smiled. "Says the man who told me he would be happy even if I were to wear sitting room window coverings!"

Darcy leaned over and kissed her nose. "I do not believe I ever said *that!*"

~~*

When Darcy announced they were entering Pemberley woods, Elizabeth opened up Anne's book and looked for the part where she described it. Once she found it, she began reading.

As the carriage rambled into the dense woods, a sudden darkness overtook them. Tall trees canopied high over them, blocking the sun. Annabelle suddenly felt cooler, despite the warmth of the day, as they traversed the shaded road.

A light caught her eyes, and she saw several rays of sunlight streak through the trees. She watched the streams of light play on the ripples in the river running alongside the road and found herself entranced as the twists and turns of the road followed those of the river.

As soon as she read it aloud to him, the thick foliage blanketed them in a muted darkness. Darcy pointed out the stream, which seemed to appear out of nowhere. The dancing water sparkled as tiny rays of sunlight touched it.

Elizabeth's heart began to pound as the next paragraph in Anne's book described seeing the manor for the first time. She could barely contain herself and craned her head to look out the window.

Darcy tapped on the front of the carriage, and it came to a stop.

"Is this the view of the manor Anne wrote about in her book?" Elizabeth asked expectantly. "Shall we now see it?"

Darcy shook his head. "No, but we will step out, anyway."

The door was opened, and the footman helped Elizabeth out. She looked around as Darcy spoke to him.

"Yes, sir," the footman said. Soon the carriage was moving along.

Elizabeth sent Darcy a questioning look.

"There are times when I return home to Pemberley, after being gone a long time, that I get off my horse or get out of the carriage and walk from here." He smiled down at her. "Are you ready for an easy walk, my dearest Elizabeth?"

Elizabeth smiled enthusiastically. "I most certainly am!"

They stepped off the road and traversed down a gentle slope. They began walking along the bank of the stream, soon coming to an area where the water pooled, and they stopped. Darcy picked up a couple of smooth rocks and tossed them into the water.

"This looks inviting enough to swim in!" Elizabeth exclaimed.

"It is." He looked at her with a raised brow. "Because it is so secluded, on many a sweltering day, I have thrown off my outer clothing and dived in."

"You have not!" An incredulous look crossed Elizabeth's face.

"It is actually quite refreshing. If you wish, we could try it now." He worked to keep a smile from appearing on his face.

"As tempting as it is," Elizabeth cleared her throat, "I wish to meet the Pemberley staff looking respectable. I cannot imagine what they would think of me if I greeted them soaking wet with strands of water weeds in my hair."

Darcy shrugged. "As you wish, but they do not think any less of me when I do so."

"You are not meeting them for the first time."

"They will love you no matter how you look."

Elizabeth looked about her, feeling as though they were getting deeper and deeper into the woods. "I hope you know where you are going, Fitzwilliam, for I am certain I would not find my way out of here if my life depended on it."

"It is easy enough. Just keep near the stream."

Elizabeth suddenly chuckled.

"What is it?" Darcy asked.

"Now I see what you have been all about. When you told me about the many paths through Pemberley woods, you were imagining getting lost in them with me. The streams where you wished me to join with you in a private swim, and the grassy knolls…" She looked at him for a moment. "I suppose they are out of view of the manor?"

Darcy nodded. "Some are."

"I see. I imagine when we set out for those knolls, you will want to bring along a large coverlet on which to lie underneath the sun."

Darcy shook his head. "No blanket is needed; the grass is quite soft. And I would much prefer to lie out under the stars."

Elizabeth smiled. "If I had known what you were thinking when you told me about Pemberley, Mr. Darcy, I cannot say I would have trusted you."

"Ah, but you are forgetting about my library."

"Your library?"

"Yes, it is quite large with many books and has a secure lock on the door. We can lock ourselves in there for hours at a time."

"And read?" Elizabeth asked innocently.

Darcy stopped and touched Elizabeth's nose with his finger, then dropped it down to her lips. "Or other things we might find to do there."

Elizabeth smiled. "I am certainly grateful we married before I discovered all these ulterior motives you had."

Darcy stopped in front of her and draped his arms over her shoulders, clasping them at her back. He drew her close and kissed the side of her neck as he whispered in her ear. "Since you claim I have had such intentions for quite some time, do you find them offensive or to your liking?"

"I must preface my answer by telling you again that it is my intention to appear quite the proper lady when I arrive at Pemberley – in a timely manner." She turned her head and found his lips, kissing them briefly. "All that aside, would you think me terribly wicked if I tell you it all sounds quite wonderfully scandalous?"

Darcy tightened his arms about her. "Not at all! And I hope soon you will come to realize I do not condone any gossiping amongst my staff about anything they see or hear; my housekeeper... *our* housekeeper, Mrs. Reynolds, keeps a tight rein on them." He tilted his head at her. "Now, Mrs. Darcy, I think that last kiss was far too brief!"

Before she had the time to protest, he kissed her again. This time much longer.

At length, they began to walk again, and Darcy pointed out his favourite paths. Elizabeth could not have been more delighted with the grounds but eagerly looked forward to finally seeing the manor.

They came to a hedgerow of trees and Darcy directed her to them. "This way brings us up to the house from the side. I go this way when I do not want to approach the house from the front."

"As when you are wet from a swim?"

Darcy laughed. "Perhaps. I would not wish to unwittingly encounter a guest or someone touring the home."

There was a slight break in the hedgerow, and Darcy held a few of the branches out of the way as Elizabeth passed him. When she came through to the other side, she gasped. A manor more beautiful and stately than she had ever imagined stood before her, reflected perfectly in a pristine lake that extended across the front and to the side. The stream they had been following emptied into it.

Darcy came up to her side and watched as she looked upon her new home for the first time. Finally, he asked, "Are you pleased with Pemberley?"

Elizabeth's eyes had widened, and she shook her head. "I do not know what to say."

He looked at her eagerly waiting for more.

"It is nice, I suppose, but it is missing something." She bit her lips and dared not look at him.

"Do you find something not to your liking? Elizabeth, what displeases you?"

She turned her head and smiled. "It has no turret!"

Darcy laughed. "I wanted to build a turret for your wedding gift, but alas, I was informed, due to the architecture of the home, it would be quite impossible."

Elizabeth smiled at him and then pressed her hand over heart. "Fitzwilliam, it is truly beautiful. It has greatly exceeded anything I imagined from all the descriptions I have heard." She let out a sigh. "I suppose I can do without a turret."

He smiled. "That is a great relief."

He lifted his hand and pointed towards the front of the manor. "Now, I imagine Mrs. Reynolds has the upper servants lined up to greet us and meet you, so shall we oblige them?"

"Yes, I greatly wish to meet them."

As they stepped around the corner of the edifice, Elizabeth saw that Darcy had been correct. Forming the straightest of lines and presenting themselves with the most erect comportment, a number of servants were waiting before the front entrance. Elizabeth detected a slight turning of a few heads as they approached. She knew they must be curious about her, as the servants had been in Darcy's London home. In London she had been treated and welcomed most graciously, and she was certain it would be the same here.

Darcy guided Elizabeth to an older, matronly looking woman. She stepped towards Elizabeth, tears glistening in her eyes.

"Mrs. Reynolds, I would like to present to you my wife, Mrs. Darcy. Elizabeth, this is Mrs. Reynolds, my housekeeper."

Mrs. Reynolds clasped Elizabeth's outstretched hand. "We have heard so much about you, Mrs. Darcy. I hope you will feel as much at home as our Master does. I believe you will be delighted not only with Pemberley, but with the staff, as well."

"Thank you, Mrs. Reynolds. I already feel quite at home."

"Mrs. Darcy, may I introduce you to Pemberley's upper servants?" As they walked to the line of servants, the front door swung open and a soft, "Fitzwilliam! Elizabeth!" was heard, prompting heads to turn. Darcy smiled at his sister, who hurried down the steps. "You are home! I have been eagerly awaiting your arrival."

Darcy drew Georgiana into his arms as Elizabeth approached. The three were soon in an embrace.

Georgiana looked at her brother excitedly. "Did you show her?" Turning to Elizabeth, she asked, "Have you seen it?"

"No, we only just arrived," Darcy replied, playfully pinching his sister's chin.

"Did I see what?" Elizabeth asked, looking from one to another.

"In due time," Darcy said. "Let us proceed with the introductions to the staff."

They turned back to Mrs. Reynolds, who was waiting patiently. Elizabeth greeted each servant with a smile, hoping she would remember their names and positions.

When they had finished and the servants had been dismissed, Elizabeth turned back to Darcy. "Now, what is it Georgiana wanted me to see?"

Darcy took her hand and clasped it between his. "Do you not wish to see the house first?"

Elizabeth looked at Georgiana, who had an enthusiastic look on her face. "I fear I am faced with a great dilemma." She looked up at her husband. "Which would you rather I see first?"

Darcy glanced at the sky, noticing the darkening of the clouds. "It looks as though rain is likely, so we shall do this first." He slipped his arm through Elizabeth's and grasped her hand. "Come with me."

They walked towards the far side of the stately manor, passing a small flower garden that encompassed a fountain. Elizabeth could not stop turning her head, taking everything in; there was so much to see. She was also eager to see what had Georgiana so excited.

When they reached the far end of the manor, they stopped. Darcy faced Elizabeth and took her hands. "It is not yet finished, but I think you will be able to see what I had in mind." He turned and pointed to the top of the ridge.

Elizabeth could see some wooden beams rising from the top but was unsure what it was. "Are they building something up there?"

Darcy nodded. "It is not quite a real turret, as that would have to be on the house, but it is a small enclosed lookout that, I think, will give you a much better view than a turret on top of the manor. It will look out over the valley on the other side of the ridge, as well as over the tree tops in the woods. Once it is finished, we will equip it with a telescope."

Elizabeth clasped her hands together. "Oh, Fitzwilliam! I cannot believe you thought of doing this! I... Oh, I cannot wait until it is finished! Can we walk up now to see it?"

When a few raindrops began to fall, Darcy smiled. "I think that is your answer." He drew in a deep breath. "Are you pleased?"

"Oh, I am overjoyed!"

"If the weather cooperates tomorrow, we will walk up. I think you will be delighted with the view it affords of the other side of the ridge."

Elizabeth smiled mischievously at him. "But does it have a view of a garden?"

"A garden?" Darcy asked.

Elizabeth raised her brows. "I would not want to catch you up there looking through the telescope as you admired some lady who happened to be picking flowers in a garden."

Darcy's jaw dropped. "You knew?"

Elizabeth smiled at him. "It was not difficult to deduce."

Georgiana looked confused. "Knew what?"

Darcy turned abruptly to his sister. "Nothing you need to know!"

Elizabeth took her husband's arm. "I believe I am ready to see the inside of my new home."

THE END

ABOUT THE AUTHOR

Kara Louise lives in the suburbs of St. Louis, Missouri
with her husband and a variety of animals,
including a dog, several cats,
and a Shetland Pony.
Their son and his wife and daughter live nearby.

Other books by Kara Louise:

Darcy's Voyage

Only Mr. Darcy Will Do

Assumed Engagement

Assumed Obligation

Master Under Good Regulation

Drive and Determination

Pemberley Celebrations: The First Year

and

Pirates and Prejudice

~~*

www.karalouise.net